SAM CRESCENT

EVERNIGHT PUBLISHING ®

www.evernightpublishing.com

AT A GLANCE

Copyright© 2017

Sam Crescent

Editor: Karyn White

Cover Artist: Jay Aheer

ISBN: 978-1-77339-344-5

SAM CRESCENT

DEDICATION

To everyone who has doubts. Believe in yourself and love yourself for who you are.

FAT

Sam Crescent

Copyright © 2016

Chapter One

"Here comes chubby."
"Fatty."
"Ugly."
"She's waddling."
"You're going to break the chair, you're so fat."

Nearly everyone in Elsa Quinn's life had judged her because of her weight. Her fellow pupils at school, her parents—even though they tried to be *nicer* about it, no matter how many times a person suggested a diet, it still hurt.

No, that was wrong. It was her mother, not her father, who cared about her weight.

Tapping the steering wheel of her car, Elsa stared up at the neon gym sign, and wished she was one of those natural beauties who didn't have to be considering this on a Saturday. She wanted to be at home, in her bedroom studying, or even going over to her friend Kimberley's house, but no, she had decided to make a change. It was the start of school, and she didn't want to keep being known as "the fat girl". She'd be going away to college next year, and the aim was for the new her to be gracing the halls of the college she picked.

First, she needed to get her ass out of the car and into the gym. She'd already paid for her membership over the phone. When she was asked if she'd like a personal trainer, she had declined. There was no way she was having some woman, or worse, some guy telling her she was too fat. If she needed that, she'd work out at school.

"I can do this. It's just about going on inside, getting my pass, and hoping no one sees me."

She had gone over to the next town in order to be covert about what she was doing. Blowing out a breath, she grabbed her bag, and just decided to go for it. She was going to go in there and start a whole new life for herself. There were a couple of cars in the parking lot, which was a good sign. Maybe everyone would stay at home, and she'd never meet another person. She'd be in and out before anyone even knew it.

I can do this.

Happy me here I come.

But she *was* happy, for the most part. Her father never judged her. He only went along with what her mother said, if he was even paying attention. Of course, her mom did love her, but she just wanted her to be better, thinner. God, she hated that.

"You'd be so happy, Elsa, if you just lost a little weight. You'd get invited to parties, and you may even have a boyfriend."

Those were her mother's words pretty much every week. Most parents wanted their daughters locked away so no guys came near them. Not her mother, no, she wanted her daughter to have a boyfriend, and maybe even go to a party.

Her father was a criminal lawyer, a really good one who made a shitload of money for his trouble. So her mother was part of some country club, and Elsa refused to participate in the games that other mothers did by entering their daughters in beauty pageants. If it wasn't for her grandmother interfering when she was five years old, she'd still be fighting to try to win.

Elsa hated beauty competitions, and there were times she hated how her mother caved to pressure from other mothers.

Anyway, that was stress for another time. She was a good student, never caused trouble, and her one downfall: she was fat.

Up until a week ago, Elsa didn't care about her weight. She liked to eat, and she liked to cook. Her paternal grandmother was an amazing cook, and had always told her that back in her day, she'd be considered a hot piece of ass, and full women would soon make a comeback. So Elsa had stayed happy in her own skin.

Then last week she'd left her bedroom to go and get a glass of milk, and heard her mother sob as she broke down in front of Bill, Elsa's father.

"I don't know what to do, Bill. I'm the complete laughingstock of the club. Elsa hates me, and all I want is what is best for her. I've seen her walking through town, and besides Kimberley, she has no real friends. No boys."

"We should be happy she's not coming home pregnant. I heard Gate's daughter had been caught last week, and he had to handle it. Now there is a shotgun wedding. We don't want that for Elsa."

"I don't want her to be miserable, Bill!"

Elsa had heard so much pain, so much fear that she had decided that enough was enough. She was going to make her mother proud of her, or at least stop stressing about her.

Entering the gym, she walked up to the main desk, where a chipper looking brunette was typing on the computer.

"Can I help you?" she asked. Her name badge read Sarah.

"I'm Elsa Quinn. I called the other day."

"Ah, yes, Bruce told me you were coming." Sarah left her chair, going to a little box behind her that she unlocked with a key. "Here is your key, your access pad. This allows you into many different parts of the gym including the, erm, pool. It's cleaned on a Saturday until nine, but after then, you can go right on in. Are you with a personal trainer?"

"No, I'm just going to do this myself."

"Oh, okay. We do advise all new starters have a personal trainer to help them see where they should focus during their workout."

"I'm just going to hit it running, and hope for the best." Her cheeks were heating, and she was so embarrassed. "I'm going to go."

"Okay, have a nice workout, and if you need anything, please let us know. We want you to have a full treatment experience at Bruce's."

Elsa nodded and made her way toward the door with a stick figure of a girl on it. "The new me is just exercise away. Once I start, there is no turning back." She held in a whimper and pushed through the door, determined to try this out.

The changing rooms were empty, and she found a cubicle, locking the door behind her.

"So far, so good."

She didn't waste any time in getting changed into her workout gear, which was a pair of shorts that were a little tight and one of her father's old ratty shirts. Her mother wouldn't allow her to buy clothes bigger, so she made do with what her father gave her.

Tying her ratty brown hair back into a ponytail, she was good to go.

She found a locker with a key, stashed her crap inside, and left.

Entering the main gym, she didn't have a clue what she was doing, but she was surprised at how many people were actually there. Entering a room with running machines, she saw at least ten people, six men and four women.

Staying at the back, she stared at the scary looking running machine. It couldn't be that hard to get started. Stepping onto it, she looked at all the buttons, and pressed for the machine to walk.

"Okay, I'm going to walk. This is going to be easy." She muttered the words under her breath wishing she'd brought some kind of music.

"Can you believe he wanted me to eat a salad with the dressing?" One of the women was talking so loud that Elsa couldn't help but listen in.

"Really? That's got like a thousand calories."

"I compromised and allowed there to be chicken, but then they went and added cheese. I mean seriously, there's no way I was going to go for that."

Great, it's a health nut.

What was the point in eating at all if you forgo the meat and the dressing? It was just a bowl full of lettuce. *Ew, maybe this wasn't such a good idea.*

The image of her mother sobbing made Elsa keep on walking, and she ignored the conversation going on up front. There was not going to be a change to herself unless she worked out, and work out she was going to do.

She only hoped her diet would allow more than a bunch of leaves in a bowl.

****

Noah Stewart made his way into the gym to find Sarah already had his key in her hand.

"Saturday morning, eight-thirty every single week

unless we're closed for holidays," she said.

"You know me, I like to be predictable."

"Yeah, why don't you work out in your own town? Don't they give you a special discount or something?" Sarah asked.

Noah sighed. He could work out in his own town, and it would be easier than making the trek four times a week, but he liked Bruce's Gym. He was left alone, allowing him to train. None of his football buddies were there, and he didn't have to worry about them trying to hook him up with some of the chicks in high school. Ever since girls had discovered he had a dick at fifteen years old, he'd experienced nothing but drama.

Working out was the one area where he got to relax. He was the kind of guy who found lifting weights, running, or swimming relaxing, but still, it's what he liked to do, and he intended to make a career out of it. If he didn't make it through football, he'd make it through becoming a sports medic, or teaching. He happened to like a lot of things, and he was smart. Bruce had even offered him a chance to earn some extra cash as a fitness instructor. The first week he was hit on three times, and that was not what he wanted for himself, so now, he focused on just practicing.

"Stop worrying about how much I'm being charged. Anything new with you?"

"I think Eric may propose. He's getting all serious."

Eric was her serious boyfriend, who she completely adored, but refused to show it. This was what his friends ribbed him about every chance he got. Not only was he known for being a hit with the ladies, but he was also a nice guy, which made girls annoyed. They couldn't hate him even if they wanted to, and also, he was a hot guy. He was tall, muscular, with messy blond hair that looked hot on a guy and ugly on girls, and blue eyes that made girls think of the ocean when he was screwing them. Not to mention he'd gotten some wicked ink during a trip to Vegas his dad took him on to see a game. It made him pretty badass, and his friends wanted to get one afterward.

It was damn good being Noah Stewart. He loved his life, and nothing was going to change that.

"You make sure I'm at the wedding."

"Shut up, Noah. Oh, we had a newbie today. She joined via the phone, wants absolutely no help."

"That's not unusual."

"Yeah? She looks like a fish out of water. I think she's just hoping everything will fall into place for her," Sarah said.

This was what he liked about Sarah, she didn't judge anyone. At some of the gyms he'd visited there was a horrible feel to the place where people trying to lose weight were made to feel like shit. Bruce, he had a motto, you came to his gym for a reason. He'd leave you alone until you asked for help.

"You know, she looked close to your age. Maybe you know her?"

"Doubt it. I go across town to avoid the chicks in my area. You know that."

"How could I forget the whole screaming girl incident, where one of your conquests tried to hit you with a weight?" Sarah asked, chuckling.

"Look, it's not all my fault."

"Yeah, yeah, being young and hot is a curse."

"You should know. You're hot."

"Shut it, and I noticed you didn't quote young."

"I can't lie."

She threw a towel at him, laughing. "Go, before your body starts to go into withdrawal because you're not working it."

He gave her a wave and made his way toward the changing rooms. There he changed into his workout clothes before heading out. He did some light stretches on his way into lifting some weights. The definition on his arms helped him to catch the girls, but it also gave him the strength he needed while playing. Noah didn't know what he'd do with his life if he didn't have the option of playing ball. It gave him focus.

Several of the guys nodded at him as they made their way to different apparatus. This was what he liked about training here, he got left alone. The last thing he wanted was a scene. He'd been there, done that, and he wasn't interested in the experience again.

After he was sufficiently warmed up, he started light on his arm reps, building up, alternating between each arm. When he was happy there, he started to do some squats, lifting the weights out either side of his body, and drawing them back in.

For the next hour, he worked the whole of his body, building up a sweat. He was warmed up, pumped, and ready to hit the treadmill. With a towel around his neck, he walked into the running room, and saw several people he recognized. Looking to his left, he froze when he caught sight of a chick he did recognize.

What the fuck was Elsa Quinn doing in a gym?

He paused, glancing around the room, and then back at the girl from his own high school. She didn't look back at him, nor did she appear to care who was in the room. She wore one of the largest, ugliest shirts he'd ever seen. He saw the signs of perspiration under her armpits. Her thighs were also swallowed up.

She had interrupted his place of peace.

Was this the girl who Sarah was talking about? No, she was going to have to go. This was his place, his gym.

Moving toward the running machine closest to her, he started at a steady walk. "What the hell are you doing here?" he asked.

She tripped, and caught herself by holding onto either side of the machine, turning to look at him.

Her eyes were so dark as she stared at him. Noah forced himself to look right back at her. There was always something … inviting about her eyes. During high school, he'd noticed how dark they were, and how they stared at something, trying to figure it out. They were beautiful eyes.

"What the hell are you doing here?"

"I've been coming to this gym for the past year. What is your reason?"

"You don't own the gym. You can't stop people from coming here."

"Are you here with a gang of girls? Did they put you up to this?" Noah looked around, wondering if at any moment one of his ex-conquests was suddenly going to pop out and make an appearance.

"I can't believe your ego. I don't have to take this. There are other rooms." She pressed several buttons, and left the room.

His peace had been ruined because he didn't trust her. Turning off his machine, he followed her, finding her standing in the weight room. She looked like a fish out of water, exactly as Sarah had described her.

"Do you have a clue what you're doing?"

"God, do you own this room as well?" She walked back into the main hall, and there were several people walking toward them. Grabbing her hand, he pushed her into one of the private sauna rooms. "What the hell are you doing?"

"You don't have a clue what you're doing here, so

tell me who put you up to this."

"No one?"

"You just happened to be at Bruce's gym out of pure coincidence."

"No, and I don't have to tell you."

"I'll make your life hell at school!"

She glared. "I dare you, and I'll make sure every single girl knows you're here on a Saturday."

They both stared at each other, neither of them showing signs of winning. "I'm here because it's the only place I get peace and quiet. You must have heard what Jessica did?"

"I heard about the scene. Who hasn't?"

"Exactly. I come here so I can work out and be left alone. Now, I've told you why, you tell me?"

She sighed. "I just want to point out that you interrupted my training time, not the other way around. You could have run anywhere else, and I wouldn't care."

"Fine, just tell me."

"I'm doing it as a surprise to my mom."

"I don't get it."

"Look at me. I know you all call me fat, cow, whale, chubby. I embarrass my mom, so here I am, trying to make her proud."

He'd heard all the names she'd been called, and he'd laughed at a couple of them. But really he didn't see a problem with her weight. So she was a couple of pounds heavier than people would like, so what? He happened to like her tits. There were many times during gym at school where he'd stared as her tits bounced. Out of all of the girls in high school, she had the biggest rack.

Damn.

Now his gaze landed on her breasts.

"Seriously? My eyes are up here, you creep."

"You don't have a clue what you're doing."

"So? I'll figure it out, and come college there will be a dazzling new me, and there will be no sobbing in sight."

"What you're trying to do is lose weight. Where is your trainer? What are your starting points? What about your diet? There's a lot more to losing weight than just getting on a treadmill, and hoping for the best. You want to be the best that you can be, then you need some help."

"I don't want to make this complicated, okay? This was just about doing something in private with no one knowing, and now you know."

"Believe it or not, I won't blab."

"Sure you won't."

Her sarcasm was grating on his nerves.

Chapter Two

This couldn't be happening. Her perfectly ordered plan of losing weight without anyone knowing was about to be completely ruined. Elsa forced back the tears as she stared back at the star of her high school.

This sucked.

"I won't. I'm not a fucking liar."

"Don't swear at me." They had never spoken more than a handful of words at each other during their time in high school.

"How do I know you're not going to tell everyone?"

"You keep my appearance here quiet, and I won't tell."

"Fine. I can do that."

"Good. Can I go now, or are you going to lecture me about something else?" she asked.

"No, you can go." He released her arm, and she made her way back toward the treadmill.

The buzz she was getting had disappeared.

The entire encounter with Noah had ruined what she wanted to achieve. She'd done an hour, and that was better than nothing. Leaving the treadmill, she made her way into the changing room. Instead of sticking around to change, she grabbed her stuff, and headed out into the parking lot.

Sarah was chipper, asking how she got on.

Elsa did her best to smile, and say thank you, but all she wanted to do was escape. Maybe get a large tub of ice cream on the way back.

"Elsa, wait."

She tensed up, glancing behind her to see Noah rushing toward her. This was the last thing she needed.

"What is it?" she asked, turning to look at him.

He ran up to her, and she refused to be drawn to his rock hard body. This was not her. She wanted something more than a pretty face to look at.

"You're serious about losing weight? This wasn't some joke to find out where I was?"

"How can you even walk with an ego that size? Yes, this was about me, and what I wanted to do for my mother. It wasn't about you."

"I'll help you."

Elsa jerked back. "What?"

"Look, I know what I'm doing, and you clearly don't. This will be awesome for me to put on my college application."

She shook her head. "No, that's not going to happen. There's no way in hell that I'm going to be—"

"I'll do it anonymously. I can take pictures without your head, or anything that will give you away."

"You can do that?" she asked, curious.

"There are a great many people who like their privacy. I can help you with this."

"And you look awesome for college?"

"It's a win-win for both of us. You lose weight, I get a good education."

She bit her lip, hating and liking it at the same time. The last thing she wanted to be doing was allowing Noah to be near her. He wasn't an awful guy, but other than being a jock, she didn't know anything about him.

"So what do you say?"

"No one can know about this. Not your friends, or family."

"It's a secret."

"Completely top secret."

"Okay, so completely top secret, let's go to my place," he said, walking away from her car.

"What?"

"My place. Let's get started. How long were you on the treadmill?"

"I don't know. I don't want to go to your house."

He turned toward her. "Do you want me to go to yours?"

"No."

"Then where do you expect us to get started?"

"What's wrong in there?"

"No, we've got some preliminary stuff to get done. We do it in there, it's got to be done through Bruce's books."

She groaned. "No, I don't want any record of what we're about to do."

"Then stop being a pain in the ass, and get in my car."

"What about my car?" she asked.

"You don't want anyone to know about this, right?"

"Duh."

"Well duh, right back at you. Your car in my driveway is going to have a lot of people curious, asking questions. Do you want them asking shit about this?"

Once again she was stumped.

"You're right."

"You know, for a smart girl, it doesn't show."

She glared at him but couldn't find a reason to tell him otherwise.

Climbing into the front seat of his car, she held her bag tightly to her, and stayed silent as he pulled out of the parking lot.

She hated awkward silences, and she felt utterly tense.

"I'm not going to hurt you," he said.

"Oh, I know. I could probably squash you anyway."

"Okay, rule one, do not put yourself down like that."

"Excuse me?"

"I don't want any fat jokes, or comments when you're with me."

She frowned. "I get called them at school. In fact I've been called a lot worse, by you and your friends."

"Actually, not by me. I don't get involved with that shit. My friends, that's their deal, not mine. I don't put anyone down. I don't believe in that. In fact I actually believe in karma."

"Karma?"

"Yeah, if I start putting you down for your weight or whatnot, then later in life I'm going to be hit by something that's going to make my life suck. So, I live in a nice little bubble, and it works for me."

"Wow, a jock who is weird, who knew?" she asked. "What do you tell your friends?"

"About what?"

"About where you work out? I thought you guys were supposed to train together or something. You know, compete for how big your dicks are."

"Oh, look at you, knowing what a dick is," he teased, and she rolled her eyes. "You do know what one is?"

"Shut up, Noah."

"You're not a very nice girl."

"I'm a little out of my comfort zone."

"You don't think I am? I intended to relax today, do some weights, some running, maybe some laps in the pool—"

"You consider that relaxing?"

"What do you consider relaxing then?" He glanced over at her.

"Seriously?"

"You say that a lot."

"I know."

"So what do you think is relaxing?" he asked.

"I don't know, anything that is not working out?" She looked over at him.

"Nope, that's not me, I'm afraid. I find sitting around doing nothing stressful."

"You don't have to do nothing. What about a walk in the park? Or maybe going swimming?"

"I would have gone for a swim. We both have different ideas about relaxing."

"There's also my personal favorite, being a slob."

His knuckles were white as they held the steering wheel. She sat back in his seat and watched the scenery go by.

"Jessica doesn't know you're here?" she asked, filling the silence.

"We're not together anymore."

"You're not?"

"Jessica is lying. I'm not with her since before her little outburst a year ago in the gym."

"Wow, a whole year. You still hang out with her."

"She's part of the cheerleading squad, I don't have a choice. What about you, nerd, do you have any guy troubles?"

"Nope, I'm lucky that way." She messed with the flap on her bag, and as she did, she couldn't believe that she was sitting in Noah's car, on the way to his house. This went against every single rule that she'd ever known.

"You're the first girl to think not having a guy is lucky. You're weird."

"Don't be mean."

"Come on, there's not some guy you want to make out with, get married and have loads of little babies?"

"Ew, gross, no, there is not." Who was this guy?

"Have you ever made out with a guy?"

"No!"

"That answers all of those questions."

"What questions?"

"If you've never made out with a guy then you've never done anything else. You're a virgin."

"Shut up!"

She couldn't believe this was even up for discussion. Actually, it wasn't. She wasn't going to get drawn into that conversation, not now, not ever.

He chuckled. "You're so funny."

"I can't believe I let you talk me into this."

"It wasn't that hard."

Blowing out a breath, Elsa decided to stare out of the window rather than talk to the insufferable guy beside her. Just because the whole school thought he was a god, didn't mean that she had to think it.

He put on the radio and started nodding his head to some kind of heavy metal music, which only made her head hurt.

Thirty minutes later they were pulling up into his driveway, which was a large one, similar to hers. They lived three streets from each other, not far to walk. She could have dropped her car off at home, and then walked.

Oh well, they were here now.

"Come on."

She followed him into his home, hiking her bag onto her shoulder.

"Both of your parents work?"

"Yep. My dad is a plastic surgeon, and my mother is a model."

"You're playing ball?"

"My dad is cool. He wants me to pursue my own

dreams, and no, he's not the kind of guy that grabs a pen, and starts marking where he wants to cut."

"I'll keep that in mind."

"Let's go on up."

Elsa didn't exactly have a choice. She followed him up to his room, and even his space had equipment inside to work out. Didn't this guy know how to do anything else?

****

"You want me to do what?" Elsa asked.

Noah placed her bag in the corner and turned toward her. "I want you take your shirt off so I can get some proper measurements." He grabbed the scales, his notebook, and his tape measure designed for the body, and waited.

"You're crazy. I'm not doing that."

"We need to start a record, or a diary," he said. This was the usual process for anyone about to lose weight.

"How about we go by just looks, or dress size? I tell you when something is loose?"

He shook his head. "That's not how this works."

"I don't care. I'm not getting on them, and I'm not letting you use some tape on me either."

She folded her arms, and Noah saw the vulnerability in her eyes.

"Look, this is going to be between us. I won't tell anyone at school. It'll be personal to us, to keep track."

Elsa nibbled her lip. "I'm not sure about this."

"You've got to start somewhere, and I'm not going to be able to use this as an example for college if I don't show the proper procedures."

"Writing it down?"

"Writing it down, keeping a record, and making sure it's all done properly."

She sighed. "You promise this won't go anywhere else?"

"It won't go anywhere."

"Do you promise?"

"Yes, I promise. Now, are you going to allow me to do this?"

She nodded. "Close your eyes."

"I've got to be able to see. Are you wearing a sports bra?"

"Yes."

"Then we're fine. Sports bras are as unflattering as they come."

"I hate this. I hate this. I hate this." She kept on repeating those words as she lifted up her shirt.

Her stomach was rounded, and her tits were squashed into a dark black sports bra. Noah had seen a lot of action in his life, even though he was only eighteen. There were a lot of girls who liked to fool around with him, not to mention women he'd picked up at random places. He was a guy. He liked to have sex, and not one of those women had ever gotten him this interested.

His cock started to swell, and he gritted his teeth, getting focused on the now. Thinking of his grandma, he stepped toward Elsa.

"Lift your arms out."

She did as he asked, and her cheeks were the color of a real ripe strawberry.

"Everything is okay," he said.

"Speak for yourself. You're not half naked."

He tutted. "Will this make you feel better?" He tugged his own shirt off so that he was as naked as she was.

"Not really."

Noah chuckled. "I'm doing my best to make you feel comfortable."

"How can that happen when you've got that wicked thing in your hand? Also, I don't want to know what it says. Don't read it out, okay?"

"Fine. May I do this now, or do you have another list of instructions for me?"

She pursed her lips, tilting her head to the side. "Nope, we're good."

"Come on, stop being a big baby."

"I don't have to remove my pants, do I?"

"No." He wouldn't mind if she wanted to, and for most fitness instructors they might ask her to.

"Cool. I can handle that I guess."

Reaching around her, he pressed the tape against her skin, and she jumped. The backs of his fingers touched her as well. He noted how soft her skin was.

"What are you doing? You're touching me."

"Not intentional, baby. I've got to take your measurements."

"Don't call me baby."

"Why not?"

"I don't like it."

"No wonder you don't have a boyfriend. You don't like being touched, or being called baby. What exactly do you like?"

"Being left alone and not called baby."

"It's my nickname for you. You're being a big baby, and so that's what I'll call you … baby." She sighed, and he waited. "May I finish now that I've started?"

"I'm waiting."

"Pain in the fucking ass."

"Shut it, jock."

"Nerd."

"Dumb ass."

"Spoilt brat."

"Shut up," she said.

"I won."

"Ugh! Just do it already."

"Wow, baby, you really like to get down and dirty, don't you?" She shot him a glare, but he silenced her with his words. "You're no fun, and I can say you're going to struggle through the whole of this."

"Fine, fine, fine. Do it."

He took the measurements for her waist and hips, making a note of them. Next he moved up to below her breasts, and she tensed.

"Be careful."

"I'm not fondling your tits," he said.

"You're crude."

"Hey, you're the one that went off halfcocked on losing weight. I'm helping you out here."

"So, I'm helping you as well."

"You're being a huge pain in my ass." He stared into her pretty brown eyes. "I'm being nice here. Stop being a bitch. I've heard you're supposed to actually be nice. We're both out of our comfort zone here, but you don't see me being a jerk. The least you can do is give me some damn credit!"

She took a step back, but he stopped her as he still held the tape around her. "You're right. I'm being a bitch, and I really shouldn't be. I'm so sorry."

"Now, can we get back to work?"

"One question first."

"What is it?" he asked, getting tired of all of her questions. Maybe he should have stayed working out at the gym where Jessica made a scene. Right now, he was starting to think he'd have been left alone for a hell of a lot longer.

"Why are you not making a big deal about this? I'm fat, and I've been bullied at school, by your very friends."

He sighed, and couldn't resist the urge to tuck a strand of hair behind her ear, so he did it. "My friends are assholes at times, I get it. I've been an asshole, and I'm sorry if I've ever hurt you, okay. All I can say is that you have my word that this will never get out."

She nodded, and proceeded to let him get the size around her breasts, and underneath them. He did her thighs, and then around her ass. After he was done with the measurements, he asked her to get on the scales, and he made a note of that as well.

"What are you going to call me for your paper or whatever it is they call is?"

"You're going to be exhibit A."

"Oh, I'm an A. That's good. I do well in school even though I'm not showing it right now."

Noah chuckled and handed her back her shirt. When she pulled it back over her head, he was shocked by the fact he was gutted to see her cover up. "So, we're onto the diet stage."

"Diet?"

"Yep, are you hoping to lose weight with a change of diet and exercise or just with exercise?"

"I don't know. If I change my eating habits my mom is going to know, and this is kind of a surprise for her."

Noah sighed. "Elsa, losing weight, it has to be about what you want, not what other people want."

"I get that. I do. I just want, I want my mom to be happy, and if she's happy, then I am."

"This isn't the right way to lose weight."

"Please, Noah. This is what makes me happy, making her happy."

He stared at her, seeing how much it really did mean to her. This was going against all of his rules.

Personally, if Elsa was happy with the way she was, then he didn't see a reason to change her. Even now, some would say she needed to lose a couple of pounds, but from what he saw, she was fucking hot. If only she wore the right clothes for her shape, she'd have half of the guys panting for her. She was a size sixteen, which wasn't all that big. Sure, compared to a size zero it was big, but she was cute, hot even.

Staring at her, Noah imagined her in one of those old vintage fifties styles dresses that Jessica had tried to wear a year ago. Elsa would pull it off, whereas Jessica just looked gaunt.

Great, now he was starting to think like a pussy by imagining her in different clothes.

"Okay, so how about you make a diary of everything you eat. I'll assess, and then we can see where you can make changes without your mother knowing."

"Sure, I can do that. It's pretty easy."

"Good, great."

"When would you like to get started?" she asked.

"I work out at Bruce's gym four times a week. Do you think you could start making trips there after school?"

"Yeah, I can make some studying excuse to my parents. It shouldn't be too hard."

"Great. Monday, we'll make a start, and next Saturday, I want to see your diary of what you've eaten."

"Will do, boss."

Later that night, Noah was chatting with his friends on social media. It was late, and he'd not seen them all day as he'd been catching up on his own workout, and then school work. His parents still weren't back, but that wasn't anything strange. There were many times when he was home alone.

Searching for Elsa's name, he found her easily

enough, with a few friends as well. Over her page, he saw a couple of pictures of her with Kimberley. The pair was inseparable at school. They were always having lunch together, sharing class.

He was about to send her a friend request, and decided against it. No one needed to get suspicious, and he'd given her a promise, which he intended to keep.

Chapter Three

"Why are you scribbling crap into a notebook?" Kimberley, or Kim, asked.

Elsa glanced up to see her friend frowning across the bench at her. She had been doing everything that Noah had asked of her. "Nothing, no reason. Mom asked me to keep a diary of everything I eat," she said, lying easily. It wasn't hard. Kim had been at her house many times when her mother talked about what to eat and the right food to take in.

"She's wanting you to lose weight again?"

"She's never really stopped."

"No offense, Elsa, but your mom is a little mean."

"Not mean, not really."

Kim raised a brow.

"What?"

"She's always pressuring you to lose weight. I don't think that's nice," Kim said.

"It's nothing. I've got a handle on it." Elsa picked her fork up, and stared down at her meatloaf. School food was horrible, and everyone had to be careful about what they picked. Three years ago, Kim had gotten food poisoning because of something she ate.

"Are you sure? I hate that your mother makes you feel that way."

"Don't worry about it, Kim."

"I'm always here for you, you know that right?"

"Yes, I do, thanks."

She ate her meatloaf while Kim talked about her father opening up another supply store. This time he was branching out, going to England with the hope of getting into Europe.

"Wow, that is a big deal."

"Yeah, it's all he's talking about, and of course

it's driving Mom up the wall. She's trying to paint every chance she gets." Kim was an artist, like her mother. "How about we hang out tonight?"

Elsa was about to answer when they were interrupted by a group of guys, Noah's friends. She tensed up, waiting for the taunts.

"Hey, paintbrush, are you ready to do some studying?" Kurt asked.

Noah leaned against the tree, and Elsa glanced at him. When he raised his brow at her, she quickly turned her attention to her friend.

"Go away," Kim said, glaring at Kurt.

Instead of him going away, Kurt took a seat beside her. Much to Elsa's discomfort, Noah took her right, while Ryan took her left. Adam, the other friend, sat on Kim's free side.

She was a little confused as to why they were getting special attention.

"Why? We're friends, really good friends."

"What do you want?"

"Seriously, this is how you treat lab partners?"

"Kurt, we have to work on one project together, that is all."

"What is going on?" Elsa asked, looking from Kim to Kurt and back again.

"Nothing," Kim said.

"Our biology teacher put us together, and we're to complete an assignment as a team."

"Have you done what I asked you to do?" Kim asked.

"Which was?"

"Find an actual disease for us to write about?"

"Nope, but I was thinking we could do one of the sexual ones."

Elsa scrunched her nose up. "I've got to head to

31

the library," she said.

"Do not leave me, Elsa."

"I can't help it, I think I'm going to throw up. Meet you there?"

"Fine, fine."

She saw her friend's cheeks were a nice shade of pink, and there was even a small smile across her lips. Kim may be pretending not to like Kurt, but all the other signs were there.

Leaving the bench, Elsa made her way to the trashcan and tipped her leftovers inside. She placed the tray back in the dinner hall before leaving. Making her way toward the library, she gave Denise, the librarian, a wave. She went to the back of the library and started looking for the chemistry book she needed to complete her homework. Scanning over the shelves, she wasn't expecting anyone, so when Noah started to talk, she jumped.

"Hey," he said.

Glancing behind her, she glared. "What the hell?" She whispered each word, looking around to make sure no one was watching.

"What are you looking for?"

"Why did you follow me?"

"I wanted to talk to you, and can I say you walk really fast?"

She frowned. "You're in the library."

"Yeah, I know what one looks like. I come here as well. I even know Denise."

"I'm sort of, erm, yeah, you're confusing me right now."

They were both whispering.

"I was just going to make sure you were coming to Bruce's tonight?"

"Yes, I said I was going to be there. I'm not going

to back down now. I told you that." She grabbed her bag and rummaged around in the chaos to grab the diary she had started. "I've even been doing what you asked. It's all going to be in there."

"Make sure to put down that you threw half of it in the trash as well. It has got to be as accurate as you can make it."

She nodded. "I will do, boss."

Turning back to the shelves, she started scanning the books. All the time she was aware of Noah not leaving.

"What's up?" she asked.

"All day Sunday I couldn't get Kurt to shut up about your friend."

"She's a great girl."

"Yep, and I've got a feeling he's seeing that."

She chuckled. "Yeah, I'm sure Kurt is going to go chasing after my friend."

"Why not?"

"Last year he was calling her metal mouth and chubbers. Now he wants to get to know her. Kim's not going to forgive him easily." She may have seen her friend being happy by the attention, but she'd never allow herself to fall for him.

"That's their problem, not ours."

"We don't have a problem, Noah." She turned to smile at him.

He pursed his lips, glancing up and down at her. She wore a baggy shirt and loose jeans. They were her comfortable jeans, and sneakers. Her brown hair was pulled back into a ponytail.

"What are you staring at?"

"Have you ever thought about wearing clothes that actually fit you?"

"That's really weird right now." She looked down

at herself. "I'm fine the way I am."

"You're right. I'll catch you later."

As quickly as he invaded her life, he was gone, leaving her completely confused. "I will never understand that guy."

By the time Kim came to her, Elsa was already making notes from the chemistry book she found.

"You took your time."

"Don't laugh, okay?"

"I'm not laughing. I'm curious is all."

"Let me grab my book, and we'll talk." Kim rushed off to grab whichever book she needed.

Writing down her notes, Elsa jumped as Kim threw her book onto the table. "Okay, so last Friday, Mrs. Donald gave us all a new assignment. She picked who we partnered up with, and I ended up with Kurt. Obviously, he's not letting me live it down, and now he's everywhere. At the weekend, he even came around to my place just so we could study."

"Do you like him?"

"Not really. He's a bully. Mean. Kind of cute, but I don't want mean and cute. I don't want any guy ruining my chances of getting into a good college."

"I know what you mean."

"Do you think I'm being mean?"

"No, not at all." She smiled at her friend. "I think it's kind of sweet. Let's hope the cheerleading squad doesn't start attacking us."

Kim nodded. "That's the last thing I want to deal with right now."

"Does Kurt have a girlfriend?"

"I don't know. He didn't say that he did, and I didn't exactly ask. The last thing I want is for him to get the wrong impression."

Elsa stared down at her chemistry book and kept

herself busy. She couldn't help but wonder what it would be like if her friend did date Kurt. He was one of the hottest guys in school, and everyone expected him to date one of the cheerleaders.

Something was happening to her head, and she wasn't sure she liked it. Guys like Kurt and Noah never dated girls like them.

****

"Are you ready to work your butt off?" Noah asked as Elsa climbed out of her car.

"I'm ready. I had to lie to my parents and tell them I was going to the library, but I got here." She held up her key card as well. "Are you ready to work my butt off?" She frowned. "Scrap that. It sounded completely wrong."

"It sounded dirty to me."

They entered Bruce's gym to find a new guy on the front. Noah didn't recognize him, and they both scanned their cards, heading toward the changing rooms.

"I'll meet you out in the main corridor."

"Sure."

He watched her disappear into her changing room, and wondered what was wrong with her. They didn't know each other all that well, but from what he did know, Elsa was usually a bubbly person, apart from her bitchiness to him on Saturday, which he could understand.

Entering the male changing room, the scent of sweat met his senses. He changed quickly and waited out in the hall for Elsa to appear. She was tying her hair back as she left the room.

"Hey," she said.

She wore a baggy shirt, this one even baggier than the one she'd worn at school, and some cycling shorts, most of which were covered by the ugly ass shirt.

"Do you not own something that fits?"

"Why would I wear something fitting to the gym? People will see my rolls and lumps."

Wow, talk about low self-esteem. His mother would have a field day with this girl. Yes, his mother was a model, but she was also petitioning to bring to light the eating disorders that occur within the industry.

"Never mind. Let's go and get warmed up."

They entered a room that had over thirty people. There was a lot of space, so he didn't have to worry about helping her out.

"We need to stretch those muscles, get them warmed up so we don't hurt ourselves while we exercise. We'll do this now, then move onto some minor weights, treadmill, and we'll cool down with more stretches."

"Okay."

Once again, she didn't seem all that thrilled. Pushing forward on what he was about to do, he showed her each stretch, and she copied him with the pose.

"Go down as far as you can, touch the tip of your toes or in our case sneakers, draw your arms up, and stretch up to the sky."

Elsa giggled. "I feel like I'm in gym class."

"It's not much different."

"So we have to do this stretch as well?" She stepped forward, stretching out her hamstring, and lifted her hands up as if to push against something.

"Yes, yes, that's right."

She impressed him by showing off a few more exercises. Noah followed her, and when they were nice, warm, and ready, he took her toward the weight's room.

"Am I going to end up looking like one of those body builders with huge muscles?"

"No."

"Good, my mom wouldn't go for that look either.

She doesn't like them."

"What exactly does your mom like?" he asked. He sat her down on the edge of a bench, and gave her some female lightweight barbells. He grabbed the ones he was using to start off. "Now, rest your elbow on your knee, and lift up." He showed her what he was doing, and she followed along with him. Together they pumped some weights, his by far heavier than hers.

"My mom just wants a blonde, size nothing doll that she can play dress up with. I'm not the perfect doll, so she tries to make me so."

They changed hands, and he watched her work the barbells. She wasn't getting out of breath, and he was able to see that she wasn't overly unfit.

He increased the weights for her, and did the same for himself.

"Have you ever thought of talking to her about it?"

"I've tried. My dad has tried, when he's not busy working on a case."

"Your father's a lawyer, right?"

"A kickass one."

"Is that what you want to be?" he asked.

"Nah. You don't want to be a plastic surgeon?"

"Nope. I can't stand the thought of cutting someone open or changing them just because they don't like it."

"Really? I bet your father makes a fortune from all the tummy tucks, and people's quest for perfection?"

"He does, but that doesn't mean he loves it all the time." Noah put down the barbell, and led her toward the machine that had her lying down on her back with her on either side of the bench. "Push this up."

"Come on, spill about your dad."

"He does work for burn victims, crime victims,

and children born with defects that their parents want changing. He's not some asshole."

"I didn't mean it like that. You know plastic surgeons have a bad rep."

"I know. Sorry, I didn't mean to snap at you."

Her body tensed, and the ugly ass shirt rode up her with each press.

Noah stared at her body, what she considered her imperfections, and he grew aroused. "Swap," he said.

She pushed up and stood. He sat down, and started to push the weights up. "There was a time that my dad was stuck up. He did tit jobs as if they were going out of fashion, and was always talking about my mom having work done to help her career. He had porn stars on his books, celebrities." He couldn't argue with Elsa's assessment. It was all true.

"What happened?" she asked.

"He was at a party, getting his name out. Mom was there, and she kept asking him to leave. She hated being with him when he was selling the perfect body. Everyone always assumed that she went under the knife to be so slender. You know liposuction?"

"Everyone knows about lipo."

"Yeah, well, my mother didn't have any of that shit. She's a model who was happy with her faults."

"She sounds like one hell of a woman, who doesn't like to be crossed."

He chuckled, swapping once again with Elsa. "She is."

"So what happened?"

"Dad was determined to stay, and so we stayed. I was twelve at the time. At around one in the morning, we decided to leave. I sat in the backseat, and they were arguing. Mom called him a pretentious prick who didn't care about anyone but himself. She accused him of having an affair, and everything. He shouted at her, told her she was nothing but a whore. Anyway, to cut a long story short as that is embarrassing as hell, Dad wasn't paying attention, and he crashed into another driver. Mom's face slammed up against the glass, and I was struck as well." He turned, showing her the scar down the left side of his body where the metal of the car had somehow crushed, striking him in the side.

"Oh my God. How did I not know this?" she asked, reaching out to touch his scar. The mark didn't bother him.

"It's not something I advertise."

"What happened?"

"Mom had lacerations to her face, and after my accident, I had to go to the care unit for kids. Dad had to switch and change between my room, and my mom's room. It was a hard few weeks. Dad got to see all these people that had suffered. I shared a room with a kid who had suffered burns to part of his face and neck. It was like my dad had only ever seen a way of making the beautiful even more beautiful. To hold them up to a higher standard than anyone else."

"The work had gone to his head?"

"Yeah. After we got out of the hospital, Mom asked for him to change, as otherwise she wanted a divorce, and she'd take me with her. There was no way her son was going to turn out like him." Noah shrugged. "Holy shit, I can't believe I just said that to you."

"I'm really pleased you did. I talk about my mom all the time." She shrugged. "Parents, huh?"

"They suck at times."

"Your dad is different now?" she asked.

"Yep. He still does the tit jobs, the lipo, and stuff. However, he now has a foundation to help those that have been hurt. It's a good job that he does."

"You're proud of him?"

"Yeah. There was a woman about two months ago who had gotten away from her ex, but he'd left her scarred. Every time she'd look in the mirror, she'd remember this guy. My dad, he healed her, and now she is doing better than ever." Noah smiled. "How can I not be proud of a guy who does that?"

She smiled, and he couldn't help but look at her. She was so beautiful.

Where the hell had all that truth telling come from? He never shared any of that kind of shit with anyone, not even with Kurt, Adam, or Ryan.

Noah didn't understand it. Sure, he'd grown up with Elsa being in the background of his life. They had gone to the same preschool, kindergarten all the way up to high school. Never had he given her more than a passing thought, and yet right now, he was telling her stuff he didn't even tell his most trusted friends. It made no sense, no sense at all.

Chapter Four

The following Saturday, and three training sessions, about to start her fourth, Elsa waited outside of Bruce's gym. She glanced through the food diary checking to make sure she'd put everything in order, and that it was easy to read.

When she spotted Noah's car, she climbed out, holding onto her bag.

"Hey, baby," he said.

Handing him her diary, she offered him a beaming smile. "Meet you in the warm up room?"

"Hold your horses." He leaned against the car and scanned the pages.

She waited patiently, flicking the ring of her keys around her finger.

"Okay, I think I can see where we can make some adjustments."

"You want to talk about it now?"

"Would you like to go somewhere else to talk about it?"

"How about we work out and then talk about it?"

"Fine, after we've worked out, there's a cute little deli a few blocks from here, and we can go over this then." He placed the diary in his sack, and together they headed into the gym. Sarah was on the front desk, and she offered them both good mornings. "This one is cranky today."

"That's because for a date you're taking her to the gym. Shame on you, Noah."

"This is not a date," Elsa said.

"It's not?"

"I'm helping her out."

Sarah looked from Elsa then at Noah, and back again. "Shame, you'd make a really cute couple."

"I'm going to go and get changed." Elsa escaped into the ladies' room, and quickly changed into her workout gear. By the time she got out, he was already there. "How did you get here before me?"

"I don't like wasting time."

They made their way down to the weight rooms where they were able to do some stretches.

"How do you feel to adding some swimming in say a week's time?"

"Sure, I don't mind. You're the boss. I'm just doing as I'm told."

"Right, I'm making Sunday our weigh in and measurements."

Elsa stopped stretching. "Why? Can't we do them today?"

"We could, but I'd rather do it before the next week. Each week we can start afresh."

"Ugh, I don't know if I can get away."

"We're ten, twenty minutes apart? We can figure something out."

"I don't want my mother to find out."

"She won't. I'm good at keeping a secret. Besides, we can always say we're working on a project together."

Elsa started to stretch up and then down, touching her toes.

Noah released a noise, and she glanced behind her to make sure he was okay. "What's wrong?" she asked.

"Nothing, I'm all good. You continue your stretches."

"Considering I'm the nerd, you're acting weird."

He laughed. "Stretch, baby."

Elsa went through all of her stretches, and this time for weights, she used her legs and thighs. She liked that Noah always alternated, and what she enjoyed was the fact they talked about everything.

"Have you heard Kurt is stalking Kim?" she asked.

"I talked to him about that. He says he's intrigued by her lack of interest in him. Sucker thinks he's got a chance with her."

She laughed. "He hasn't. I can assure you."

After thirty minutes on the weights, they headed into the treadmill room.

Climbing onto the machine, she waited for Noah to program her. He always ran beside her. She would start on a steady walk, building it up to reach a run. She hated running. No matter how tight she put her sports bra on, her boobs always bounced, and not only did it hurt, it made her aware of how big they were. The boys made fun of her running, whether it was her body moving, or her boobs bouncing. Ever since she'd grown breasts, she had avoided running at all costs.

Starting off on a walk, she accepted the water from Noah, and watched him out of the corner of her eye as he climbed on the treadmill, and started off jogging.

"You just like to show off, don't you?"

"My smoking hot body is used to showing off."

She closed her eyes, enjoying the feel of her body just taking a steady walk. The machine she was on beeped, and she picked up the pace. Noah always leaned over, messing with the setting to make sure she kept on walking. It was easier to do this.

More beeps, and she went a little faster.

He pushed further until she was running, and again, she did so with her eyes closed. It was strange at first, but she found the only way to run comfortably was by pretending no one was watching her. Also, it allowed her the chance to pretend she wasn't running. It didn't stop her from getting out of breath.

She wouldn't open them until he started to slow everything back down to a walk. Time passed, she didn't know how much, and when she was back to walking, she looked over at Noah and smiled. "I'm getting used to this."

"You look weird with your eyes closed. Don't ever go running in a park or something. You'd crash into stuff."

"I trust you. Besides, I can do the whole running thing with my eyes closed, not open."

"Is that some kind of sickness?" They had stepped off the treadmills, and Noah handed her some water.

"Not sickness."

"Then why?"

"You really don't know?"

"I wouldn't ask if I knew."

Elsa sighed, and then told him the story of the boys, and her body when she ran. She was even telling him stuff she hated admitting out loud. "You should know. You were there, and one of the guys laughing your asses off because some of us girls have been cursed with big ones. If I was allowed, I'd get them reduced."

"Don't do that!" He snapped the words out, making her jump.

"Whoa, where did that come from?"

"You don't need to change yourself. Your tits are fine."

She frowned at him, but decided to let it go. "There you have it, the reason I hate running, or working out in general. My body, it moves with me. I'm just not comfortable doing stuff like that, and a treadmill means I don't have to worry about it. Are we stretching again?"

"Yes."

"When do you want me to bring a costume for the pool?" She didn't actually own one so she'd have no choice but to go ahead and buy one.

"A week after next?"

"I can do that."

After they warmed up, Elsa made her way to the changing rooms, grabbed her stuff, and waited outside for Noah.

She didn't have to wait long. Neither of them had changed out of their workout gear. There was no way she was going to take a shower here. She hated the feel of exposure while everyone was moving around.

They headed out, dumped their bags in their cars, and walked toward the deli. Elsa was starving. She looked forward to finding out what Noah thought of her diet. Personally, she didn't think it was all that bad. Yes, there were a few snacks and stuff she could cut out, which she'd do easily.

The deli was busy, so they stood in the queue together.

"What are you in the mood for?" he asked.

"Seeing as you're the guy in charge of my diet, why don't you order for me?"

"Will do. Do you want to go and get us a seat?"

"Sure." She left the queue, and found the private table toward the back. Checking through her cell phone, she saw there was a message from her mother.

Mom: **I'm at the country club. Call me if you need me.**

Elsa wouldn't call her mother. One of the few things that was guaranteed to put a smile on her mother's face was that club.

Deleting the message, she glanced across the deli to see Noah being served. She didn't know why she was telling him all of this stuff, and it really unnerved her with how easy it was to talk to him. He didn't judge her.

This guy, he was like an entirely different guy

from the one in high school, and yet, he wasn't.

Thinking back hard, Elsa couldn't actually recall Noah doing or saying anything mean to her directly. The only drama she remembered was that of his ex, Jessica.

It didn't matter.

She didn't understand why she was thinking about him or their past together. They'd always been near to each other, just never friends. Pushing her crazy thoughts aside, she watched as he placed a bagel with low fat spread and chicken in front of her.

"Wow, I have to say I thought I was going to get cardboard," she said.

"Nah. Believe it or not, I do have a need for proper food. Preferably homemade. I don't like crap in my diet. I even believe in eating dessert as well, but that's a strict treat."

Elsa chuckled. "What do you think of my eating diary?"

"I can see where you can make some changes. I grabbed a pen from the lady behind the counter."

He opened her book and started making notes.

****

Noah didn't know what to do. On the one hand, he wanted her to lose weight for her mother. When he actually thought about it, he didn't want to help her for her mother. Elsa was fine. Yes, her figure was bigger than a lot of the girls he'd been with, but she was fucking hot. He wished he could get her into clothes that actually showed off that hourglass figure. She'd have guys drooling after her. Of course, then when he thought about it, he didn't want to allow her to have others know.

It had been one week of training with her, and he liked her. He really liked her. She was fun, and honest. When they were together, she wasn't always holding a mirror up to her face, or thrusting a camera begging for him to tell him how he felt.

For once in his life, he really liked a girl.

There had been lots of girls, and women, along the way ever since he'd discovered how much he liked sex, and he liked it a lot. None of the women had ever made he feel like this. He'd certainly never felt relaxed in the gym, working out with one of them.

Having Elsa close her eyes while she ran, gave him the perfect opportunity to observe her, without her even knowing it. Her tits, they had given him a boner, which he had to think of his grandmother to get rid of.

Earlier, when she had been bent over, he'd been unable to ignore how hot she was. Her ass thrust up, almost begging for him to sink his cock inside her.

Damn, he was bad. Fuck. Elsa was trusting him, and all he could think about was getting her naked, and fucking her.

They were both eighteen years old, and he'd never pressure her.

She doesn't even know that you like her!

Staring down at her food diary, he saw that she actually ate pretty well. There were exercises that Elsa could do that would keep her figure, improve her fitness, and it meant she'd stay the shape she was but be healthy.

"What is it?" she asked. She took a bite of the bagel he'd bought her, and she moaned, her eyes closing as she licked the cream cheese from her lips. "That is so damn tasty. How did I not know about this place?"

"It's a closely guarded secret."

"Well, I'm glad that I'm on your side. I get to share in your secret." She winked at him. "So, boss, where do you think I need to improve my awesomeness?"

"We can cut out the snacks, and change your soda for some smoothies or water." He made a few more notes and handed it back to her. "I want you to keep up with this, and at the end, we'll do some results." He took a bite of his bagel, and watched as she nodded.

"None of this will alert my mom?" she asked.

"None at all. The smoothies can just be down to a preference. Maybe say you had it with a friend."

"I like that. I must get Kim to like those smoothies."

He grabbed his cell phone, and started locating a great website. "What's your phone number?"

"Why?"

"I can email you this good site with great smoothie recipes."

"Oh, of course, silly me." She gave him her number and her email address.

"Great." He took another bite of his bagel.

"This is really good stuff."

"You're doing really good. There is one thing I'm going to ask though, and I'm not sure you're going to like it."

"Hit me with it."

"I should have asked you last week, but I forgot, and to be honest I didn't think you'd stick with it."

"What is it?" she asked.

"I need to take a picture of you, for my paper."

"Why?"

"It's a before, and then I'll take an after shot."

"You want a before picture of me?"

"Yes. It will help with my paper. It's no big deal, and it doesn't even have to be with your head on."

She laughed. "Yeah, it kind of does, but I know what you mean. A picture from the neck down. I've seen a lot of them. Erm, sure, where do you want to do it?"

"Maybe back at my place again. We can drive over now, after lunch, I can take some pics, and that'll be it."

"Oh, wait, what about tomorrow?" she asked.

"Tomorrow?"

"Yeah, I'm walking to your place to get measured, why don't we just do the pictures then? It could be fun." She finished her bagel, licking her lips.

"Sure, we'll do it then." He was happy to have an excuse to spend some time with her tomorrow, but he was also gutted that he'd not been able to think of something reasonable to keep them together longer today.

Fuck!

"What are you doing today?" she asked.

"I don't know. Probably do some more weights when I get home."

"Seriously? You don't think you work out enough?"

"What else is there to do?"

"I don't know. Watch a movie, go and see some beautiful sights."

"We live in a neighborhood where everything is pristine, and beautiful, and there's nothing out of place. It's clinical."

She rolled her eyes. "You've just not been looking hard enough. Come on." She stood up, throwing him some notes.

"What?"

"Go pay, and I'll grab my car. Come on." He found her giggle intoxicating.

Paying for their food, he met her outside. Climbing into her car, he did his seatbelt, and waited. "Okay, where is this fun?"

"Relaxation, my friend." She pulled away from the deli, and went up onto the highway.

"Where are we going?"

"Just relax. I know what I'm doing. So, about two years ago, Dad was super stressed about a murder case he was working on. It was a big deal. Mom and Dad were fighting, and everything was going to shit, if you don't mind my saying so."

"It's just us here."

"I know. I know. Anyway, Mom threatened him with a divorce unless he slowed down. To be honest, I think he was going to die from all the stress anyway, but, one weekend he took us on a camping vacation. I don't mean hotels either, I mean actual camping, tents, beds, a gas stove, you name it. It completely rocked. Probably the best weekend of my life with my parents."

"Why are you telling me this?"

"All you do is work out, and I know it's for fun, but I want you to have a chance to relax, and just to see the world a little differently. I'm not saying stop, and turn into a slob. You still need all of those girls to lose themselves over you."

"Wow, Elsa, are you paying me a compliment?"

"Yeah, come on, you know you're hot. Everyone knows you're hot. You hang out with the hot brigade."

He laughed. "I didn't know you were an admirer."

"So, what I'm thinking is I show you the world through a new perspective."

"How did you get on with camping?" he asked.

"At first I didn't like it. In a tent around lots of people with bugs, and the risk of getting murdered in my sleep, but being around my parents with nothing to distract them, it was awesome. No phone, no laptop, no other world but the one we made."

"It sounds great."

"It was."

They drove for over an hour, and Noah relaxed, enjoying the ride. She didn't pull up into a camping zone, however. She pulled up in a parking lot that had several cars already there. Some people were packing away equipment.

"Come on."

"This is where you camped?"

"Oh, no. That weekend, we explored the beauty surrounding the camp, which is probably an hour's walk that way." She pointed somewhere west. Leaving the car, she grabbed his hand. "Let's go."

There was a walkway with trees on either side, and within seconds they were surrounded by woodland.

"Where are we going?"

"You'll know it when you see it."

Noah followed her up a steep incline, using the excuse of steadying her to hold onto her hips to help her up.

They had been walking and climbing for a good twenty minutes, and then there was a clearing at the top. Everything opened up, and he saw a railing in place. Moving toward it, he looked down and gasped. It was really high up.

"Some people use this to parachute, but look," she said, pointing across.

He followed her finger and overlooked the beautiful country. The mass of forest, and he even caught sight of a lake—it was the most beautiful thing he'd ever seen.

"Wow," he said.

"It's pretty awesome right? Bird watchers come here, hikers, and photographers alike. They all love the view, and it's so magical."

He saw it. Noah saw it all. "I've never seen anything like this."

"I come here to think about the world, and what I'd like to be. This, the beauty, the nature, it puts everything into perspective."

Noah stared at her, and he was struck by how

beautiful she was. "Yeah, it really does."

Chapter Five

"Where are you going?" her mother asked.

Elsa glanced across the kitchen island to see her mother staring at her. "To a friend." She tapped her bag. "We've got to work on our English assignment."

"Oh, you didn't say anything about going out today."

"I'll be back for dinner."

Lorna, her mother, nodded. "I was hoping we could go to the country club today, maybe have some dinner. I put you a dress on your bed. I thought you might like to wear it."

She'd seen the dress. It was an old fifties style dress that nipped in at the waist, and flared out. Elsa had tried it on last night, and of course she couldn't do it up. The dress was a size too small.

"Erm, I'm sorry."

"I don't want to go to the country club, Lorna. I'll take you out to dinner. We can bring something back for Elsa, right?"

She perked up. "Yeah, I'd like that. Seriously, you don't need to worry about me. I can fend for myself."

"How is school?" he asked. Bill, her father, took a seat at the counter, and accepted a glass of juice.

"It's going great. I've got this project in English to finish up." She finished her toast, dusted off her hands, and walked around to her father, kissing his cheek. Next, she kissed her mother before she left the house.

Once she was safely outside of the house, she let out a breath, pleased that she'd been able to escape.

There was no way in hell she was going to the country club.

Several of the girls from school went there, including Kim, and she knew her friend hated going there. Fortunately, Kim's mother never made her.

She started walking toward Noah's house.

Her cell phone binged, and she grabbed it out of her pocket.

Kim: **What u doin today?**

Elsa: **Not a lot. Busy right now, homework. C u l8r?**

Kim: **Sure.**

While she had her cell in her hand, she sent a quick text to Noah letting him know she was on her way.

Noah: **Cool, c u soon. I'm timing.**

Picking up her pace, she made her way toward Noah's, and was knocking on the door. She noticed two cars in the driveway. Neither one of them was Noah's.

He opened the door, holding his watch up. "Impeccable timing."

"How long?"

"Ten minutes."

"I wonder if I can get that down." She entered his home, which was similar to her parents' in size.

"My mom and dad are home. Don't worry, they're outside having breakfast."

"Noah, show off your little friend," a feminine voice said.

"Ugh, that's my mom."

Elsa smiled. "Parents!" She shrugged, trying to pretend she wasn't nervous when the truth was, she was as nervous as hell.

He held her arm and led her down a long corridor toward the back room.

"If I don't do this, they're only going to keep on nagging, and they will find a reason to embarrass me."

"I'd rather like to see you all embarrassed. It could be cute."

Noah raised his brow, and she was struck again by

how handsome he was. This had been happening to her quite often, and it had only been a week. When she saw him at school, during their training together, she noticed little things. The twinkle in his eyes when he was teasing her, the way he stood too close to her. All of them had become something that she really enjoyed when she was in his company.

They entered a large garden with a patio area that led down to a pool.

On two chaise lounges lay his parents. His mother sat up and pushed her sunglasses up on top of her head. She was so breathtakingly beautiful.

"Hello, I didn't know it was a girl."

"I told you I was working on a history paper."

"Hello, Mrs. Stewart," Elsa said.

"Hello, dear, I don't know your name as Noah failed to mention it."

"It's Elsa, Mom."

His father turned around, and Elsa tensed up. Wow, she was being faced with a plastic surgeon and a model. This had to be one of the worst moments of her life.

"It's nice to meet you both."

"Tell me, Elsa, what do your parents do?" his father asked.

"Er, okay, my father is a defense lawyer, Bill Quinn."

"I've heard of him."

"My mom doesn't have a job. She looks after us."

"Is your mom's name Lorna?"

"Yes."

"I've met her. She's a charming woman," his mother said.

Elsa simply smiled.

"We're going to go and work on that paper."

"What is it about?" his father asked.

"The plague."

"World War Two."

They both answered something different.

"I see," his father said.

"Leave them. They clearly know what they're doing," his mother said.

"Let's go." Noah took the lead once again but his father called his name. "What, Dad?"

"Bag it, will you."

Elsa's cheeks went a bright red, and Noah released a groan.

"So fucking embarrassing. They're not like that around anyone else."

"What were they like around Jessica?" Elsa asked.

He grunted. "They hated her, and gave her such a hard time. My parents are very intelligent, so when they don't like someone, or want to see how good they are, they ask stupid questions, or at least, intelligent ones. Jessica failed."

"Well, she's only known for her athletic ability." *And for her ability to suck and fuck.* Elsa was a virgin, but she knew a great deal of rumors, and had heard a lot of people talk. She was a virgin that knew what everything was called, and knew what to do. It was simply down to the physical, which she hadn't done.

"Come on, Jessica is known for a lot more, and I bet it's all true."

"You broke up with her for cheating on you. Did it make you sad?"

"You'd think it would, but it didn't. I was pissed more than anything else. I knew it was going to be a big deal at school, do the rounds of Jessica cheating on me. There was even some kind of bet on if I was going to put the guy in the hospital."

"Didn't you like her?" Elsa asked, switching her bag onto another shoulder.

"Not really. She talked a whole lot, and she did a lot of screaming. To be honest, I was only interested in the sex. I didn't have to work hard to get any."

She wrinkled her nose.

"Shit, sorry, I forgot you don't like sex."

Holding up her hand, she shook her head. "Don't worry about it. I've never done it. It's completely different from actually not liking it. I don't yet know if I like it."

"Oh."

"This is getting a little uncomfortable."

"Thankfully for us, we are at my room." He opened the door, and she stepped inside. Noah took her bag from her and threw it onto his bed.

"Just so you know I told my parents that we were working on an English paper."

"We have English together."

"Cool, that works then. We can make something up." She looked around the room, noticing the different exercise equipment again. Nothing had changed since her visit here last. "So, pictures. How do you want to work this?"

"I've got some workout gear that I bought for you. I want you to try it on, and then we can take pictures. It has to be similar to what we see in magazines. A before and after shot."

"Okey-dokey." He handed her some clothes, and she glanced around the room. "Where do you want me?"

"I've got a bathroom."

She followed behind him, liking the look of his butt.

Get over yourself.

Nothing is going to happen here, nothing will ever

happen here.

He opened the door, and she stepped into a small en-suite bathroom.

Elsa closed the door, and stripped down to her underwear. Grabbing the workout gear, she tugged on the running shorts, followed by the sports bra. Next, she put on the sneakers, and stared in the mirror.

She groaned.

Everything was there, it was visible.

He saw you last week.

Not only had he seen her, he'd also done some touching as well.

Dropping her head into her hands, she shook herself, trying to bring some focus to her life.

"This sucks."

"Is everything okay in there?"

"Yeah, it's fine," she said, calling out louder for him to here. "I'm just wishing I didn't eat lots of ice-cream and pies." The last bit she said quietly.

Opening the door partially, she stared out at him. "I'm not sure about this."

"Why?"

"I look horrible."

"Have some trust. I've proven myself, and look." He handed her a piece of paper. "It's all above board. I'm not lying to you."

She took the college advisor's letter, and read through it. Based on what Noah had discussed, there were several key points that he could improve on. One of them was creating this assignment, providing he could get someone to agree.

"Okay, I get it."

"I won't laugh, I won't mock. Trust me, Elsa. I won't let you down."

She was seeing that.

****

Noah had to put on a long shirt to hide the length of his cock pressing against his damn pants. What was it about Elsa? He was asking that of himself a lot lately, and she was driving him crazy, completely and totally crazy. He didn't understand this hold she had over him.

Well, it wasn't a hold.

She turned him on.

He liked spending time with her, and yesterday, he'd hated separating from her. The brief interaction with his parents, he knew they liked her, which was a big step. His mother had voiced her dislike of Jessica so many times. In the end, he'd been blunt with his father, and asked him for help.

His mother stopped commenting on Jessica, and blanked her whenever she was around.

Elsa opened the door, and her hands crossed in front of her over her stomach. He'd gone out, and bought clothes to fit her size, and yeah, the clothes highlighted her curves.

"What's the problem?" he asked.

"Everything is on display." She opened her arms. "Look. My belly, it's not flat, and you can't see my hipbones. Aren't hipbones supposed to be sexy as hell?" Next she lifted her tits, and he watched them bounce. "They're too big."

They're just right, baby.

"And my ass." She turned and bent over. "Look, it is huge."

His cock pulsed, and he stepped back, hoping he wasn't tenting his pants. Damn, he was fucking hot and ready for her. "You look fine." *Sexy, hot, and I want to fuck you so hard that I stop you looking at every other guy.*

"I'm never wearing this stuff again."

Stepping forward, he took her hands, and urged her out of the bathroom. "You're beautiful."

"Stop."

"No, I'm not going to stop. You look beautiful, and here, this doesn't matter to me."

"Are you some kind of chubby chaser?"

"Shut up, Elsa." He placed her in front of the only wall in his room that was plain white. "Now, I'm going to take a series of shots, and you're going to be happy, and enthusiastic, and not look like I'm the one who forced you to do this. It's all in the body. Now, hands on hips."

He pulled out his digital camera, and held it up, seeing her on the screen. Zooming in, he cut her head from the shot, and started to take different shots of her body. "Turn to the left." A couple more shots. "Then turn to the right." He pressed the button.

Once he was done with all the necessary shots, he didn't want to call a stop to it.

"Pull a funny face for me," he said.

"What? Why?"

"For some fun. You looked like I was torturing you, now show me I wasn't, and let's have some fun."

"None of these will be for your paper?"

"None."

Hands on hips, she stuck her tongue out, and crossed her eyes. Noah laughed. She rushed toward him. "Come on, now you."

She took the camera from him, and he pulled the same face as she had, only he flexed his muscles.

"Ohh, sexy, give me that body builder's, come hither look."

Several more shots, and he took the camera. "Show us that nerd come hither look."

She pouted for him and leaned forward.

Fuck, she was so damn hot, and she didn't even

know it. He loved that about her, how natural she was.

"Oh, some selfies, come on." They stood together, and she held the camera up. Of course that didn't go far enough, and he took the camera, holding it up a little further. He wrapped a hand around her waist and pulled her up against him, trying his hardest not to spoil the moment, or show that he was enjoying her being close to him.

They collapsed onto the bed, and still holding the camera, they laughed and giggled. He must have shot over a hundred pictures, but it was a lot of fun.

Together, they lay on his bed, and he enjoyed the feel of her against him.

"That was fun. Thank you for making it up to me." She looked up at him, and smiled. Without thinking, he leaned down, and pressed his lips against hers.

Elsa jerked back. "What was that?"

"I wanted to give you your first kiss."

She lifted up, and tucked some hair behind her ear. "I can't believe you just did that."

"I'm sorry. It doesn't have to be weird. It was wrong of me to think you'd want your first kiss to be by me."

"I've not really thought about my first kiss to be honest. It's not high on my list."

Noah shrugged. "It's no big deal." Her lips had been so soft, and he wanted another taste.

She glanced at his lips before looking back up at him. "It means nothing."

"Nothing at all," he said.

"Okay. I'd like to try that again without me being nervous."

Noah nodded, leaning up on his hands. "Come and kiss me."

She moved a little closer and leaned in. Her lips

touched his, light and soft. He wanted to kiss her some more, but she pulled back and smiled.

"I've never done this before," she said.

"I couldn't tell." He tried to lighten the mood.

She groaned and climbed off the bed. "I better go."

"Wait, Elsa. You don't have to run off."

"This is embarrassing. You're probably used to girls not slobbering all over you, and besides, we're just friends." She went to grab her bag, but he held it out of her way, following her back.

With each step he took, she took a step back until she hit the wall.

"Kissing is simple, it's natural." He cupped her face, tilting her head back. "Follow my lead, and go with what feels right. Relax, and know it's me here. Enjoy it."

He closed the distance, watching as her eyes grew a little wider. "Everything is okay here."

"I know."

Pressing his lips against hers, he gave little pecks to her mouth. When her eyes closed, he tilted his head, and sealed his lips over hers, sliding his tongue across them. She gasped, opening up, and he showed her exactly how good it was to be kissed by him. Sinking his fingers into her hair, holding her close, he ravished her mouth.

It started out as just a tester kiss, and now it was something more.

He wanted Elsa with a passion that scared him, yet it excited him all at the same time.

Loving her mouth, he tasted her lips, and savored her.

Finally, when he couldn't make the excuse of kissing her any longer, he released her, stepping back.

Her lips were red and swollen, and he wanted to do it all over again.

"I just thought you should know what a real kiss was like."

"That was amazing," she said. Her cheeks were flushed. "Er, I better go. You know."

"Wait, we haven't done your measurements yet," he said.

"Yeah, crap."

"Elsa, this doesn't have to be weird between us."

She frowned, looking doubtful. "Are you sure? I mean, we just kissed."

"I'm not feeling weird." *Other than wanting to bend you over my bed, and fuck you.* He didn't know where these possessive feelings were coming from, but he couldn't ignore them.

"You're not?"

"Nope. We kissed, and I'm hoping you enjoyed it."

She touched her lips, and nodded. "It was nice."
Victory.

He hoped she thought about him every time she touched her lips.

"If you ever want to make out, fumble, or anything, let me know."

"Fumble?"

"Yeah, let's pretend I didn't say that."

"Can we keep it strictly private friends where you're helping me?"

"Sure."

He was disappointed, but he hoped in time, and some pesky little tricks he had, he was going to win her over. What did he have to lose?

Chapter Six

One month later

"Is your mom still bugging you about that country club prom thing?" Kim asked.

Elsa was having a sleepover with her friend, and they had both opted for Kim's house.

"Yes. It's some kind of dance that shows off people's kids."

"It's horrible, but I've agreed to go," Kim said.

Elsa glanced up from her homework, in shock. "Really?"

"Yeah, it could be fun. We get to dance with some guys, and eat something nice. I'll be there, you'll be there, it'll be fun. We'll make it fun."

She laughed. "We'll make it fun?"

"If it's not fun, we can always behave like the worst daughters in the world, and we'll never get invited again. It's a win-win, either way. Do you want to see the dress?"

"Sure, why not."

Putting her paper down, Elsa stood up going toward her friend's clothing closet. Like hers, it was large, and filled with items their mothers had purchased for them.

It was right in the back, covered with a protective bag. Kim brought it out and unzipped it. The pale pink dress was beautiful. It had a long skirt and small straps for the arms.

"Would you like to see it on?"

"It fits?"

"There's a first for everything in my world. Mom made sure to get my measurements." Kim removed her clothes and stepped inside. Elsa helped her with the zipper in the back. Moving in front of the mirror, Elsa loved it.

"You look beautiful."

"Mom thinks if I have my hair up like this, with some butterfly pins—what do you think?"

"Dreamy. Do you hope to meet your dream guy?"

"No. I've got way too many plans before I think of falling for a guy." Kim gave a little twirl. "A girl can still dream of the guy who'll sweep her off her feet, and offer her some loving."

Elsa thought about the kiss she had shared with Noah. Neither of them had spoken about it in the last four weeks, which she liked. Nothing was weird between them. She did find herself thinking about his kiss, and what more could have happened between them.

"Did you know Kurt sent me a friend request?" Kim asked.

"He did?"

"Yeah."

"What did you respond?"

"I didn't." Kim wrinkled her nose. "I'm not going to be friends with Kurt."

"Did you finish that paper?"

"Yep, we did. He even did half the work, which was a surprise, and he won my mother over by charming her."

"No!"

"Yes. She asks about him as well. The polite young man." Kim rolled her eyes.

"Maybe he likes you."

Kim sighed. "He called me a lot of horrible names, Elsa. Names that if I even think about them, it makes me want to cry."

"Kim?"

"No, I can't. I don't want to think about it. He

called me fat, a whale? I'm not going to be that girl that has this big crush on the guy that bullied her. It would be too sad."

Elsa nodded. "So what are you going to do?"

"I'm going to ignore him. Before this blasted assignment, he didn't know I existed. I'll just keep on going until he doesn't know I exist again."

"That's the way to do it."

"See, I knew you'd understand."

Kim removed the dress after having a final twirl, and for the first time, Elsa was a little envious.

"Mom bought me a new dress and keeps asking me to wear it. It doesn't fit." Elsa left the closet to give Kim some privacy.

Sitting on the bed, Elsa hated how sad she felt.

Losing weight was something she was doing to try to make her mom happy. Just that morning, Elsa had to listen to her moan once again about the bad stuff inside pancakes. What her mother didn't know was that Elsa was trying out lower fat versions of the recipes. She'd found a really cool food blog online, and had started to be inspired. Nothing she did was ever good enough for her.

Her cell phone pinged, and she crawled off the bed to the floor to see who it was.

Noah: **U seemed sad today. Want to talk about it?**

Elsa: **No.**

It was only Thursday night. She'd have to see him tomorrow and Saturday. For the first time since she started her new healthier regime, she didn't want to go.

Noah: **Come on. I'm your motivator, your hot little body builder. Talk to me.**

Elsa: **Can't. I'm with Kim. Talk to you later.**

She turned her phone to silent, and smiled at Kim as she came out.

"Don't let your mom get you down. She does love you." Kim sat beside her. They leaned against the bed, and Elsa sniffed up, trying to stop the threat of tears. She hadn't cried in a long time, and she really didn't want to do it now.

"Oh, Elsa, what's wrong?"

"I'm tired of being fat." She covered her face with her hands. "With the way Mom is, anyone would think I'm this disgusting, horrible ... thing that can't stop shoving another cookie in my mouth."

Kim wrapped her arms around her, and held her close. "Ignore her."

"Why can't my mom be like yours? She supports you, and she doesn't nag you."

"She nags me all the time."

"Only because you don't always wear dresses. Your mom wants to pretty you up. Me? My mom just wants me to be slim, to lose weight so I can look pretty like all the other dolls that are there."

"Then how about we go shopping for you?" Kim asked.

"What do you mean?"

"Come to this prom party, and instead of going in something that is going to be too tight, and leave you uncomfortable, you and I will pick something out."

"You know my mom always picks my clothes."

"Yeah, and she can still pick out the dress. You don't have to wear it."

Elsa thought about it, and it actually made her feel better. "Thank you, Kim."

"You're like a sister to me. Don't let your mom change who you are. You're a beautiful woman, Elsa, inside and out. You don't need to be a size zero to be amazing. I think you're amazing." Kim rested her head on her shoulder. "Best friends forever?"

"BFFs all the way."

Holding her friend's hand, Elsa let the last of the tears fade away.

****

"Do you think I'm an asshole?" Kurt asked.

Noah looked up from his phone toward his friend. "Why do I feel this is going to be a trick question?"

"I'm being serious. What do you think of me?"

"Dude, if this is your way to come out, don't try to get with me. I like girls. If you're gay, I'm cool with that."

"I'm not gay."

"You sure?"

Kurt launched a pillow at him, and Noah caught it, throwing it back. He was pressing some weights as Kurt was pretending to study. They were having a sleepover, which was so fucking lame. Noah couldn't remember the last time this happened. Kurt just turned up with a bag, and a pizza, expecting to spend the night.

Noah stared at his phone wondering if Elsa would call or text. He hadn't responded to her last text, but he really hoped she'd tell him what was wrong.

Today in school he'd seen how upset she had been, and throughout the day he'd wanted to ask her. No chance opened up for him to go and see her, or to even talk to her.

"Are you listening to me?" Kurt asked.

"Sorry, dozed off. What?"

"I'm your best friend, and you've dozed off. What kind of friend are you?"

"The kind you crash on at night to have a lame ass sleepover as if we're kids." Noah released his weights, and stood up, rotating his arms. "What were you talking about?"

"I think I've got a problem."

"If it itches, smells, or has swollen up, go and see a doctor."

"Noah, shut the fuck up. I'm having a real crisis right now, and it's pissing me off."

"Fine, fine, fine." Noah took a seat, and stared at his friend. "What is it?"

"Girls, we like them right?"

"Yes."

"Do you have a … type of girl you like?"

"One that likes me back usually gets me going." He thought about Elsa and the kiss they had shared. She was the only girl who was getting any kind of response to him. Today in gym, Jessica had come up to him and tried to rub against him. He'd not been interested. She held no appeal to him whatsoever.

The moment he caught sight of Elsa, that was a whole different story. He wanted her badly. Most of his nights were spent dreaming about her. Each morning he'd wake up with a boner, and no matter how many times he tried to get himself off, he couldn't stop the need from stirring up again.

"No. I mean, do you like big tits, round ass? No tits?"

Noah stared at his friend, frowning. "I have no idea what you're trying to get at. I'm confused."

"Fuck, I just need to come out and say it, don't I?"

"Usually that happens to people, yeah."

Kurt stood and started pacing. "I've noticed her all the fucking time, and I was a total asshole because of my older brother Lewis."

"Sit down, and just tell me what the fuck your problem is." Noah lost his patience.

"My lab partner Kim, I like her." Kurt sat down and stared at Noah. "I mean I really like her, Noah."

"So?"

"So? I've bullied her for fucking years. She's not slim. My brother told me never to become a chubby chaser, it's like fucking death."

Noah held his hand up. "You like Kim? Like a friend?"

"No, I want to sleep with her. I want to get naked with her, fuck her, screw her, but I don't want to be a jerk about it. I actually want this. Tell me what the fuck is wrong with me?"

"Kim's hot."

"I've been calling her a whale since we were in kindergarten."

Noah chuckled. "I did warn you about being a bully. Guess what, this is karma, buddy. Straight and simple karma."

"You're being a rat bastard, you know that." Kurt collapsed on the bed. "I can't get her out of my mind. She's all I can think about."

"Don't you have a girlfriend? Britney?"

"No. She's just a girl who likes to have a booty call." Kurt sat back up. "What the hell am I going to do?"

"I don't know."

"I don't even know anything about her other than the fact she can't stand me." Kurt rested his hands on his knees. "I'm going to have to stop being a jerk."

"I'd start with not calling her whale, or anything relating to her size."

"I don't know what it is. At first when Donald partnered us up, I couldn't believe it. I thought I was going to have to deal with this chick offering me shit on a silver platter. She got to have a piece of the Kurt action."

Noah stared at his friend, smiling. Kurt had this coming. "What changed?"

"She fucking ignored me. Throughout the whole

lesson, she ignored me, and started her assignment. When the bell went, she looked at me and asked me if I knew what I was doing. I nodded, 'cause, that's what I do. She told me what I should work on, and left. I called 'round to her house, and she growled at me. It took me having to sweet talk her mother before I was allowed in the house."

"So, you like the chase?"

"I thought that, but nothing has happened."

"Nothing?"

"Not a thing. No kiss, no groping. I didn't even get to talking about each other. Every time I asked her a question, she'd avoid it. I know next to nothing about her."

"You know where she lives, and where she goes to school."

"I also know she hangs out with that other chick, Elsa. The mousy one, kind of cute."

Noah tensed up, gritting his teeth. "Leave her alone."

"Oh, I will, I promise."

He was pleased Kurt was so distracted, as otherwise he'd have witnessed that Noah was having a hard time keeping his shit together.

"What do you think I should do?"

"About what?"

"About Kim?"

Noah stared at his friend. "Does this really bother you that much?"

"I've never felt like this. Not about anyone. I've not even spoken to Britney. Seriously, I can't get her out of my mind."

"If all you want is just sex, then you're going to have to find someone else."

Kurt shook his head. "It's more than that."

"Then start by trying to get her to talk to you."

Noah got to his feet, slapping him on the back.
There wasn't more to be said.

Chapter Seven

For the next couple of months, Elsa spent her time between school, working out with Noah, and spending time with Kim. She picked out a dress for the country club prom, and she'd kept it at Kim's place. Her mother was nagging her to still lose weight, and according to Noah, she was losing weight, and she was toning up.

Alone.

Staring in the full length mirror in her bedroom, Elsa turned around. She was completely naked, and she was assessing her own body. Her stomach appeared flatter, and her ass was not as saggy, which had to be a good thing. Lifting her hair up, she saw her back still showed more signs of her weight. Her thighs still jiggled when they walked, and a few touches of cellulite remained.

Her body wasn't all bad, and she was getting used to being around Noah semi-naked. She liked it when his fingers touched her. Sometimes she was sure he touched her breasts. Cupping her breasts, she looked into her eyes, and wondered what the hell was going on with her.

Noah wasn't her type. He was the most popular boy in school, which to her equaled, not for her.

"Get over it, Elsa. He's not for you. Not now, not ever."

The sound of the front doorbell going had her frowning. She didn't know why it would be ringing this late at night.

Grabbing a robe, as she didn't have time to put on anything else, she made her way downstairs.

Glancing through the peephole, she let out a sigh of relief. Noah was at the door, no one else. She frowned and opened the door. "What's up?" she asked.

"Hey. I heard you saying to Kim that you were

alone tonight, and I thought I'd come and keep you company."

"You just happened to be in the neighborhood?"

"I don't live that far from you," he said, chuckling.

Moving out of the way, she let him past. "How did you hear I was on my own?"

"I was passing by when you asked Kim what she was doing tonight. I figured I'd stop by to keep you company." He held up a bottle of whiskey and some movies.

"You've brought me alcohol?"

"I've got us both alcohol."

"Are you trying to get me drunk?" She closed the door and followed him through to her kitchen. It was rather surreal to have one of the popular guys at school offering to spend time with her. She was also completely naked beneath her bathrobe, and she needed to remember that.

"I know you're all pure and innocent. Consider this a little walk on the wild side." He grabbed down a glass, opened up the whiskey, and poured out some dark liquid. She watched as he took a sip before offering her some.

She shook her head. "I'm not going to get drunk. I've got to go and get dressed."

"Why? You're okay in your pajamas."

"I'm not wearing any." She slapped her hand over her mouth. "Crap, I can't believe I just said that to you."

"You're completely naked underneath your robe?"

"Yeah, I am." She crossed her arms over her chest. "I wasn't exactly expecting company tonight. With Mom and Dad gone, I was just doing some, erm, some checking."

"Of what?"

"Nothing."

"You're confusing me."

"I was looking at myself in the mirror. I was hoping to see some results, and even though I see something, it's not exactly a lot. I was hoping for something more."

"Elsa, you do know you don't need to lose weight?"

She snorted. "Yeah, right."

"I'm being serious. You're fine the way you are."

"You don't live with my mom."

"You've got to do what feels right to you, not to your mother." He put the glass down and took a step toward her. "I'll be with you every step of the way. I'm helping you because I couldn't watch you torture yourself with running."

They had soon moved from the treadmills to the pool. She'd never forget how awkward she'd felt when she had to go to the main pool. He'd been in boxer briefs, and the modest one-piece costume she had didn't hide enough for her liking. She'd spent most of the time in the pool underneath the water so no one saw her, especially Noah. His thoughts about her concerned her. No guy had ever gotten this close.

Even Kim had noticed that she was distracted lately.

"Why are you being so nice to me?" she asked.

They had never been close. Sure, they had been together a lot throughout their lives. They had shared classes, teachers but never getting to know each other.

"Why can't I be nice to you?"

"I don't know. You've never taken the time to get to know me. We don't know each other. Take your pick."

"Our lives have never connected. I get that until

this moment. I'm not going to be mean to you, Elsa. In fact I've done nearly everything in my power to make you as comfortable as possible. I don't know what more you want me to do."

Rubbing her temple, Elsa couldn't argue with him. He was right. "You're right, I'm sorry."

He walked toward her and wrapped his arms around her, pressing a kiss to her temple. "Don't worry about it. I'm here."

She held onto him, resting her head against his shoulder. His hand rubbed her back, and the other stroked over her hair. Closing her eyes, she found herself basking in his scent, and the strength of him. Noah was a large man, and he worked out a lot.

The hug changed. It went from one of comfort to awareness, or at least to Elsa it did. Biting her lip, she chanced a look up at him, and Noah was staring down at her. The hand on her hair moved to her cheek, and he brushed his thumb across it.

"What are you doing to me?" he asked.

She didn't have time to respond as he pressed her up against the fridge, sinking his fingers into her hair as he slammed his lips down on hers.

Elsa moaned, holding onto him by wrapping her arms around his neck.

His tongue ran across her lips, and she melted, opening her mouth to accept him. He plundered inside her, and she gasped at the contact, needing every single touch of his hands. Noah thrust his pelvis against hers, making her aware of his rock hard cock.

While he was kissing her, ravishing her mouth in ways she'd only seen in movies, his hands slowly started to descend. She should stop him, but the truth was, she couldn't, nor did she want to. This was going to happen. She wanted it to happen, more than she wanted anything else to.

"Fuck, I've got to stop," he said, pulling away.

The rope she wore was partially opened. "You don't have to stop."

"I'm not going to do something you don't like."

"I didn't tell you to stop." Feeling bold, she untied her belt, and let the robe open up and fall to the floor. She stood before him naked, and even though she felt a little sick to be completely naked, it also felt right.

Noah wasn't repulsed by her, far from it, and being around him made her feel alive.

"I want you, Noah." She had been fighting her desires for a long time, and she was tired of always denying herself. "Are you with someone?"

"No. The only person I want is you, Elsa. You're all I can think about. All I want. I spend most of my time having to hide my dick from you."

She loved that. "I'm here. I'm yours. You can have me."

He stepped toward her again, and his hands landed on her hips. His gaze swept down her body, making her wet. "I only came to spend time with you."

"We get to spend it the way most people do our ages." She smiled at him, and pulled his shirt up. Scoring her nails down his back, she went onto her toes and kissed him. "What do you want?"

****

Noah grabbed her hand, leading her upstairs. "Which one is your room?" There was no way he was about to pass up the opportunity of a lifetime. Elsa had been on his mind forever, and he couldn't let her go, not now, not ever.

For the first time in his life, he was actually having feelings for a woman, and it consumed him daily. He understood why his father married his mother. Love, marriage, commitment, it had all been a foreign concept to him. With Elsa, he could see himself doing that— loving her, marrying her. He was turning into a pussy, and all she wanted to do was fuck.

He'd take it. For now, he'd take whatever she wanted to give him.

"The last door down here," she said.

Making his way into her room, he opened the door, closed it, and pressed her up against it, claiming her lips as he did. "If we do this, we do it my way."

"Don't you know I'm getting used to you being the boss for me?"

"Oh, baby, I know all right." He ran his hands down her body, cupping her tits before sliding down to cup her ass. "Do you want to set out some ground rules?" She always talked about the ground rules.

"No one in school can know. I don't want to be laughed at."

Noah gritted his teeth. No one would laugh at her as far as he was concerned. "Fine. You won't give me any leeway with this."

"None. Please, Noah."

"Fine, fine. What else?"

"I won't be seeing anyone else. I'd like you to do the same."

"Are you asking for a commitment?"

"Yes, I guess I am. I've never done this before, Noah. You'll be my first."

Squeezing her ass, Noah took possession of her lips. "You've got nothing to worry about. Can I set some ground rules myself?"

"Sure."

"You're mine, and when I want you, you're to come to me. I'll never force you, but I'm a man with a lot of desires." He only had desires for her, but right now, he doubted she needed to hear that. "I've not been with a woman for a long time."

"You want me?"

He pressed his cock against her. "Can't you tell?"

"I can't believe we're doing this."

"How did you imagine your first time?" he asked.

"I don't know. I didn't even imagine I'd have a first time, or a second. I guess I only ever imagined going away to college, and being great at my job."

"Rather boring." He took a step away from her and removed his shirt. "I've got a way to spice up your life." Removing his pants, he made sure to keep a little distance. His cock stood out, long, thick, with pre-cum leaking out of the tip.

Her gaze ran down the length of his body, and he loved it. Wrapping his fingers around his cock, he ran his hand up and down, showing off the size. He wasn't embarrassed by what he was packing in his pants. "Do you like what you see?"

"Wow," she said. "Erm, do you have any condoms? I don't."

"I've got it covered." Reaching into his pants, he pulled out a single condom.

"Were you expecting this when you came here?"

"I wasn't expecting anything. I'm always prepared, and I'm always going to be protected. This is about protecting the both of us."

"Okay."

"Come here, baby."

She took a step toward him, giggling. "Baby?"

"Haven't you noticed it's my word for you?" When she was close to him, he banded an arm around her waist and pressed his face against her neck. "Fuck me, you smell good. You know I have to be careful when I'm around you."

"Why?"

"You make me want you so damn bad. Half of the time I'm fighting a boner." He kissed her neck, nibbling on the pulse that was beating frantically.

"I don't know what I'm doing," she said.

"Don't worry. I'll teach you."

"Exactly how many women have you been with?"

"Enough to know what I'm doing. I'll make it really good for you."

"Have you had a virgin before?" she asked.

"No. You're my first." The girls he'd been with before had all known what they were doing, and after sex had admitted they'd been with someone else.

Turning her toward the bed, he eased her down and sank to his knees. "Trust me, baby. I'll make it good for you."

She nodded, biting her lip.

"Lie back."

She lowered down to the bed, and he spread her thighs, staring at her creamy virgin pussy. Sliding his fingers between her lips, he touched her clit, watching her gasp. She was wet and ready for him.

In his need to have Elsa, he'd gone online looking for ways of taking a virgin, and the only solid piece of information he was given was to take his time, to love the woman for the first time.

That was exactly what he was going to do. Leaning forward, he slid his tongue between her slit, flicking her clit.

"What are you doing?" she asked, jerking up.

"Have a little trust, okay? I'm not going to do anything to you that you're not going to like."

"Are you sure?"

Noah chuckled. "Believe me, I'm going to have you screaming from the rooftops before the end of the night."

She lay back down, and he tongued her clit, getting her all nice and wet. He gripped her thighs, keeping her open even as her pussy grew sensitive. Keeping his tongue on her, he flicked, sucked, and nibbled on her clit, heightening her arousal. He knew exactly what to do to take her over the edge, but instead he kept her there, making her even wetter. There was no way he was going to spoil this opportunity. When he was finished, he wanted her to think of nothing but him. He wanted her to be so consumed by need for him that she finally admitted to wanting him. Noah took his time, making sure she was at the edge of the abyss before he plunged her over, and she screamed his name.

Reaching out to grab the condom, he tore into the foil packet, and rolled the latex down his cock. He eased her up the bed and followed her as he went.

"Noah?"

"It's okay. I'll take my time."

"You're, erm, the rumors about you are true."

He chuckled. "Forget about all of them. All that matters is you and me, and what we're about to do right here and now."

Kissing her lips, he caressed down her body, going to her tits. He stroked over her nipples, pinching the hard buds, and then soothing them out with the palm of his hand. Cupping one breast in his hand, he released her lips, and flicked his tongue across one hardened peak. His cock was desperate to get inside her, but he'd wait.

Noah was coming to find for Elsa, he'd do anything.

She was in his head and everywhere.

No matter what he tried to do, he couldn't forget about her, and his need for her only kept on growing.

Moving to her other breast, he sucked her nipple

into his mouth, using his teeth to create a bite of pain.

"Please, Noah, I want you," she said, moaning. "I can't take much more."

"You want me to fuck you?"

"Yes."

"Then say it to me."

"You want me to talk dirty to you?"

"I want you to tell me what you want."

She sighed. "Noah, please will you fuck me?"

Her cheeks were a lovely shade of red, and he decided against torturing her some more. "Yes." Reaching down, he gripped his cock, and pressed the tip against her pussy entrance. She tensed up, and Noah forced himself to slow down. "This may hurt a little." He hoped it didn't hurt at all, and everything he'd read was fucking wrong.

Pushing the tip inside her, he stared into her eyes as he slowly started to sink into her pussy. She was incredibly tight, and when he found the small piece of flesh, he kissed her lips, and slammed every inch of his cock inside her.

She cried out, tensing beneath him. If it wasn't for him being stronger than she was, he was sure she'd have pushed him away.

"It's okay. I know it hurts." He stayed still inside her, kissing her neck, and moving up to her lips.

"Ouch," she said.

Seeing the tears in her eyes angered him. The last thing he ever wanted to do was hurt her, and that was exactly what he was doing. "Fuck, baby, I'm so sorry."

"I wasn't expecting that," she said.

"I'm not going to move until you're ready."

She nodded. "That's good."

Stroking her cheek, he kissed her lips, loving the way she moaned as he did.

"Did it hurt for you?"

"No. Guys don't suffer like girls do."

"Damn, you get a better deal than we do."

Noah stared into her eyes, wishing for this moment to never end. He'd really only been coming to see her to keep her company. Now, he didn't want to leave. They had been working out for well over two months, and she was making some serious progress. He hated school, how they walked by each other, neither acknowledging the other's existence. When they were working out, they talked, and she was fun. They had a lot in common.

She'd come out of nowhere, and now he couldn't let her fade away.

"I'm ready, Noah," she said.

"Are you sure?"

"Yes."

Noah slowly eased out of her tight pussy and made sure she was still with him the whole way. "Is this okay?"

"Yes. It's amazing. Oh God, that feels so good."

He started some slow thrusts, building up the pleasure, and she gasped, moaning, and gripping his arms as he started to plunder her pussy.

"You like?"

"It feels so good." She looked between them, and he followed her gaze, seeing his cock sliding inside her.

He slammed all the way in, making her moan.

Noah made love to her. He'd never made love to any other girl, or the women he'd taken. This was a first for him, just like it was a first for her.

Locking their fingers together, he held her tightly as he claimed Elsa. In his head, in his heart, in that moment, Elsa belonged to him.

Chapter Eight

One week later

"You look different," Kim said.

Looking up from her book, Elsa stared at her friend. "What?"

"This week, you've been a little different. Every now and then your cheeks will go bright red. Are you coming down with something?"

"No, nothing at all." They were in the library, and Elsa closed her book. "I'm going to change this." She got up from the table and made her way between the shelves. It had been a crazy week. Last Friday, she'd lost her virginity, and it had to be the weirdest, yet sweetest moment of her life. Noah had made love to her, and they had only done it the once because he only had one condom.

After they'd had sex, he even cleaned away a little blood that had occurred because of them being together. She couldn't believe it when he did that, wiping away the blood as if it was no big deal. He'd not left her though. No, he'd stayed the night, and left before her parents arrived. At nine, she'd met him at the gym where they walked out. Throughout it she'd been aware of him, and Noah had taken advantage, touching her, reminding her of how good it was between them.

By the time they made it home, she'd been ready to jump him. They'd gotten to his bedroom, he closed the door, and they had fucked on his bed, and in the shower. At his place, he had condoms, and she couldn't go buy them. She'd tried to go, but failed. Noah had promised to be the one to provide the condoms.

Neither of them had gotten a moment alone since then. She was still working out, but with his parents home, she wasn't comfortable having sex with them being so close.

Moving between the shelves, she placed the book back and started to look for a different one. She really needed to ace this biology test next week, and the only way to do that was to study.

Suddenly, she was grabbed from behind and spun around. "I can't fucking wait any longer."

Noah pushed her against the books, sinking his fingers into her hair and claiming her lips.

She wrapped her arms around him, needing him. Her pussy was on fire.

"I haven't been able to get you out of my head. I'm tired of you being close, and not being able to touch you."

"We shouldn't be doing this here."

"Why? I'm single, you're single. What law are we actually breaking?" he asked.

Biting her lip, she couldn't look away from him. "Look at you, and then look at me."

"I *am* looking at you, Elsa. It's all I do."

"You're hot and I'm not, okay? If you're seen with me, everyone will think it's some kind of joke, a game."

Noah sighed. "This is your mother again."

"It's not. Think about school. Your ex is the hottest girl in school."

"She's not hot, Elsa."

"Don't lie."

"I don't see what's on the surface. Jessica is a bitch, and she's a bitch to the core. Don't you get that?"

She shook her head. "You just don't see it."

"No, what I see is you think I'm fickle. You think I care what people think."

"This isn't about you."

"No, clearly. It's about you. You know what, I'll see you later, when no one can see us."

He walked away, and Elsa closed her eyes, leaning against the bookshelves. She had hurt him, and that had been the last thing she wanted to do.

This was getting complicated.

Why couldn't Noah just fit into a nice little box where she didn't have to stress about anything?

Grabbing a book, she made her way toward the front desk.

"Are you okay?" Kim asked.

"I'm fine. I just, I've got to head out of here. Meet you for gym?"

"Believe me, if I could miss it I would."

Elsa chuckled. She handed the book over to Denise and waited for her to place it on her account. When she was done, she made her way toward the bathroom. She just needed to take a minute before heading out to gym.

Entering a stall, she locked it and leaned her head against the back. Noah had taken her virginity, and she had shared a lot with him. It was hard for her to keep him at arms' length, but how could she not?

Tears filled her eyes, and she sucked them in.

Crying wouldn't solve any of her problems, and it only ever made her feel weak.

I've got this. I can do this.

Getting off the toilet she was about to leave the stall when people entered.

"Can you believe him? He turned me down. Kurt! He turned me down for sex, and I was offering to blow him. God, I don't understand men," Britney said.

"Come on, look what Noah is doing. He's totally acting like a big baby over that one time fling. We're young, and we're going away to college. Does he expect me to not taste everything out there?" Jessica asked.

"I can't even get Ryan to look at me," Lola said.

"Don't look at me. I'm doing okay with Adam," Sienna said.

"Whatever," Jessica said.

Great, she was trapped in a toilet with four of the most popular girls in school.

"I thought Noah broke up with you?" Britney asked.

"Oh, he did, but he'll come crawling back. They always do."

"He's not like other guys though. Noah doesn't even pay you attention, and he's not even groveling for you," Sienna said.

"Look, when Noah gets his stick out of his ass, everything will go back to normal. All he has to do is stop being so boring talking about exercise. I'm a hot piece of ass, and he should see it. Do you really think he'd lower himself to any of the other girls in school?"

"Wish I could say the same about Kurt. He's been panting after that fat bitch, Kim. You know, the one who dresses funny. They had an assignment, and now he won't leave her alone. It's so embarrassing. He could do so much better," Britney said.

"I don't get what people see in fat people. They're gross and disgusting. I'll never get fat. I'd rather die of starvation than look that ugly," Jessica said.

Elsa closed her eyes, trying to drown them out. These were the girls her mother wanted her to hang out with.

They were shallow, mean people. How on earth could she ever be friends with them? Noah had gotten a lucky escape.

"Well, we've got cheerleading practice. Maybe we could show them exactly what they're missing out on," Jessica said. "No one picks lesser women, when we're around."

Minutes passed, and finally they left, leaving the heavy scent of perfume.

Kim was waiting for her outside of the gym. "What took you so long?"

"I had to wait for the cheerleaders to preen themselves."

Her friend wrinkled her nose. "I've heard it takes them hours to get ready."

"Did Kurt tell you that?"

"Yeah, I think so. It was one of those things that he said I was better at."

"Are you and Kurt a thing?"

"Ew, no. Bully, remember? I'm not going to fall for that kind of shit. I do have some self-worth, you know."

"I know." They entered the changing rooms and made their way toward the back. Elsa changed quickly, trying to avoid being seen without her clothes on.

"What the hell, Elsa?"

Kim moved up beside her.

"What?"

"You've got bruises on your hips."

Quickly pushing down her shirt, she brushed it off. "It was nothing. I've been clumsy this week. With any luck my mom will back off with the idea of me helping do the country club prom."

She'd noticed the bruises on her hips earlier in the week. Noah had left his mark on her, and it did delight her.

He liked to grip her during sex, holding her in place.

"If something was going on, you'd tell me, right?"

"Of course, Kim. Why wouldn't I tell you?"

"I don't know. You've just been a bit different lately."

"It's college next year, and my mom. You know how she gets."

"Yeah, I know, but I don't like it. You know you can stay over all the time."

"I know. Your mom is a wonderful woman."

They finished getting changed and made their way out onto the field. It was close to middle autumn, so it was starting to get colder.

For now, they were going to be running track while the football team practiced, along with the cheerleading squad.

Their teacher set them to do laps, and staying beside Kim Elsa started at a steady pace. There were clusters of different groups as they worked out. Elsa couldn't help but look toward the football field. She spotted Noah instantly.

She quickly averted her gaze. She didn't need this.

"Kurt keeps trying to talk to me," Kim said.

"He does?"

"Yeah. He's also being really nice, and when he's nice, it's hard to remember that he's a bully. Do you think I'm a horrible person?"

"For not falling for Kurt? No. Do you *want* to give him a chance?"

"No. We don't have anything in common. He's mean, and he's a jock. Like you said, we're going to college soon, and I don't want to start something up like that."

Elsa watched as the cheerleaders who had been in the bathroom made their way toward the football team. Adam, Ryan, Kurt, and Noah were all grouped together, talking. She forced herself to look away.

This was why she never wanted her relationship with Noah to come out in the open. They would only mock something she loved.

****

Noah watched his friend, who was watching Kim. The gym class had just come out and been told to run. He'd clocked Elsa instantly. She was wearing those ugly ass shorts with the large, baggy shirt. Once again she was with her friend, and he was mad at her.

She wanted to keep their relationship a secret, and it was starting to piss him off. He had proven to her he wasn't some asshole who was going to hurt her, and yet that was exactly how she was treating him.

Her weight didn't bother him. He was thankful for her curves. Not only had it given them a reason to come together, he loved holding onto her during sex. The night they had spent together had been the best of his life, and he couldn't wait to explore her some more.

In time she would come to see that he was the perfect guy for her.

"You're not getting anywhere with her?" he asked.

"No. I'm the guy that has bullied her. I'm surprised if she'd ever look at me."

"It sucks."

"Hey guys, Sienna has given me a warning that Lola, Jessica, and Britney are pissed with us."

"What the fuck did we do?"

"I don't know, but they're pissed." Adam looked at him. "Are we missing something?"

"No."

"Why did you break up with Britney?" Ryan asked.

"I got tired of her whining. There's more to life than screwing a bunch of cheerleaders."

"You're insane, right?" Ryan asked.

"I'm not going to say anything. Sienna has told me she's only cheering to pass the time. When we go to college, she's concentrating on economics," Adam said.

Out of all of the cheerleaders, Sienna was the only one who didn't seem to judge people.

She also wasn't bound by some fucking law that stated she had to follow her friends wherever they went.

"Speaking of the cheerleaders, here they come," Ryan said.

Noah glanced toward Elsa and Kim, seeing them talking. He'd lost his temper in the library, and he really shouldn't have. She was just so infuriating, but being a bitch wasn't going to make him stop wanting her. If she didn't want to go public, then he was more than happy to wait for her. He didn't *want* to wait, but he'd do it for her.

"Hey, Sienna," Adam said.

Drawing his attention back to the field, Noah watched as Jessica walked up to him. When she put her hands around his neck, he shook his head, stepping away. "Not going to happen."

"You're seriously going to keep holding that shit against me?"

"That shit means something to me."

"Oh, come on, Noah. Stop being a big baby."

"You think I'm being a baby? You fucked another guy. You think I should just let that slide as if it didn't happen."

"He didn't matter. It was just a bunch of fun. Why can't you see that?"

Noah ignored her.

"Seriously, you're going to pick a fatty over me. Do you even have eyes that are working right now?" Britney asked.

"I don't want you. We're done. I told you we

were done before we even got back to school, but like always, you refuse to listen." Kurt took a step away. "We're done."

"So, it's those fat sluts that you want?" Britney asked.

"Don't even think of getting Kim involved in this. I don't want you anymore."

Jessica tapped Britney's arm. "It's okay. It's their loss. We can find what we want anywhere, can't we, ladies?"

Noah didn't like that, and he watched as the cheerleaders left the field.

"What the fuck do you think that's about?" Ryan asked.

"I don't know."

After a few seconds, Ryan turned back to look at them. "You've got a thing for chubby?"

Before any of them realized it, Kurt had slammed his fist against Ryan's face. Suddenly Kurt and Ryan were fighting in the mud.

Noah stepped out of the way.

"What the hell is going on here?" Mr. Wood asked.

Kurt and Ryan were separated. "This fucker pissed me off," Kurt said.

"What? Can't handle the truth that you're a fucking chubby chaser?" Ryan asked.

"Both of you, my office, now!"

Noah watched his two friends leave, and he shook his head. He couldn't believe that they had just fought over this shit.

"What the hell was that all about?" Adam asked.

"It was nothing." Noah glanced over at Elsa and Kim.

Kim looked ready to cry, and Elsa stared at him.

He could just hear her words in his mind, or at least what he imagined she'd say. "Do you see?"

Yeah, he saw, but like Kurt, he'd fight for her.

No one would say a bad word about her when they were near him, and if he found anyone hurting her, he'd fuck them up.

After practice he waited for Kurt in the parking lot. Ryan and Kurt both walked out. The four of them stood together, waiting.

"What happened?" Noah asked.

"We're suspended from two games until we can work our shit out," Kurt said.

"We? You're the one that went fucking bat-shit crazy," Ryan said.

"I've got a crush on Kim, the chubby girl, the whale, the girl I have fucking bullied all my life. You want the truth? That's it. I've been with Britney, and for a brief moment, I was able to see Kim, talk to her, and even though it was about the fucking assignment we were working on, she saw me as more than a fucking cock, and a guy to show off." They were the only ones left in the parking lot as most of students had left.

Noah was supposed to be meeting Elsa in an hour, but he'd sent her a text letting her know he was running behind.

"Whoa, dude, I'm sorry. I didn't have any idea."

"No, no one has any idea. Kim won't even give me the time of day. I can't win her over. I shouldn't have hit you. I'm sorry."

Noah watched his friends shake hands. "Is that it? None of you are going to give him shit?"

"It's not our business. If you like a girl, then you like a girl. Nothing to worry yourself about."

Noah rubbed the back of his head. He wanted to tell his friends, but he decided against it. The last thing he wanted to do was break Elsa's trust.

Chapter Nine

"I wasn't being fair to you," Elsa said the moment Noah climbed out of his car.

"Kurt got into a fight because of your friend."

"What did Kim do?"

"Where do you see us going?" he asked.

"What?"

"Us. Is this just something for fun, to pass the time?"

"No!" She didn't understand why he was yelling.

"Then what is it?"

"I don't know. I don't want to lose you."

"You don't want to lose me, and yet you won't tell me what the hell this is. I can't tell my friends about us. I can't tell anyone about us. I've just watched Kurt defend Kim—you know what I mean, he defended her, and I can't do that. I had an opportunity to tell them about us, and I kept it a secret, for you, because of you."

"I'm sorry."

"I'm not some asshole, Elsa. I'm not going to walk away and leave you, okay? I'm not going to make you a laughingstock."

"But look how your friends reacted. Look at your exes!"

"They're exes for a reason. I'm not here because I want to be with Jessica. I'm here because I want to be with you. I like you, a whole hell of a lot, and that fucking scares me. My whole life, all I ever had was college, football, and my plans. Now I find myself changing my plans for you."

"Changing your plans?"

"Yes. I have feelings for you, Elsa. Is that so hard for you to understand? I don't want high school to finish and us to be over. I want this to be the start of something amazing."

"I don't know what to say."

"Don't say anything. Just promise me you'd think about it." He climbed back into his car.

"Wait, where are you going?"

"To clear my head. I can't do this right now."

She watched him go, and she hated herself.

Going to her car, she climbed inside and made her way back home. Her mother was already home, and Elsa let herself in.

"Elsa, honey, is that you?"

"Yeah."

"Excellent. I'm experimenting with some quinoa. It's really healthy, and it will help with your little weight problem—"

"Mom, do you love me?"

"Of course—"

"No, do you like the way I am, how I look, how I dress, how I weigh?" she asked.

"Honey, don't do this."

"I want to understand why I'm not good enough for you."

"You are."

"Really? You see, I don't think I am good enough. I've just had a really great guy in my life, and I felt I had to keep him a secret because I wasn't good enough for him. Every time I thought I was doing something great, you'd always come back to my weight. I'm even exercising in fucking secret because of you."

"Elsa!"

"It's not fair that I have to be like this. I hate it, Mom. I hate myself, and I hate you." Turning on her heel, she walked out of the house, rushing to her car.

"Elsa, come back here."

She ignored her mother and jumped into her car.

She reversed out of the driveway and headed toward Kim's. When she realized that would be the first place her mother would look, she made her way toward the local town, parked her car, and walked toward Noah's house. He wanted space, but she really needed to talk to him.

If he sent her away, she'd understand. On the way toward his house, it started to rain, and by the time she got to his front door, she was already crying.

There was no sign of his parents, which she was thankful for.

Noah opened the door.

"Elsa, what the hell?"

"I'm really sorry. You deserve someone a hell of a lot better than me." She turned to leave, but he caught her around the waist and pulled her into his home.

"You're freezing." He pushed her jacket off and walked her into his front room. Within seconds she was down to her underwear, and he had a blanket wrapped around her, rubbing her body in an attempt to warm her up.

"It was all supposed to be simple, you know? I was supposed to go to the gym, work out, and at the end of school, I'd be this new and improved person. I never expected to see you there, Noah. I didn't think this would happen." She wiped her eyes. "My mom doesn't love me. Well, she probably does, but she doesn't like me very much. She wants me to be slim, but I can't be slim. I'm fat."

"What have I told you about calling yourself that? You're not fat. You're beautiful."

"I'm not blind. I look in the mirror."

"Yeah, you are blind. I think you're the most beautiful woman I've ever seen, and I've seen a lot of women naked."

"Yeah, Jessica is one of them. I heard them talking in the toilet. They didn't know I was there. I've never heard such horrible things. I really don't know what guys see in them."

"They're easy, Elsa. No guy has to work hard to get in their pants."

"Is that all guys think about, sex?"

"Elsa, we're eighteen. We're in our sexual prime. Believe me, we're horny all the time. You've got to admit that you're horny sometimes."

She nodded. Around Noah she had felt it more times than she cared to imagine. She'd never known something so consuming before.

"I didn't expect to fall for anyone, Elsa. I shouldn't have left you alone at the gym, or run off. I don't know. For the first time in my life, I actually feel something for someone else, and you want us to hide. I just want to tell everyone that we're together."

"You do?"

"I'm not ashamed of you. I'm not embarrassed to call you mine." He cupped her cheek, running his thumb across her bottom lip. "As crazy as it sounds, I think I may even be in love with you."

She gasped. "You love me?"

"Yeah, fucked up huh? We've wasted so much time."

"How?"

"I could have had you since kindergarten."

"Oh," Elsa said. "Yeah, we did go to kindergarten together."

"You've been in the background of my life for so long, and I've taken you for granted." He kissed her lips. "What have you done to me, Elsa Quinn?"

"I've done nothing to you."

She caressed his cheek, kissing him back.

"I've got a condom in my back pocket." He lifted up and brandished the square foil packet. "We could have some fun."

Elsa pushed the blanket off her, and pushed Noah to the sofa.

"First, are we going public with our relationship? I'm tired of being taken advantage of. You have your wicked way with me, and then I get tossed aside as if I don't matter—"

"Shut up. You do matter." She kissed his lips, sucking on the bottom one and using her teeth to create a little bite of pain. "We're going to go public, but you may be laughed at."

"I know how to use my fists."

"Noah Stewart, are you saying you'll defend my honor?"

"Yeah. Anyone who tries to hurt my girl will have to come through me." He gripped the back of her head and pulled her down for a kiss. "Let's put that condom to good use."

Sinking her fingers into his hair, she gripped him tightly, holding him close. Slowly his hands moved down her body, flicking open her bra. She helped remove it, and then he tore her panties off, surprising her with his strength.

"I always get what I want."

She giggled, moving out of the way so he could tug his pants down his thighs.

He tore into the latex, and she watched as he rolled the condom over his length.

"Very impressive."

"I practiced my technique with a banana. My dad made me one afternoon. He was determined his son wouldn't get anyone pregnant, so that is what I did during father-son time."

"Really?"

"Yep. Come here."

She straddled his waist and gasped as the tip of his cock started to slide inside her. Once there was enough within her, he gripped her hips and lowered her over his shaft. Biting her lip, she tried to contain her moans.

"No one is here, Elsa. Scream how much you want me from the top of your lungs."

He slammed her down, and she couldn't contain her need. She screamed his name, which only got louder as he reached between them to stroke her clit.

"Fuck, do you really think I'd want anyone else, Elsa? You're it for me."

Damn, he was it for her as well.

****

"I'm so nervous," Elsa said.

Noah smiled. Not only had Elsa spent the night with him from Friday into Saturday, she had also taken him home to meet her parents. He'd never forget the look on her mother's face when he walked through the door, or when Elsa introduced him as her boyfriend. Her mother didn't have a clue how amazing she was.

Of course he got the grilling from her father, which was scary as hell. He was never going to be breaking any laws if he had to go against Bill Quinn. The guy was a force to reckon with.

"Don't be nervous."

"Have you told your friends?" she asked.

"Nope. Have you told Kim?"

"No. I just said I was getting a ride into school, and I'd tell her everything then. I can't believe this is happening."

"Don't hyperventilate on me." He held her hand as he pulled into the school.

"I'm going to be laughed at."

"They can laugh all they want."

"This is really happening. I'm not going to wake up to discover this is all a dream?"

"Nope. We're about to enter high school hell, and everyone is going to know that you're my girlfriend, and I'm your boyfriend."

"Oh God."

"This is it." He pulled into the car park, and made his way toward where his friends were standing.

Parking the car, he climbed out. "Morning," he said. He couldn't stop smiling, and he didn't want to ever stop.

"Hey, Noah," Ryan said.

Rounding he car, he helped Elsa out. She tugged her bag onto her shoulder, and he felt how nervous she was. Her hand shook within his.

"What's going on?"

"Guys, I'd like you to meet my girlfriend, Elsa Quinn."

"She's your girlfriend?" Kurt asked.

"Yep, she is, and I'm damn happy about that. Do you have a problem?" he asked.

His friends looked at her, and then back up at him. They all shook their heads.

"You're Kim's friend right?"

"Yeah."

"You can help me."

"It's not going to happen. You want to win Kim over, you've got to do it on your own."

"Elsa?" Kim asked.

"Hey, Kim." He watched as she walked over to her friend.

Elsa had asked him to let her talk with Kim. He didn't see a reason to butt in.

"You and Elsa?" Adam asked. "Wow."

"Don't even start. You got a problem, we can settle this right here?"

"Dude, you do realize everyone is talking to you, right? Jessica is going to find out, and she's going to find a way to hurt her?" Ryan asked.

"She's my girlfriend, and I'm not going to let some snotty ex ruin it for me. It was over with Jessica a long time ago." He walked up to Elsa, turned her, and claimed her lips in a searing kiss that made him hard within seconds. "Hey, Kim."

"Hey, Noah."

"Do you want me to walk you to your locker?"

"Why not? You coming, Kim?"

"Sure."

"You're loving this, aren't you?" she asked, whispering the words.

"Totally loving it." He walked her to her locker, and Kurt joined him as well, trying to make polite talk with Kim.

Noah felt sorry for both Kurt and Kim. He saw that Kurt made her nervous.

"I'll see you at lunch," he said.

"Bye, Noah."

Walking by Kurt's side, they made it to registration before the questions started.

"What the hell, man? How long has it been going on? What did you do?"

"It has been going on for a couple of months, and we've only just gotten together. Elsa wasn't comfortable coming out as a couple. She's not had the best experiences so far." He hadn't seen Jessica, but with the people who'd seen them, she was bound to know.

"Why won't she help me with Kim?"

"Because Kim's her friend, and you were a real

bastard to her. Why should she help you?"

"I'm not a bad guy."

"*I* know you're not a bad guy. You've got to prove it to Kim. It's going to take a little time." Noah did his best to offer his friend some advice. It was hard to do considering Kim was his girlfriend's best friend.

"Yeah, you're right."

"Don't pressure her, and you know what, I'm going to be around Elsa a lot more. You're my friend. Promise me you won't be a dick, and you can join us."

"I won't be a dick. I promise. Thanks, man, you're the best."

Chapter Ten

"What the hell, Elsa?" Kim asked.

"What?" Elsa smiled. "Surprise."

"Something has been going on, and you're going to tell me." They sat down, and with it being early, Elsa decided to tell her.

"I made a decision to lose weight to please my mom. I wanted a fresh start, so I joined this gym. I was there one Saturday, and I didn't have a clue what I was doing. All of a sudden, Noah was there, and before I even knew what was happening, he was offering to help me."

"To train you?"

"Yes, to help me lose weight, and to satisfy my mom. I want to point out, though, that Noah told me I shouldn't be losing weight for my mom. He kept trying to stop me, and for me to do what I wanted to do, not what someone else wanted." Elsa smiled. "He's met my mom."

"He has?"

"Yeah, he came to meet my parents yesterday. It was kind of cool to see her shocked. Yeah, her fat daughter can get a man."

"Don't say stuff like that."

"It's what she is thinking. We both know it. Even she knows it, which is why she gets embarrassed about it." Elsa shrugged. "It doesn't matter anymore."

"You like him?"

"Yeah. He, erm, he told me he was falling for me."

"Have you had, you know?"

She couldn't stop smiling as she nodded. "Yes."

"Oh, wow, no wonder you've been acting strange. Did you want to tell me?"

"Yes, I wanted to tell you all the time."

"We're both a little crazy right now."

"Do you forgive me?" Elsa asked.

"Of course. I can see how happy you are. What are you going to do though? Are you going to the same college?"

She shrugged. "I don't know. We've not really thought that far ahead."

"You're not going to get pregnant, are you?"

"No. We made sure we were okay." Tucking some hair behind her ear, Elsa smiled at her friend. "I'm kind of scared."

"What about?"

"His ex, Jessica. She's not exactly known for being nice, is she?" In the past both of them had been bullied by Jessica.

"No. We'll deal with that together. I'm sure Noah won't let anything happen to you."

"He won't." He had asked her to trust him, so that was exactly what she was going to do.

For the rest of the morning, she was aware of the stares and the pointing from fellow pupils. She did her best to ignore it, but it was hard. There were no classes with Noah, and she didn't see him lingering in the halls. Her morning was spent with Kim, going from one class to another. Elsa was happy that her friend didn't hold it against her.

On the way into the dinner hall, Elsa looked around for Noah but didn't see him. Grabbing her tray, she made her way toward the back of the queue. "Will Noah be taking you to the prom?"

"Probably. I'm not going to be dancing with anyone else. Do you still have my dress?"

"Yes, it's a Christmas prom."

She remembered. Her mother did nothing but talk about it, boring her half to death with all the details.

Elsa picked a chicken salad, followed by a slice of

cheesecake for her dessert, and had just paid when Jessica and her three friends came walking over to them.

"Well, well, well, isn't it lard and butter, feeding their fat faces again."

Elsa's cheeks heated, and she hated how those words could upset her. Just once, she'd love to not have her weight bullied about. "Hey, Jessica," she said.

Don't take this crap.

You don't have to take it anymore.

Fight back.

"So, I heard a nasty little rumor that you think you can take my boyfriend."

The whole of the lunch hall had gone quiet.

Elsa stared down at her food.

"Don't think you're out of the firing line," Britney said. "Do you really think Kurt wants you over this?" She pointed at her own tight body. "No guy wants something that jiggles, over this."

Jessica stepped forward and started walking around her. Elsa tried not to tense up, but it was hard. It had been a long time since something like this had happened, and she hated how sad she was.

"You're fat, you're ugly, and Noah is only going to use you before he comes crawling back to me." Jessica tugged on her hair, and she jerked away, spilling her drink. "You disgust me." She had picked up a drink, and she poured it over Elsa's head. At the same time, Britney attacked Kim, throwing the cheesecake into her face. Kim cried out, and Elsa gasped as Jessica punched her in the gut.

"Get away from her," Noah said.

Elsa looked up in time to see Noah grabbing Jessica's arm and pushing her away.

"What a joke, do you expect me to believe this?"

Kurt stood between Britney and Kim.

"I don't care what you believe. Don't you ever come near her again!"

Jessica laughed. "This is what it has come down to? You're going to fuck a tub of lard."

Noah growled and took a step toward Jessica. "You want to keep with those insults, I suggest you think back, Jessica. I wonder what your father would think of you if he knew the truth about who you really are."

Elsa watched her go pale.

"You wouldn't."

"Oh, I would. I'd make sure everyone knew exactly what a whore you are. You stay away from Elsa, or else I will make sure you wished you'd never even looked in her direction."

Jessica laughed. "You're kidding."

Noah grabbed his cell phone, pressed some buttons, and all of a sudden, the lunch hall was filled with Jessica screaming to be fucked. "You've messed with one guy too many, Jessica, and they're out for revenge."

Elsa watched as Jessica took a step away. When Jessica looked around the lunch hall, everyone avoided her gaze.

"There's plenty more where that came from."

Jessica, Britney, Lola, and Sienna left the lunch hall.

"Elsa is my girlfriend. You fuck with her, you fuck with me, got it?" Noah didn't wait to hear responses. He turned to her. "Are you okay?"

"I think so."

Noah led her out of the dinner hall with Kim and Kurt following close behind.

"I'm so fucking sorry that happened."

"I should have been expecting it. Jessica wants you."

"She's a skank."

"What did you mean exactly?" she asked. "In the dinner hall, your threats."

"A couple of months ago, Jessica sent me some porn video that she was in with other guys. I think she tried to make me jealous, and she knew I wouldn't share them. I never talk about private stuff."

"You just broke your rule?"

"Yes, I broke my rule for *you*. No one threatens you. I won't let it happen."

Glancing behind her she saw Kim was barely keeping it together. "Do you want to go home?" Elsa asked.

"Yes, I really do."

"I can drive you," Kurt said.

"It's okay, I really want to be alone."

"I'll follow you," Elsa said.

"Okay."

Noah cupped her cheek. "It's fine."

"I'll meet you at your house."

She nodded. There was no point in arguing with him. Noah always liked to get what he wanted.

"Let me drive you. Noah can bring me back to school for my car," Kurt said. "You don't look in any condition to drive."

Kim caved, accepting Kurt to drive her car back home.

Elsa waited for Kurt to pull out of the parking lot before she followed him down toward Kim's home.

Once they pulled up outside, she climbed out, and saw Kim inside. Kurt had jumped into Noah's car, and was already on his way back to school. "Are you going to be okay?"

"Yeah, I am. Did you see what Kurt did?"

"He stepped between you and Britney."

"Yeah, I wasn't expecting that." Kim smiled. "I'll

see you tomorrow?"

"Yes."

"I'm really happy for you, Elsa."

She hugged Kim tightly. "Take care, okay."

"I'm going to take a shower, and then park my butt in front of the television."

"Text me if you need me," Elsa said.

"I will."

****

Noah waited outside of Elsa's house. He was so damn pissed at what Jessica had done. Someone had been taping the whole thing, and it was now all over social media. Fortunately, Jessica was disliked by everyone, so he didn't have to worry about anything happening to Elsa.

She pulled into the driveway, which was empty apart from him. He expected Lorna, her mother, to be home.

"Hey," she said, climbing out of the car.

"What happened today at the cafeteria, was that the reason you wanted to keep us a secret?"

"It was part of the reason, yeah, why?"

"I had no idea Jessica would do something like that."

Elsa shrugged. "She's popular, just not always for the right reasons."

Noah wrapped his arms around her, pulling her in close. "I don't care what other people say."

"Seriously, Noah, do you want this?"

He tilted her head back with a finger beneath her chin. "I want this with you."

"Kim asked me what we're going to do when it comes to college, when it comes to the future."

"Let's plan it."

"Our future?"

"Yeah, we don't need scholarships to get into college. I can go to whichever college I choose. What about you?"

"My dad has already told me to pick one."

"See, we've got an opportunity to make this work." He pressed a kiss to her lips. "Why don't we shock everyone, and actually do that?"

Elsa smiled. "Shock the world?"

"Show them that two complete opposites can make a go of this."

"I do like that idea."

"First, when are you going to invite me to the Christmas prom at the country club?"

"You want an invite? I thought you'd go, and maybe sweep me off my feet?"

"I've done enough sweeping, thank you." He tucked some hair behind her ear. "We've got to head to Bruce's gym."

"Yes, we want your paper to be perfect."

"I don't care about the paper. I'm happy with you the way you are. You don't need to lose weight with me."

"I know, I get it. I'm totally awesome, but you see, I happen to enjoy working out with you."

"You do?"

"Hell, yeah, I get to see you all buff. Watching you lift weights has become a favorite hobby of mine." She pressed her body against his. "Do you know what else?"

"I can think of a few things."

"Mom's not home, and it has been awhile since we've been in my bed. What do you say to having some special kind of fun?" She kissed his lips, and Noah groaned, his cock already filling, ready to fuck her.

"You're a damn evil woman."

"But I'm your evil woman."

****

After the craze inside the cafeteria, life seemed to return to normal. Elsa's and Noah's relationship created a huge stir, and no one seemed to want to forget about it. She didn't mind so long as people stopped staring. Kim wasn't always happy about being around Kurt, but she did talk to him now. Elsa refused to get involved. Kurt had hurt Kim a lot over the years, and that was a great deal of pain he needed to handle himself.

Her mother finally backed off, and even though she was exercising with Noah, Elsa had stopped changing her diet. She ate what she liked, and was working out to keep herself healthy. She loved it, and she loved Noah as well.

They had stuck to their promise and had both planned for their future. Their college of choice was one that excelled in sports and business. They had applied, and were waiting to hear if they had both been accepted.

"So, Elsa, are you going to wear the dress I got you?" her mother asked.

"Lorna, enough," Bill said.

"But?"

"No. I'm sick and tired of this. Our daughter is a great young woman. You should consider yourself lucky after everything I've heard. Elsa is a great student, wonderful daughter, and Noah is a brilliant boy. I'm fed up with you trying to change our daughter. She's fine."

"But her weight—"

"Has only ever been an issue with *you*. I've seen the way that boy looks at her. Our daughter is healthy, she's happy, and as far as I'm concerned, you need to back the fuck off."

Elsa tensed up in her seat. She'd never heard her father yelling before. Cursing, she'd heard him do a whole hell of a lot, but never at her mother.

"I've already got a dress I'm going to wear. Noah's going to meet me at the prom."

"Stupid prom, stupid county club," Bill said. "I've lost my appetite." He threw down his napkin and stormed off.

Elsa no longer wanted to eat.

Silence fell on the dinner table.

"He's right," her mother said.

"What?"

"I've been a horrible mother to you." Lorna covered her face and started to cry. "Oh, Elsa, I'm so damn sorry."

Looking around the room, Elsa frowned. Was she sleeping?

"You've been a good daughter, and I've turned into someone I hate so much."

Elsa frowned. "What do you mean?"

"Your grandmother, when she was alive, she was so strict." Lorna got to her feet, and Elsa helped clear the table. Her mother wasn't talking about her father's mother, her paternal grandmother, who had said she was fine the way she was. "I was on a diet most of my life. I don't even remember not being on a diet. I was a bigger girl growing up, my grandmother being an exceptional cook. I loved going there, and eating her gravy and biscuits, fried chicken. Mom, she wasn't so happy about that, and she hated anyone saying stuff about her daughter."

Leaning against the kitchen counter, Elsa listened as her mother talked about growing up with a strict mother, her own grandmother, who she didn't see very often.

"I can't believe I actually turned into her. I promised myself growing up that no daughter of mine would ever have to live what that kind of crap, and yet I did it anyway." Her mother broke down. "I'm so sorry, honey. I'm so sorry for everything. I love you the way you are, and I wouldn't change you for the world."

Elsa felt tears spring to her eyes, and when her mother opened her arms, she went to her.

"I love you, Elsa."

"I love you, too, Mom."

Chapter Eleven

Noah waited at the country club for Elsa to arrive. He was in one of the few tuxedos he actually owned, and he was looking forward to seeing his woman.

"She'll be here soon," Kim said.

"Why did you arrive before her?"

"My mom is one of the caterers. She wanted to be here to make sure everything arrived okay." Kim sipped at her drink. "You dress up nice. Elsa is a lucky girl."

"When are you going to give Kurt a chance?" His friend was due to arrive any minutes. At first, Kurt wasn't going to come to the Christmas prom. It was lame, which Noah agreed with. However, once he learned that Kim was going to be there, Kurt had made sure that he was going as well.

"This is really none of your business."

"He's not hurt you, or bullied you. I'm just trying to figure out what the problem is."

"There is no problem."

"Yeah, there is. You won't give him the time of day."

"You're being unfair, Noah. He *was* a bully."

"He's trying, Kim. Give him a chance."

Kim sighed. "I talk to him, Noah. I'm nice to him. You and Elsa have something special. Others, they don't."

Noah stared up at the ceiling before returning his gaze to her. "I tried."

"Did he put you up to that?"

"No, he didn't. Kurt, he's an asshole, but he's a good friend. I care about him."

"That's nice to know. I'm not going to hurt anyone, Noah. I'm just not going to fall for a guy I've spent most of my life being afraid of. I don't expect you to see it from my side, but that's it."

Noah nodded. "You're right. I've never been bullied before."

Kim smiled, but it didn't reach her eyes. "I'm going to go and see my mother."

He watched her leave and wished he'd kept his mouth shut.

"She's struggling to get over the name-calling and the bullying," Elsa said, coming round the corner.

Noah saw how beautiful she looked in the prom dress that molded to every curve. "Hey," he said. "You were stood there the whole time?"

"Not the whole time but I heard enough. She needs time."

"I'm getting that."

Elsa smiled. "What do you think?" She gave him a little twirl, and he grabbed her hand, pulling her close.

"You're so beautiful. I want to take you home right now."

"We can't go home right away. We've got to enjoy this party."

Noah groaned, pressing his face against her neck. "Fine, we'll stay and dance for you." He kissed her lips and took her out onto the dance-floor.

He noticed how she couldn't stop smiling.

"What is it?" he asked.

"This is the first time I've been to a dance. I never go to them, and technically, this is my first date with you."

"Come on, we've been on loads of dates."

"Not really."

Noah sighed. "Really?"

She nodded.

"Fine, you're going to make me get all mushy. Elsa, I consider every single moment that I spend with you a date."

"You do?"

"Yeah, I do. You're smart, funny, beautiful, and you make my world complete. Every moment with you is special for me. I never thought it was possible to fall in love but when I'm with you, and when I'm away from you, you're the only person I can think about."

"You love me?"

"I've told you that I do plenty of times."

Elsa reached up and kissed him. "You said you thought you were falling in love with me."

"Oh, well, I know I've fallen in love with you. Can't you see that, feel it when I'm around you?"

"I love you, too."

He sank his fingers into her hair and locked his lips with hers. She opened her mouth, and he went on inside, taking possession of her lips. To him she was his world, and he wouldn't change a thing. Noah had found her, and knew he'd discovered a real gem, and he wasn't going to let her get away, not now, not ever.

Noah danced with Elsa in his arms, and couldn't believe how lucky he was. When he spotted Kurt entering the country club, he and Elsa made their way toward the table where Kim sat.

"Hey, man," Kurt said, shaking his hand. "Hey, Elsa, Kim."

They all smiled at him, as did Kim. She wasn't mean to Kurt. Kim just didn't give him anything more than friendly interaction.

Sitting around the table, they all started talking about their futures.

"Are you both excited that you're going to the same college?" Kim asked.

Noah took Elsa's hand and nodded. "I wouldn't dream of going anywhere else."

"What about you, Kurt? What are you going to do?"

"At first I was just going to rely on football to live my dream. Since talking with this guy, I've decided to make sure that I've got a backup. I'm going to college that also has dramatic arts."

"You're an actor?" Kim asked.

"According to my parents I'm a bad one, but our careers' professor seems to think I've got a flair for it. What about you? What are you going to do?"

"I'm going to art and design school."

"That's fantastic. You like drawing?"

"Pretty much. I like sculpting as well."

Noah smiled as he watched the two start to hit it off. When Kurt asked Kim to dance, she accepted.

"Well, that is a little progress."

"Kim's not a bad person. He's got a long way to go for her to trust him, if she ever does."

"Come on, Elsa, let's go and dance."

The rest of the night, Noah romanced Elsa, dancing with her. They had a lovely dinner, and he hoped that he gave her a night to remember. It was what he wanted to do.

****

Christmas came and went with Noah and Elsa still together. They had defied the odds of their relationship. They were both accepted into the same college. Kurt and Kim had gotten into separate colleges. Elsa was right about them. Kim was friends with Kurt, but they hadn't gotten further. He never gave up though, which was kind of sweet to watch.

Jessica and her friends left them alone. Sienna came to talk to them though. She was still dating Adam, so she'd made it work.

For Elsa it was still kind of surreal to be dating

one of the most popular guys in school.

Her mother had backed off with her losing weight demands. Elsa still exercised with Noah. They'd done the before and after shot of her. Even though she hadn't lost much weight, she had toned up her body, and she had lost a little weight, which was fun.

He'd kept to his promise about her identity remaining a secret.

Tomorrow was graduation, and soon their futures away from high school would start.

They both spent time at each other's houses. They'd become one of those close couples that actually enjoyed spending time with each other. Now she stood in his room, talking with him.

"Can you believe at the start of the school year I didn't know you at all, and now I know that you like the color green? It's crazy."

He laughed. "Yeah, you like the color blue, love chocolate ice-cream, and hate having your picture taken."

"You still keep taking it, which drives me crazy."

Noah was tapping away at the keyboard, and she walked over to him, tucking her hair behind her ear as she did.

"What are you doing?" she asked.

"I have worked on a little high school memory board, photography, thingy," he said.

"Show me."

He leaned out and tapped his thigh. "Take a seat."

She lowered herself to his knee, and he clicked a button. Elsa frowned as the first picture was a group photo of them all in kindergarten.

"Oh my God, you still had that?"

"Yep, and I've got a lot more."

Elsa watched as the photographs showed them growing up, different pictures of each of them, until after a few minutes they came to the shots they took together. The first were of her as he made her turn from side to side so he could get the shots for his paper.

"You must hate me," she said.

"Not at all. I found it really hard to just take pictures of your body. I wanted the whole package."

She kept on watching, and she saw as they'd changed it up, pulling funny faces at each other. Even now, she was so happy.

Noah wrapped his arms around her, kissing her shoulder.

"You're so beautiful. Going to Bruce's and seeing you was the best thing that had ever happened to me."

"I was so scared to even enter that gym. I wished there was a magical cure to lose weight."

"I'm pleased there wasn't."

There were more pictures of the two of them together, one at the Christmas country club prom and several at school while they'd been studying.

"Elsa, there's something I want to ask you, and I don't want you to freak out, or start panicking, okay?"

"Why start off with saying something like that?" she asked. "Now I'm nervous as hell."

He chuckled. "I'm sorry. Try to forget all that I've just said."

"That's even harder to do." She smiled. "What is it?"

"We're going away to college, and I want to do something that will guarantee you stay mine. It's also completely crazy, and I don't even know if you'll accept." He held a small velvet box in front of her. "Elsa, will you marry me?"

She gasped. Not once had she even considered for a second that he'd propose marriage.

"You want to marry me?"

"I was going to ask you tomorrow at graduation, get down on one knee in front of the whole crowd, and then I realized you hated scenes, and people staring. This is it, me, here, putting my heart and my future on the line for you."

"It's not on the line."

"I love you, Elsa. I know I want to spend the rest of my life with you. I want us to be the crazy teens that get married young, but I want to be the ones that prove everyone wrong. We are right together, we are good together."

Elsa silenced him with a kiss. "Shut up, Noah. Yes."

"Yes?"

"Yes, put the ring on."

He pulled the ring out and slid it onto her finger. "Holy shit, we just got engaged."

"We're going to have to tell our parents."

"They already know. I asked your father for your hand in marriage."

"What did he say?" Elsa asked.

"I'm alive, and after some pretty hard grilling, he accepted that I was the right man for you."

"People are going to think we're pregnant."

"I don't care. I kind of like the thought of you being pregnant though."

She chuckled. "Not right now."

"No, we've got a future together, and I intend to enjoy every second of it," Noah said, taking her lips in a possessive kiss, making her forget everything else but him.

Epilogue

Elsa and Noah got married before college, and they became known as the wedded couple. Neither of them strayed, and no one could tear them apart. Even their college peers made bets on how long they'd stay together.

Throughout the next ten years they defied all expectations, staying together and being happy with each other.

They both graduated college, Noah going on to be a physical therapist for sports injuries. Elsa changed her path and majored in law, much to her father's happiness. After college, Elsa trained at different law firms, fulfilling the requirement to get experience away from her father. She took challenging cases, winning plenty and losing a few.

By the time they were both twenty-eight, Elsa was ready to settle down, so together they moved back to the childhood neighborhood.

They were moving into a modest three bedroom house. Elsa placed a box on the kitchen table and stared around at her space.

Noah came up behind her, wrapping his arms around her. "What are you thinking?"

"We're back home, and we're still together."

"Did you know Mrs. Donald, our chemistry teacher, was in on the bet?"

Elsa laughed. "You're kidding?"

"Nope."

"What was her limit?" Elsa asked.

"She didn't have a limit. She actually believed we'd be together for a long time."

"How do you know all this?"

"I just bumped into her. She tried to give me the winnings from the bet, but I wouldn't take it."

"Winnings? How is that possible?"

"She was the only one to bet on a lifetime, and no one else had gone this high."

"Wow, they really didn't believe we were real, did they?"

"Nope." He kissed her neck. "We proved them wrong."

"I can divorce you now."

"I doubt it. I'm the only one that does that thing with my tongue."

She groaned, pressing her thighs together to stem the flow of arousal. "Stop."

"Nope. We've got some time before Kurt and Kim arrive to help. How about we get started on filling up that nursery?"

Kim and Kurt were *not* together. Over the years, they had both stayed in touch with their friends, and even arranged to see each other as well. Kurt owned his own company and was making a name for himself in the business world. Kim was more modest, and grasped life as an artist. She was rather sensual in her art, which Elsa put down to her lack of satisfaction with life.

"Do you think they'll ever get together?" Elsa asked.

"I don't know. I'm hoping to get together now, with my wife."

"You've got a one track, dirty mind," she said.

"And you love it."

"That I certainly do."

****

Kim was shaking. She couldn't believe this was happening. The studio that she worked for, and that she had a contract with, had gone bust. She didn't have any money herself, and now she was standing in the studio, waiting for the businessman to arrive. Mr. Coal had wanted his asset to be present when the guy showed up.

She didn't know why. Over the years she'd proven time and time again that she sucked at social situations. This wasn't going to be any different.

The doors opened, and she froze. Kurt, the guy from high school who'd bullied her, was entering. He stared at her, and without looking away, spoke.

"Leave us, Mr. Coal."

The boy from high school was gone, and in his place stood a man that Kim didn't recognize.

"Hello, Kim, it has been a long time."

"Hey, Kurt."

"Let's get down to business."

The butterflies dancing in her stomach went crazy. Whatever was about to happen, Kim doubted she was going to like it, but what choice did she have? This was her livelihood, and now it was in Kurt's hands.

The End

SAM CRESCENT

DEDICATION

In the hope that people can change.

SAM CRESCENT

BULLY NO MORE

Sam Crescent

Copyright © 2016

Prologue

"Here comes the cow," Kurt Michaels said.

Kimberley James, or Kim to her friends, tried her hardest to ignore him. He was one of the guys who was popular, had it all, so he picked on people who were less than he was. Kim wasn't slim. She wasn't pretty, and she didn't even bother to try to fit in. She didn't care to.

"Ignore him," Elsa said.

Kim didn't know what she'd do without her best friend, Elsa.

"I'm surprised she can even walk."

They were all the same taunts. Kurt hadn't figured out anything original. It was always the same.

"Fatty's coming. Move out of the way before she squashes us."

"I bet you just eat lard by the tub full."

"Why don't you go on a diet?"

"Can you even fit into a car?"

There were more hurtful words along the way, but she tried not to think of them. Her life was made easier by ignoring him, pretending he didn't exist. She was overweight. At a size sixteen, she was the same size as Elsa, which they loved, as they could share each other's clothes. They didn't have to worry about each other giggling because of their size. Some of the girls in the female changing room during gym would laugh and point. It was embarrassing. Kim loved Elsa, and knew she'd found a friend for life.

"Just think, one day he's going to wake up, fat, miserable, and alone, thinking about his glory days in high school. We're not going to have to worry about that."

Kim forced a smile, and together they made their way into the main building of their high school. Most of the time she ignored Kurt, and gladly she did it. He was just so … mean. Why did he have to be so mean? She imagined it was down to his friends who urged him on. Noah, one of his friends, didn't join in. He seemed locked in his own little world. Even still, she didn't like Kurt, and wanted nothing to do with him.

Later that day when Mrs. Donald set a chemistry paper, and then proceeded to partner her up with Kurt, Kim truly thought that would be the end of it.

It wasn't.

****

They had been doing this paper for two weeks, and Kurt didn't like the way he was feeling. Kim sat on the opposite end of the table, and even though they were supposed to be studying together, she wouldn't give him the time of day. She only spoke to him when she had to, and most of the time, she gave him instruction on what to do via text message. Seriously, the bitch had issues.

No, you have issues, asshole.

"So," he said, and paused as Kim tensed up. He noticed that every time he spoke, she always tensed up as if he was going to attack her. "Okay, why the hell do you keep doing that?"

"What?"

"I've never hurt you. I've never raised my hand to you, thrown a ball at you. Why do you keep flinching when I've never fucking hurt you in my life?"

Kim sighed, and looked up at him. "Words hurt a lot harder than your fist, Kurt."

It was like a complete slap to the face.

Fatty, cow, pig, chubby, chunk, lard.

All the names he'd ever called her ran through his head all at once, and he finally saw himself the way she did. He wasn't a good-looking guy who was nice. No, to Kim, he was an asshole, a bully, and as he thought about it, no wonder she flinched every time like she did. He was the worst person in the world.

"Look, I don't want to cause trouble. I don't think you do either. Let's just do this assignment, so we can get out of each other's lives."

Kurt didn't like that. When it came to Kim, he was enjoying her company more and more. Gritting his teeth, he stared down at his sheet, and knew there wasn't a damn thing he could do about what happened.

"What would you like me to do?" he asked.

****

"I'd like to take you out on a date," Kurt said.

Kim stared at the guy who had done nothing but pester her all the way up to graduation. He was the bully, the jock, and now it seemed he wanted to date her. She didn't get it. Nothing had changed. He was still an asshole. Sure, ten months of him being different, compared to the last eleven or so years of him torturing her. Yeah, of course she wanted to go out with him. *Not!* Even though her mother liked him, Kim wasn't fooled.

"No."

He stood at her door, and she glanced up and down the street, wondering if this was some kind of prank. She knew all about Elsa and Noah. Kim was really happy for her friend. Elsa was happy with Noah, but then he'd never been mean to her either. Kurt on the other hand, he was a first class douche, and she wasn't going to be one of these pathetic people that caved. She had read so many books where the heroine caved, and she wasn't. Kurt was not likeable.

"Kim."

"Kurt."

"Look, just give me a chance is all I'm asking. I'm good. I can even give you an orgasm."

"Kurt, as nice as it is to know that you can show some care and attention to the women you're with, to me, all of this, it's wasted on me. I don't want anything to do with you. I don't like you."

"I know I was an asshole. Okay. I get it. I hurt you. I tortured you—"

"And the fact you can say that with even the remotest hint of sarcasm is one of the reasons why I'm always going to say no to you. I don't like you, Kurt. I can't trust you, not now, not ever."

She closed the door and leaned against it. She wouldn't be that one girl that fell for his crap.

****

"Can I have one dance?" Kurt said.

He stared at Kim. She was dressed in a beautiful deep blue dress, and her blonde hair was bound up on top of her head with curls coming down, framing her face. Her green eyes once again stared at him with doubt, and a little fear. He'd not attempted to hurt her, or call her names. In fact, now he actually went out of his way to hurt anyone who tried to hurt her.

She hesitated, and seeing it broke his heart.

"One dance, nothing else."

"Sure." She placed her hand within his, and he escorted her onto the dance floor.

"So we're just going to dance."

"What are your plans for after graduation?" she

asked.

"I've got a job lined up at my father's company. I intend to start on the ground floor and work my way up. When I'm in college, I'll work there part time."

"Are you taking over from your father when you're older?"

"I don't know. I've got my own plans, you know. What about you?"

"I'm going to art school. My mother thinks I have what it takes to make it on my own with my work."

"That's pretty good." Kurt hadn't seen any of her artwork. She'd always been so quiet about it. Whenever he tried to talk to her to get her to open up, she just seemed to close up even more.

"Yeah, I think so."

He pulled her into his arms, placing his hand on her waist and holding her close. Across the hall he saw Elsa wrapped in Noah's arms. His buddy had always been different, never really running with the rest of the pack. Now he understood why. Noah had never gone out of his way to hurt Elsa, whereas Kurt was suffering for being a constant jerk to Kim.

"Kim, I'd like for us to start over. We're leaving high school, and I want to leave all the memories behind."

She pulled away, looking at him. "No."

"Please."

"Kurt, I understand that you're different. You've seen the error of your ways, but it doesn't work like that. This is my life. I get to choose what I do, and I don't choose you." She stepped away from him. "Thank you for the dance."

Even as she stepped away, he knew he couldn't be angry. He was the one who fucked up, and now he was paying the price. Going toward the long table, he grabbed one of the drinks, disappointed to see it hadn't yet been spiked.

"You okay, man?" Noah asked, coming toward him.

"She'll be mine one day."

"Why don't you just cut your losses?"

"No. I want her, Noah. One day, she'll see I'm not that bad of a guy."

He finished his punch and left the prom. Kurt had danced with the only girl he was interested in. One day, Kim would belong to him, and she would see that he wasn't the same asshole who had hurt her.

Chapter One

Ten years later

"What the hell are you doing here, Kurt?" Kim asked. It had been ten years since she'd seen her tormentor. Ten years of wondering what had happened to him. Toward the end of high school, Kurt had changed. He'd been different. She didn't know why, other than he'd just decided to change. A lot had happened, especially between their two friends, Elsa and Noah.

"You know why I'm here."

She stared at him. He was handsome, and he hadn't gotten fat, bald, or ugly. Kurt looked much better now than when he was in high school. Some people have all the luck.

"You're looking to buy this business."

"I couldn't give two shits about this business, Kim. The only reason I'm here is because you are."

"Me?"

"Yes." He looked around the room, moving toward one of the paintings she'd done not long after prom night. Kim hadn't wanted to bring it, but Mr. Coal had insisted that it was one of her best works. She found Mr. Coal strange at times. He was constantly blowing hot and cold when it came to her work, never taking her to the next level. The scene was of a sunset outside of her bedroom window. She'd been so impassioned she hadn't been able to stop, whirling the colors together so that it was all blended. "This is your work?"

"Yes."

"You never showed it to me."

"I thought you owned your own business."

"I do. I own a lot of things."

They hadn't seen each other in ten years. Their

only connection to each other was through Elsa and Noah.

"You got what you wanted then?"

"Always. You were picked up by a failing business, and Mr. Coal, for all of his niceness and eye for art, he's bad for business." Kurt kept moving around the room.

He wore an expensive designer suit, and she couldn't help but tell that he screamed money. Biting her lip, she locked her hands together, trying to stop the shaking that was overcoming her. She was so scared, and she hated that.

Many times over the past year or so, she had noticed that Mr. Coal didn't have any business sense. Her work, to her, was good. Others thought her work stunning. Her mother had wanted to exhibit it herself, but Kim had wanted to do it on her own. She didn't want to earn credit where none was due.

"So you're interested in art now?" she asked.

She wanted to keep him constantly talking.

"No."

Kim frowned. "If you're not interested in art, why are you here?"

He turned toward her. "You."

"Me."

"Yes, always you, Kimberley James. This is amazing work. Why have you never been up for an exhibit?"

"Mr. Coal hasn't seen anything that he thinks would be worthy of an exhibit." It had confused her completely. Mr. Coal would say she was brilliant, and then not put any of her work in an exhibit, always finding someone else, or failing to even book an exhibit with his personal issues. She had noticed several artists had taken their work and gone elsewhere. She hadn't done that.

Kim believed in sticking around. Her mouth was so dry, and she was so nervous about what Kurt thought of her work.

"He's a fucking asshole, and he doesn't have a clue what he's talking about. These are amazing."

"Thank you."

Kim stared at him, noticing that Kurt had gotten bigger, filled out, and become more muscular. Averting her gaze, she stared at the floor, hoping this meeting would just end.

"You know this place is in the fucking ground, don't you?"

"You're the reputable businessman that's supposed to bring it out of the mire of debt?"

Kurt smirked. "That's right, babe."

"I thought businessmen had a little more … tact about them."

"Never really cared for being predictable. Learned that at my dad's place years ago." He pushed his hands into his pockets and turned toward her. Staring into his brown eyes, she felt a little out of place.

Ten years had passed since they'd been peers.

"You should be far more advanced than this."

"What do you mean?"

"You're much better than this. Mr. Coal is an asshole. To consider you an asset, and not sell your work, I don't get it."

"Kurt, what are you doing here?"

"Let's get right down to it. I'm here to offer you a deal."

"How did you even know I was here?" Kim hadn't kept an eye on all of Kurt's whereabouts.

Kurt paused and stared at her. "Do you really think I've not kept an eye on you after all this time?"

"It has been ten years. I shot you down every

time."

He shrugged. "This place is dead in the water, Kim. I have no desire for it. I have desire for your work, and I have a proposition for you."

"I don't know what to think right now," she said.

He'd been keeping an eye on her? Had he been stalking her? No, this was not really stalkerish, was it? Shouldn't a stalker make her feel threatened? She was so confused right now, and she didn't like it.

"You don't need to do anything. You're broke. This shop's not going to last the week, and I'm not saving it. The only person I'm interested in is you. Your work, it needs to go to the right places."

"Garbage?"

"No. A real exhibit for people to come and see what beauty you give to the world. I know you're broke, and you're too damn proud to go to your parents. So, I have an offer for you. I have a place set up in the countryside. I've got a room for all of your art equipment. I want you to paint for me."

"Paint for you?"

"Yes. I'd like to be the boss, and to tell you what I want you to do."

"I'm not going to sleep with you."

Kurt smiled. "One day you will."

"Seriously, ten years, and you're still hung up about the fact I said no?"

"I'm not hung up on it. I know why you said no. I got it. I'm showing you I'm a changed man."

"By what? Making me draw for you?"

"Then go home. Go back to your parents, and wait for another chance to come along. You can do that. Your mother will set you up for an exhibit. Your dad will pay your bills, and when people ask how you did it, you can say your parents helped."

Kim gritted her teeth. The reason she was in this predicament was because she didn't want her parents to help.

Running fingers through her hair, she stared at him. "So, what? I leave with you, take my work, and what?"

"Consider it a live-in position."

"A man of such high power can leave his job?"

"I'm the boss, Kim. I do whatever the hell I want, and I want you."

She closed her eyes, and she froze as he took a step toward her. Lifting her head, she found he stood a little too close. "How often were you watching me?" she asked.

"I know you've not had a steady boyfriend. You keep everyone at arm's length, refusing to give anyone a chance. Did I really cut you that deeply?"

"This is not about you, Kurt."

"Okay. I'm offering you a chance."

"I have an apartment."

"Your lease has run out. You're flat broke, and you're proud. This place is finished, you know that. Give me a chance."

Looking around the room, she saw the crumbling building around her. She hated the thought of going back to her parents a failure. She had a goal, and she was determined to meet that goal. Sure, her parents would help her out, but like he said, any achievement would be met through them.

"How do I know that this is going to be through my merit, and not yours?"

"Sometimes in life you have to take a chance, Kim. The key to greatness is knowing when to take the hand that has been offered. I'm offering to introduce you to the right people, but the rest will be up to you. I know how to take you to the next level, or at least the people who can do it. After that, it will be up to you."

"You won't ask for any favors?"

"No."

"And all you want is for me to move in with you and paint?"

"Yes."

"I don't know."

"I'm going to offer you a million dollars to come to my house and paint."

"That's too much."

"For the year. I want you to be at my house for the next year, painting, giving me a chance."

"You want me to be a whore?"

"When we fuck, it will be because you want it to happen. No other reason." He tilted his head to the side, and she found the action strangely erotic. He was assessing her. The way he looked at her, it was like she was naked, and he knew exactly how to read her. "I want you to paint for me, and live with me."

"This is completely crazy."

"You're going to agree. You're too stubborn not to."

****

Damn, he'd missed her. Kurt finished packing away her stuff, looking around the shitty apartment she'd been staying in. If her family even knew what she'd put herself through, they'd have put a stop to it. Ten years had been a long time of waiting, of planning, and if he was honest with himself, he'd been trying to move on from her. Kim in that last year of high school, had taken his world, twisted it, turned it, and completely obliterated every part of him. She had shown him exactly what it meant to be a bully, and how his actions could come back and bite him in the fucking ass.

Kurt had spent many days cursing his behavior. Each time he went to her, Kim always had that fear in her eyes. He hated that more than anything.

He never wanted to hurt her.

Since growing up, getting a decent pair of balls, and fighting in the main corporate world, Kurt had learned a lot. He'd learned to fight for what he wanted, and also the error of his past mistakes.

"Your parents would be horrified if they saw this," he said.

"I know."

"Why do you have to be so stubborn?"

She stared up at him, pulling the strap up on her shoulder. "When you were working for your father, did you get special treatment?"

"No. They worked me harder." He wouldn't admit that it had been harder than he anticipated. People at his father's place thought he was an entitled prick. In the beginning, he had been. It had taken months to convince them that there was more to him than met the eye. Through the time he worked for his father, not once did he complain, or try to get special treatment. He took everything they gave him, and he made his father's company more profitable.

"Oh," she said.

"The guy that bullied you. The guy that hurt you, and treated you like shit, that guy is gone. Long gone. He's not coming back."

"Kurt, I don't know what to do with this," she said. "I'm scared, okay?"

"Look, I'm not going to hurt you. I just want you to fulfill your passion for painting, and to know you don't have to worry about me."

"Sex?"

He smiled. "That's going to happen."

Kim smiled, too. "I can't even believe you think that's going to happen."

"Babe, we've been going around in circles for years."

"We've not seen each other for years."

"So? I bet you've thought about me." He saw the way her cheeks went a glorious shade of red, and knew she'd thought about him. "I'm free, I'm single, and I'm hot stuff."

For the first time in his life, Kim laughed along with him. She covered her mouth, but he saw the humor. "You're bad."

"I'm only just getting started."

"I can't believe I'm doing this."

"You're the first chick I know to carry light. You've not even got a case for shoes."

"I have two bags of art equipment." She patted the ones lying on the ratty old sofa.

Kurt sighed. "This is everything you want?"

"It is, yes."

He shook his head. "It has amazed me how you've survived out in this world all alone."

"Shut up. I've been doing just fine."

"Please, your loyalty has been a problem. You're way better than what that fucker was going to do for you. He didn't really care about the business anyway. He's been looking for a buyout for years," Kurt said, talking about Mr. Coal. The only reason he organized any meeting was to finally get to talk to Kim. He knew unless he organized it in secret, she wouldn't have taken the time to talk with him.

"Why did you come then?"

"You. Like always, you."

They headed toward the door, and he waited for Kim to lock it. They made their way downstairs. The elevator was broken. Kurt didn't say anything as she posted the key through the landlord's letterbox, along with a letter.

Outside at the car, he opened up the trunk and placed her bags inside. He'd expected her to have more stuff.

Still, there were plenty of things for him to buy her. Kurt wanted to treat her, to show her that she could be herself around him. Opening the passenger door, he waited for her to climb inside, and then got behind the wheel. Turning over the ignition, he pulled away from her shitty apartment, and her shitty life, determined to help her create a new one.

"Are you seeing anyone?" Kim asked.

"No."

They were silent for several seconds. "Are you going to ask me if I am?"

Kurt glanced over at her. "You better not be."

She chuckled. "You only want me to paint for you."

"Are you seeing someone?" he asked. Kurt knew that she wasn't. He'd kept an eye on her, knowing she hadn't given any guy a chance in the last ten years. Sure, she went on dates, which went nowhere. Even Elsa and Noah had tried to set her up, but all of them had failed. Kim was a unique beauty, and he intended to have her all to himself.

"No."

"You ever had a long term boyfriend?" he asked.

"Don't need one."

"Doesn't it ever get lonely?"

"I have my art if I need companionship."

Kurt hummed. He thought about the art he'd seen, the changes in each piece. "Where do you keep all of your artwork?" he asked.

"Mr. Coal is sending you every single piece. I've also got multiple sketchbooks if you'd like to see them."

"Yes, I would. You're willing to show them to me now?"

"You're paying me to. I don't see why I can't share them."

Kurt nodded. It wasn't much, but it was a start. She wasn't keeping him out. It was a small victory.

Chapter Two

"You really did well for yourself," Kim said, looking up at the high ceiling in the country house. The place was huge. Too big for a single guy, yet this was Kurt's home. She couldn't believe it, not really.

"Thank you. I like to think so."

"And now you're taking some time out?"

"Consider it a much needed break for the future."

"You've got future plans?" she asked.

"Always. Life is about living, and I intend to live it to the fullest, don't you?"

She turned toward him to find him leaning against one of the doorways leading to other parts of the house. "I don't know. I've always been more focused on the now, rather than the then, or whatever they say for the future, if that makes sense."

"It does. You're not really living. You worked for Mr. Coal, and you took a job as a waitress. Why?"

"I had to make ends meet."

"Again, you're all about independence and stubbornness. It's a good quality most of the time."

Kim smiled. "You don't sound like you believe that."

"I don't know. The world is made up of favors, friends, help. You wouldn't ask anyone for any help. I find that a little sad."

"I wanted to make it on my own."

"You will. The problem is, sometimes you just need one person to put you in touch with the other. It's how it all starts. Think about it; movie stars, billionaires: it's not just about what you know, it's who you know. Also, you never used your last name, James, why?"

"How did you know about that?" she asked. Kurt was confusing her at every point. She didn't know which way was up or down.

"I know everything. It's the power that I have."

"My mom's name is James. She did a lot of her art under the James name, so I changed it so I didn't have to be compared to her." Not that she minded being compared. It was all about her pesky independence.

"Huh, you are one stubborn woman. No help from parents, friends, family, no boyfriend, and you're determined to make it on your own. Quite a hard combination to help."

She sighed. "I feel like I should be saying sorry."

"Nah. Not sorry. I've known several … stubborn people. You're not the first, and I'll help."

Kim pressed her lips together. She didn't ask for his help, but she also didn't want to leave either. The house, the grounds; what she'd seen, she loved. Also, she had … missed him. How weird was that? She had missed the guy who used to bully her, which sucked. Toward the end of high school, he'd become a really nice, loving, caring kind of guy. She missed that with him. Even though it was hard for her to relax around him, after some time, she'd find herself laughing at his jokes, his stupidity. He was a fun person.

She hadn't had a lot of fun in a long time.

Stubbornness is going to hurt you.

"Your paintings should be delivered tomorrow, and I've got several rooms set up for them. Would you like to see your art room?" he asked.

"Yes, please." She quickly grabbed her two art bags and turned toward him.

"I'll take those." He lifted them onto his shoulders as if they didn't weigh a ton, and she knew they did. They were really heavy. Even she found them hard to lift. She wouldn't leave anywhere without at least one that was filled with her sketchpad.

"I don't mind carrying one."

"I'm sure you don't. I can manage this, sweetie."

"Sweetie?" she asked, walking beside him.

"Term of endearment. You never heard of it?"

"I've never been called it."

"Get used to it. It's a … thing I do."

"Okay, *darling*."

"Be careful, pooch, I'll expect it all the time."

"Sure thing, babe!" Kim found herself laughing.

"Good, love."

"Honey."

"Sweetness."

"Hot pants."

"Sexy."

Kim blushed and stopped playing along.

"I won," he said.

"Hey, you went dirty."

"You could have as well. I've got a nice long cock."

"Kurt!"

"What? Just letting you know. Advertising what I've got packing."

She looked around the house, catching glimpses of the hominess of it. This wasn't a bachelor pad. It felt like a home. "I don't need to know what you're packing."

"Fine. I also know how to use it. I can give multiple orgasms with my dick, and my tongue."

"This is sexual harassment."

"Your work is not even here yet. Besides, we're old friends bantering with each other. You know I wouldn't hurt you. My hands are on myself until you beg."

She shook her head and couldn't help smiling. He was so charming and sweet. For the first time in over five years, she felt happy.

They walked past the dining room, library, study, kitchen, toward the back of the house that overlooked the garden. Kurt opened a door, and she stepped into heaven. The room was completely plain. The walls themselves looked like a canvas with several lights hanging down so when it got dark, she could choose her own lighting. The windows were large, and nothing masked her view of the outside, which, as it was summer, was stunning in color.

She spotted several easels, boxes, and a large storage cupboard at the end.

"I got everything so you'd know what to do." Kurt placed the bags down. "Later on, I'll show you down to your other art room, past the garden near the lake. I believe deer come, so it's something to look forward to."

"Wait, I have two rooms like this?"

"Yes. I understand as an artist, you find inspiration everywhere, and I wanted to be prepared for all of it."

Kim couldn't help it. She ran into his arms, wrapping hers around his neck, and holding onto him tightly.

"Thank you so much."

"If I knew it just took a couple of art rooms to get a hug, I'd have purchased them years ago."

She giggled.

"I'm serious. What does it take for a kiss?"

Kim laughed, pulling away. "Don't push it. My kisses are sacred."

"Have you ever been kissed?"

"Sure." She hadn't, not on the lips. Whenever a guy had gone to kiss her after a date, she panicked, and turned so that he grazed her cheek.

"You've not been kissed."

"I totally have."

"Prove it, kiss me."

She frowned. "How is that supposed to prove anything?"

"If you've kissed guys before, it shouldn't scare you."

"That makes absolutely no sense."

"Then don't kiss me. You're afraid."

"I'm not afraid."

"Then kiss me."

"No. I'm not going to be pressured into kissing you." She was chuckling, finding his teasing endearing.

"Chicken."

"Whatever."

"Chicken." He then started to cluck like a chicken.

"Fine!" She stormed up toward him, went on her tiptoes, and slammed her lips against his. The kiss took her completely by surprise. His lips were a little firmer than she imagined. Closing her eyes, she ran her hands up his chest. Part of her was prepared to push him away, yet her hands kept on moving up. She locked her hands around the back of his neck, putting her body flush against his.

Kurt held her hips.

Tilting her head to the side, she opened her mouth, and he ran his tongue across her lips. She released a little moan.

A cell phone ringing had them both pulling apart. Her lips tingled. Kurt stared at her. "The phone's not mine."

She frowned, then remembered her own cell phone. Glancing down, she saw it was Elsa, and told him so.

"Answer, I'll show you to your room."

"Hey, Elsa," she said.

"Did I catch you at a bad time? You sound a little breathless."

"No, it's not a bad time."

"It's totally a bad time," Kurt said.

Kim ignored him, following him back the way that they'd come.

"I phoned Mr. Coal, and he said you were no longer working for him. What's going on?"

"Well, I have a new job now, one you're not going to believe."

"Oh, tell me all about it."

Kurt grabbed her bags, and they made their way upstairs. She walked quickly, trying hard not to think about the kiss they had just shared together. Her lips tingled, and if it hadn't been for Elsa, she'd have kept on kissing him. He took her to the third room on the right, opening the door.

"Let me know when you're done. I'll be in the kitchen."

He left her alone, and she sat on the edge of the bed.

"Who was that?" Elsa asked.

"That was Kurt Michaels."

"Wait? Noah's Kurt? Bully Kurt?"

"Yep to both counts."

"What are you doing with him?"

"He came to offer me a job, and I'm currently at his country home getting settled in."

"Okay, I've missed a shitload of information here. Tell me all."

"I kissed him, Elsa."

"You kissed Kurt? Your sworn enemy?"

"Yes, and I enjoyed it. I didn't want it to stop."

"You really need to start from the beginning."

****

Pulling out his cell phone, Kurt dialed Noah's number.

"Stewart here," Noah said.

"Don't you ever see who is calling?"

"Nope. Where would the fun be in that? I was hoping you were my wife, but clearly not."

"You love that don't you?" Kurt said, smiling.

"I'll never get tired of it. What's up?"

"I wanted to let you know that I've given Kim a job, and she's telling Elsa about it now. Thought I'd do the nice thing for you, so you're not in the dark."

"Wait? You're hiring Kim."

"Yep, to paint."

"Kurt?"

"Yeah."

"What's really going on?"

Noah had always been able to see through him. There had once been four of them. Him, Noah, Adam, and Ryan. Now, it was just the two of them. The other friendships had failed whereas theirs had remained strong. He was really proud of what they'd been able to do together.

"Nothing."

"Kurt, you've not had a serious relationship in years. Every time we talk, you ask about Kim. When you went to college, you banged your way through freshmen right up to actual professors. You were trying to fuck her out of your system. Ten years on, you're her savior? It's me, man, Noah."

Rubbing the back of his head, he let out a breath. "She needed help."

"How did you know that? I never told you about the guy she was working for."

"You should have told me sooner that he was a real piece of work. He told her that she was brilliant, even though her work wasn't good enough to do an exhibit for. Did you know I did some research, and the people he helped, paid him? Can you believe that?"

"You're very protective of Kim, even after all this time."

Kurt let out a sigh, and stared up at the sky. "What are you getting at, man?"

"Ten years, Kurt. Ten years, and you're still chasing after her."

Staring across the kitchen, he placed his fingers against his lips. It had been ten years, but that kiss had been totally worth it.

"I'm not going to hurt her."

"You and Kim have this strange kind of relationship going, and don't pretend you don't, because you do. Back in high school, you hurt her, and since then, you've done everything to try and get in her pants."

"This isn't about that. I'm not that same asshole from high school, Noah. This is about more than that."

"Do you love her?" Noah asked.

"What?"

"Do you? I think I know the answer. It doesn't take a rocket scientist to guess that you have feelings for her."

"I do. I love her." He'd loved her for a long time, and even as he'd been with other women, trying to forget her, it hadn't happened. Kurt's feelings for her hadn't gone away.

"She doesn't have a clue how you feel about her."

"I know." Kurt wanted to tell him about the kiss, but instead, he chose to remain silent. That was his, and no one was going to take that away from him. The kiss belonged to him, no one else.

He wondered if she was telling Elsa?

Didn't that mean something good if she was?

Women told each other everything that was important.

Crap. She was making him think about girly stuff.

"I don't want to see you hurt, Kurt."

"I won't get hurt."

"Kim wasn't able to get past you bullying her in high school. I don't want you to get your hopes up, in case she has the same fears now as she did back then."

"I'm not going to get my hopes up. I know you mean well, I do. I just, I've got to do this. I have to help her."

"Okay, okay, I'm here if you need me."

"Thanks, man, I appreciate it."

Kurt hung up the phone and tossed the device onto the counter. *Fuck.* He was completely exhausted. Turning toward the cupboards, he started opening them up, hoping that he'd have some idea what to cook for dinner.

He didn't cook.

Unlike Noah, he was happy to order takeout, or let others cook for him. Kurt had been more interested in getting his company off the ground than learning to cook.

"Elsa says hey," Kim said, startling him. He turned around, forgetting that he'd partially opened one of the cupboards, and slammed his head against it. "Oh, ouch. Crap, I'm sorry. I didn't mean to scare you."

He held onto his head and winced. She came over to him, grabbing his waist, and forcing him into a chair.

"Let me check it out."

The moment he sat down, his gaze landed on her large tits. The shirt she wore pressed them together, and he got a nice view of her cleavage. The temptation to sink his head against her breasts was strong. He held back. This was not about allowing her to be uncomfortable.

"It doesn't look like it's broken the skin. I think

you'll be fine. A minor headache, if that."

"I'm totally fine." He rested his hands on his knees, staring up into her eyes. The tension changed between them, and he saw her eyes dilate as she stared at him. She licked her lips, and he wondered if she was getting wet thinking about him.

"When you speak to Elsa again, tell her I said hey."

She nodded.

Did she realize that she was thrusting her chest out, cocking her hip to the side? The way she licked her lips was more of an invitation. One he didn't want to turn down.

"Why were you looking in the cupboards?" she asked.

"I was going to make us something to eat."

"You cook?"

"No."

"Then how would you cook?"

"Figured it was easy."

She laughed. "Oh my God, your ego. Seriously? You think cooking is so easy?"

"Why not? Everyone does it."

"And some die from not doing it right. Wow, I can't believe you." She placed her hand on his shoulder. "I'll cook."

"You cook?"

"Of course. I spend time with Elsa, and she cooks. It's something my mom enjoyed doing. She found food brought her family together, and in doing so, it inspired her. Her family inspired her to paint."

Kim started looking through the cupboards, and he wasn't about to complain. Every time she bent over he got a nice view of her full ass.

She rummaged through the ingredients and went

toward the fridge. "Wow."

"Second wow in one day," he said.

"Your fridge is totally full. You have chicken, beef, lamb, pork. There's even shrimp in here. You're not going to eat all of this in one day."

"My cleaner goes shopping for me. I throw out what is bad."

"Not anymore. I know how to keep this food for longer, and if I'm right, you have an empty freezer. Throwing good food away."

"You're going to stuff it in the freezer. Isn't that throwing it away?"

She shook her head. "You have three pounds of fresh shrimp. Separate them down, you've got enough for at least three dinners, even more. Before we cook, I'm splitting it down. I'm not having any waste. If you don't mind."

"Make yourself at home." It was what he wanted her to do. This home had been bought for a reason, and he was hoping that Kim would help him fill it with children, and happy memories.

Sitting at the counter, he watched as she got some freezer bags and started to put away the meat. He noticed she smelled it first, before packing it away. Once that was all done, she threw anything that couldn't be recycled into the trash.

Once her hands were washed, the meat and fish in the freezer, she then got started on preparing the shrimp that she left out. He watched as she started to add some spices that had been displayed on the counter.

Watching her was enthralling. He couldn't wait to get to watch her paint.

She sliced up a lemon, and started to add the juice, capturing any seeds that fell into her hand.

The scents were already amazing. His cock was

stiff as with each movement, her tits would move, her body showcased in ways that made him desperate. Kurt wanted her naked and underneath him. No, he wanted her over him. Then he wanted to take her from behind, riding her doggy style.

He just wanted her, and he'd take her anyway he could have her.

Kim made them spicy shrimp tacos, which were so delicious, and heavenly. After which, he took her for a tour of the grounds, showing her everything she needed. By the time he was done, it was late, and Kim was struggling to stay awake. Walking her to her bedroom, he waited for her to go inside.

"Thank you, Kurt." She kissed him again, and he watched her go in. Moving toward the bedroom beside hers, he entered his own room.

Two kisses on the first day.

Kurt looked forward to more.

Chapter Three

The following morning, Kim stared at the three rooms, which displayed her art. She had also placed a large box on the table for Kurt to have a look at. She stood beside him, explaining when she painted certain pieces, and what they meant to her.

"This is amazing." Kurt stopped at a particularly sexual piece.

The night she painted that, she'd stumbled onto a porn site online, and there she had watched fucking in its rawest forms. Even as she'd been aroused, she'd also been struck by the different couples on screen. She had watched some who were fucking as a job, others that were attracted to one another, and then even some of the amateur porn videos.

Instead of closing it down, and pushing it to one side as a dirty experience, she'd embraced it and found a great deal of inspiration.

"These can't be shown around kids," he said.

"No, they can't."

Was it her, or was his voice deeper, a little cracked?

He didn't speak as he moved from one painting to another. When he was finished with her work, Kim waited for him to speak first.

"What inspired you to do those pieces?"

"Porn."

Even as she said the word, her cheeks heated.

"Porn?"

"Yes." She told him how those paintings came to being.

"Are you a virgin?" he asked.

"That's a little personal?"

"From the paintings alone, you seem to envy what

they're doing."

"You can't tell all of that from some paintings," she said, knowing she lied as she spoke.

Kurt started at her. "You know you can."

"I'm a virgin. I've not had sex." She expected him to laugh, but instead, he just nodded, and made his way toward the table where the box of sketches lay. "Is it okay if I go and get set up?"

"Yes."

Kim didn't wait around, and made her way straight toward her room. Entering, she went straight toward the windows, allowing fresh air into the room.

It was such a plain room, and she went to her supplies and started to mix her colors. She didn't know what to paint, but the moment the paintbrush touched the color, and she placed it on the wall, inspiration took over.

Kurt hadn't made fun of her.

He'd not ridiculed her lack of a sex partner.

A simple nod, and he'd gone to her other work.

She didn't understand it.

She was a twenty-eight year old virgin, who had only kissed the guy who bullied her in high school. Kim couldn't even think why she'd remained a virgin so long.

Sex didn't scare her.

Connecting didn't scare her.

She wanted to have sex.

The men she'd dated, they had left her cold.

Her mother always said to make sure that you trust the person you give yourself to. Kim hadn't trusted any of the men she'd dated. Going on blind dates, double dates, they all sucked.

The only constant in her life was her art.

She didn't know how much time passed before Kurt came into the room. He was carrying a glass of juice.

"I thought you might like this."

When she checked the time on his watch, she saw it was already past lunchtime.

"I didn't even know the time. I'm sorry. Do you want me to do lunch?"

"You're not my maid." Kurt stared past her, and when she turned to look, she gasped to see that she'd painted Kurt, only it was the face that haunted her. The way he would look when he'd say horrible names. She'd even put the names in a bubble near his lips. The painting looked more like a comic book illustration. "I've got a lot to do to make you trust me."

"I didn't even realize I'd drawn it."

Only now, she felt … happy. The drawing had been locked up inside her, and now she felt free. He saw what she had seen all those times. On from the writing, which she'd done large, she had started to draw a vast field, and in the distance, two people, hand in hand.

She would have believed she'd drawn Noah and Elsa, if it wasn't for the blonde hair. She had blonde hair.

"You've never had sex with anyone?"

"I said that. It's what virgin means. Untouched."

"Why?"

Kim shrugged. "Never been the right guy." She turned to look at him. "You're not that boy anymore."

"You would flinch when I came near you." Kurt didn't look away from the drawing on the wall. "Your artwork touches the soul."

"I don't mean to hurt you."

"This is what I looked like, saying that shit to you?" he asked. "Hurting you."

"Words cut deeper. They last longer than a bruise."

He turned toward her, and she gasped. The emotion, the pain, the hurt, all of it was there for her to see. "I'm sorry."

For the first time, she truly believed him.

The remorse was there. The pain. The guilt.

"I forgive you."

She did. Turning back to the wall, she stepped up toward the couple, and carried on painting. Even though Kurt was in the room, she kept on painting. "You're not going to tease me about the porn?"

"No."

"Being a virgin?"

"No."

"We have come a long way."

"Noah called. Elsa wants us to go to dinner over at their place."

Kim chuckled. "Do you think they're planning on keeping an eye on us? Make sure we're good?"

"I bet they are. Nothing will get past them."

Kim took a deep breath and turned toward him. "Thank you so much for giving me this opportunity." She had already placed a call to the diner to let them know she wouldn't be back. Kurt had given her an opportunity to focus on her art, and she was going to take it. There was no way she was going to let this chance go.

"I'll do anything for you, Kim. All you have to do is ask, and it's yours."

He left her alone, and for several minutes, she stared after him.

They had changed once again. Neither of them was going to be the same. Staring at his image, Kim could look at him, and know the Kurt of now wasn't him. This boy on the wall, he meant nothing. He was gone.

The hurt he'd caused was over.

****

Kim's work had the power to cut him to the core. Kurt walked into his office and took a seat, spinning around to stare out over the garden. Ben, the gardener, was pruning some flowers, and stopped to wave at him. He waved back, staring out at the beauty that was before him. This was all for her. None of it was for him.

The only thing Kurt had wanted was Kim. She was his reason for buying this house, for doing so well. In the early years of college and work, he'd tried to build a life for himself. Kim had always been there in his head, refusing to leave. She didn't have a clue of the hold she had on him.

Rubbing his eyes, he tried to clear his head of the image she'd painted. It was so brutal. That was who he'd become to her. Some vicious monster who spewed abuse in her direction. He didn't want to be that man ever again.

Firing up his computer, he checked his emails to see that his company was doing fine without him. He'd left a manager in charge, a man he trusted, so that he could take this time away.

When boredom started to set in, he got to his feet and started for a walk in his garden.

He went outside the front door and along the paths until he was near her art studio. Kurt was about to move on, when she saw him.

"Hey," she said, moving toward the door. "Would you like some company?"

"Sure?"

"I have to check. You being the boss and all." She walked toward him. The jeans she wore were covered in paint. The thin strap of her crop top slid down her arm, showing the white strap of her bra.

"I'm such a hard ass boss."

She chuckled. "Total hard ass."

Kurt nodded for her to start walking, but she surprised him by linking her arm through his.

"After Noah's dinner invitation, I was thinking of

accepting one for a charity event in three weeks. I was wondering if I could showcase some of your work," Kurt said. He held his hand up before she could complain. "It's for charity. People within the community are going to be there, and I think it's a perfect opportunity to showcase you."

"Okay."

"You're not going to argue?"

"I want to, but I also see what you mean about having help. I need to learn to accept help that you offer."

"In my company for one day, and look at the change in you. I'm so proud."

"I'm kind of nervous about going to dinner with Elsa."

"Why? They're our friends. It'll be fine."

"They're going to ask questions."

"So, we tell them the truth. I want to help."

He paused near the water fountain, and Kim stopped touching him to bind her hair up into a ponytail. Kurt wanted her hair down so that he could run his fingers through it.

"You don't think that's strange?"

"A little, but what does it matter?"

"You said we're going to end up fucking."

"Big words for a virgin," he said, tugging lightly on a loose strand.

"I'm learning from the best."

"I should be offended, but I'm not. I'll have you cursing like the rest of us."

"You're so different," she said.

"I don't know what that means."

She shrugged. "Back in school you were an entitled prick. Now, you're like a real adult. When did that happen?"

"I take care of thousands of people, Kim. My

business is their job, and their livelihood falls to me. Sometimes you just have to grow up."

"Huh."

"What?" he asked, seeing her assessing gaze.

"Never thought I'd see the day that you were all about being sensible."

"People change, Kim. Sometimes you have to have a little faith."

They continued walking, this time in silence. The sounds of birds chirping, trees rustling, calmed him. Kim placed her arm through his once again.

"Change?"

"Yes. You should try it some time. You might find some surprises."

"Um."

They moved down to the lake near her other art studio. "I may as well show you this now that we're here." He grabbed a key, handing it to her. "Whenever you're looking for another source of inspiration, you can come here."

Kim took the key, and he opened up the door, flicking on the light. The studio was like the one at the house, only on a bigger scale.

"You have completely spoilt me, and I've just been a bitch."

"It's okay. It's a woman's prerogative to be a bitch."

"It's not good enough. I'm so sorry."

"Don't stress about it." He turned around. "This is all of yours."

When he looked toward her, he saw tears in her eyes as she stared at him. "This not good?"

"This is perfect."

"You've not even looked."

"You're right, I haven't looked properly. I guess it

takes an intervention to really see someone."

Kurt frowned as he stared at her. She wasn't looking at anything else but him. "Well, you can do whatever art you feel like. Decorate it, screw it around. It's all yours."

He stepped outside of the studio and stared up at the house. So many dreams, and yet, he didn't even know if he was fighting a losing battle. Kim was an enigma to him.

Kim closed the door, flicking the lock. She came toward him, grabbed his face, and slammed her lips against his.

There was no denying her lack of experience. Her lips landed toward the corner of his mouth, and only when he took over, cupping her hips, coaxing her lips apart did Kim melt against him. Kurt wouldn't have her any other way. He would be her first, and her last. His dick thickened at the thought, and he forced himself to release her.

"You don't have to thank me with a kiss."

"I wasn't. I kissed you because I wanted to. Thank you for the studio, Kurt, and for believing in my work enough to give me this."

He didn't just believe in her work. He believed in her. She was a strong woman, a resilient one. Kurt hoped for her to see it soon.

"I think we should make a deal," Kim said.

"I'm all ears."

"I'll cook and bake for you as a thank you for the wonderful gift you've given me."

"How about you cook and bake period, I'm never one to turn that shit down. Also, you'll give me the pleasure of your company, whenever I want it."

"Oh, bargaining are we?" she asked.

"I think your company is not too much to ask.

Take a chance, Kim. Be careful though, it might be fun."

"Hey, I can have fun."

He snorted. "No, you can't."

"I'm the queen of fun."

"I doubt it."

She rushed toward him, patting his arm. "I'm fun."

"Then prove it. Give me the pleasure of your company."

"It's already a deal, Kurt. You know that."

He took hold of her hand, and they made their way back toward the house. Kim paused, and he stopped.

"You have a pool?"

"Yeah, I have pretty much everything. I also have a gym in the basement as well." Kurt smirked. "Prove you're fun." He reached down, lifting her up. Kim screamed at him, trying to get away. Her body wriggled against him as he got to the pool edge, and threw her in. She dropped into the water.

Kurt watched as she broke the surface, screamed, and suddenly sank.

"Kim?"

Shit, he couldn't be sure if she could swim. Diving into the water, he grabbed her, and pulled her up. His heart was racing, and as she broke the surface, she burst out laughing.

"What the fuck? That wasn't funny."

"I couldn't get you in the pool any other way. Come on, that was funny."

"No, it fucking wasn't. I was fucking scared." He turned his back on her, trying to gain his composure. Kurt had never been so scared before in his life.

"You threw me in the water. I was just fooling around. I'm sorry."

He turned toward her and watched as she wiped

her face. "I overreacted."

"You were scared for me?"

"I couldn't bear the thought of anything happening to you." Kurt loved her, damn it. She didn't have a clue how much she meant to him.

"I didn't mean to scare you." She wrapped her arms around him.

He breathed her in, feeling her against him, which helped to calm him.

"I told you I was fun."

"Babe, you're fucking dangerous."

Chapter Four

"How is baby making going?" Kim asked. She stood inside Elsa's kitchen, stealing some grapes from the salad as her friend finished up some food.

"It's going great, thank you for asking. Had any sex yourself?"

Kim swallowed the grape, and started to cough. Elsa slapped her on the back, helping her. "Thanks."

"No problem. So, no sex then?"

"No."

"Kurt would gladly get rid of that V-card for you."

"I'm not looking to get rid of it. What has gotten into you?" Kim asked.

Elsa paused. "You're right. I shouldn't be asking about that stuff. You didn't ask for my advice. I was just worried about you, and I'm trying to be cool and hip."

"Do you think you're really old?" Kim couldn't help but laugh.

"I'm twenty-eight. I'm married, trying for kids. I love my life, and my friend is going through something. I don't know. I want you to know that I'm here, and with Kurt, he can be a little overbearing, and scary."

"I get it, I do," Kim said. "Believe me, you don't have to be cool and hip. Save that for when you have a bunch of kids."

"Do you think twenty-eight is old?"

"No. I'm twenty-eight. Calling you old is like calling it myself."

Elsa sighed, staring at her.

"What?" Kim asked.

"I just, don't you want to know what it's like? To be with someone? To share that kind of intimacy?"

"Yeah, I do."

"What has taken you so long?"

Kim took another grape, looking around to make sure Kurt wasn't around. "When you and Noah went there?"

"To sexland?"

"Sure, to sexland, did you enjoy it?"

Elsa wrinkled her nose. "At first it was quite painful. He made it good after that though. I trusted him, and he loved me. It was special."

"Exactly. You trusted each other, so no matter what, it was special. I've never had that kind of trust with anyone, apart from you." She shook her hand. "I don't want to have sex with you."

"I get it. You've not been comfortable enough to go to the next level."

"It means something, and when I do it, I don't want to wake up in the morning, wishing I'd not done it."

Elsa nodded. "I can see that. When Noah and I went to sexland, in the morning I was sore, but I was happy."

"This is way too much information for my liking."

"Friend here, remember? Total loving friend."

Kim rolled her eyes just as Noah and Kurt entered the kitchen. She stole another grape, watching the man who had turned her world upside down again. He'd come out of nowhere, and changed her life. It had been six days since his visit to Mr. Coal. Since then they had spent a lot of time together. They walked around the gardens, shared the pool, meals, watched television. He also came to her art studio, watching her.

She found herself watching him.

He didn't seem to understand what he was doing to her with his presence. Kurt had changed. He wasn't a bully anymore, or a guy trying to have sex. Kurt was a man with a heart. A man with so much depth that she found herself wanting to draw him.

Still, her art aside, she found him to be quite funny.

"That must be exciting," Elsa said.

Kim looked at her friend with wide eyes. "What?"

"Kurt was just saying about the charity gala, several of your pieces are going to be on show."

"Erm, yeah. I've even called my parents. They want to go. They understand it's not strictly for my stuff."

"The right person sees your stuff, and you'll get to host your exhibit."

Just thinking about her work on display filled her with nervous excitement.

"And you two? How is it going?" Noah asked.

"We're both still alive. Kurt keeps running from my claws."

They all laughed. Kurt moved behind her, gripping the back of her neck. Her nipples hardened, and her pussy grew slick at the way he held her. "I can handle her, can't I, babe?"

"Sure thing, sugarplum."

"They have secret names for one another," Elsa said.

"It's love," Noah said.

Kim looked up into Kurt's brown eyes. Her heart began to pound. Was it love? In their last year of high school, she didn't want to be one of the girls that fell for the guy who'd hurt her. Now, she was falling, and it was hard to remember the guy who sneered at her. The names that spewed from his lips.

That guy was gone.

The boy had turned into a man.

Over dinner they drank some wine and chatted about high school. Noah talked about the new role he'd taken on the weekends, teaching kids at the local high school to play ball. All the time, Kim was aware of Kurt's gaze as he stared at her across the table.

At the end of the night, she hugged Elsa tightly to her, with the promise she'd keep in touch. Climbing into Kurt's car, Kim waved one final time.

"I want you to trust me, and when morning came, you'd still be in my bed. I wouldn't give you a chance to regret being with me."

She gasped, turning toward him. "You heard?"

"Yeah, I wanted to let you know I was there. Noah thought it would be rude, and Elsa might be pissed."

"So embarrassing."

He reached over, squeezing her knee. "Not embarrassing. You never have to feel that way in front of me. I mean that."

****

"I give it another week," Noah said, putting away the leftovers into the fridge. He looked forward to lunch tomorrow. Elsa always made sure he was well fed.

"That soon?"

"Did you see the way they were looking at each other? I'm surprised they didn't fuck on our table in front of us."

Elsa laughed. "There was some fuck me action going on with their eyes, wasn't there?"

"The eyes are the keys to the soul. Those two are meant for each other." He moved up behind his wife, kissing her neck. "Think about it. Ten years they've been apart. They were there for our wedding, but neither of them spoke to each other, apart from dancing with each other. Kurt's always had a thing for her. Do you think she's stayed a virgin for a reason?"

"No. She said she wasn't comfortable with

167

anyone else."

Noah sighed. "They're in love with each other. Kurt knows it, but I don't think Kim does."

"He hurt her."

"A long time ago. If you ask me, he's more than made up for it."

"Kim's a complex soul. She'll see it, and I hope Kurt is ready for her."

"What do you mean? Will she go stalker on his ass?"

"No, nothing like that. Kim's an artist. Her soul is fragile at times. I've seen it with her mother. Her father, he dotes on her mother. It's a connection that is bound so tightly together. I think whoever loves Kim, they have to give it their all."

"You love her," he said.

"She's my best friend. Of course I do. That's the point though. No one else in high school would take the time with her quirkiness. I did. Kim's like a light. You just have to turn her on."

Noah placed his hand to her stomach. "Can I turn you on?"

She laughed. "You turn me on just by entering the room. I didn't mean sex, you big doofus."

"I know what you meant. If anyone is going to turn her light on, it'll be Kurt. He needs someone like that in his world. Kurt fights for everything. It's what makes him hungry. The love he has for Kim, it'll be there for life. You won't have to worry about her."

"I know." She leaned her head against his chest. "Enough of our friends. We both checked, and they're both still alive, and well. Take me to bed."

****

The following afternoon, Kurt returned home. He'd gone before breakfast leaving Kim a note to let her know an emergency had come up at work. If his manager hadn't been able to deal with it, Kurt had no choice but to go.

Entering the art studio, he saw that Kim wasn't there. She'd decorated the whole of the walls. The image of his bullying was still there, but there was also another picture of him on the opposite wall, this time the man he was now.

In the center were the words, "which one is the truth". Kurt wondered if she even knew what she was doing when she painted. She seemed to get lost, completely absorbed into the world of art that she was creating. He loved watching her, found a great deal of peace from doing it as well.

The door to the studio was open, so he followed it out, going down the path to her other art studio. He found the door slightly ajar, and when he eased open the door, he saw she was listening to music. Her back was to him, and she only wore a shirt.

She stood on her toes, letting him see her muddy feet.

The walls were covered in paint as was the floor, and Kim herself. Kurt couldn't look away as he admired her body. The shirt went to mid-thigh, and each time she moved, the shirt showed off her glorious curves to perfection.

Now, some men liked their women on the slender side. Some even liked their women with bones showing. There was a time he thought he enjoyed skinny women. Since Kim had gotten under his skin, he found fuller women attractive. He didn't like grabbing onto a woman's hips and it actually hurting him as he touched bone, or to be riding a woman, and be worried by the thought of hurting them.

Reaching down, he moved his dick to make him a

little more comfortable. He was lucky as he stopped doing it just before Kim turned around, stared at him, and screamed.

In turn, Kurt screamed.

"Holy crap, I'm so sorry. You scared me," Kim said, yelling the words. She removed her headphones, and he heard some rock music playing.

"No wonder you couldn't hear me. Rock music?"

"It helps me to think."

"That crap helps you to think?"

"Well, yeah, of course it does."

He shook his head. "I don't get it."

Now that Kim had turned around to look at him, his gaze landed on her tits. Her nipples were rock hard, poking against the front of her shirt.

"So, not getting dressed today?"

"I saw your note, and I figured why not come down here. Once I did, I kind of forgot to go and get dressed."

"You made a great deal of mess," he said.

"I know. Isn't it wonderful? Chaos, it's nice."

"You did this on purpose."

"Yeah, look around. Nothing is in order, it's clean, and I could do whatever I wanted."

"So you played?"

She turned to him, practically glowing. "I've never done anything like this. My heart is pumping, my body is on fire. This is all because of you." She stood in front of him. "Thank you."

Kim wrapped her arms around him, and he held her tightly against him. "Anything for you, baby."

She didn't release him straight away. The hug prolonged to the point that he became aware of how good her body was against his.

"Kim?" he asked.

"Yeah."

"Really hard right now."

"I know. I can feel it." She didn't move.

Closing his eyes, he ran his hands up and down her back. "Struggling here."

"I want to kiss you again."

"Kim?"

"Please, would it be so wrong to have one kiss?"

He moved his hand from her waist to cup her face. "With you, it's more than just a kiss. You take a part of me with you every time." Running his thumb across her lip, he shook his head. "No. The next time we kiss, it's going to mean something. You're going to trust me with your body, and your heart, and know that I'm going to love and protect you for the rest of my life."

Kurt forced himself out of her art studio and made his way back to the house. He meant what he said.

Yes, when he'd gone to find her a week ago, he'd intended to give her an ultimatum. He'd even gone so far as to look in the mirror and practice his speech. The moment he saw her, all of his plans had gone up in smoke.

Kim undid him.

She made him want things he'd never thought he would want.

Entering his home, he went straight up to the shower. He needed the icy cold to get his thoughts back in line.

Closing his door, he removed his clothes, dropping each item on his way toward the shower. Turning it on to the coldest it could go, he climbed inside, and let out a growl.

It was freezing.

Staring down at his dick, he watched it slowly start to disappear. Only the cold could make a man not perform. The cold, or being really intoxicated with booze.

"Kurt?" Kim said.

He closed his eyes, counted to ten, and when he opened them again. She stood in front of the shower. The glass wasn't foggy, and he watched her.

"What?" he asked.

"You stormed away, and I shouted at you."

"Kim, don't you realize that I fucking care about you?" Kurt didn't know how much longer he could take with constantly giving.

"I know. I just…"

"You just what?"

"I don't know. Okay. This is really confusing to me. You were the guy that was there. You called me names that hurt. Everything hurt because of you. Then all of a sudden out of the blue you're acting like we're friends, and I'm supposed to be okay with that?"

"It was ten years ago."

"Yeah, and before that, it was ten years of pain! I know I come across as a bitch, and I am sorry for that. It's hard for me to trust so easily. You've come back into my life out of the blue this different person. You're like a damn alien in comparison."

They were having this conversation with his cock now flaccid from the cold, and her standing in a paint covered shirt.

"I get it."

"No. You don't, because even as I think of all of that, I can't get over how you make me feel right now. You've given me the chance to be passionate about what I do. Not one but two art studios. I've spent more time with you in the past week than any other guy. I've kissed you. I've done nothing but think about kissing you, and other … stuff."

"What other stuff?" he asked.

"I'm not telling you."

"For fuck's sake. I'm standing here with my dick out and you can't even be honest with yourself."

"I think about us having sex. There, are you happy? The fat cow has finally succumbed to you. You win, Kurt, do you see that?"

He turned the water off and opened the glass door. Without reaching for a towel, he stepped right up to her, butt ass naked.

"Do you really think this is what I want? What I think?"

"I promised myself I wouldn't give in to you. You were mean, hurtful, and now you're like some completely different guy. You swoop in and give me so much stuff. You're surrounding me, and I can't keep fighting."

"Then don't. I'm not that guy!" He yelled the words at her. "I'm not the same guy who called you fat, cow, chubby, whatever. When are you going to see that I'm changed? I'm Kurt Michaels. I'm not after anything but your happiness. After ten years I'm here, waiting for you."

"I don't know what to do."

Tears were streaming down her cheeks, and he hated the fact he'd been the one to put them there. The last thing he ever wanted to do was make her cry. He loved her. She needed to see that he wasn't the same guy. She had to open her heart to him, and her mind.

"This is on you, Kim." He opened his arms wide. "No games, no teasing. This is total honesty for you. I'm open to you right now. I'm not going anywhere. What do you want? Trust in me."

He didn't know what else to say to make her believe. This was just the two of them.

She stepped up close to him, and he watched in awe as she removed her shirt, then used it to wipe away her tears.

Kurt saw her visibly shaking.

"I want to take a chance on you."

Wrapping his arms around her, he pulled her close, lifted her up, and carried her back into his bedroom. Placing her on the bed, he laid her down and stared into her eyes.

"Are you going to?"

"Not right now, no."

"Why?"

"You're shaking. I don't get my rocks off with women who are scared."

"I'm giving myself to you."

"I know. It's what I always wanted."

"Then why are you holding back?" she asked.

"I'm showing you that I care about you. This isn't about *you*. This is about *us*."

Chapter Five

The following day, Kim woke up in Kurt's bed, still a virgin. Yesterday had been entirely surreal. She was alone in bed. After getting naked for him, they'd lain down, and stared at each other. Then she'd gone to fix them both some dinner. Together they watched a movie, and at night, she had gone to sleep in his bed.

"Ah, you're awake," Kurt said, coming in with a tray.

"Did you make some breakfast?"

"I didn't cook, no. I poured cereal into a bowl, placed a jug of milk, and chopped up some fruit."

She sat up in bed and tucked her hair behind her ears. He placed the tray on her knees, before taking his place beside her.

"I think we should talk."

"I thought we'd talk yesterday."

"You were shaking. I couldn't talk with you being afraid."

"I wasn't afraid."

He didn't look convinced.

"I was nervous. I'm not afraid of you."

"Shaking like that, I don't want you to ever feel that again." He took a banana, peeled back the skin, and started to eat.

She poured some milk into her cereal, took a spoon, and started to eat. "I meant what I said."

"About?"

"Wanting to be with you. Sex."

"Ah, sexland."

"Don't tease."

He shrugged. "I told you I'm not going to judge you. This has to be what you really want."

Kim licked her lips. "I do want it. I want to be

175

with you. Have sex."

Kurt stared at her. "Can you believe we're trying to have this conversation right now?"

She smiled. "No. I promised myself I wouldn't fall for you."

"I was a bastard." He shook his head. "I'll always regret what I did and said to you."

"You didn't really *do* anything. You only said hurtful stuff."

"It still stuck with you though. So, we're going to take this slow. Every time I come near you, you're not going to flinch away."

Kim leaned over and pressed her lips against his. "You're being awfully patient with me."

"I'm a good guy. It's my thing now."

She chuckled.

"So, I had this boutique send you over a couple of dresses to wear for this charity gala event. It's going to be a big deal, so shirts covered in paint aren't going to cut it."

"We could both go like that. Be rebels."

"As much as I'd love to see your ass, it's not a good impression to make for a first event. Maybe in the future."

"Deal," she said. "I'd love to see their faces if you walked in without the suit, looking like a penguin."

"Please, I'm the best looking penguin there is. I'd be the alpha of the pack."

"I think that's wolves."

"I'm a wolf."

"More like a baby cub."

He laughed, kissing her back. "Enjoy your breakfast. I've got to make a few calls."

Like that, he was gone again, leaving her confused. Kurt hadn't just taken her, and laughed it off.

He was a changed man, and Kim found herself enjoying him.

Finishing her breakfast, she took a trip to the bathroom, to freshen herself up. By the time she came out, there were several dresses laid out. Grabbing her cell phone, she called Elsa. Her friend was much better at these things. In fact, her mother was, but she didn't want to have to deal with her mother right now. She was more interested in the guy she was staying with.

"What's going on?" Elsa asked.

"I want to have sex with Kurt."

"Wow, I wasn't expecting that for a conversation opener."

Kim placed her hand on her head, completely stressed out. "We argued yesterday, and I ended up getting naked. He carried me back to his bed, and refused to sleep with me. Isn't that a bad thing?"

"Not necessarily."

"How can it be anything other than bad?"

Elsa paused.

"Please, I want to understand."

"Fine. You and Kurt, you've got a past that's not a good one. You've said yourself you're not going to fall for him, and yet here you are, wanting sex. Just a few days ago you spoke about sexland, and how you didn't want to regret it."

"He heard that conversation as well."

"See, how do you think he's doing to behave? Kurt's not a bad guy. He was an asshole in the past. Not now though. Now he's grown up, and he wants you, Kim. Don't mistake his hesitancy for a lack of desire."

"How do you even know that when you're not living here? You don't see him."

"It has been ten years, Kim. Ten years and he came to your rescue. From what you told me the other day, he's done nothing but show that he's taking care of you. Tell me, is the guy you want to have sex with the same guy you hated for most of your high school years?"

"No."

"Then look at it from his side, okay? Kurt cares."

She had seen the regret in his eyes many times when they'd been talking.

"Give him the chance to be the man you always wanted."

Kim sat on the edge of the bed, open, raw, exposed.

"Was there anything else you wanted to talk to me about?" Elsa asked.

"Yeah, this gala, charity thing. Do you have any suggestions for what I should wear?"

After picking the dress, and chatting a little, Kim hung up the phone. Putting the dress she was wearing into Kurt's closet, she left the other one on the bed, and made her way downstairs. There was no sign of anyone, so she went to the art studio at the bottom of the garden. Instead of running, she just walked, taking in the beauty of the sights. Flowers of all different varieties were in full bloom. The colors blended together, showcasing the entire summer.

Opening her art studio, she entered, and started to open the windows. It was really warm, and she looked around at the fun she'd had the day before. The fun all because of Kurt. Sure, her parents would have given her something like this, but it wouldn't have been the same.

Moving toward the center of the room, she stared at the chaos around her. Thinking about Kurt, and everything in life, she found herself at peace.

For so long she'd been fighting this guy inside her head, and the stereotype that had been plaguing her. She didn't want to be the girl to fall for the hot bully.

"Can I enter?" Kurt asked.

"Sure."

He entered the studio, dressed in a crisp white shirt that had a couple of buttons open at the top. His pants were those she thought of businessmen wearing.

"Are you hot?" she asked.

"Of course I am. I'm hot stuff."

"No, not that. The clothes you wear. It's hot out. You don't have to be the businessman with me."

"I'm comfortable like this." He took a seat right in front of her. "I want to play a game of truth."

"Truth or dare?"

"No. Just truth." He reached out holding her hands.

"What is going on?"

"Trust. I want to be truthful with you, and I want you to do the same with me."

She nodded.

"The last ten years, I haven't lived like a monk. I've fucked a lot of women, and while I was doing a lot of fucking, you would somehow, come into my mind. It was like no matter what, I couldn't shake you."

"I'm a little worried about that."

"I wanted to move on, but I couldn't. You were always there."

She licked her lips. "For the past ten years, I've thought about you as well." She smiled. "It wasn't about your murder either. I just wondered what you were doing, how you were doing." She took a deep breath. "There were moments when I wondered if you thought about me."

"Now you know I did."

"I also regretted not going on a date with you."

"You did?"

"Yeah. I wondered if we'd actually be good

together. Hearing all these wonderful things about you from Elsa and Noah, it made me wonder if you'd changed. I know you did."

"You helped change me," he said.

"How? I've done nothing."

"You showed me that I was a bully. I'd never thought of it like that. The way you reacted to me, and how I was. You showed me another way, and for that, I'm grateful. You made me a better person."

"And I've been nothing but a bitch to you."

He chuckled. "Maybe you should start being nice to me."

"I offered you my body."

"It's not the only thing I'm interested in."

"What are you interested in?" she asked.

"That is something you're going to have to figure out on your own."

Kim stared at him, wondering what he could possibly want. They were two different people. Neither of them the same.

He's different.

I'm different.

"I've never been on a rollercoaster," she said, picking a more suitable topic.

"A rollercoaster?"

"Never been to an amusement park."

"The charity event is going to be an amusement park."

"Why?"

"A lot of big type people giving away a lot of money. It's a big event. A political playground for everyone, businessmen, politicians, actors, you name it. And you, Kim James, are going to be my date."

"So exciting."

"It should be. You're spending your time with

me."

****

Kim looked absolutely stunning in the floral blue dress that molded to every single curve. Kurt couldn't keep the smile off his face, he was so damn proud to have her on his arm. He spotted Noah and Elsa already at the event. Even with cameras flashing, Kim held onto him like a lifeline.

"Please don't leave me."

"Are you afraid?"

"Terrified. I've never done well in social settings."

"You'd never know." He enjoyed teasing her. "Don't worry. I've no plan of leaving you."

She pushed some hair off her face, and they were stopped by some of his business associates.

"Michaels, how have you been?"

"Busy, John."

"Who is this charming lady?"

"Kim James, she's my girl, and you'll see some of her work displayed toward the back."

"Ah, a budding artist."

"A professional one I believe. Real talent," Kurt said.

"He's just being nice."

"Nah, I know Kurt. If he's giving you that recommendation, it's for a reason. He believes in your potential." John took her hand, laying a kiss to her knuckles.

A couple of other businessmen asked where he was, to which Kurt introduced Kim.

Finally, after twenty minutes they were able to get to their friends.

"Enjoying the attention?" Elsa asked.

"No. It's scary." Kim took a glass of champagne

from a waiter who was passing. "I don't know how anyone can do it."

"Your mother did it just fine," Kurt said.

"Where are your parents?" Noah asked.

"They're here, I think. I got a text just as we arrived. Mom was looking at my work."

He saw her cringe, and shook his head. She had so many doubts about herself they were unreal at times. He didn't understand it. Her talent rivaled so many, and yet she was always nervous about showcasing her stuff.

Kurt kept his arm around her, holding her close as people kept on talking to them.

"How are things on the baby making front?" he asked when Kim and Elsa were deep into conversation.

"They're going great. Can't complain."

"But?"

"But nothing. Baby making is fun. What about you and Kim? Any progress?"

"We're on a date."

"Does she know it's a date?"

"Yes, and she doesn't want me to leave her side. I'd say that is total progress. I expect congratulations any day now."

Noah snorted. "She's falling for you."

Kurt looked toward her. "Do you think so?"

"Yes, I do. Look at her. You've got her glowing. Kim's always been on the depressive side. Sad, artistically stunted at times. With you, I see her smile. I can actually see why Elsa likes her. Beforehand, I did have to wonder how the two of them were friends. They're like chalk and cheese."

Kurt stared at his woman as she once again pushed some hair out of her face. She did that quite often, and he saw her hand was shaking. She was really nervous, yet she didn't have any reason to be. Kurt wanted to protect her. Tonight would go well, he was certain of it. Her work was exemplary.

"Baby making is fun?"

"Yep. Married life is fun. You don't know what you're missing."

He wanted to be married. There were so many plans he had, and all of them were devoted to Kim.

When it was time to move on, he held his arm out for Kim to take. They met up with her parents, both of whom were clearly proud of her.

"Darling, you have hidden away too long. It's time the rest of the world sees how far you've come," her mother, Esther James, said. "It's so good to see you again, Kurt."

"Hi, Mrs. James."

"Please, call me Esther. Donald, this was the young man I was telling you about."

"Donald James." A large man with huge hands greeted him.

"Nice to meet you."

"Kurt Michaels. You're David's son?"

"Of Michaels Industry. Yes."

"You're on your own now though, right? Technological industry, social media, and all that."

"Yes, sir, yes I am."

"Huh, I've heard a lot of things about you."

"Dad, leave him alone."

"You're here with my daughter. You're paying for my daughter. What exactly are you doing with her?" Donald asked.

Kurt expected this. Most fathers were protective of their daughters.

"Dad, do not embarrass me."

"I'm hoping to get your daughter to agree to date me. I'm helping her meet the appropriate people for her work. She wasn't given the right opportunities before."

"You think you can help her."

"Yes, sir, I do." He showed her father respect.

"Donald, enough please," Esther said.

"Why didn't you come to us, Kim? We could have helped you."

Kim sighed. "Because I want to do this on my own."

"You've got this boy to help."

"Donald, that is enough with your father's duties for one night," Esther said. "Our daughter doesn't want our influence to affect her work. I understand. It's what I didn't want to happen with my own work when I married you, and it could have quite easily done that. I'm thankful you're taking care of our daughter, and I appreciate it." Esther hugged him, pulling away.

Kim's father, however, glared at him. "I've got my eye on you."

"So embarrassing, even now after all this time. Do you know how horrible that would have been if you'd come calling for me in high school? He'd have given you the third degree."

"We're not in high school? I feel like I've just been stripped down and whipped because I asked you out for ice cream."

Kim threw her head back and laughed. "It would be pretty close in high school. He wouldn't have been happy."

Her father had never been home when Kurt visited her. Esther always had been, but she worked from home with her work.

"You survived the parental encounter," Elsa said, joining back up with them.

"I noticed you two disappeared when they arrived," Kurt said.

"Of course. We have to give you time to shine or not when it comes to parents. No one was there to help Noah with him." Elsa shrugged. "Not even Kim."

"I think it went well," Kim said.

"You think that went well?" Kurt asked.

"Yeah."

"How?"

"You're still walking, and we're both heading into the room to check out more items for auction." Kim patted his hand, kissed his cheek. "We're doing good."

Wrapping his arm around her waist, Kurt pulled her close, not wanting to let her go. They made their way around the charity gala, looking at little trinkets of jewels, rare books, and other items that had been given to put up for auction. Kurt hadn't given anything, but he was more than willing to pay for some of the items he saw. There was a large ruby necklace, which would look glorious on Kim's body. He wondered if she'd paint completely naked while wearing it. When they got to the art room, he recognized several of her paintings that he'd picked. She was happy for them to go up for auction.

Kim didn't believe they would sell.

Her lack of confidence grated on his nerves. He knew they would sell. They were all too good for them not to. Kurt didn't argue with her though. He figured the only way for her to see the talent she possessed was for others to realize it as well.

Several people were gathered around her pieces, and he saw people putting down numbers, and making notes. He also happened to spot Randy, who he knew worked in the art world.

Moving toward him, he nodded at the piece. "What do you think?"

"This is like a dream come true."

"It is."

"Seriously, whoever this person is, they have a serious eye for color, for depth, and for imagination. Absolutely stunning. I've not seen work like this for so long. Captures the eye and the soul."

Randy had always been a strange one, but he knew art.

"I know the artist," Kurt said. "She doesn't believe her work is that good."

"An artist, gifted, and deluded. I don't suppose I could meet them."

Just then, Kim came toward him.

"Randy, I'd like you to meet Kim. The mind and hands behind the paintings." He made sure not to mention her last name, or her association with her mother.

"H-hello," Kim said, looking nervous.

Kurt didn't leave her side as Randy started talking. Kurt listened, doing his utmost to offer support to his girl even as others noticed, and turned to listen to the conversation. He was so proud of her for not running away, when it would be so easy for her to do. Instead, she stayed, kept up talking, answering questions. When it got too much for her, she gripped his hand tightly, and he held her back.

Later that night, Kurt watched as each of her paintings was sold for a large price. The competition had been fierce, and with it, a star had been born.

Chapter Six

"I'm in shock," Kim said, coming out of the bathroom.

Kurt stood in a pair of shorts, and smiled. "I told you there was real potential."

"Randy wants to see my other stuff. He told me that exhibits are not all the rage anymore. There's benefits and socials, where people like to rub shoulders, buy art, and pretend they know what they're talking about." She moved toward the bed, taking a seat.

He entered the bathroom to brush his teeth, and found her kneeling on the bed, hands clasped in front of her, waiting.

"What's up, babe?" he asked.

"I can't stop smiling."

"Good. It's what I always wanted." He moved toward her, gripped her hip, and tugged her close. Slamming his lips down on hers, he kissed her. When she opened her lips, he slid his tongue inside, teasing her. She pulled away, breathless.

"I had a really good time tonight."

"Me too. I never thought I'd say it about one of those things." He'd purchased the ruby necklace, and forced himself to stay out of competing for some of her paintings. "Your parents bought one."

"I know. I told them I'd paint them anything they wanted, but they wouldn't hear of it. Crazy, don't you think?"

"Nah, they want to support their girl."

"I also noticed you told Randy my name was Kim, not James, no association to my parents. Thank you."

"I promised to help you. The rest is up to you."

"You looked really handsome in the tux." She

rubbed his chest, and Kurt stroked her hip.

"Thank you."

The air thickened between them, and his cock went from flaccid to hard within seconds. Kim's gaze went from his eyes to his lips, then back again.

He watched as she bit her own lip, and he couldn't contain his moan. "You've got to stop doing that. All I want to do is taste you."

"Then taste me."

The hand she teased up and down his chest, started to move down. This time, Kurt didn't stop her. He didn't pull away. This was about her, what she wanted to do.

She rubbed his cock, and she took a deep breath. "You're so hard."

"It's what you do to me, babe."

Kim slid her hand into his shorts and cupped him. It was late, and he wasn't wearing any boxers. The only reason he was wearing the shorts was to make Kim much more comfortable with him. She worked from the base of his cock, up to the tip, then back down again.

Sliding his hands up her back, he cupped her shoulders, then moved to tilt her head back. "You're playing a dangerous game."

"I trust you, Kurt. I know you won't hurt me."

"Whenever you want to stop, just tell me to stop. I won't push you any further."

"I know." She leaned in close and kissed him. Sinking his fingers into her golden locks, he tugged her closer, deepening her kiss, and taking control. He didn't want her touch to stop. His body was on fire with the need of her.

Only Kim had this kind of power over him, no one else.

"Feels so good," she said, breaking from the kiss.

He didn't stop there. He kissed her even deeper, sliding his tongue into her mouth, hearing her moan as he did.

All the time, she teased his cock, running from the base to the tip.

"This porn you stumbled on, did you learn something?"

"I learned a lot. I felt a lot, and it made me curious about a lot."

She moved off the bed, so that she was standing before him.

He slid his fingers beneath the thin strap of her nightshirt, and worked it down her arms until it fell away from her full breasts.

With her tits free, he watched as she went to her knees before him, taking the shorts with her, sliding them down to his knees. His cock sprang forward, and she wrapped her fingers around him, covering the head of his dick with her lips. He closed his eyes even though he didn't want to. The feel of her warm mouth against him was so good. He was worried he was going to look like a teenage boy, and shoot his load right there and then down her throat, and that wasn't something he wanted to do. He had a lot more control than a mere boy.

She released him long enough to run her tongue down the thick vein at the side of his shaft, before bobbing on the tip of his cock.

"Um." She moaned around his length, taking more of him to the back of her throat.

"This is what you wanted?"

"I saw a lot of cock sucking," she said.

He saw her cheeks heating even as she said the words. "We're going to have to make you used to dirty talk. No one can hear you. Is this something you've been curious about?"

"Yes." She worked his dick with her hand while

she spoke. With her gaze on him, she flicked the tip with her tongue. "I watched a lot, and it inspired my work."

"I saw the passion in your paintings, and the yearning."

"Yearning?"

"Yeah, you wanted something like this, were desperate for it, but always afraid to ask."

Kurt hissed as she used her teeth, scoring down the length of his dick until he got to the back of her throat once again, and then coming up off him.

"You're not a small man."

"I know. When I take your pussy, it'll fit me."

"I watched that as well," she said.

"What?"

"I watched a man fill his woman up, and then see his release come out of her. There's a lot of dirty stuff on the internet."

Damn, he had a twenty-eight year old curious virgin on his hands. Kim was the ultimate dream, and he didn't intend to ever let her down.

He touched her head, stroking her hair back and wrapping the length around his fist so that it no longer got in the way. He pumped into her mouth watching as she took more of him. Kurt let her set the pace. She used her hands and mouth, working him. It had been too long since he'd been with a woman, and with a quick warning, he pulled out of her hands, and came all over her tits.

She moved her head out of the way.

"Why did you stop me sucking you?" she asked.

"I didn't want you to be forced to swallow."

Her cheeks were already the color of a ripe strawberry, and the conversation wasn't helping. Her cheeks seemed to go a shade darker.

"Oh, I wouldn't have minded."

Sinking to his knees, he cupped her cheek, and

claimed her lips, sliding his tongue into her mouth.

He grabbed his shorts, which were near his feet, and wiped his cum from her chest. When she was clean, he stopped her from moving.

"What?" she asked.

"Do you think that is it?"

"You've come. Doesn't it stop now?"

"No, it doesn't." He got to his feet, and helped her up, moving her back toward the bed. Kurt eased her down on the edge, going back to his knees this time. "Open them wide."

"You don't have to do this."

"Do you want to feel good?"

"I do."

"Do you trust me?"

"Yes."

"Then lie back. I want to give you the same kind of pleasure you're giving me."

At first she hesitated, and only as seconds passed did she lie down.

"Now, open your legs."

She released a sigh and opened her legs. Kurt placed his hands on her knees, and slid them up the inside of her thighs, opening her a little wider, getting her to splay them open. Her shorts were in the way, and they were loose enough that he only had to move them to one side, to see her perfect cunt.

Fine pubic hair covered her pretty pussy, and her lips were open, showing her clit. Her slit was wet, and he eased a finger between lips, touching her clit.

Kim gasped and sat up.

"I know you're a little nervous. Will you be willing to remove your shorts?" he asked.

"I've never been naked for anyone."

"You got naked for me the other day."

"I know. I mean, I've never been touched there before."

"Not even yourself?"

"Erm, yeah, I've touched myself."

"Show me," he said.

"What?"

"Touch your pussy, show me what you like." He gripped her shorts, easing them down her thighs and pushing them away.

Kim was the one to throw away her shirt, and now they were both completely naked with each other. Her body was so full and curvy. He couldn't wait to be inside her. Kurt wasn't in a rush though. They had to get to the same place with each other, and he'd be more than willing to wait a long time for Kim. He'd waited ten years, and he'd wait longer as well.

She owned his heart, mind, body, and soul.

****

With the shorts gone, nothing was there to protect her.

You don't need protecting.

Kim's body was on fire, and only Kurt could put it out. He opened her thighs then the lips of her pussy. Staring up at the ceiling, she closed her eyes, basking in each touch of his hands on her body. He took his time, letting her get accustomed to him.

"You've got such a nice wet pussy, baby."

"Kurt?"

"What? I'm going to tell you how much I like it."

She cried out as his tongue slipped between her folds, licking from her entrance all the way up to her clit. He circled the bud then flicked his tongue from side to side, each little touch sending little lightning bolts of pleasure through her. She lifted her legs up, resting her feet on the edge of the bed.

Kurt removed his tongue, then ran his fingers over her fine hairs.

"Show me how you touch yourself," he said.

Kim had thought he'd forgotten about that. "You want me to touch myself?"

"Yes."

There was so much stuff that she hadn't done. Watching porn didn't make anyone an expert.

"It's just the two of us. No one is going to see you but me."

She liked how possessive he sounded. The way he spoke about them was as if they were never going to be parted. Their future was with each other, and no matter what, she liked that.

Their future together.

Sliding her hand down their bodies, she kept her eyes closed as she touched her wet pussy. Kim had usually had to use lubrication to help her, but now, she was so aroused, her natural juices were enough.

Using two fingers, she stroked over her clit, going slowly.

Kurt opened the lips of her pussy, and she heard him groan. "Now that is a sight I'll never forget. Oh, baby, you're so wet." He covered her pussy with his fingers.

Kim paused.

"Show me what you like."

She placed her hand on top of his and guided him against her pussy, using his two fingers to work herself.

Kim arched up against him, wanting more, needing more, and yet, holding back at the same time.

He moved her hand out of the way and covered her pussy with his tongue. There was no fear, only excitement. This was Kurt Michaels between her thighs, licking her pussy. Unable to stop herself, she went to her elbows, and watched as he tongued her clit. He stared up at her, showing her exactly what he was doing.

No one had touched her so intimately before in her life. Collapsing to the bed, she thrust her pelvis up against him, crying out as he sucked hard on her clit. His hands went to her hips holding her in place as he ravished her pussy.

Kim came against his mouth, screaming his name. Kurt didn't let her go. He kept on licking, sucking, and drawing her orgasm out. She couldn't believe it when he thrust her into a second orgasm.

The pleasure was out of this world, and only when she stopped shaking from the second orgasm, did he stop and climb up the bed. Opening her eyes, which she'd closed against the onslaught of need, she saw him licking his lips.

"I'm going to be licking you out a lot."

She laughed. "I can't believe we just did that."

"We're rebels."

"You're technically my boss."

"You know I'm much more than that."

"You are."

He grabbed her hand, locking their fingers together. "I was so proud of you tonight."

"Thank you for setting it all up."

"I didn't set anything up. I only helped guide you to the right person to see your work. I've heard that Mr. Coal has retired. Even as his business was going under, he was still a wealthy man."

"It makes no sense."

"Let's just say he wasn't an entirely nice man."

He held her hand close to his chest, taking her lips once again. Staring up into his eyes, Kim couldn't believe she was lying in bed, exhausted from two orgasms, because of this man. The same man she'd been hurt by so often growing up. She had forgiven him, but Kim was starting to believe she had a lot more feelings for him than just forgiveness.

"When do you think Noah and Elsa will have a kid?"

"I don't know. I'm hoping soon. Elsa wants a kid, and they waited a long time."

"They had their careers, and each other."

"Would you want a kid straight away?" Kim asked.

"No. I want to spend a lot of time with it being just the two of us."

"I wasn't assuming it would be me you wanted a kid with."

"I know. Still, you know we're going to have a kid."

"Your ego knows no bounds," she said, loving it. "We're going to have a kid, what? Get married?"

"Yes, you're going to marry me, Kim."

"I am."

"Yep, and you're going to be totally in love with me."

"I like the way you're talking."

"Good. When we do finally have sex, you'll see."

"We can have sex now."

"Soon."

She chuckled. "You're the first guy to turn down sex."

"I'm not turning it down. I'm … postponing it."

"Fine."

"That doesn't mean you don't sleep here."

"You want me to sleep in your bed?"

He nodded. "Yep, and seeing as tonight you're going to be completely naked, I expect you to be naked every single night."

"I don't think so. I don't sleep naked."

"You do now."

He wrapped his arms around her, tickling her.

Kim burst out laughing, trying to wriggle away from him.

The thought of being married to Kurt didn't scare her.

Nor them having a future together.

For the first time in her life, she saw them together, like the two figures in her painting in the art studio downstairs. She saw them as one: happy, complete, and in love.

Chapter Seven

"Where are you off to?" Elsa asked.

Kim smiled at her friend. It was a late Saturday evening. The guys were in the kitchen, grabbing some food to grill up on the barbeque. Noah was being trusted seeing as Kurt couldn't cook.

"It's nothing."

"Is everything okay?"

"Of course. Why wouldn't it be?"

"You just seem a little dazed, and it's kind of scary to see you like that."

She waved her hand in front of her. "I'm fine."

Elsa looked toward the kitchen. "You and Kurt? Everything fine?"

"It's great, actually. We get along so well. It kind of makes me wonder what it would have been like in high school if I hadn't been such a bitch."

"You can't regret what happened, and neither can Kurt, not really."

"Why not?" Kim did regret it. She'd been a bitch, and she never really considered herself one at all until Kurt.

"It was so long ago, and you had your reasons. Kurt bullied you. I understood why you held back. Now, you're both older, and both of you know what you feel. You're both working past everything. It means it will always be good now."

"Yeah, we are."

They were. Kim found herself missing him at every point in the day. She would leave her work, to go and find him. Sometimes he worked on his computer, and other times he was in the studio, watching her. They hadn't had sex yet, even though they fooled around, doing a lot.

Every single night she went to sleep, naked in his arms, sated by the pleasure his hands and mouth had given to her.

"Do you want to take a walk?" Kim asked.

"Sure. Let me grab some juice."

Kim stood, pulling her long hair back into a rubber band. Elsa came out seconds later with two bottles of juice, each bottle holding a straw.

"They're having some kind of football game argument. Never understand it, but they're boys. They're allowed to play."

Kim smiled, thinking about all the games Kurt had been catching up on. He carried around his laptop, headphones in, listening to a match from two years ago. When she asked him about it, he told her that with work, he didn't get to do much in the way of socializing. He'd missed a great deal of life.

"What's up?"

"Nothing."

"Kim, you wanted to get away to talk. I'm your best friend. You can tell me anything."

"Okay, erm, I'm struggling right now."

"What with?"

"My feelings. How I feel about Kurt, and what's happening."

"Is this because of him bullying you?"

"No. I've forgiven him. That's not the issue, and hasn't been for a long time."

"What is the issue?"

Kim paused, letting out a long breath. "We've not had sex."

Elsa took a sip of her juice, saying nothing.

"We've not had sex, but we've fooled around."

"Are you asking me for sexland advice?"

"Yes, I am. I want to know how I can get Kurt to

have sex with me."

"Get naked. It works for most men."

"I've gotten naked. We've fooled around, and he still won't do it."

Kim paused to take a sip of her drink.

"Kurt wants you to be ready," Elsa said.

"I am ready."

"Maybe he doesn't think you are. This is a big deal. You're twenty-eight. Even I'm shocked that you're a virgin after this long. You're an artist, and you feel everything. Sex, intimacy, it's all part of that."

"Since being with Kurt, my work is lighter, more passionate. I love it."

"Then talk to him. He's taking your pace, so no one else is going to convince him you're ready other than you." Elsa wrapped her arms around her, and Kim held her close. "I've not told Noah yet, but I missed my period."

Kim gasped, pulling back. "Really. Do you know for certain?"

"No. I haven't taken a test. I'm scared. What if it's not positive?"

"Then you keep on trying. You could be pregnant," Kim said, covering her mouth with her hand. "I won't say anything."

Elsa held her stomach. "There could be a little guy or girl in here."

"It's magical."

"It really is," Elsa said.

They walked around the garden until they heard Kurt and Noah shouting for them to join. When they got to the table, Kim wrinkled her nose at the shriveled up, blackened meat that was resting on the plate.

"Don't eat that. I think it's poisonous," Noah said. "Kurt threw one over the grill, and told me he knew what he was doing."

"He's never cooked a day in his life," Kim said, taking a seat.

"Babe, keep my secrets to yourself."

"Nope. He thought cooking was so easy, he didn't even need to practice. I could have died the first night I was here."

"I make a rather good dinner."

"He makes death," Noah said. "That is gross."

"How did you burn it to a crisp?"

"I don't know," Kurt said. "I bet it tastes good."

Kim grabbed the plate, a knife and fork, and waited. "Go on, give it a try, and see if it's fit for human consumption."

"Fine!" Kurt grabbed the cutlery, and took a small, very small, sliver off the meat. Kim winced as he took a bite. It sounded like his teeth shattered.

He wore a poker face really well. Only his cheeks, which were red, gave away his embarrassment. He kept on chewing, not looking anyone in the eye. She wondered what would happen.

After what felt like minutes, but probably wasn't that long, he took a long swallow of beer, chugging down the liquid.

"Is it good?" Kim asked.

"Fucking nasty. I think I chipped a tooth."

Noah burst out laughing while Kurt pulled his lip to one side, getting her to inspect his tooth. She laughed along with their friends, shaking her head. "Your tooth is fine."

"I heard Randy is making quite a big deal about your work," Noah said.

"Yeah. He wants me to do a selection of paintings based on passion. I've done some work already, and I showed him pieces. He thinks I'm locked, or blocked, and I need to just let it all go. To be one with my work."

"Randy talks a lot," Kurt said. "All good things."

"Do you think I'm blocked?" Kim asked.

"No."

She frowned when he shot her down. Filing it away, she would ask him after their friends had gone.

Noah served up some steaks and chicken, and they dug into their food, enjoying conversation and laughter. Kim wondered if her friend was in fact pregnant. If so, she'd be happy for her.

Later that night, Kim entered the sitting room, finding Kurt already flicking through the channels. Taking a seat beside him, she turned toward him.

"What are you real thoughts on what Randy thinks?" she said.

"Darling, he knows what he's talking about."

"Kurt, I trust you, and your opinion means a great deal to me. Please, tell me what you think."

He sighed and looked toward her.

"Have you felt passion before?"

"Yes."

"There's a lot of things to feel passionate about. I'm there with my work, my company, I want to see it succeed. Your art is your passion. What about sexual passion, desire, need?"

"I feel that as well."

"Your work is beautiful, and with it, it showcases that innocence. Randy doesn't know you're a virgin. What I think he means by you being blocked, is that you haven't opened yourself up to that kind of intimacy."

Her heart was pounding, and her pussy flooded with arousal. Kurt's shirt had several buttons undone, showing off his chest. He didn't look like a boy, but a man, and she was finding it hard to deny herself.

Fed up with waiting for him to take the next step,

Kim took matters into her own hands.

"Intimacy is an interesting point." She straddled his waist and held onto the back of the sofa. Grinding her pelvis against his dick, she found he was hard. "You see, Kurt, there's this guy. He's a rather complex soul, and I've been trying to get him to be intimate with me for a little time now. I've taken my clothes off. I've sucked his dick." She still blushed, but kept on going. Nothing was going to stop her. "I'm ready to take the next step. How do you think this guy will feel?" she asked.

Kurt held onto her hips. "Marry me."

Kim paused and jerked back. If he hadn't been holding her, she'd have fallen onto the floor. "What?"

"It's an easy question."

"I know."

"Marry me."

She stared at him, not sure if she was hearing this right. "Marry you?"

"Yeah."

"I wasn't expecting a proposal."

"You're asking me to fuck you."

"Yes."

"I want something a little more." Kim moved off his lap, and Kurt sighed. "You're running away?"

She stood in the sitting room. The television played in the background. "I'm in shock right now. I've never been proposed to."

Kurt reached into his pocket and took it one step further. "I bought this for you prom night. I saw it in the jewelry store, and I wanted to give it to you."

"Ten years ago?"

"Yeah, imagine that. I fell in love with the girl I used to bully."

Her heart started to pound. "You're in love with me."

****

Kurt didn't know what came over him. One moment he'd been watching television, but then Kim had straddled his waist, and all thought had left his mind. It had been another glorious night shared with their friends. Kim had sat against him, and he'd held her. She had fit so perfectly against him that he couldn't imagine life without her.

Now she was straddling his dick, begging for him to fuck her, and he couldn't hold it back.

"Yeah, I am." Kurt stared at the ring in his hands, then up at the woman who had destroyed him for all others. "I just want to see if it fits." He took her hand, and she didn't pull away. Kurt slid the ring onto her finger, finding it a perfect fit. "You know, I think I read somewhere that if you buy a ring and it fits, it means you're destined to be together for life."

Tears glinted in her eyes as she stared down at him.

"How am I supposed to say no? How did you get so romantic? Was there a class, or was this always you?"

Kurt took a deep breath. "Is that a yes? Will you belong to me?"

"We've not had sex."

He laughed. "You're the first woman to think about sex before marriage." He pressed his head against hers.

"Yes."

"What?"

"I'll marry you. First, you've got to have sex with me."

Kurt smiled down into her blue eyes. "You're a crazy woman, you know that, right?"

"Completely crazy, and I'm saying yes. I'm saying yes to you. Wow, I'm saying yes to marrying Kurt

Michaels. Do you know how weird that—"

Kurt silenced her with a kiss. Claiming her lips, he slid his tongue into her mouth, moaning as she melted against him. He sank his fingers into her hair, pulling her against him. Running his hands down her back, he grabbed her ass, tugging her against him. He was so damn hot for her. "You're going to be my wife."

"I'm going to be your wife. Elsa's going to be so excited," she said. "I'm getting married."

"You certainly are. Damn, we're going to be husband and wife. Seems totally surreal," he said.

"Surreal? You asked me to marry you. I was happy with us being together."

He pushed her hair off her shoulders. "We're going to have to tell the parents."

"Ugh, do we have to? We could get married in secret, come back, and ta-da, we're married."

"I doubt your father will be happy with me. I'm not sure he even likes me now." Kurt leaned down and lifted her up. "Now, you want to be made love to, and that's not going to happen on the couch."

"You're carrying me to our bedroom?"

"Haven't you noticed I've been moving you in?" he asked.

"I've noticed a lot of things actually. Would you like me to tell them to you?" She wrapped her arms around his neck, and Kurt carried her upstairs to their bedroom.

"I would." He'd been wondering if she'd noticed the world that he'd created for the two of them.

"The house, it's fit for a family. Is that for our family?"

"Yes."

"The two studios, you made them for me?"

"Yes."

"You can't cook, and yet the kitchen is fit for a queen. Did you make that for me?"

"Of course. Everything in this house, Kim, it was made for you." Every time he'd thought of just turning it into a bachelor pad, he'd changed his mind, and turned it into a home. Kurt hadn't wanted to be a bachelor for a long time.

Kim was the only woman he wanted.

Entering their bedroom, he put her down on her feet and moved toward the wardrobe, opening the doors. While she'd been busy, he'd been moving her stuff to rest beside his. "I've wanted you for a long time. In high school, it wasn't about fucking you. I liked being around you, Kim."

He turned toward her, stepping up close, cupping her cheeks. Kurt hadn't been running from his feelings. All this time, he'd simply been waiting for her.

"You really want to marry me?"

"Yes," he said. "The question is, do you want to marry me?"

"You're not my bully anymore." She touched his chest, running her hands up to cup his face. "I can't believe we're here, at this moment. Of course I want to marry you."

Sinking his fingers into her hair, he pulled her close, taking her lips. Every time she kissed him, Kurt felt on fire. He'd never known feelings like it, and he didn't want it to stop.

"We've got to tell our parents."

"We will."

"And Noah and Elsa," she said.

She spoke in between his kisses. "We're going to do all of that." He ran his fingers underneath the strap of her vest stop. "First, I'm going to make love to you. Then I'm going to fuck you."

"You talk dirty, Mr. Michaels."

"Kim, babe, I've got ten years of fantasies to make up for."

"For ten years you've thought about me?"

"Every single day. Not a moment went by that I wasn't thinking about you." He teased her shirt down her arms, watching her breasts as they fell out.

"They're big," she said, complaining.

"They're perfect, and they're all mine."

The vest rested at her waist; he was reaching up, and cupping her large breasts. They were so firm and full. The nipples were large, deep red, and his mouth watered for a taste. He loved watching her walk toward him, or even better, run. During high school, he'd loved when it was gym, and there was running while he practiced. There were a lot of times he found himself watching her, wondering what she'd look like naked. Now he knew.

"What are you thinking about?" she asked.

"How many times I used to watch you, and wonder about these moments. You used to drive me fucking crazy with needing you."

"We were two different people back then."

"No more, we're not. We're one." He ran his thumbs across the tips of her nipples, watching as her eyes dilated. She arched her back, trying to get closer to him. "You have no idea how much I've waited for this moment."

She moaned in response, and he moved his thumbs out of the way, to claim her left nipple. He continued to tease the other with his thumb. Using his teeth, he bit down on the plump flesh, then soothed it with his tongue. Moving across the valley of her tits, he took her other nipple, sucking it deeper into his mouth. She stood on her tiptoes, trying to get closer to him.

"Damn, you feel so fucking good," he said.

Wrapping his arms around her, he ran his hands down her back, gripping her ass, and squeezing the plump flesh. Spreading the cheeks of her ass, he thrust his pelvis against her.

Kim cupped his dick, rubbing him through his pants. She opened his belt, slid her hand inside, and started to tease his dick, the tip already leaking pre-cum as she touched him. Kurt released her long enough to remove his shirt and the rest of his pants. Within seconds he was naked, and his arms were filled with Kim.

He pushed her shorts down her thighs, and watched as she wriggled out of them, pushing them away. Cupping her flesh, he groaned. He didn't give a fuck about her cellulite. He loved her. The love he had for her went deeper than what she viewed as imperfections. She was meant for him.

She ran her hand up and down his cock, running her fingers across his cum, and rubbing it into the tip.

"I want you, Kurt."

Stepping her toward the bed, he claimed her lips, took hold of her hands, and locked them together. He felt the ring he'd given her against his finger, and he was filled with so much excitement.

He followed her down to the bed, never once breaking the kiss. She opened her legs, and he rested between them. Releasing her hands, he started to tease her body, touching her breasts, running down to touch her pussy. She was totally slick, wet, and ready for him. Kurt wasn't happy though. He wanted her dripping.

Kurt didn't have firsthand experience with a virgin, and suddenly, he froze up. "Erm, I've just got to go and get some condoms."

"Kurt?"

He didn't wait around. Rushing out of the room, grabbing his cell phone as covertly as possible, he made a dive toward the bathroom, then realized she'd be able to hear. "The condoms are in my office. One moment."

"Seriously?"

"Yes, erm, wait there, don't do anything." On the way out, he cringed at his own words.

Rushing toward his office with a hard on had to be the single most embarrassing things of his life.

Finding Noah's name, he dialed. For several seconds he heard the ring, and finally Noah answered.

"Kurt's calling."

"Don't answer it," Elsa said.

"I already have. It could be important."

"Unlike your wife who was on the verge of orgasm?"

"Sorry."

Kurt faced planted his desk, while also holding the phone. "I called at a bad time."

"No, it's not a bad time," Noah said.

"That's it, you can use your hand for the rest of the night."

The sound of a door slamming made Kurt wince. "Crap."

"You better make this worth my while."

"I don't know if it will."

"Fuck, Kurt, couldn't this have waited until the morning?"

"If you want you can tell Elsa that Kim and I are engaged."

"You finally asked her?"

"What do you mean finally? You had no idea I was going to ask her."

"Please, I know you, Kurt. That house you bought didn't have a first art studio, let alone the second. You've spent a great deal of time adapting your life to meet her needs. What's up?"

"Virginity."

"You're not one."

"Kim is."

"So?"

"I'm about to erm, take it. I mean, she's giving it to me so I'm not forcing her or anything. I'm starting to sound like a bumbling idiot."

"You are," Noah said. "Why are you calling me?"

"I'm sitting in my office with a mega hard on because I've never taken a virgin."

"You call me?"

"I take it Elsa was a virgin."

Noah sighed. "Fine. What do you want to know?"

"What do I do?"

"Well, first things first, you're in a good place seeing as you actually got her there of her own free will. That is always a good point."

"No jokes."

"Take your time with her. If she's ready, everything will come to you. It'll hurt at first. It did with Elsa, but take your time, don't rush. This isn't about getting caught by parents."

"Take my time?"

"Yeah. Caress her body, love her, and everything will fall into place."

"You said it's going to hurt."

"I did."

"What if she can't stand it? What do I do?"

"I feel like I'm talking to a baby here. Kurt, you're not stupid. You own a corporation, and are responsible for millions of dollars worth of investment. Peoples' livelihoods depend on you. You can figure out how to make love to your woman."

Chapter Eight

"Elsa, babe, it's me."

"You're not coming in here," Elsa said. She folded her arms and stared at the door, which she had locked. What kind of husband took a call from his best friend during sex?

"I'm sorry."

"How would you have liked it if I put a call to Kim? Huh? Would you be so forgiving?"

"You're right. I'm wrong."

"Ugh, you're doing that thing again where you always agree with me, and you know that drives me crazy."

"Kurt was worried."

"About what?"

"He and Kim are taking the next step."

"He called you why?"

"Kim's … a virgin."

"So?"

"Well, he figured you'd been a virgin."

"The cheek," she said, shaking her head.

"They're getting married."

Climbing off the bed, she rushed toward the door, flicking the lock, and opening it.

"What? Kurt proposed?"

"Yes."

"And now they're having sex?"

Noah nodded, stepping into the room. "I'm hoping you'll forgive me now."

"I'm not in the mood anymore."

He wrapped his arms around her, lifting her up off the floor. "You're not in the mood?"

"Nope. I'm not ready to have sex again."

"Babe, you're pregnant, and I heard that's

supposed to make you horny as hell."

"It might not. The books said each person is affected differently." He dropped her to the bed, following her down. Noah eased up the shirt she was wearing and tugged it off her head.

"I'm hoping you're horny as hell."

"What if you're not here to serve my needs?" Elsa asked.

"Babe, I'll always be here to serve you. If I'm not, I'm just a phone call away."

"Did you tell him?"

"No, I didn't."

They had stopped off at the pharmacy when she told him she'd missed her period. They had done the test together, which had been weird. She'd been so embarrassed, but Noah wanted every single part of it.

"We're going to have to tell them soon."

"Soon, now I've got to make up for taking a phone call you didn't want me to take."

****

Kim lay on the bed, her hands on her stomach as she stared up at the ceiling. He had smooth ceilings, nothing textured. Kurt hadn't returned, and it was making her nervous.

The moment he entered the room, she sat up, noticing he held his cell phone, and had a red mark on his forehead.

"What's going on?" she asked. "You didn't go for condoms?"

"I've got condoms all over the house. I made sure that each room had enough. I wanted to take you in every single room so that I'd always have a memory of us together."

She sat up, lifting the blanket to cover her breasts. "Okay, so if you don't have condoms, and you have a cell phone. Did you hit yourself in the head with it?"

"No. I didn't. I called Noah."

Kim frowned. "Why would you call him?"

Kurt took a seat on the bed, and she noticed he was still hard.

"Did Noah do that to you?" she asked.

"Do what?"

She pointed at his rock hard dick.

"No, that's what you do to me. It's kind of hard not to be aroused even though I'm nervous as hell."

"Why do you have to be nervous?" she asked.

"I've had a lot of sex. I've been with a lot of women."

"You know, this isn't something I want to hear about naked in your bed." In fact it was making her really uncomfortable. "Did you bring them back here?"

"What? No. This bed, this house, it's all new. I wouldn't do that to you. Not the asshole anymore."

"Okay, so what's the problem?"

"I've never been with a virgin."

"Oh."

"I don't want to hurt you."

"What did Noah say?"

"There would be some pain, and I can't stop that from happening, but I can make it better for you."

Kim tucked some hair behind her ear, wondering what they were supposed to do now, and said as much.

"Do you want me to make love to you?" he asked.

The moment had been lost. Kim frowned. "Not tonight. It's kind of creepy that you went to your friend." She smiled. "I'm cursed to stay a virgin forever."

Kurt moved to lie beside her, taking hold of her face, and capturing her lips. "Not for much longer."

They didn't have sex that night, or the night after that. Kurt got called away for a week on a business deal that took him to half way across the globe. Kim spent some time with Elsa, but other than that, she painted. Randy came to visit her, letting her know that her work in his shop at a high-end mall was getting some really interesting offers. People were asking after her, and with Kurt gone, Kim went to Randy's shop to meet some of the people there.

She took Elsa with her for company as she wasn't entirely comfortable around new people.

Kim answered questions, and was surprised by the enquiries of doing her painting on commission.

One gentleman wanted her to paint his garden, and another wanted her to paint his woman. Several offers opened up, but Kim didn't take any of them.

On Sunday, after a week without Kurt, she was missing him, and decided to go for a swim. She climbed into the pool with the sun beaming down, heating up the water. Kim did several lengths, then floated up. When she came across a shadow, she opened her eyes to find Kurt staring down at her.

"You're finally home," she said.

"Yes. I couldn't find you." He sat down on the edge of the pool, and she moved toward him, resting her arms on the ledge and looking up at him. He wore a pair of gray slacks and a white shirt. It seemed to be his entire wardrobe, business suits.

"Did your meeting go well?"

"It went as well as to be expected for a meeting. I wasn't exactly in the best of moods, so I wasn't good with negotiations. In the end, I gave an ultimatum, and left." Kurt shrugged. "I got a call on the flight back that I'm too much of a hard ass, and they agreed."

"I have no idea what you're talking about."

"It's not something you need to worry about. Randy called me. You've had some commission pieces offered."

"Several actually, and more keep coming. I'm not sure. I'm not really comfortable."

"Would you like me to come with you to a few of them? I can do my big caveman growl, and send them all off?"

"You'd do that?"

"Yes. If I wasn't so much of a distraction I'd even stay with you."

"What makes you think you're a distraction?" she asked.

"Babe, I'm hot stuff. I know you can't stand to not look at me. Your eyes are drawn to me."

Kim moved, grabbing onto his legs and tugging.

"Then, hot stuff, come and swim with me." She let him go, and splashed him with some water. "Come play, businessman, or is this too much for you?"

He jumped in the water, and she screamed as he charged for her.

Kim couldn't get away as he lifted her up, and then pulled her down. They were both laughing as they broke the surface. "You're a crazy man."

She started to unbutton his shirt, and slide it off. Kurt began to pull down the strap of her costume, but she stopped him.

"We're all alone. I've missed you."

There was no one around. Unless they invited friends over, they were always alone on a Sunday. Removing her costume, she waited for his clothes to come away, and then she threw herself into his arms.

Kurt gripped her ass, and she wrapped her legs around his waist, holding onto him. "Fuck, baby, I've missed you. I've missed you so much."

Taking his lips, she wrapped her arms around his neck, pressing her pussy against his erect cock.

One week she'd been without his kisses. One week of regretting not being with him.

Kurt had broken down her icy walls and demanded that she pay attention to him. Now, she couldn't stop thinking about him. Kurt inspired her. He filled her with passion, longing, and desire.

She was in love with him, and knowing that, any doubts she once had ceased to matter. The only thing that mattered to her was him.

Reaching between them, she gripped his cock, which was already hard. Distracting him with a kiss, she found her entrance, and even as Kurt tried to pull away, she eased her pussy onto his cock.

"Babe?" Suddenly, he pushed her up against the edge of the pool, capturing her hand, and holding it above her head. "What the fuck are you doing?"

"I'm showing you that I'm ready. I want you, Kurt, please."

She tried to wriggle on his cock, to make him see that she wanted him, but he wouldn't let her move. "Make love to me."

"We're in the pool."

"I don't care. I'm ready. I don't want to stop now."

He stared at her for several seconds. The only sound she could hear was that of their heavy breathing. Kurt didn't move. The tip of his cock was within her, and she wanted more of hm. He released her hands and gripped her hips.

"Don't look away from me," he said.

****

Kim was so incredibly tight. Kurt had known she would be, but he'd not been prepared for it. Who was prepared for a tight pussy? Gripping her hips, he stared into her eyes, seeing how wide they were, and how filled with lust she was. Kim was ready for him.

He'd been ready for her for a lifetime.

Even though they were in a pool in his backyard, he intended to make it the best experience in the world.

Inch by glorious inch, he sank inside her, going deeper. When she looked to be struggling with his length, he took his time, pausing, kissing her lips. All the time, he made sure her eyes were on him. She was with him the whole time.

At the last inch, he slammed her down, and they both cried out. She wrapped her legs around his waist, holding him tightly.

"You're so fucking tight," he said, muttering the words against her lips.

"It feels so good."

"You're not hurting?"

"No."

Running his hands to her ass, he rocked gently within her, feeling each spasm of her cunt around his dick. He closed his eyes, counting to ten to stop himself from coming so deep within her, so quickly.

Her nails dug into his back, marking him.

Staring into her eyes once again, he pulled out of her pussy and watched the change in her gaze as he began to fuck her. There was no rush even as his body just wanted to pound within her, and fuck her. Kurt didn't.

He released one of her ass cheeks and started to tease her clit.

"Oh, wow," she said, leaning against the wall. She moved her hands, to hold onto the edge of the pool, thrusting her tits up. He couldn't resist. Latching onto one of her tits, he sucked it into his mouth, moaning as her pussy tightened around his dick.

Kim started to rock on his cock, trying to get him to speed up, but he wouldn't do it. He took his time, fingering her pussy, sucking her tits, and making love to her, slowly.

"Feels so good. I don't know if I'm going to last, Kurt."

He teased her clit, slow strokes until she came, her cum sliding down the length of his cock. Wrapping his arms around her again, he ravished her mouth as he fucked her a little harder this time.

It had been so long without her, and without a real release that with a few strokes, he quickly pulled out, and erupted into the water.

"We didn't use a condom," he said.

When it was over, he stroked her neck, back, breasts, holding her close.

Kim smiled at him.

"Any regrets?" he asked.

"None. That was perfect." She kissed him back. "We're going to need to get someone to clean the pool."

"I'll handle it, don't worry."

"Kurt," she said.

"Yeah, baby."

"I love you," she said.

He pulled back, looking into her eyes, and wondering if he'd been imagining it. "You love me?"

"Yes, I do. Kind of crazy, don't you think?" she asked.

"No. I don't think it's crazy. I love you, too."

"I just lost my virginity in a pool," she said.

"Yes, you did."

Kurt couldn't believe she took charge and put his dick inside her. It was the single most erotic thing to ever happen to him, and he knew every time he looked at this pool, he would always remember their first time together.

It would hold a special place in his heart. With Kim, she owned every single part of him.

Chapter Nine

"Congratulations," Kim said, raising her glass of water to her friend.

They were celebrating Noah and Elsa's pregnancy. There had been a small party organized by the happy couple at Noah's parents' house.

Kim saw her own parents talking with the soon to be grandparents. This was the first time she had come back to town since leaving after graduation.

"Thank you. It's kind of surreal don't you think? Being here?" Elsa asked, voicing her own thoughts.

"I was just thinking that. I can't believe we're here in Noah Stewart's backyard," Kim said. "Seems like a lifetime ago with high school and everything."

Kurt and Noah were talking with a couple of their old friends who had been invited back to the party. Kim recognized Sienna and Adam. They had gone away to college in the last ten years, and were happily married with two kids.

Ryan had also appeared, and part of her wondered if she would see Jessica, but there had been no sign of her. Britney, one of Kurt's exes, had not been there either.

Kim smiled at everyone and did her best to be there for her friend.

"You're really hating this, aren't you?" Elsa asked.

"It's fine. I'm here with you, and this is home."

"You've not been back home?"

"Not really. I mean sometimes I go back home, but I don't go to other peoples' homes if that makes sense."

"It does. You only come to see your folks."

"Yeah, and if they're away, I don't come back.

Mom's and Dad's work usually takes them away."

"They're here tonight."

Yes, her father hadn't taken Kurt's proposal all that well. Donald James didn't put his trust in a lot of people, and she was his only daughter. He worried.

"They are."

"I see your father is glaring at Kurt."

Kim looked toward the man she loved and her father, and sighed. "It's not going to be easy with those two."

"It never is with parents."

"Your parents were happy with Noah."

"Up until they realized that I would be sleeping with him, planning a future, and one day hoping to have kids." Elsa smiled. "Which we are now."

Kim laughed. "You're glowing. It's amazing to watch."

"Thank you. I really do appreciate you coming here, and being with me. I couldn't imagine going through something like this without you."

"I'll always be here for you. I know in the past I went to a different college, and we've been in and out of each other's lives, but we're still here, and we're still together." She hugged her friend. "I can't wait to find out if it's going to be a boy or a girl."

"I know. Can you imagine a little Noah?" Elsa asked. "He'd be so cute."

"I want another little Elsa around," Noah said, coming up behind Elsa and kissing her neck.

Kim smiled, leaning back against Kurt as he placed a hand around her waist.

"Are you having fun?" he asked, whispering the words against her ear.

"I am. Yes."

"We've been talking and planning. Elsa and I, we

were wondering if you two would be willing to be godparents?"

"Us?" Kim asked.

"You're getting married, and you're going to be together. Kurt is my best friend, you're Elsa's—it made perfect sense to me."

Once again, Kim couldn't stop smiling. "I'd love to. Absolutely love to."

She hugged her friend, holding onto her tightly.

Elsa and Noah left them alone, talking to their relatives.

"We're going to be responsible for a kid," he said. He took her hand, and pulled her along toward the front of the house.

"Where are we going?" she asked.

"Seeing as we're staying at my folks', and they're enjoying the party, I thought I'd delve into a little fantasy."

He kept her hand as they left Noah's house, walking along the streets. She recognized the street that she used to cross to get to Elsa's.

"So many memories here."

"Is it hard for you because of me?" he asked.

"No. I'm not going to hold that against you." She rested her head against his shoulder. "You're not a bully anymore. Besides, I'm marrying you. I couldn't back out now. You're rich."

"Ah, you're after me for my money."

"Yes. I intend to live a life of luxury."

"Which you can support yourself if you began to take the commission jobs."

"Yeah, I will. The money, it doesn't bother me," she said. "I've lived without for a long time."

"Do you like the house I bought for you?" he asked.

"Yes. I do. I love it." It still seemed surreal to her to be living in a house that was bought for her. It was a nice thought, a loving one.

The streets were dark and silent. Kim started to embrace the present rather than constantly look back toward the past. Kurt was not the same guy. He was a bully no more.

"You know I regretted a lot back then," Kurt said.

"I know. You've said so."

"No, that last year of high school. It was a killer. At first, it was the best time of my life. Last year of school. I thought I was going to rule the world." Kurt laughed. "Then Mrs. Donald had to give us that assignment."

"I was so scared," Kim said. "I remember tensing up and glancing over at you, and seeing you smirk. I thought my life was going to be a nightmare."

"I sat with you, and I don't know, something changed. Something snapped inside me, and I didn't want to call you names."

"Why did you?"

"I don't know. I was an asshole. I didn't get it? Name them, and I'm sure I wouldn't have a good enough reason. You went from being the girl I tormented for a bit of fun, to being the girl that I thought about all the time. I hated how you flinched away from me. You wouldn't give me the time of day, nor would you smile at me the way I saw you smile at Elsa." He paused at the front door of his house. "I wondered what it would be like to have you call for me."

Kim bit her lip. "I was never going to call for you."

"A guy can dream."

He opened up the door, and they walked inside. This was her first time in his world. They had invited their parents over for dinner to break the news of their engagement.

Kurt closed the door behind her and locked their fingers together.

"Are you okay?" he asked.

"I don't know. Do you have any monsters or demons lurking?"

"No. It's just me, which could suck either way."

She laughed. "It's fine."

"I'm going to be a guy right now, and take you up to my room."

"Your parents kept it the same?" she asked.

"Didn't yours?"

"Yeah, I didn't know if it was different for a guy."

"My room is the same." She followed behind him, catching a glance at all the pictures. The evidence of Kurt's family was all around. He was well-loved.

They got to the third floor, to the door right at the back. "My dad decided I needed a lot of privacy growing up."

"Why are you blushing?"

"He may have walked into the bathroom when I was becoming acquainted with my dick."

"Oh my God, no?"

"Yes. We decided to put the entire incident behind us, and um, he got me my own floor, own bathroom. Told me to keep that stuff to myself, and to always wear a condom."

They hadn't worn a condom. Kim knew there was still a risk even though he pulled out of her. Since then, they had been using condoms.

Entering his room, Kurt flicked on the light, and Kim got a good look at the guy who'd tormented her, and become the love of her life. There was a little gym area in the far corner. Elsa told her that Noah had the same.

Exercise still played a huge part of Kurt's life. She'd gone to the gym in their own house to watch him work out. Kim had her sketchbook with her, and of course made sure to use every aspect of inspiration he created.

Along one wall were several cabinets with trophies, pictures of him getting the trophies, several newspaper articles, along with some of the football team as well. On the other wall, she saw pictures of him with Noah. Then one of him, Noah, Elsa, and her.

What surprised her was a picture beside his bed, and she took a seat, picking up the framed photograph. It was of her sitting on the grass outside of the school, her chemistry book splayed open. Her throat felt thick as she stared at her past self.

****

Ten years ago

It was really hot indoors, and rather than try to teach, Mrs. Donald had brought them outside to bask in the fresh air. Several of their classmates were sunbathing, holding a book up, and pretending to learn. Kim sat in the shade of the tree. She'd not brought a hat, and if she wasn't careful, she'd burn and be in agony for days.

Kurt didn't seem to mind. Rather than walk away, he stayed by her side, flicking through emails, and munching on the apple he'd found in her bag.

"Don't you want to sunbathe?" she asked, opening up her book.

"Nope."

Kim cursed in her head, looked down at her book, and started to work. She just couldn't shake him. If she was mean, he was nice. If she was nice, he remained nice. If she ignored him, he kept on talking. Now he was eating her food, sitting way too close, and she was scared. What if he spat some apple at her?

Glancing over at him, she saw that he had finished

the apple, and tossed the core in the trash.

He's never thrown stuff at you before.

Just vile words.

"If I get some sun lotion, I can rub it on you," he said, leaning on her shoulder.

Kim growled and shoved him off. "Stop being … you. Just work. There, can't you do that? Just work, and leave me alone."

"Wow, are you due on or something?" he asked.

"Due on?"

"You know, menstruating."

Why did she allow herself to get dragged into these conversations? "You're disgusting."

"And I thought there was a reason for girls to be a bitch. Don't you have a law or something that allows you to be a bitch three days a month? Come on, that's pretty good going. You've got a reason to be a bitch, and us guys, we don't."

"That just comes naturally to you. We can't help it. Ours is because we're women."

He stared down at her chest and winked. "I know."

She shook her head, turning her back on him. Staring at the page, she tried to think of what it actually said. Kurt had fried her brain, and she noticed he did that a lot. Distracting her. She didn't want to talk to Elsa about it, as her friend would be convinced she had feelings for him. She didn't. He was a horrible, horrible person.

Kurt got up, stretched, and called her name.

She looked up, and he took a picture.

"Hey, what are you doing?"

"I'm making sure I have some kind of record. Kim spent time with me, oh yeah." He looked at his camera, staring at her. "Come on, don't be a bitch. Show me that beautiful smile."

"Stop it."

"Come on. I can make you laugh."

She dropped her book. "Fine, make me laugh, and then you can take a picture."

He pulled a face at her, and she smirked.

"Ha, the cold witch can melt."

"That was being stupid."

"I can do better," he said.

"Go on."

She gave him her full attention.

The facial expressions he started to make were hard for her *not* to laugh at. "What are you doing?" she asked.

"I'm showing my lady my best 'come to me' smile. My charm. I'm going to light you up, and have you eating out of the palm of my hand."

He started talking in a French accent, and she didn't know why she found him so funny. Kurt took the picture and sat back beside her.

"Don't share that on a horrible site."

"I won't. I'm going to treasure this forever."

****

Kurt had treasured her picture forever. After he'd taken the snap, and gotten home, he'd hooked up to the computer and printed it off. He'd gone out to buy a frame for it. He took a seat on the bed beside her.

"We've come a long way," she said.

"Yeah, and I bet it was all down to the faces I pulled."

She threw her head back, laughing. "It wasn't. You looked like a dork, and what made it worse, you knew you looked like one."

"I made you laugh though."

"That you did."

She put the photo back and turned toward him. "I had completely forgotten about that until I saw it."

"Yeah, I was a weird kid." He kicked off his shoes, and moved back to lie against his pillow. Kim turned toward him, lifting her leg up. He stroked her knee, needing to touch her.

"So, you had some secret fantasies while you were here?"

"Yes. I am the dashing man in all the fantasies, here to meet your every desire."

"Stop joking around."

"I'm not. Okay, maybe a little. Most of them involved you getting naked, climbing on me, straddling my dick, and fucking me."

"How romantic, Kurt."

"It was in my head. You said nice things to me all the time."

"Like what?" she asked.

"Oh, Kurt, you big boy. You've got the nicest cock I've ever seen."

She chuckled. "Is that what every eighteen year old boy thinks?"

"You've watched porn. It's what we hope to experience."

He stared at her, seeing all the thoughts running through her head. Kim got to her feet and closed the door. There was no need for a lock. His parents didn't come to his private space. She turned toward him, holding the cardigan a little away from her body.

"Hello, Kurt. I really enjoyed doing our chemistry project together." She tilted her head to the side, let go of her cardigan, and fingered a strand of her blonde hair.

"I know you struggled with it, babe. I'm here when you need me. I know all about chemistry."

She moved toward the edge of the bed. Kurt was

curious about how far she'd be willing to take this little game.

"I've been thinking a lot lately about chemistry, and how important it is."

"It is very important." He made sure to emphasize the word "very".

Kim removed the cardigan, sliding it down her arms, and letting it fall to the floor. "Do you like me, Kurt?" she asked.

"I like you very much." His dick pressed against the front of his pants, creating a tent. She was turning him on.

"Really? I didn't think you did."

"Neither did I, but I love you, Kim. I always have, and I always will."

She leaned down, showing off her impressive cleavage. He watched, his mouth going dry as she started to lift up her dress. Fuck, she looked so good already. "I've only ever been with one guy, and he's so amazing. His dick is so big."

Kim threw the dress aside, showing off the pastel blue lingerie he'd purchased for her. The cups lifted up her tits, almost in offering. His mouth watered, and he wanted them swinging above him as he plowed inside her.

She crawled on the bed and straddled his hips. He watched as she lifted her arms above her head, taking her hair up on top of it.

Kurt cupped her hips, groaning as she rolled her pelvis, rubbing his dick as she did.

"Kurt," she said. "I'm so horny, and I'm all yours."

"Yeah, baby, you are."

He held her hips in place and started to thrust against her. When he couldn't stand any more tormenting, he sat up, flicked the catch of her bra, and watched her tits spill free. Cupping them, he ran his thumb across each tip. Taking one nipple into his mouth, he sucked it hard, biting down on the flesh.

"Oh, yeah," she said.

Gone was the fake voice. This was his Kim, not fantasy Kim. Gripping her shoulders, he buried his head against her breasts, and remembering his mirror, he turned to look. There in the mirror he saw his woman, straddling his waist, her chest thrust up to him.

"Look at us, Kim."

He moved her head to see, and he heard her gasp.

"That is us, and that is what I dreamed about. You're so fucking beautiful. I can't wait until we're married. The whole world will know that you belong to me."

Kim cupped his face, silencing him with her lips, and he let her. He was at the point of arousal that he'd do whatever she wanted. She tore at his shirt, opening a few buttons, and then tugging so that they sprayed across either side of the room. Her nails sank into the flesh of his back.

Gripping her back, he turned her on the bed, so that he straddled her.

Plunging his tongue into her mouth, he tore the panties from her body and stood up. Opening his belt, he pulled down his zipper, and removed the rest of his clothes.

Kim's gaze landed on his dick, and he saw her lick her lips.

"Do you want a taste, babe?"

"Yes."

Wrapping his fingers around the length, he started to play with himself, while watching her. Kim crawled to the edge of the bed.

He ran his fingers in her hair, holding on, and pressing the tip of his cock to her mouth. She looked up at him, taking him deep into her mouth. The confidence she showed him was out of this world.

"You completely fucking undo me." He wasn't lying.

Turning toward the mirror, he watched as she sucked his cock. Her hand went over his, and together they worked his length.

He groaned.

Kurt refused to close his eyes. The feel of her lips around him was the best. Pumping into her mouth, he set up a pace so that she didn't gag on him.

"Fuck, baby, you look so damn hot taking the whole of my dick." He pumped inside her, and finally pulled out. Kurt didn't want this to be over. Flipping her onto her knees, he lifted her ass into the air and opened her cheeks. He saw her pretty pussy and swiped his tongue against her cunt. Plunging inside, he fucked her with his tongue, teasing her clit with his fingers.

Kim screamed his name, and he loved hearing the sounds she made. She always seemed shocked by the pleasure he gave her.

"Oh, it feels so good, Kurt."

"You like my mouth on your pussy?" he asked.

"Yes, I do."

Kurt stepped back, gripped his cock, and placed it at her entrance. His dick was bare, and he cursed.

"Don't worry about it. Please don't stop, Kurt. I need you inside me."

"Are you sure?"

"We're in this together, right? We'll handle everything."

The image of Kim swollen with his kid was the biggest turn-on in his life.

Gripping his cock, he pushed the tip into her entrance, and when there was enough of him inside her, he held onto her hips, and slammed in deep.

They both cried out. Kim reached behind her, and he caught her hands, holding them at the base of her back.

"I've got you now, babe. I'm in complete control."

She released a little whimper, and Kurt made sure she was still there with him. When he was satisfied that she was, he started to withdraw from her tight cunt.

He watched his dick, covered in her cream, and then pushed inside her again. Each time he pressed inside her, they both groaned at the pleasure.

"That's it, babe, fucking take my dick. I love you, Kim. Fucking love you."

He slammed inside her, going as deep as he could, then pulling out, staring at her pussy. It was dirty, but when it came to Kim, he never had enough. He saw her pussy open, wet, and waiting for his dick, and he fed it to her.

Reaching between them, he fingered her pussy, using his grip on her hands to keep on fucking her.

The only sounds in the room to be heard were those of flesh hitting flesh, and their combined heavy breathing.

He pounded inside her, and glanced over at the mirror to see Kim staring at their reflections. "Do you like what you see?" he asked.

"Yes, yes, I do."

Kurt couldn't hold back, so he slammed inside her, going deeper within her.

Kim gasped out. "I'm so close.

He fingered her pussy, gritting his teeth, and her orgasm set off his. Kurt tried to pull out, but she held him so perfectly, that it was impossible for him to leave her pretty pussy. Holding onto her, he spilled his seed deep within her.

Seconds passed, and when he opened his eyes, he saw Kim smiling at him. "Oops."

"Yeah, we keep having oops."

"Did you enjoy your fantasy?"

"You made it more than a fantasy, you made this a reality."

He pulled out of her, and Kurt was just about to grab some tissues when he saw his seed spilling from her pussy. There was no way he was going to waste that. Covering her, he pushed his cum back inside her, hoping that it would take.

"What are you doing?" she asked.

"I want to get you pregnant."

"Kurt, that is a big deal. It's not something you can undo."

"I don't want to undo it. I want to get you pregnant. I want to fuck you knowing that we created a life together."

"Oh," Kim said, flushing.

"Don't you want that as well?" he asked.

"Yes, I do. Do you think we're ready for that?" she asked.

"We're not kids anymore. I think we're ready for anything."

"Being a mom and a dad. That's huge."

"Elsa and Noah are handling it."

"They're destined to be together forever."

Kurt dropped a kiss to her lips. "So are we."

Chapter Ten

Kim stared at the image in front of her. The image was of Kurt in his bullying days. She'd painted it when she first got to the studio, and looking at it now, the image wasn't true to him.

Kurt was on the phone in the corner, organizing the final details for her to go and paint for commission. She was nervous about it, but he was going to be there to help her. It didn't matter how much time passed. Social interactions were always difficult for her.

She needed to change this picture. Kurt was not this guy anymore. Neither was she, and no matter how many times she stared at it, her hatred of the piece only kept on growing.

"It's done. We go over there Saturday. Do you have everything you need, or do you want me to go and order you some stuff?" he asked.

"No, I have everything. Are you sure about this?"

"You enjoyed the garden he wanted you to paint, didn't you?" he asked.

"Yes, I liked it." She turned toward him. "I just wonder if it's a good idea. I usually only paint what I feel. Randy didn't seem to mind people asking. His advice was not to let my art get affected by demand, if that makes sense."

"It does. You're an artist with a lot of talent, and you're soon to be my wife. I'd happily cancel the appointment if you'd prefer."

Kim looked around the room, unsure of what to do.

"I don't know."

"Do you want to talk it over with your mother before you make a decision?"

She nodded.

Kurt handed her a cell phone. "I'll be in my office. Let me know what you decide."

Kim dialed her mother's number. Esther answered on the third ring.

"Kurt, what's the matter? Is something wrong?"

"It's not Kurt. It's me, Kim."

"Honey, what's wrong? How are the wedding plans going?"

"They're going well." At night, they made their decisions. They had settled on a church, in their home town, the irony of it. She was wearing a white wedding dress at Kurt's demand. As far as he was concerned she'd been a virgin bride.

"Good. Good. I know some places where you can find the best lemon cake, and let's not forget the flowers. Roses or daisies?"

"We're not sure. Flowers aren't that big of a deal."

"Oh dear, every woman should have flowers."

"Mom! It's actually work I wanted to talk to you about."

"Oh, work. Your art, of course."

Kim rubbed her temple, and explained what was going on and how she was feeling. "Of course, I want you to be involved in the wedding. Kurt and I have handed most of it. If you want to deal with the cake and flowers, you can."

She heard her mother's excitement. "I'd love to do it. Of course I would. Don't you worry about a thing, sweetie. Now, back to your art. There is no right or wrong answer to this. Do what you think is best. Yes, I know it's an awful answer. You wanted me to tell you what to do. Your art is your world. You make the decisions on what works for you. What inspires you? Ask yourself all the right questions. What inspires you? What makes you draw? How do you feel at the thought of going to these places for people? Will it be forcing your craft, or enhancing it? Art is not something that can be taught. Drawing and painting can be taught. Art, emotion, love, all of it, it's down to a feeling, and that, my dear, cannot be taught. That's what is inside you."

Kim had her answer, and after saying goodbye to her mother, she hung up the phone, staring at Kurt's hateful image. This was not the man she was marrying. This was not the man she fell in love with.

Putting the cell phone on the counter, she grabbed her pallet and started to mix the paint with her finger. Staring at Kurt's face, she knew exactly what to do. What she loved about painting was everything could be changed. His face could be transformed into a scene of beauty. There was room for faults within painting. It only made the artist work a little harder.

Her life had taken a huge turn from the girl she was ten years ago, to the woman she was now. There were really no comparisons. Even Kurt was different, and she couldn't keep thinking he was that same guy. She *didn't* think that, and that was why she had to change this picture.

She would do the current commission pieces, but after that, no more. Her art was her soul, and she wouldn't draw or paint for the sake of it.

****

Kurt collapsed back against his office chair and released a huge sigh of relief. They had been going through their wedding stuff, and he was exhausted. He knew planning their wedding was tiring out Kim. She'd picked her dress, they'd picked their church, and they'd also picked their honeymoon. There was so much to plan, and he hated it. What was the point in picking flowers? Then he had to think about his best man. It was easy of course, Noah.

Rubbing his eyes, Kurt wondered if he should have taken her to Vegas. It would have been a hell of a lot easier. Their parents were involved now, so everything should be better.

He fired up his computer and started to do some work. There were times like this when he left Kim to make her own decisions. She never needed to paint again. He'd support her for the rest of their lives.

For the next couple of hours, Kurt worked, going over several emails, and dialing up his manager to make sure certain investments were still going ahead. He wasn't there every single day, but he was still in control.

At the end of the day, he frowned when he saw the sun had already set, and it was in fact dark. The light of the screen had distracted him, and now he got up and stretched.

"Kim?" He called out her name, wondering where she'd gotten to.

Kurt had expected her to come and find him. He drew the curtains in his office, and started turning on a couple of lights. The kitchen was completely bare, so he went to the only place where he'd be able to find her.

There was light coming from the art studio, and when he entered, he saw Kim was staring at the wall. She was staring at his picture, the one she'd drawn when she considered him a bully.

He looked at the picture, and paused.

The picture was of the two of them. Kurt tilting her head back, and the look on his face was one he recognized. It was pure love. Along the top of the painting were the words, BULLY NO MORE.

Kim turned toward him. "This is how I see you now."

"Babe, this is …"

"It's mine. It's not going to be put on sale. This is what I feel when I think about us. You're not a bully, Kurt."

He took a deep breath, touched that she had changed her thoughts of him. "I spoke to my parents, and to yours."

"Ah, did my mom tell you I'd given her permission to go crazy on all the extras?"

"Yes, my mom's joining forces with her. It'll be an interesting wedding." Kim got to her feet and walked toward him. He opened his arms, and she went right into them.

"I love you, Kurt Michaels."

"Love you too, angel." He kissed the top of her head, and they turned to look at the painting.

****

Ten years ago

Kurt stared across the dinner hall as Kim entered with her best friend. They had been given an assignment together, and he'd been trying to spend time with her.

"Yo, man, what's up?" Noah asked, drawing his attention.

Shaking his head, he smiled. "Nothing, I'm fine."

No, he wasn't fine. Something was seriously wrong with him. Since spending a little time with Kim, she'd been in his head, and not the usual way. He used to call her fat and be mean to her. Now, he didn't know what to do, as when he looked at her, he didn't think of her as fat.

She was curvy, and when she turned to look behind her, twisting, from all the way over at his table, he saw the fullness of her tits, and he wanted her.

His dick thickened.

"Hey, you're not going to say some shit about her?" Ryan asked, leaning in close. "Don't you like to torment that girl?"

"Not in the mood," Kurt said.

His stomach twisted thinking about what he used to call her.

"You okay, man? You look like you're going to throw up."

"I'm fine. Okay, I'm fine." He got up from his seat, and took his tray, emptying it into the trash. Leaving the school grounds, he took several deep breaths of air. Gripping the back of his neck, he tried to loosen his muscles. When he was calm again, and nothing seemed to be fucking with his head, he started to walk around the back of the school. When he got close to the edge of the building, he stopped when he recognized Kim's voice. Glancing around the building, he saw Kim and Elsa were sitting near the wall on the grass verge. They couldn't see him, but he could see them.

"You okay?" Elsa asked.

"Yeah, I'm fine. Just a little stressed with this assignment."

"Kurt seems to be being nice to you. That's a good thing."

"Yeah, until it suits him. I'm waiting for him to strike, you know? He'll probably put a 'kick me' sign on my back, or pour soda into my bag. It's why I'm carrying my books. I've even started to put my hair up, in case he puts something in it." She sighed. "Just once I'd love to come to school, and not worry about what he'd say or do."

She sounded so sad, so hurt, and it was all because of him.

Kurt stepped back, knowing he had to change. She didn't deserve the pain he'd caused.

One day he'd make it up to her.

****

Staring at the painting of the two of them, Kurt knew he'd done well. This was their future.

"Who would have thought we would be here when we were two complete opposites?" she asked.

"I'd say we were more likely to work. Opposites attract, and I'm attracted to you." He kissed her neck.

Kim turned in his arms and smiled up at him. "How long do you think we're going to stay married for?" she asked.

"The rest of our lives. I'm not divorcing you. You can rant, rave, and curse my name, but as far as I'm concerned, we're in this for life." He took hold of her hand that had his ring on. "Think about it, Kim. You're not going to get rid of me." He pressed a kiss to her ring. "For life, forever, with me, even when I'm an asshole."

She rolled her eyes. "I suppose someone is going to have to put up with you. Not many people would."

He nuzzled her neck, biting on her flesh.

Kim laughed and moaned, the tension changing between them.

Kurt couldn't wait, so, taking her to the floor, he made love to her, and showed her with actions exactly how much.

****

"I, Kurt Michaels, take Kimberley James, to be my wife. I promise to love, honor, and cherish her, and to love her fiercely." Kurt smiled at his wife. Their families were in the church that they would have passed many times growing up. "I will be a loving husband, a brilliant father, and best of all, your friend." He turned to look at Elsa. "Obviously not your best friend, you already have one." Tears filled Kim's eyes, and he reached out, wiping them away. "I promise to try to never make you cry, to care, to provide, and give you a life that doesn't fill you with regret. I love you, Kim. I'm yours. Always."

"Wow, I don't know if I can follow that kind of vow. I, Kimberley James, take Kurt Michaels as my husband. I'll love, honor, and cherish you. Of course I'll love you fiercely. There's no doubt of that." She took a deep breath. "I'll be the best wife I can be, and a mother to your children. I will devote my life to you, to our family, and to our future. You came into my life, and turned it upside down. You made me see myself differently, and I love you, Kurt. I'm yours."

Kurt gripped her hand tightly as the priest bound them together in marriage. It didn't matter to Kurt. To him they had been married in their hearts. When it was over, he pulled her into his arms, kissing her.

Noah and Elsa clapped and wrapped their arms around each other, Elsa's large stomach making it hard for her.

After pictures were taken, they all climbed into the limousine, making their way toward the reception.

"I feel like this is going to prom," Elsa said.

They had traveled with Elsa and Noah toward their dates. "We're all married, and there's already a kid on the way," Kurt said, smiling. He wrapped his hand around the back of his wife's neck, pulling her back. "We need to start working on our own kid."

"We're doing just fine," Kim said.

"We're going to have to start early. We've wasted ten years."

"I wouldn't call it wasting ten years. I'd say we were preparing for each other. Neither of us was ready."

"Speak for yourself. I've been ready for a long time."

Kim looked up at him. "Then thank you for letting me be in the right place."

"I'll wait forever."

He kissed her lips, and their friends faded into the

background. This was the start of the rest of their life. A life he was determined to make perfect.

Epilogue

Kim sat in the waiting room, rubbing her own stomach as she and Kurt waited for the news on Elsa's labor. Her best friend had gone into labor last night, and had been in the hospital for a couple of hours. She was trying not to freak out as she was six months pregnant herself.

"Everything is going to be fine," Kurt said, taking her hand.

"You're right. She's in the right place."

"Did you see how freaked out Noah looked? He was telling me last weekend how awesome he was. He was totally in control."

"Will you be driving me crazy when I go into labor?"

Kurt caressed her stomach, shaking his head. "I'll be completely in control, and you'll not have to tell me to calm down, or to relax. I'll be there, by your side, always."

She stared at him. "I'll believe that when I see it."

Noah came through the doors, and they stood up. "I have a baby boy."

Kurt shook his hand, clapping him on the back. Kim hugged him. "Can we go and see Elsa?"

"Yes, yes, she wants to see you. Come on."

Noah took them through the doors, back toward the main wards. Kurt rested his arm across her shoulders, and she held his hand, locking their fingers together. They entered a room, and Kim gasped. Elsa sat up. She looked a mess, but the love in her eyes was what Kim saw. In her arms was a little blue bundle.

"Oh my God, he's so beautiful." Releasing Kurt, she made her way toward her friend.

"Isn't he a dream?"

Kim smiled down at her best friend's son. "He is. Did it hurt?"

"I don't care. I really don't care. Any pain I felt disappeared. Just look at him, Kim."

She giggled. "How was Noah?"

"I was brilliant."

"He fainted. Nurses had to pull him out of the way."

"I did okay."

"I'll do better," Kurt said.

Three months later, Kurt was a complete mess to the point that Kim even recorded him on her cell phone before they got to the hospital. It was so funny to watch.

She gave birth to a little girl, without Kurt as he'd fainted and was out cold. When he came around, it was to hold his wife and his daughter.

Their life was perfect, and after three more children, along with rabbits, cats, and dogs, Kurt gave her the perfect life, the best life. In return, Kim never held back again. She loved him with the whole of her heart.

The End

DEDICATION

To Teddy, you came into my life, and gave me so much love, and then was gone before I even realized it. Thank you for at least showing me how damn important it is to spend time loving. It broke my heart losing you, but I will always have my memories. Rest in peace, buddy.

Teddy is the rabbit I adopted, and left me so fast. I never knew grief like this. I thought it was crazy, crying over my rabbit. I want to thank everyone on Facebook, on my blog, for their kind words, and their complete understanding. Your words of love, and support meant so much to me.

UGLY

Sam Crescent

Copyright © 2016

Chapter One

"Do you want some help, Dad?" Blake Carson asked.

Her dad was working on the engine of his car in the driveway of their house in the little quaint village of West County.

He glanced up, staring at her. She saw his frown, and his lips pressed together.

"No."

It was a simple word, and yet it was loaded with so much heartache, at least to her. Being an only child, Blake was aware her father wanted a son. There had been complications with her birth, and now her mother couldn't have any more kids, so he wouldn't be having a son. All they had was Blake. And she was such a disappointment to him. He'd never outright said it. She had only heard his yearning when it came to wanting a son.

"Oh, okay."

"Blake, shouldn't you be in school?" He was still frowning, but this had to be the most he'd ever spoken to her in a single morning. Actually, not so much. She did recall times when they used to talk. At least, she did all the talking.

"I'm heading there now."

"Go on then," her father said. "You don't want to be late."

Blake went to say something more, but what was the point? Her dad wanted nothing to do with her because she wasn't a boy. Even now she was used to him saying, "if only you were a boy". He never said it to her face, and never aloud. Many times over the years she'd tried to fill the boy role, watching football, attempting to read a car manual, even trying to design things. Nothing. She wasn't interested in cars, or a bunch of guys running around.

She wasn't a boy, even though as far as she was concerned, she had a boy's name. Leaving her home, she made her way toward the County high school. On the way she was going to stop by Isabella's—or Izzy as she liked to be called—house, and wait for her.

At seventeen years old, Blake was used to her father's lack of interest in her. Her mother was the same. Even though she had been born a girl, her mother had wanted a blonde starlet for her to show off. Blake was the complete opposite. Brown hair, brown eyes, plain features, and she was really shy. It took her six years of school to finally make friends with Izzy. They were the complete opposite of one another. Izzy was outgoing while she wasn't. Blake never felt the need to impress the people at school. She didn't care about the style of her clothes, or what was the latest fashion. She simply didn't fit in, and she didn't care that she didn't.

"Morning," Izzy said, running out of her front door. "Today is such a beautiful day."

"Why?"

"There's a new boy coming today. Well, I hear he's a bit of a rebel, and I intend to be the one he looks at."

The new boy that was going to be attending their

high school. Someone new coming to County High was big news. No one knew anything even as they all pretended to know something.

"You're beautiful," Blake said.

"So are you," Izzy said. "Don't sell yourself short."

If Izzy wasn't so determined to fit in, she'd be the most awesome friend. Izzy gave in to peer pressure, and there were many times that she left Blake in order to go with the popular kids. Regardless of her somewhat flaky attitude, Izzy's comments were sweet. Blake's mother found her ugly, and told her regularly she had to work on her looks if she ever hoped to get a guy.

That hadn't been recently though. Lately, her mother had started asking her about school, and what she liked. Blake found it was easier to stay out of her mother's life. Her father didn't think much of her either. He certainly never contradicted her mother. She was used to being plain, boring, ugly. They were words that actually gave her some semblance of comfort. She was the plain Jane, the boring person that was left alone. There was nothing she could do about it.

"I'm not interested in stuff like that." She offered a smile, hoping Izzy wouldn't push. They were chalk and cheese. "So have you heard anything about him?"

"Not a lot. He's moving here with his mom. Bad divorce, and she got custody or some crap. I don't know."

Izzy's family was the epitome of a family portrait. Everything looked great in the photograph, but it wasn't the truth in real life. Her mom and dad fought a lot. Blake didn't know if it ever got violent or physical, only that Izzy never liked her staying over.

Where Izzy's parents were happy to voice their problems, her own parents did the opposite. They rarely spoke to one another. Sure, they had date night, and sometimes they ate as a family. For the most part, they were all separate beings. Blake didn't really understand the dynamics of a family. She watched it on television, but that was it.

"You don't know anything else?"

"It's all just gossip. I heard he was a real rebel, and even though he's like only eighteen, his arms are like totally covered in ink. He's supposed to be some real fighter, gets in trouble a lot."

Blake listened wondering if any of this was true, or if today all of her friend's fantasies was about to be shot down. She couldn't help but smile imagining a guy in a tweed suit, buck teeth, and a science nerd. That would be a refreshing change. She'd get on well with him.

"Oh, did you know I totally broke up with Sean? That guy is a total asshole."

"Did you sleep with him?" Blake asked.

"Yeah, that's not the point. I'm so done with him. I mean, totally done."

"You still slept with him. I thought we agreed no more loose sex." Blake held onto her backpack, glancing over at her friend.

"Yeah, I know, but he was being so nice to me, and I like him. You don't even know how good sex can be."

"Thanks," Blake said. She'd not had a boyfriend, what with the whole ugly girl thing. One boy a few years ago offered to kiss her but later told her he'd have to put a bag over her head to actually do it. "We both know that's not going to happen."

"Ugh, what is with all this negativity? You're not an ugly person, Blake. You're sweet, you're kind, and you are pretty. You just let it sink you down into everything you're not."

"Izzy, you don't have to—"

"Someone does. You're a beautiful person, and your mom telling you that you were ugly because you weren't a blonde whore is just wrong. Not that all blondes are whores, because you know, I'm blonde."

"I don't think all blondes are whores. I hate that statement, and the stupid thing as well. My bestie is a blonde, and even though she likes sex, I don't think she's a whore."

Izzy sighed, linking arms with Blake. "This is our last year of school before college. I want this to be a perfect, bright, fun year."

"I was thinking of going to Europe to college," Blake said.

"Wait, Europe? That's like really far."

"England, they have some decent colleges. Of course over there it's university. Could be kind of cool." Blake wanted to do everything to disappear from West County and move on with her life.

"You'll be far away from me. I thought we were going to the same college."

Izzy looked genuinely upset.

"It's not a sure thing. I can change my mind."

"It's something that you've thought about?"

"Yeah, it is." They hadn't talked about going to college together. Izzy always changed the subject. Today was a different day it seemed.

"I don't know. England, that's like, really far away."

"I know." She forced a smile. "Forget it. I was being stupid. It's not like I've talked to my parents about it. It was just a thought." It did seem reckless, going all the way to England on her own.

Izzy stopped and turned to her. "You shouldn't be running away. Your folks are complete and total idiots."

"I don't need the pep talk, but it is appreciated."

They entered the large parking area of their high school, and it was already abuzz with activity. Izzy release Blake's arm as another girl, a cheerleader this time, came rushing toward her.

"Oh, my God, he's so hot. He takes hotness to another level," Tiffany said.

"What's his name? Do you know how old he is? What's he like? Tell me, tell me, tell me." Izzy spoke a mile a minute, and kept on talking.

Wow, anyone would think this new guy walked on water. Blake stayed beside her friend, only because when she left, Izzy tended to do the girl pout that made her feel guilty.

"Logan Black, eighteen years old, no criminal record, but I think there was—oh, his arms are covered in like tribal ink, very bad boy. Sean and his crew swarmed around him. Don't know if he's into sports, but you never know."

Blake tried not to burst out laughing. They were all making assumptions.

"Izzy, I've gotta go. See you later," Blake said.

"Sure, catch up with you at lunch."

Blake was walking away, but she still heard Tiffany's question.

"Why do you hang out with that weirdo? You can do so much better, Izzy."

"Shut up. I like her."

She didn't catch anything more, but that was about it. Most of the people at school often wondered why Izzy chose to hang out with her. Blake didn't really care what people thought. She'd gone through her life knowing she was a disappointment, and ugly. When she looked in the mirror, Blake couldn't see a single thing pretty about her. Her hair was dark brown, and she pulled it into a ponytail. Glasses hid her brown eyes, which were dull, and her face was just plain and pale. Either way, she didn't spend much time trying to improve herself. There was simply no point in it.

Opening her locker, she grabbed her books, and placed the ones she didn't need back inside. With that done, she made her way toward homeroom. She was earlier than everyone, so taking out a book, she started to read. Everyone would be more interested in the new guy than anything else.

****

Logan Black's mother wanted him to have a fresh start. West County was supposed to be that. When his parents divorced he had two options, go to this little town with his mom, or stay listening to his dad have a serious mid-life crisis and fuck his way through every single bit of pussy that spread their legs for him.

He decided to split, staying with his more stable mom. Neither option had been that good as he didn't have that good of a relationship with either of them.

That was a lie. He happened to get on well with his mom. He just didn't like the fact she had stayed with his cheating, lying, rat bastard of a father for so long. They provided him a home, and in turn, he didn't bring the cops to the door. His father didn't have any paternal instinct within his body. His mother, on the other hand, deserved a hell of a lot better.

"You the new kid?" a jock asked.

Staring at him, Logan wondered if he slammed his fist in the guy's face whether he'd be as cocksure afterward. This was clearly his kingdom.

"What do you think?" Crossing his legs, he leaned against his car waiting for this guy to make the next move.

"Name's Sean. You're already quite the news."

And this guy wanted to be first in on the action. For his first day, Logan held his hand out, shaking Sean's. "Logan." His mother didn't want him getting into fights.

"Good to meet you, Logan." Within minutes there was a swarm of people introducing themselves to him. "You're one of us now, Logan." Sean clapped him on the shoulder as if they had been best friends all of their lives.

"Hey, handsome," one of the girls said. She was a perky little redhead, thrusting her chest out. She wore a short skirt, and she was game for a fuck. Everything about her screamed for him to take her.

"So, where did you get the ink from?" Sean asked.

Glancing down at his arms, he smirked. "Vegas."

"Shit, man, you've been to Vegas."

"Used to live there. My father's a lawyer." Who also liked to fuck all of his young assistants. Logan had been around sex, drugs, alcohol since he was able to get his dick hard enough to use. This town was going to be a piece of cake. He even got involved in fighting. Too much anger and aggression and his parents put him in a fight club, a legal one that was supposed to be tame. It didn't take him long to break out of that shit, and go for the big leagues. He liked fighting, hurting, breaking things within reason.

"Hi, I'm Tiffany," another girl said.

"And I'm Izzy." This time a blonde spoke. She looked a little different from the rest. Her smile was sweet, and genuine.

"This here is my girl," Sean said, wrapping his arms around her shoulders.

"In your dreams. We broke up, asshole." She pushed him away and shook her head. "I'm going to catch up with Blake."

"Babe, leave Blake. She's a fucking drag."

Izzy shoved Sean hard. "Leave her alone. You're a first class asshole."

She stormed off, heading toward the school.

"Blake's a girl?"

"Yeah, fucking weird girl." Sean shook his head. "Don't know why Izzy even hangs out with her. She's plain, and she doesn't put out. She's ugly as fuck as far as I'm concerned. I'm sure you'll see her soon."

Logan didn't think much about it. Once the bell rang he headed inside, and went straight to the reception desk to get set up.

The principal, a balding guy, didn't like him. Logan knew he wasn't liked, and once again, he didn't care. Mr. Blaine could go and suck his dick as far as Logan was concerned.

"We don't tolerate disrespect, Logan."

"I'm not giving you any."

"This is a good school, and we expect you to be the best that you can be."

It took every ounce of control for him not to roll his eyes. This was ridiculous.

"We also don't allow fake tattoos. Those will have to go."

"They're not fake." Logan swiped a finger across his tongue, and slid it across the black ink. "It should be in my files."

Mr. Blaine looked annoyed. "Fine. Here are your books, your locker, and your class schedule. We'll be keeping an eye on you."

The same old crap, and Logan couldn't care less.

He left the principal's office and made his way to homeroom. For the next couple of hours, he simply did what any other guy did. He was forced to stand up, say stupid shit about his own life, listen to people coo over him. By the time lunch came, he was sick of being the new kid.

Grabbing a couple of burgers from the cafeteria, he took a seat at Sean's table. It was just fucking easier to stick with the bastards he knew. The jocks seemed to know what they were doing for the most part, even if he didn't like them. He already had most of them pegged. For instance, Sean was an asshole, and believed he was God's gift to women. He doubtless cheated on every single chick he was with, including that Izzy he saw earlier. Brian was a follower. David was a closet gay. Paul was fucking two girls from the cheerleading squad, and Ben was a nerd. They all had their little weaknesses, and they all tried to bully others for theirs. He'd been sitting in class and had to listen to all of them say shit about others. They wanted him to join in, but he wasn't down with that kind of crap. There was a friend in his last school, one of the reasons he started to get ink, who had ended up taking her own life because of the shit that happened to her.

He never thought about her, or at least he tried not to think about her, as otherwise it just made the pain hurt even more. The world was an ugly place, and with her death, he had vowed to make sure no one ever suffered because of him.

Yeah, it was totally out of fucking character seeing as he liked to hurt people in a fight, But fighting was different. They were both there for a reason, to hurt, and to earn money. Bullying, that was something dark, sinister, and nasty. He didn't agree with it.

Biting into his burger, he watched as Izzy walked into the cafeteria.

"Your girl is going to do her street cred no good by hanging out with Blake," Brian said.

"I've told her all the time not to hang out with

ugly, but does she listen? No." Sean leaned back, shaking his bottle of soda.

"I thought she dumped you," Paul said, talking in between chewing.

"She'll dump me until she needs me for a quick fuck. My door is always open."

The fucker didn't even see that she was using him.

"Yeah, and for every other chick," David said. "You want any ideas of which cheerleader to fuck, go to Sean. He knows what they like and how best to get them on their backs with their legs spread."

"Who's the girl?" Logan asked.

Izzy was clearly doing all the talking while the brunette beside her listened. She had a rucksack on her shoulder, which he found to be incredibly cute. Her hair was pulled back into a ponytail, and she wore glasses, large ones that distracted people from her eyes. She was a fuller girl as well. The clothes she wore were baggy, so he couldn't be sure of her size. If he had to guess, he'd put Blake at a size sixteen or eighteen. He liked her curves, and her large tits. Even with the baggy shirt, he saw how big they were.

Logan knew women. Being in Vegas most of his life, he got to fuck a whole load of available women, even married ones.

He wasn't about to scream rape either. Logan had been more than willing, especially with the women who were happy to give him tutorials on pleasing a woman.

"Who?" Sean asked.

"The one next to your girl. I've not seen her."

"Blake? The ugly fat chick."

Logan frowned, looking toward the girl. She wasn't like the cheerleaders, and she didn't seem to be in a huge rush to run with the crowd. "I've not met her.

Why not?"

"She's not in your classes today. Izzy hangs out with her, but she doesn't spend time with us."

"The ultimate virgin," Brian said. "Not that anyone would want to screw that chick. So many other fish in the sea."

"You may be in luck, Logan. Izzy's bringing her right over," Paul said.

There was a table close to theirs that seated all of the cheerleaders. Logan watched as Blake tried not to scrunch up her nose. She clearly didn't like sitting with Izzy and a bunch of cheerleaders.

"Hey, girls," Izzy said, taking a seat after she forced Blake to sit.

"Seriously, you're letting *her* sit with us?" another girl asked.

"You got a problem with that, Blair?" Izzy asked. "Last time I checked I could be friends with whoever the fuck I wanted to be."

"It's okay. I can move."

Logan stared at Blake. She wasn't even a little shocked by their outrage to have her sitting with them.

"No, Blake, you're eating with me."

"She'll probably eat you," Sean said.

"I'd let her eat me before I'd let you," Izzy said.

"Wow, so now you're sticking up for her. I remember a time when you'd let her be alone. What changed?" Sean asked. "She'll be back to being on her own tomorrow!"

"Izzy?"

"Blake, eat!"

He watched as she grabbed her fork and speared a piece of chicken, putting it to her mouth. "Happy?"

"Yeah, now eat all of it."

"Blake," Sean said.

The way he said her name wasn't very nice. She tensed up and glanced down toward Sean. "Yes."

"Logan wanted to meet you."

Chapter Two

This had to be some kind of ploy. Blake looked at Sean, then at Logan. His name was Logan Black, and he wasn't much of a talker, or so she had heard.

"He wants to know why he hasn't seen you yet," Sean said.

The smirk on his face let her know he was up to something. She didn't know what exactly, but it wasn't exactly comforting. Sean was never nice to her, which she didn't mind. Blake hated the way he treated her friend.

"Hey," she said, glancing at the tattooed guy.

"Blake, right?"

"Yep."

Her heart was pounding. This was the first time since kindergarten that anyone had taken the time to actually talk to her, apart from Izzy.

"Guy's name?"

"Parents wanted a boy," she said.

In the beginning she used to say it with so much pain, but now it was easy to tell people she wasn't wanted, and she wasn't. There was no point hiding from the fact. Her parents didn't abuse her in anyway. They were simply truthful.

"They tell you that?"

"Yep."

She took a bite of the salad she'd gotten herself.

"It's their loss," he said, startling her.

"What?"

"Some parents can't have any kids. Yours got you. Regardless of you being a girl or boy, they should be grateful."

It was the first time anyone had said anything. She noticed that people were staring at him, and then back at her, clearly shocked.

"Erm, thanks." She frowned, glancing down at her food. This was uncharted territory for her. "I just remembered I had to do something, Izzy. Chat soon."

She didn't like the attention, and Logan clearly didn't know what he was doing talking to her like that. They could all turn on him, and she'd seen other guys regret it. Grabbing her lunch tray, she threw it in the trash quickly, and exited the dinner hall.

The next lesson was gym, so she didn't want to be working on a full stomach either. Placing a hand to her chest, she found her heart pounding. Why the hell would he do and say something like that? It made no sense.

"You run away from a lot of people?" Logan asked.

Blake paused, and slowly turned around to find him standing there. He held two sandwiches in his hands, and she glanced at the food before looking back at him. "What's going on?"

"You ran out without really eating. Figured we could eat?"

"You're friends with Sean."

"Not really. I was standing by my car, and he came and spoke to me. Not really much of a big deal. He's a dick, that's not hard to see."

"I don't think you should be friends with me." She spun on her heel, walking toward her locker. Her gym clothes were in that locker.

"Why?"

"I don't have that many friends, and in case you didn't see, I'm not exactly on the cheerleading squad."

"Do you see me playing sports? I'm not a jock. I'm the new boy. The fresh young new boy that everyone wants to not know."

"Not know?"

"They don't really care. Sean saw an opportunity this morning. I take it County High doesn't see a lot of new kids."

He kept on following her, and she didn't get it. "What are you doing?" She stopped next to her locker and opened it up.

"Talking to you, which I'm starting to see is a foreign concept for you. Did you know this locker is mine?"

He pointed to the one right next to hers.

"Is this some kind of ploy or scam, or something to bully me?"

"Nope. Just a sandwich. Figured it would be fun to chat."

She grabbed her gym clothes, stuffing them into her bag. "You'd rather chat with me than with Sean?"

"Why not? You seem way more interesting. Besides, I already know which cheerleaders to fuck, and who'll not only suck my dick, but allow me to do every hole."

"Ew, that is disgusting."

He chuckled. "You're cute."

"I'm ugly," she said, stating the obvious.

Logan tilted his head to the side, staring at her. "Delusional."

"Are you insulting me?"

"I find it interesting is all. You're a nice looking girl, and everyone seems to think you're ugly. Strange."

"What's strange about it? I'm not like Izzy, or anyone else."

"And if you were like them, I wouldn't be standing here now."

"You confuse me."

"Good, it's the start of a good friendship." He held up the sandwich. "You want to eat with me."

She stared at the food, and her embarrassing stomach started to growl.

"Take the food, Blake, and take a chance."

Closing her locker door, she followed him outside to one of the benches beneath a tree.

Logan unwrapped her sandwich for her, before presenting it. "Enjoy."

Lifting the sandwich up, she took a bite, enjoying the spicy chicken with cheese. Her mouth watered for more.

"Good?" he asked.

"Good. Where are you from?"

"I was from Vegas. My father worked there, as did my mom, which all changed."

"You decided to come here to West County?"

"Yeah, it got tiring seeing my dad screw every chick that crossed his path."

She swallowed her first bite, and looked at him. "You're going to be very blunt, aren't you?"

"No other way to be in life."

"Vegas?"

"Yep. I was around sex, drugs, criminals, you name it."

"I doubt that's all you were around."

"No, I gambled a little as well," he said.

"Inked on, too." She couldn't help but smile. "So what is this?"

"This?" He pointed between them. "This is about me making a friend, and I hope you're more than happy to be my friend."

"I don't know. I'm bad for your street cred."

He tensed his hands into fists. "These are my street cred. I can survive on my own."

"You're very confusing," she said.

"I know. It's what I planned to be." He winked at

her.

Staring down at her sandwich, Blake wondered, not for the first time, what he was doing.

"I had a friend like you once," he said.

"What?"

"Yeah, my old school. I'm only going to say this once. She was the best person I ever knew."

The passion in his eyes was easy to see. Taking another bite of her sandwich, she was kind of jealous about the girl who'd claimed part of his heart, and she had.

"You want to be my friend?"

"Why not? It's not like you have many."

"Izzy, I have her."

"One friend out of a high school of, what, a thousand? And from what I see Izzy's friendship isn't exactly the best."

It was true that no one ever wanted to be her friend. Blake found it hard to connect. Izzy was different though. Izzy didn't care about what others thought of her. She liked Blake, and so as far as she was concerned, she'd remain friends with her.

"Are you saying I should be friends with you?"

"I don't see why not. What do you have to lose?"

Seconds passed, maybe even minutes, and she stared at him, not knowing what to do. "I'm not worried about me."

"It seems to me that a lot of people haven't given you a chance," he said.

"You ever thought that I'm happy to be on my own? Have my own company?"

"Must get very lonely."

"Not really. Not when you like it," she said.

"Your family wanted a boy."

Blake tensed up, finding it hard to stare at him.

She distracted herself by eating a little more. The sandwich no longer held any appeal, and the thought of talking to him didn't either.

"I see that is a sore subject for you."

"It's not. What about your parents' divorce?"

"I don't really care."

"You moved here with your mother. When do you expect to go and see your father?"

He shrugged. "When I want."

"It doesn't bother you that you're living separate lives?"

"Does it bother you that your parents wanted a boy?"

"No." The answer was instant, and even as pain struck her heart, she still came up with the same answer.

"Do you have a brother?" he asked.

"No."

"Why not?"

"None of your business."

He paused, then took a bite of his sandwich. It seemed to be a playoff between the two of them. Tit for tat.

Her heart was racing as she stared at him, and she didn't know what to make of it, or what to expect next.

"You're an interesting person."

"No, I'm not."

"Yet saying that makes you interesting."

Finishing off her sandwich, she rolled the wrapping up in her fist. "I find you strange. You'd rather sit out here with me than inside with your friends."

"I've spent a few hours with them. They're not my friends. I bet Sean makes a lot of people's lives a misery. Am I right?"

"I don't know. He's not my friend." She didn't know Logan, and wasn't about to tell a total stranger the truth of their high school.

"I've seen it, and I know he's an asshole. You should warn your friend he only sees her as a great fuck."

"Sure. Izzy comes across as being stupid sometimes, but she's not. She's using him as much as he is her. He's a sure thing, and when she wants something, she goes to him."

He tilted his head to the side. "Where do you go?"

"I don't go anywhere." She was a virgin, complete and true. "Look, I've got to go, thanks for the sandwich."

"This is the closest you've ever opened up with someone."

"I didn't open up to you."

"Then what would you call it? Because I'd say we got some interesting discussion out of the way."

She climbed away from the bench and stared at him. He was a force to be reckoned with. Logan sat there with his thick corded muscles, decorated in ink. Most of the boys in school couldn't even begin to come close to this guy. He was a man in his own right, and he owned it.

"I've got to go."

****

"How was school?" his mother asked the moment he walked through the door that afternoon. Logan looked across the large main hall. His mother had certainly gotten plenty out of the divorce, this being one of the first homes his father acquired for her.

"Interesting."

"I see that look in your eye. What was interesting?" she asked. One of her hands was poised into the box, the other on her hip, as she stared.

This was what he found curious about his parents' marriage. His mother was a straight up calm, collected, down to earth woman. She never cared for fancy shit, and was always the first one to take a family meal in her own home over one outside. In the beginning, his father adored her, and they were a strong couple. Now, at his mother's choosing, they were further apart than ever before.

The divorce was the only time Logan recalled his father being sad even though he tried to hide it.

"A girl at school."

"Oh, is she a cheerleader?"

"No. She's a nobody."

"Logan, don't."

"This isn't about *her*. She has one friend who doesn't treat her like shit. Everyone thinks she's ugly, and even her own parents don't want her."

"What do you mean?"

"They wanted a boy, and she went all tense when I brought it up. Blake is an open book."

"Blake's a girl's name as well."

"Yeah, but I don't think her parents gave her that name on purpose. She's lost, and I think she sees herself as ugly."

"How horrible. Let me guess, my son was nice as usual, or did he go the other way, and become rather invasive?"

"I was nice, and I simply asked a lot of questions."

"You've just found your new friend, haven't you?"

"Well, I could be friends with some of the jocks who have already told me what girl does what. I can get oral sex, or anal—"

"Gross, gross. Enough. I do not need to hear what is available on the sex market at school. I take it this is all consensual."

"From what I saw, yes."

"Disgusting."

"No different from back home. Only you don't always have to pay for it here."

"Logan!"

"What? Sorry?"

"Look, I know you have the little rebel inside you, but you wanted to come with me so everything was different. I love you very much, and I need you to show a little more respect right now."

"I will. I won't get into trouble. Principal doesn't like me."

"You try everyone's patience at times, Logan."

"You love me though."

"I'm your mother."

He smirked. "You'll always love me." He moved toward his mother, looking into the box that contained several pictures. "Want some help?"

"Sure."

The first picture he pulled out was his parents' wedding picture. "You keeping this?"

"Yes. I think it's always good to look back."

"Doesn't it hurt?"

"Not all the time. I had good memories with your father, and he didn't want to divorce. I refused to be the wife while he had all of his extra women. Especially when I tried to get a man for myself, and he was up in arms about that."

"Ew, Mom, don't need to know you have an actual life."

"Don't worry, dear, I don't need to know that you're not a virgin either." His mom kissed his cheek. She took the picture from him, and placed it on a basket of washing. "So, do I get to meet the elusive Blake?"

"I don't know. She doesn't seem to get I want to be friends with her."

"Did you ask?"

"Of course I asked. She doesn't think it'll do well for my street cred if we're both friends."

He placed several pictures of the two of them on the shelf running the far side of the main hallway.

"Interesting girl."

"The guys are total assholes."

"No fighting. Remember, I told you to leave that crap behind in Vegas."

Logan stared at his mother. "I won't fight at school." If he discovered fighting of another kind, he'd gladly take it. The fighting he enjoyed was the kind without a ref.

"I mean it, Logan. You think I'm just talking about the school fights, I'm not. I mean all kinds of fights. The ones that you may not walk away from."

"Mom——"

"No, I get it, okay. Shauna died, and she left you behind. You started taking on fights, and then I heard that you were doing the illegal, underground fights, the ones in hidden locations."

Logan turned to his mother, seeing the hurt in her eyes. "I don't hurt anyone."

"Fighting hurts people, Logan."

"They're there because they want to be."

"What about those guys in the high school? You fought them without them asking."

"They deserved it." He held onto the shelf, taking several deep breaths.

"Logan?"

"What? The shit they did, they pushed her to that, Mom." He'd lost his temper plenty of times over the shit that got said to Shauna. The moment she was gone, the guys who'd caused it, Logan had gone hunting for them, and he'd not stopped. He never hurt anyone, unless they asked for it. Those bastards had ended up in juvie, but he'd wanted them to serve cold, hard time.

"I know, sweetie. It's one of the reasons I knew it was time to go. You could have ended up in a juvenile facility or something else if it wasn't for your father. I know, I know, you'd have taken whatever punishment that they dished out. You shouldn't have to deal with that kind of pain, Logan."

"I like Blake," he said. "She's different."

"You're changing the subject."

"We can't change what happened, neither of us can. I won't start any fights."

"Will you go looking for them?" his mother asked.

He sighed. "I can't promise that."

This time, she sighed. "I worry about you. Those fights, they're not to help. They're to make a quick buck, and to leave."

"Can we not talk about this?" he asked. "I know the risks. I'm eighteen years old, but I'm not a child. I get it."

"Do you? Do you really? I worry where all this anger has come from."

"I know. I used to be such a good boy."

"Logan, don't. You can be an asshole, but don't ever try to use sarcasm on my memories." His mother grabbed the basket and made her way upstairs.

He was a total dick!

Out of both of his parents, his mother had always been more understanding. She was the one he went to whenever he had a problem. His father, well, he'd been useless at everything else, and Logan hadn't trusted him after finding him screwing his latest secretary across the desk.

He finished removing the pictures and placed

them around the room, wondering what the hell he was supposed to do with his future.

Once he was done, he headed upstairs and apologized to his mother, who gave him a hug in return. She never could stay mad at him for long. Entering his room, he dropped down on the bed just as his cell phone rang.

His father was calling.

Logan didn't want to talk to him. Not right now, but if he didn't, Dad would phone his mom, who would then get him to talk anyway.

"Hello," he said.

"Logan, great to hear from you."

"You called me."

"Right, right, how was school?"

"Fine."

"Really? Fine."

"What more do you want me to say?"

"Did you knock them dead? Make friends? Get a girlfriend?"

"It was fine," he said again.

"Logan, talk to me."

"Why?"

"I'm trying here."

Logan sat up and opened up his bedside drawer. He stared at the single picture he had of him and Shauna together. It had been taken on a day out to the mall. His father had taken it. Logan had his arm around her shoulders, and she was smiling. She'd been his best friend.

"Dad, the reason I'm here is I don't want to try with you."

"Logan?"

"No, you don't get it. I never wanted a dad like you. I moved with Mom because I wanted to. I wanted to get away from that life. That is a life *you* embraced. Not me."

"Son, I miss you both."

"You should have thought about that before you were balls deep in women that were not your wife, and young enough to be your daughter." Logan closed the cell, ending the call. He loved his father, and he hated him. It was an equal feeling.

Staring at Shauna, he thought about Blake.

He wasn't going to give up on being her friend.

****

Mitchell Carson watched as his daughter headed upstairs. They had set the dinner table, and like so many times before, Blake sat in the kitchen, not joining them. His wife, Linda, she stared down at him, and they both were in pain.

"She asked if she could help this morning," he said.

"Did you let her?"

"No. I … I didn't want her to be late for school, and Anna said small steps."

Anna was the therapist who had been helping them to see the error of their ways. They hadn't always been like this, this cold. When Blake had been born, they had both been so happy. The first five years had been utter bliss, but that had soon turned to darkness. One miscarriage after another. Time had disappeared, and now all that remained was a daughter they had failed.

"I love her," Mitchell said.

"I do as well. God, when I think of the things I've said, she must hate us both." Linda placed a hand over her mouth to keep her tears inside. "We're the worst parents in the world."

He got up from his chair, and rounded the table, to hold onto his wife. "We can fix this."

After years of pushing each other away, of hiding the pain with anti-depressants, and secrets, they had finally caved six months ago. They had gone to a therapist to help them. Mitchell couldn't even remember what had happened to make him see the monster he'd become. Blake had been talking to him, and he'd snapped at her. Shouting at her to get out. That time, not only had he seen the pain inside Blake, he'd witnessed the monster he was. The mirror on the wall when he'd snapped had woken him up. The way he looked, and then the flashes of anger over the years.

The father he'd wanted to be was not the father he'd become. Years of pain, of feeling like a failure, and he'd pushed all of that on his little girl.

"We can make this right, Linda, we have to."

Chapter Three

It was too hot for gym, but she didn't have much choice. Blake stood off the main track and started stretching out her body. Several of the girls in her class were all huddled together. Three days had passed since Logan joined their school. Three days of him getting her lunch, and forcing her to sit with him. If they had classes together, he was there beside her.

During the past three days, she'd watched as Izzy had started to crumble to peer pressure like she always did. Every other week, she had a couple of days where Izzy didn't seem to care. Then it was like someone gave her a warning, or something happened, and she went back to her *other* friends.

Back to Logan. He made a point of standing beside her locker first thing in the morning, and at the end of the day. Izzy had asked about him, but what could she say? The new guy was persistent in wanting to be her friend. It made no sense to her.

Sean and his little group had also been paying attention to their little conversations, which she didn't like.

She was so tired. Last night she had stayed up trying to study for a chemistry test that she was sure she failed on. Tilting her head from side to side, she tried to ease out the tense muscles as best she could. Thinking back to last night reminded her of her parents' current stalemate.

Her mother wanted to move, and her father wanted to stay. Both threw out each other's shortcomings. High on her father's list of problems was the fact he didn't have a son. Her mother had screamed that he didn't pay attention enough. It didn't matter what either did. They would both still continue to argue. What did surprise her was the moment she walked she into the room, they had stopped arguing, and smiled at her. The entire situation had seemed surreal as they asked about her day, and what she thought of moving. Instead of giving her thoughts, she had made her escape.

"Penny for them," Logan said right behind her making her jump.

"What the hell?" She spun around to find him so close she almost fell over, and if he hadn't reached out to grab her hips, she would have.

"You seemed a little lost. Just thought I'd make sure someone was home."

Pulling out of his arms, she frowned. "You really don't give up, do you?"

"It's not in my nature."

He stood in front of her in a white vest top and running shorts. The latest shocking rumor surrounding this guy was the fact he didn't want to try out for any of the sports available. She'd heard Sean, Brian, and their little group complaining about it. Of course the cheerleaders were pissed about it. Izzy had let her know there was a little revolt going in the group seeing as Logan wasn't going to be on any team, and he was the one they all wanted to have sex with.

High school politics were never her strong point. Sex was never something she thought about either.

It was like overnight all anyone cared about was sex. She found the subject boring.

"We're running."

"You're really not going to try out to be on the team?" She pointed toward the center of the field where the football team was waiting.

"I don't have time to be into sports."

"Fighting? You mentioned your fists the first day."

"It's the only thing I do."

"There may be a wrestling team," she said.

"I don't fight for sport."

"You like it?"

"Sometimes."

She stared at him. He was a large guy, much bigger than any of the other guys at school. The tribal ink helped him to stand out from the crowd. Even now she saw several of the girls eyeing him up. Logan didn't look at them. He was focused on her.

"You're confusing, you know that?"

"You clearly don't see friendship all that much."

"I see friendship, I just don't get why you're wasting your time with someone who is ugly?"

He took a step toward her, the smile on his face disappearing. "Don't call yourself that."

"What?"

"You're not ugly, Blake."

"You've known me a few minutes."

"I've had my eyes for a long time. I know what ugly is, and when I look at you, I don't see it."

"You're just trying to confuse me now."

"I'm not. You're just not used to someone saying nice things to you," he said.

"Let's see what summer vacation did to you all. I want laps around the track, no slowing down. Steady pace throughout," the gym teacher said.

Taking a space on the track, Blake tried to focus on everything else rather than the confusing thoughts that Logan inspired. He looked good in gym clothes, she'd give him that. They left nothing to the imagination as it showed off how muscular he was.

"Do you work out?" she asked.

"Like what you see, babe?"

"Don't be a pig."

"Believe me, I wasn't. Just like your eyes on me, and I get a chance to show off my rocking body. Yes, I work out. You can stop by and watch me."

"No thanks."

"My mom doesn't like it unless I take a shower after. I stink real bad."

She started to laugh. "Seriously?"

"After a good workout, I stink. I have a manly smell." He lifted his arm in the air, and proceeded to tell her to sniff.

"Stop it, you goon. I don't want to sniff your armpits. Gross." She touched his waist and gave a little push.

He took hold of her hands and kept them resting on his stomach. "I can be your friend."

She stared at his hands, which covered hers.

"Logan?"

"Black! Carson! This is not a social, get your butts moving."

She started to run, hoping that she could leave him behind. *Ha! As if that would ever happen.*

"You never answered," Logan said.

"Ugh! You just don't give up."

"I like the thought of us being friends. I'd be a good friend as well. Someone you can rely on."

"Why? Why are you seriously pushing this?" she asked.

"Why are you not? I'd be a damn good friend. You know it, I know it. We'd be good together."

She kept on running, noticing he was close beside her as they did. Izzy kept looking back at her, and she smiled to reassure her friend.

"Fine, you want to be friends."

"But not secret friends. I want us to braid each other's hair, and paint each other's toenails."

She frowned. "You're crazy."

"Also, my mom is doing this amazing stroganoff Friday. Want to come?"

Blake didn't talk. She didn't want to talk. This man defied every kind of stereotype she knew. He was trying to be friends with her, and she was pushing him away in the hope he would see where he was going wrong. Yet he did neither. He didn't walk away, nor did he back off.

"You really don't care what people think?"

"I've come to learn that people are going to hate you and like you, no matter what. I'd rather be around people I want to be around."

"You're a hot guy. Don't you want to be around hot girls?"

"What makes you think you're not hot?" he asked.

She rolled her eyes. "I look in the mirror every single day. I know what I'm looking at."

"And I know what I like looking at. I think you spend too much time believing what other people see, rather than what you think."

"I know what I've been told my whole life."

"You're not good enough?"

"Yeah, why shouldn't I believe it?"

"Okay, for argument sake, you believe it," he said. "Why don't you give me a chance to be something different? I'm new, and I'm a good guy. Why not take a chance?"

"I don't ever take chances." She spent most of her time wishing to be a sex she was never going to be. Her mother always cooed about the beautiful girls, while looking at her as if she was a huge disappointment. Izzy had to spend all of her time justifying to others why they were friends. People at school reminded her daily that she was ugly. For Blake, she just wanted to stay hidden, to help her constant open wounds a chance to heal.

Life sucked!

Yet even with life sucking, Logan had come from nowhere, and done nothing like that. He'd been nicer to her than her own parents.

"Sometimes it's easier to hide from chances. There's no risk of getting hurt. I'm offering to be your friend. Let me know what you think."

She kept on jogging and watched as Logan picked up his pace. He didn't go to the other girls. He stayed alone running.

"What harm would it really do?"

****

Logan waited by his car at the end of the day. He'd planted the seed inside Blake's head. He now just had to wait for it to blossom. Leaning against his car, he ignored the messages on his cell phone. Ever since that initial talk with his dad, it had been nonstop messages asking about his day. He wasn't interested in talking to his dad. There were some things that couldn't be undone as far as he was concerned.

Sean, Brian, David, Paul, and Ben exited the building and headed toward him. Sean spotted him first, and he saw all conversation cease when they all saw him.

Staring at the Sean, the leader, he wondered if this was about to be his first fight. He'd be a good opponent. Logan stayed beside his car, not making a single move even as all three guys stood in front of him.

"What?" he asked.

"You don't play sports?" Brian asked.

"I told you that. I don't do tryouts. I don't do sports of any kind." He was waiting to see what Blake would say. He'd given her the rest of gym, and the last couple of lessons to figure it out.

"You're aware we're the popular ones in this school," Sean said. "We decide who has a good time, and who doesn't."

"You threatening me there?" Logan asked.

"I'm telling you how it goes."

"Blake's not one of us. Izzy's always hung out with her, but she knows not to bring her friend to parties, and our shit. No one wants her there," Paul said.

"You're telling me who to be friends with now?" Logan asked.

"We're letting you know what happens in County High, and Blake, she's social suicide. Even her own parents don't want her. She's a dud, a waste of space," David said.

"You can't hang out with us, and her," Sean said.

Logan burst out laughing. "First, that sounds utter shit. Second, Izzy hangs out with her. Third, I never said I was any of your friends. You little fucks came to me. You think you can make my life hell, go ahead. You'll fail."

"This is County High. We're the ones that make the rules." Sean pointed a finger at Logan's chest.

Logan reacted. Grabbing Sean's arm, he twisted, and slammed him against the car, pulling the same arm up his back to the point that a little pressure would snap it. Sean cried out. Logan held him and looked at his friends. "You were the ones that ruled County High, and you can go on ruling it. I'm going to be friends with whoever the hell I want, and if that means Blake, it will be her." He looked at the guys, who were shocked to see Sean locked against the car. If Sean moved, his arm was going to be in some serious trouble. "He needs this arm, doesn't he? You see, I don't give a fuck about football, sports—I fight. I've got no problem snapping this little shit's arm because of it. Try me, you will lose. I have never lost a fight, and I will take on each and every single one of you. The difference between me, and everyone in this school, I don't give a shit if I break something. It's just a bonus to me. Do you want a broken arm, Sean?"

"Fuck you."

All it took was a little press, and Sean screamed.

"Fuck, stop. I don't want it broken."

"You can all fight me if you want. Rush me, Sean will end up out of the season, and County High will not win. I'll take you all down."

"They'll arrest you."

"My dad is the best fucking lawyer in Vegas. I'll be out within the hour." Logan glanced at Sean, who was now sweating. "I'll be friends with Blake, and you won't mess with me. Push this, and I'll be having more than a chat with your broken bones."

He finally released Sean and pushed him against his friends. "Nice chat, boys."

Blake was standing beside the car, and her eyes were wide.

They all scampered away, and he focused his attention on Blake.

"How much did you see?"

"How much did I miss?" she asked.

He smirked. "You're not pissed?"

"Why would I be pissed? Sean and his boys have made people's lives a misery here. One guy went to tryouts, and he was much better than David, and because of it, they broke his fingers. It could never be proven, but we all knew who did it."

She watched them walking away, a smile so wide on her face it took his breath away. Blake needed to smile more often.

"Sorry, I just, wow, can I have your autograph?" she said.

Sean was nursing his arm and pushing everyone away from him. Clearly, he thought he was strong.

"You can have anything your heart desires."

"I want to see that again," she said. "From the start to finish. That was so totally awesome. I mean, wow."

He chuckled. "You're not used to seeing that then."

"Well, I'm used to seeing some guys fight. Nothing like that."

"I'm glad I could finally give you a reason to smile."

Blake held her bag on her shoulder, and her hair was out of the ponytail. The long length cascaded around her, and he wondered if it would feel as soft as it looked. "I was thinking about what you said at gym."

"Good. It's why I was waiting for you."

"You were waiting for me?"

"Of course. I'll always wait."

"That's really sweet."

"I'm a sweet guy, with a dark side."

"I'd like to be your friend," she said. "I imagine it's going to be a lot like that. Some are not going to like you befriending me when they think they're much better. Anyway, I'd like to give it a shot."

"You would?"

"Yeah."

"What about stroganoff Friday?"

"I've never had it, so it's going to be an interesting Friday."

"My mom is going to love you."

She chuckled. "Anyway, I better go with Izzy."

He glanced in the direction she pointed, and saw Izzy staring down at her phone while she waited for her.

"I don't mind her coming for the ride. I'll take

you home."

"Oh, you will?"

"Yeah."

"Two seconds," she said.

She made her way toward Izzy.

"Izzy, babe, let's go!" Sean barked the order across the parking lot, and he watched as Blake approached. He didn't hear their conversation, but he saw the indecision in Izzy's eyes. She was torn between going with her friend, or going with the guy who would cause some problems. The pressure was clear to see. Still, Izzy could do whatever the hell she wanted. All she needed to do was not give a shit about fitting in.

Seconds passed, minutes, and he watched as Blake gave her hug and walked back toward the car, alone.

"What she doing?"

"She's going with Sean. She thinks it would be better."

Logan knew what had happened. Izzy had picked her boyfriend over her supposed best friend.

"That's okay. I was wondering, do you have a ride into school?" he asked.

"No, I walk."

"I'm going to start picking you up."

"Do I have a say in that?"

"No. I'm officially friendless. I have you."

She giggled. "Join the club. Izzy's still my friend. It's not the first time she chose to go with Sean. I've made my way home a few times."

He opened the car door for her and waited for her to get inside. Climbing behind the wheel, he started up his car.

"Sean's an asshole."

"That he is. He's an asshole that is determined to

let everyone know how important he is. Kind of sad really," she said, grabbing the seatbelt.

He pulled out of the parking lot, aware of the people watching them. Logan smiled. He was public enemy number one, and he was okay with that. It felt good to be himself. There was no way in hell he was ever going to join forces with a jock or a bully. He had his own self-respect to think about.

"Will your parents have an issue with you coming Friday?"

She started laughing. "No, not a chance."

He glanced over at her, seeing she wasn't lying.

Sean had mentioned that her own parents didn't want her. He followed her directions all the way back to her place. In the driveway he saw a car parked out front with the hood up. Blake tensed up.

"That's my dad," she said, pointing to the guy. He looked up, saw Blake, and then went back to fixing his car. When Blake turned toward him, he saw the guy look up once again. Logan didn't know what was going through the guy's mind, but he was clearly struggling. He had a death grip on the cloth he was holding.

"Do you want to meet my mom?" he asked, deciding not to think too much about her father's reaction, which Blake hadn't seen.

"Erm, do you think that is a good idea?"

"Yeah, she'd love to meet you. I've already talked about you."

"You have?"

"Yep." He pulled away from the drive, noticing that her father looked up, and stared at the car, but he didn't do anything else. How strange was that? Her father did love her. Logan was sure of it. What he didn't get was his complete lack of actually showing it. "He always like that?"

"Yeah. It drives Mom crazy that he spends so much time working on his car."

"I don't mean the car."

"Oh, what do you mean?"

"He ignores you, and then when you weren't looking, he looked all confused and shit."

"You clearly didn't see properly. He never comes out from under his hood to check that I'm okay," she said.

Logan truly believed that was a lie, or at least Blake didn't see the truth. There was love there, and pain, and guilt. He didn't know what to do to help her.

"It's fine. Dad never has worried. If I walked past him, he wouldn't say hello. He'd be more upset that I distracted him from work. It's okay."

No, it really wasn't okay.

The people around her didn't have a clue. Either that, or Blake didn't have a clue what was going on with her parents.

Chapter Four

"You live in a mansion?" Blake said, staring up at the large house.

"Dad's guilt money."

"I thought your parents were divorced."

"They are. He still bought this for her."

"Why?" she asked.

"Guilt. He feels he has a lot of shit to make up for, and guess what, he does."

"This is crazy," she said, climbing out of the car. "Is he a good lawyer?"

"Sure. When he wants to be."

There was no affection for his father. She heard the anger, the resentment every time he was mentioned.

Her family was not rich. They were not poor either. This was wealth on a scale she didn't even know if she could feel comfortable.

"Don't do that shit."

"What?"

"Make out this is more than it needs to be. It doesn't. I'm no different."

"It does make me wonder how your parents put up with you. I mean shouldn't you be wearing a shirt and tie or something. Maybe even some slacks." She started to giggle. He'd look totally ridiculous in clothing like that.

"You're being an ass," he said.

"But it's so much fun to be so." She winked at him.

His blue eyes seemed to twinkle as he looked at her. All animosity toward his father disappeared, and she found it hard to look away. She forced herself to break the stare.

Logan took her hand as they walked inside his

home. The main hall had to be as big as her parents' place. It was huge.

"I bet Sean would have loved to throw some awesome parties," she said.

"No, I don't think so," a woman said, coming downstairs. "I don't have parties, and certainly not for kids."

"Mom, I'd like you to meet Blake. Blake, this is my mom, Renee."

"Nice to meet you," Blake said.

Renee wrapped her arms around her, giving her a hug. "You're the one that was giving my boy a hard time."

He'd told her about that?

"It wasn't really—"

"I'm kidding, sweetie. Logan told me all about you. He likes to pretend he's this rough, tough boy, but I know he has a good heart." Renee tapped his cheek, and she saw the affection between mother and son.

It made her throat feel incredibly tight. Her mother didn't even hug her anymore.

"Are you staying for dinner?" Renee asked.

"I don't know."

"I'll let you both decide. I've got to head to the supermarket, and to the drop the boxes off in town. You two good to behave?" Renee asked.

"Sure," Logan said. "We're going to get drunk, smoke a spliff."

"Logan!"

"Ah, rowdy old kids," Renee said. "Have fun."

She walked out, and Blake was in a fit of shock.

"She doesn't think we're going to do that shit. Believe me, she had me tested a lot of times, and I passed every single one of them."

"What? She made you pee in a cup?"

"Yep. Like I said, I was around sex, drugs, and alcohol. I failed the alcohol one though. Damn, that had consequences," he said.

"How?"

"She made me do community service. I had to go around the school picking gum off the bottom of tables. I was then told to pick up litter off the ground."

"Wow," she said.

"Yeah, Mom's firm but fair. It kind of pisses me off that I can't argue with her. She always knows what to say and do."

"Isn't that supposed to be a parent's prerogative?" Blake said.

"It is."

He didn't need to say the rest. Blake would never know what it was like to have parents like Renee.

"How about a tour?" he said.

"Sure."

He took her bag and placed it on a chair beside a desk with a telephone. "Stop stressing." Logan took her hand once again, and proceeded to show her around his mansion. There was a large dining room, a breakfast room, study, cinema room, kitchen, pantry, basement, and games room. Upstairs were his room with en-suite bathroom and his mother's room, then four more bedrooms with bathrooms and an attic. Outside he had a basketball court, a pool, and a garden.

"Talk about guilt," Blake said.

"You can come over at any time," he said. "Mom liked you."

"How do you know?"

"She left us both alone. That's Mom's code for, 'everything is okay, and I trust you'."

Blake laughed. "Oh, okay."

They both sat down on chaise lounges near the

pool. It was still really hot, and Blake removed her jacket, hoping a patch of sweat didn't show through.

"This is lovely," she said.

"It's a nice house. Mom always wanted more kids though. I know she wishes she could fill the extra rooms."

"If you don't mind me asking, why did you move here? West County is nowhere near the gloriousness of Vegas, surely?"

She watched him lean back, closing his eyes.

"There are a couple of reasons I don't want to go back to Vegas. My dad, for everything, is an asshole. I don't want to be around him. I can't even stand to talk to him, and believe me, he makes sure I do."

"Oh."

"Yeah, oh. The life in Vegas, it took a turn for the worse. I'm glad Mom decided to get us both out."

"You know that just causes more questions than answers. You said that there was someone like me back home. Won't you miss her, or him?"

"It doesn't matter. Shauna, she's dead."

"Shauna was the friend?"

"Yeah, I don't want to talk about this right now."

"Okay," she said. "I'm sorry I brought up something so painful." She glanced down at her hands, wondering what the hell she was supposed to do now.

"You didn't. Shauna is still fresh to me, and it's still raw."

"Logan, I'm not one of these people that need a lot of explaining too."

"Seriously? I had to stalk you to get you to be friends with me."

"Only because I was concerned about your street cred."

"My street cred is more than fine."

"You fought in Vegas, didn't you?" she asked.

"Yeah, I did."

"Were you good?"

"What do you think?"

"The way you handled Sean, I'd say you were very good."

He smiled. "I don't like Sean."

"Join the club," she said. "I think he's a total ass, and I can never understand why Izzy sleeps with him. He's a giant pig."

Logan leaned forward, sitting up. "So, bestie, I think it's time we got to know each other."

"We will. Don't rush it," she said.

"Tell me one thing you wish for more than the world. Don't lie to me either."

"If I tell you something, you've got tell me. Total honesty."

"Okay."

"I wish one day my parents would look at me, and tell me they loved me." She forced the tears to stay down. Blake wasn't going to lie to Logan. This friendship was weird, but she liked him. Besides, he put Sean in his place, which had been awesome to witness. She'd never known anyone else to do that. "You?"

"I hate my father, and I blame him for Shauna's death. I wish that could have been different."

****

"I like Blake," Renee said, leaning against his bedroom door.

"She's great, isn't she?" he said, looking toward his mom.

"Your father's been calling me. You won't return any of his calls, and he's trying to get a hold of you."

Logan tossed his phone toward his mom. "Go ahead, read it."

"I don't need to read it, Logan." She moved toward the bed, taking a seat next to him. "You're hurting."

"Nah, I'm moving on, and I figured us moving here, it would stop him trying to interfere."

"He's still your father."

Logan sat up. "I defended myself today," he said.

"Logan—"

"I didn't start it. There's this asshole at school. He threatened me because I wanted to be friends with Blake. I'm only telling you because of this whole honesty crap you wanted."

"Logan!"

"It is crap. He calls Blake ugly, Mom. In fact, there's a lot of ugliness in her life. You know her own parents have never said they love her."

"What?"

"Yeah, I'm getting to know her." He was drawn to her. Logan couldn't describe it, and even though it had been three days, she captured his attention.

"She's not Shauna."

"I know. I'm not going to stand by while some guy pummels me. I will win."

She touched his hand. "I get it. Don't go hunting for fights, Logan. That's all I ask."

"I'm not a monster."

"I didn't say you were." She kissed his cheek. "Talk to your father."

"Not yet."

She sighed. "You're going to be difficult, aren't you?"

"No. I'm not."

"You sound like a petulant child. Talk to your father when you want. Just know I want you to have a good relationship with him."

She got up and left him alone. His door remained open, and he flung himself back on the bed.

Today with Blake had gone better than expected. She had even shared some personal crap with him. Admitting that she wanted her own parents to say they loved her had been hard, even for him, to hear. His parents told him all the time that they loved him. Even his father, which pissed him off.

Logan couldn't even begin to imagine what it was like to go through life thinking you were unloved, unwanted … ugly. That was what Blake felt, that she was ugly.

Lifting his cell, he pulled up the messages icon, and typed in Blake's name.

Logan: **what u doin?**

Blake: **How did you get my number?**

Logan: **easy. I got it from ur cell when u went to the toilet. *smile emoticon***

Blake: **Fine. I'm doing fine. You?**

Logan: **Mom wants me 2 talk 2 asshole.**

Blake: **asshole?**

Logan: Dad.

Blake: **then talk to him.**

Logan: **Why?**

Blake: **He's your father. I'd give anything for my dad to want to talk to me. At least he's trying.**

Logan paused. He hadn't thought of it like that.

His father was trying to get him to talk while her own was doing everything in his power to avoid her very existence.

Logan: **sorry.**

Blake: **Don't be. Don't act like it matters either. It doesn't. I'm used to it.**

Logan: **Doesn't make it right.**

Blake: **Neither is texting without using full**

words. I don't complain about all of that either.

He laughed. She didn't understand how much he enjoyed talking to her.

Suddenly her name appeared on the screen, and he accepted her call.

"You're calling me now? Should I be worried about a stalker?"

"Not at all. I'm sure there's plenty of room in your life for one of those. I don't like texting. It takes too long. Why don't you want to talk to your father?"

"You know what I said this afternoon."

"I know. You didn't elaborate, and I figured you'd be ready to tell me the whole story."

"I'm going to pick you up," he said, changing the subject.

"This is going to turn out to be an interesting couple of days."

"You think our friendship will last a couple of days?"

"No, I think it'll take a couple of days for people to realize you weren't kidding about being my friend. Things could get tough."

"Awesome."

"Sean could make life really difficult."

"Cool, I look forward to it."

"Logan, has anyone ever told you that you were a little strange?"

"No. You see, Blake, the thing is, I don't give a shit what other people think."

"So tomorrow, we're going to do this?"

"Hell yeah."

She chuckled. "You're a loon. I've got to go. Goodnight, Logan."

"Night, BFF."

He was sure he heard her call him weird before

she hung up. After talking to her, he felt much better.
****

"Hey, sweetie, I made breakfast," Linda said.

Blake stared at her mother, who was standing in the kitchen. "Shouldn't you be at work?"

"Not this morning. I wanted to make you breakfast. It has been so long since I made it for you."

"You used to make me breakfast?"

The smile on her mother's face disappeared. "Yes, I did. You used to love the pancakes and blueberry syrup."

Blake couldn't remember her mother ever going to that kind of trouble. The food in the cupboards was mostly fast food items that made meals in minutes.

"I don't remember."

"We used to eat a large stack of pancakes, and go out to the park. You loved the swings, and I'd push you, and you'd scream at me to go higher."

"I don't remember any of that." Logan's car horn made her jump. "I've got to go."

"I can drive you to school. I thought we could catch up."

"It's fine. I know you're busy." Blake rushed out of the house, leaving the pancakes behind.
****

Linda stared at the pancakes as tears filled her eyes. Blake didn't remember the times that had been pretty damn special. It killed her to know that she'd pushed her daughter away. She had stopped showing her affection, love, and always criticized her. Locking all of her feelings away, she had hurt her baby, and now after all of these years, she was paying the price.

Her cell phone started to ring, and she picked it up. "Hello."

"Did it work?"

"No. Blake stared at me like I was an alien. She doesn't remember the breakfasts, or the parks. I bet she doesn't even remember our vacations, Mitchell. What have we done?"

Mitchell sighed. "Anna told us we couldn't rush this. So we don't rush it. It's as simple as that."

Letting out a sigh, she agreed with him. "This boy, what do you know about him?"

"He's a new kid. I've not heard anything bad, but I do keep an eye on them. Fixing my car allows me to watch her. We don't want to scare her, remember."

"I know."

Hanging up the phone, Linda walked around the house, and noticed there were very few pictures of them together as a family. She was going to change that. This had to change. The darkness inside her, she fought. The miscarriages were not her fault. It wasn't Blake's either.

She had to make amends, and win her daughter's love back. Linda wouldn't stop.

Chapter Five

It took nearly a week for people to realize that Logan had befriended Blake. For a week she went to school in his car with people staring open mouthed at them arriving together. Logan didn't help matters either. Whenever they were together, he held her hand, or placed his arm across her shoulders. On the phone, she really thought he'd been kidding about not caring what others thought.

He proved time and again, he really didn't care.

They were two completely different people, and for the most part had different classes. Logan always showed up to either escort her, or just to hang out. Sean hated him, and Izzy had yet to talk to her. She spent Friday at Logan's, enjoying his mom's stroganoff then watching movies until he dropped her home. The weekend was divided between helping out at home, and going to see Logan. He wouldn't call ahead, and she found him constantly turning up at her home.

Her parents didn't care. So far her mother hadn't seen him, and even though her father had, there was no mention of him.

By Friday the following week, Blake was at her locker when Izzy came to her.

"Okay, so spill," Izzy said.

"What do you want me to spill?" She saw Izzy's friends were standing just down the corridor. They were back to Izzy caving to her *other* friends' demands.

"For over a week now you've been arriving and leaving with Logan. He's the new kid, and we both know he's a rebel."

"So?"

"What gives?"

"Izzy, we're friends, just spit it out."

She saw her friend looked embarrassed. "They want to know why he's hanging out with you. Sean also won't shut up about it."

"You could have shared a ride with me and Logan. I offered. You picked to go with Sean, who is an asshole."

"I know. I just, this is difficult, okay?"

"You mean because you like me, but your other friends make you pick other people."

"Thank you, you get it."

"No, I don't get it. I don't agree with it. I'm friends with you, and I've never made you pick." She put her bag into her locker, and closed the door. Not once in her friendship with Izzy had she ever questioned her.

"What are you trying to say?"

"Maybe you should think about who your friends are."

"What's going on?" Logan asked, stepping up behind her. He placed his arm across her shoulders, and Blake leaned back.

There were times where she felt their friendship had become solid in a short space of time, and then it was like they had known each other forever.

"She wants to know why you're friends with me instead of them," Blake said.

"That's rude."

Izzy looked uncomfortable. "Sean's upset."

"Then tell that fucker to come to me. He wants to cause a fuss, tell him I'm more than ready to start breaking shit. Don't ever upset Blake. You're a shitty assed friend, you know that?"

"Excuse me?" Izzy said.

"Logan?"

"No, it's not okay."

Blake touched his chest, not wanting to cause a

scene. "It's fine."

He stopped, his nostrils flaring. "Fine. I'm friends with Blake because I like her. Tell your fake fuckers to get gone."

Blake closed her eyes, hating the pain she saw in Izzy's.

Seconds passed, and the corridor was suddenly empty. Leaning against her locker, she took a breath. "This is crazy."

"What is?"

"I don't really know you, and yet, we're friends like this."

"I'm a nice guy."

"This is more than being a nice guy. This is craziness."

"You going to stop being my friend?" he asked. "We've been friends over a week."

"So? Don't you think that's a little soon for me to be cutting ties with my only other friend?"

"Do you really think Izzy was your friend?"

"She was."

"Friends don't have to decide on who to hang out with. Friends don't turn their backs on each other. I never turned my back on Shauna."

He rarely mentioned her, and Blake was intrigued by the mystery girl that Logan cared about.

"It's Friday. You want to come to my place tonight?" he asked.

"Sure."

"Mom said you could sleep over if you wanted." She nodded. "Okay."

"Don't look so terrified," he said, smiling.

"I'm not."

He stared at her for several seconds. "You okay?"

"Yeah."

"If you want me to slow down, let me know. I don't want to scare you."

"It's fine, Logan. Honestly, I'm just not used to being this close with someone in such a short time. It's all new." She ran fingers through her hair and stepped away from the locker.

"I got us lunch." He slapped his backpack, and she followed him into the dinner hall. This was one of his requests that they share lunch together. They took a seat a few tables away from the popular kids.

"You know all those fights you got into," she said. "Did you lose any?"

"None. I love fighting as much as I love fucking."

"I'm underage. I don't need to hear bad language."

"When's your birthday?"

"March, why?"

"Just curious. I need to think of what to get you, and then there's Christmas as well."

"I love Christmas. West County has an amazing festival on with all the traditions of the season. Sometimes we have European markets, and stuff. It's pretty cool," she said.

"What are you doing for graduation?" he asked.

"Not a lot. I'm currently looking for a job. I'm hoping by the time graduation comes, I have a job, and I'll save to find my own place. I don't want to be stuck with my folks."

"That I can relate to."

"The diner is always hiring, and then there's this music shop in town, oh, and the video store, but I have to be eighteen to be there, which sucks," she said.

"What about the mall?" he asked.

"There's several jobs there, I just, I guess I'm scared. People shop at the mall."

Logan laughed. "Everyone goes to the mall. If you want, I can study at the mall wherever you get work. How's that sound?"

"You'd do that?"

"I'm not doing anything else with my time, and why not? It'll be fun. I get to watch you attempt to be controlled by the man."

"One day, you're going to have to get a job. You know that?"

"Until then, I can work off my dad's hard earned guilt."

"You still not talking to him?"

"Nope. I have no reason to."

Blake didn't even try to convince him. What was the point? Logan did everything he could to avoid his father, even changing his cell number.

"Your mom still wants you to talk to him," she said.

"I know. Mom wants me to have a perfect relationship with my father. I just, I can't."

This all went back to the mystery Shauna. Blake didn't pry. There was no point. If he wanted to tell her more, he would. Sometimes she wished she knew this girl. Whoever she was, she'd left her mark on Logan, and helped to turn him into the man he was.

"When are you looking for work?" he asked.

"I've already started. I grabbed the local paper, and there's a jobs section."

Logan handed her a fork, and opened a large tub of spicy pasta salad. It was one of his mom's creations, and she'd just fallen in love with it. She kept trying to make it at home. Her mother decided she hated it. Her mother never failed in her quest to make her feel like crap.

Blake glanced past Logan's shoulder and saw

several of Sean's friends glaring at him. "You're getting glared at again."

"Comes with the territory of being hot. These jobs, any of them decent?"

"Not really. It's for high school kids to make their first way into the world. Most of them start at five and finish by eight. Three hours' work a day."

"You're not going to college either?"

"Nope. I asked my parents about support, and they refused. Said I couldn't go unless I got a full scholarship." Blake shrugged.

"I officially hate your parents."

"Which is why you're never going to meet them for dinner." She took another bite of the pasta, and rolled her eyes, moaning. "Seriously, your mom is amazing. She could be on television or something."

Logan nodded. "If you want I can drop you off at work, stick around, study, and take you home."

"Why are you being the good guy? I've heard your mom. You were a complete pain throughout high school."

"I made an agreement to come here. My mom was more than happy for me to stay with my father through school, and go to her on the weekends. She didn't think she could handle my rebellious attitude. I told her I wanted to go with her, period. After a lot of glaring, she told me I had to get good grades, stay out of trouble, no fighting, and try to make something of myself. If I agreed to all of those terms, I could go."

"Your mother is very loving. I couldn't imagine her doing that."

"I got into a fight every single day, landing guys in the hospital. Believe me, I deserved the warning, and the ultimatum."

She tapped her fork on her lip, staring at him. "Is

that why you've become friends with me? I'm a sure deal in being nice."

"You think you're a sure deal? I had to convince you to be my friend. I think if it wasn't for me nearly breaking dick's arm, you wouldn't be."

She opened her mouth in a gasp. "Totally wrong. I'd have actually kissed you for doing that, but I think friends is as good as it gets."

"I'd take a kiss any day."

Blake chuckled. "Sure you would." She patted his arm, and went back to eating her pasta, not wanting to think about how his words made her heart race and her body come alive.

Not going to fall for you.

****

"I heard your dad is coming here for Christmas," Blake said, moving to stand beside his table.

Logan looked up at her. She was dressed in an ugly ass serving uniform that only Bill's Burgers would make her wear. The burgers were great, but he didn't like her working here. Blake wouldn't listen even though he offered to pay twice the going rate for her to clean his room. He thought it was a brilliant offer. She didn't. So five days a week, he brought her to the mall, where she stood, serving burgers, wiping down tables, as he waited to take her home.

To top it all off, Christmas was now a month away, and his dad was already making arrangements to come here. Their relationship hadn't progressed in ways his father would have liked. Logan kept changing his number, and his father kept on finding out what it was. Drove him crazy.

"He is."

"You're really not happy about that?"

"Nope."

"He loves you, Logan."

He took hold of her hand, locking their fingers together. They had been friends for nearly four months now, and he felt closer to her than ever before. She trusted him with so much. He'd not gone to dinner at her family's place yet, and had yet to meet her mother. She spent more time with him at his mother's place now. Logan did wonder if her parents would call to find out if she was okay, but nothing.

Blake tried to pretend she didn't care. He knew the truth. Her parents lack of caring hurt her. The thing was, he saw their concern for her, and the troubled looks they gave each other. Something was happening there, but still, he didn't know what. Blake preferred not to talk about her parents.

"So."

"Will I get to meet him?" she asked.

"Yep. I'm not stopping our dates just because he wants to pretend to be a father."

"What if it's not pretend?"

Logan shrugged. "Either way, I'll play by Mom's rules."

She gave his fingers a gentle squeeze, and made her way back to the counter. Releasing a sigh, he glanced down at his biology work. Writing notes, he flicked through the pages, doing some of the tests at the end of the chapter. He wasn't a stupid kid, but with Blake not going to college, he wasn't interested. His mom wanted him to go, as did his father. Glancing toward the counter, he watched as she served burger after burger to the long line. A lot of people took their burger to eat out, and didn't take the time to sit and eat.

Logan tensed up as he watched Sean and his little gang enter Bill's Burgers.

There was no change in Blake as she finished

filling in another person's order. He was too far away to hear, and he watched as Blake started to deal with Sean's order. She tilted her head to the side, showing no signs that she was upset or angry.

Tapping his pen on the side of the book, he watched, unable to look away. Each second that passed, Blake continued to show no sign that she was upset. All he needed was one clue, one clue from her, and he'd take matters into his own hands.

The group left Blake, and she smiled over at him, the message clear in her eyes for him to read.

"Please don't do anything stupid."

In the last four months since Sean's little ultimatum, nothing had happened. No one tried to step in his way, or Blake's.

There were some of the cheerleaders who tried to get his attention, but he wasn't interested.

"You're stalking her now?" Sean asked.

Logan ignored him, and went back to studying.

"Maybe he's fucking her," Brian said.

"I tell you, the ugly may know how to suck a dick. None of us has tried it."

The pen Logan held within his grip snapped, some of the plastic cutting him as he dropped it. Getting to his feet, he stepped up close to their table. "What the fuck you saying?" he asked.

"Just wondering if Blake's pussy is good. Something must be keeping you near her," Sean said.

For months he'd ignored the snide comments, the jibes, and the taunts that they threw Blake's way. Logan could take them, and he'd ignored it because Blake asked him to.

Months of doing nothing had finally come to a head. He wasn't going to take any more.

Grabbing the back of Sean's head, he slammed it

on the table.

"Logan!" Blake shouted his name, but he didn't turn toward her. Paul shot out of his chair, coming toward him.

Slamming his fist into David's face, Logan kicked Paul, then took on Ben and Brian. Sean got to his feet, landing a blow to Logan's stomach. He was a little surprised. Sean seemed like a wimp, but he was showing that he could hold his own.

He bent down, grabbed Sean's dick, and twisted it. Sean went down, spewing up as he did. None of the guys were stepping down, and kept on attacking him.

The fight escalated until Logan was grabbed from behind, and cuffs strapped around his wrists.

Blake was crying, and seeing the tears cascading down her cheeks gutted him. He fucking loved her, and it was more than the love of a friend. She was in his heart, and he didn't ever want to get rid of her.

"Call my mom," he said.

"She's going to be pissed."

"I know."

"She'll call him."

"I know."

She followed him outside, wearing that ridiculous uniform. He saw a couple of ambulances, and knew he was going to be fucked for this. His mother may even send him back to Vegas with his father.

He was fucked either way.

"They were saying shit about you," Logan said.

"I know. I heard what they said. You should have ignored them." Blake rushed beside him, trying to talk with him as the officer escorted him into the back of the car.

"Everything will be okay," he said.

"Try not to start another fight," Blake said.

Before he could respond, he was shoved into the police car, the cuffs digging into his wrists. Leaning back, he took several deep breaths. His mother was going to be so pissed.

****

"You have no right to keep my son. He was defending a young woman, his friend. I have already spoken to the judge, and from what I believe the families of the injured party will not be pressing charges. Those boys surrounded my son, and last time I checked six against one is not a fair fight," John Black said.

Logan heard his father and closed his eyes.

If John Black was here, it meant the moment Blake told his mother, a call had been put through to his father.

"With all due respect, Mr. Black, it was five boys."

"Let's hope they learned their lesson, and don't try to hurt an unsuspecting innocent. It was still five boys against one."

Within the hour, he was leaving the station with his father right beside him. He was near the doors when John stopped him. "You're not going to say thank you?"

"Do I have to? It's your job."

"I'm your father."

"So? I didn't ask you to come down here."

He slammed open the doors, and saw his mother step away from the car. "What did I tell you?" Renee said.

Blake leaned against the car. She wore his jacket with the hood placed over her head. It was fucking cold.

He was only interested in her.

"No, no, young man. We had a deal." Renee tapped him on the chest.

"Yes, we had a deal."

"What the hell happened?" Renee asked. "Five boys? What the hell could five boys have done to you?"

"They spoke shit about Blake."

"What kind of shit?"

"They figured Blake had a golden pussy because I was friends with her," Logan said, moving toward Blake. He placed his arm across her shoulders, pulling her against him. "You telling me I should have let that happen?"

Renee groaned.

"It's why the boys are not pressing charges," John said. "Thank you, Blake, for putting your own statement in to that effect."

"Do you need me to do anything else? I don't want Logan to get in trouble," she said.

"Not right now. I have a deal with the boys' parents. Nothing should have to be done," John said. "Just a big misunderstanding."

"Yeah, everything is a huge misunderstanding, right, Dad?"

"Logan—"

"Mom, can I take Blake home?" Logan asked, cutting his father off. The last thing he wanted to listen to was the man he had little to no respect for.

"Your father is going to stay with us," Renee said.

"Cool, he can drive you home." He held his hand out for his mother's keys.

She released a sigh. "We are so talking when you get home."

He knew they were going to talk.

****

"She's not answering her phone, Mitchell!" Linda kept dialing the number, but it just kept saying that the number wasn't available. Did she have the right number?

This hurt her. She couldn't even believe that she

may not have her little girl's number.

"We'll find her, Linda. She's going to be grounded. I don't care what Anna says. We caused this, and we have to make amends with Blake. She's going away to college next year, and we won't have a chance."

"She hasn't even applied." Linda wiped away the tears. "Not even to try for a scholarship."

"Why? She didn't come to us to ask."

"But why would she come to us? She probably thinks we wouldn't support her. Look what we've done? We've been the worst parents."

"We didn't beat her, or hurt her."

"But we neglected her! When was the last time you cuddled her? When was the last time we sat down with her, and talked? We haven't done it! We're the bad guys, Mitchell. Us."

Linda's cell phone started to ring, and she answered it. "Thank God. Thank you. She's home."

Mitchell spun the car around, and headed home.

Chapter Six

"Did you need to talk to your mom like that?" Blake asked.

She locked her fingers together in her lap and glanced over at the guy who hours ago had gone mental. Logan had completely lost it, not that she blamed him. The stuff Sean and his friends had been saying was awful, horrible really.

"I'll apologize when I get home. You know it's a little after eleven."

"We called your father at five-thirty, he was here by nine. I'd say that was really fast," she said.

"The company he works for owns a plane. It was how he got here so fast."

"Your mom called, and he came running. That's got to mean something."

"Yeah."

"Don't take that for granted, Logan. I mean it."

"Seriously, you're going to give me that talk right now, how I should allow my parents to decide my future and shit."

"I'm sitting in a car with you, and it's past eleven at night. I've been at the police station for the last few hours, and I haven't gotten a single phone call from my parents. Your parents care, Logan. I could probably run away, and they wouldn't for a second care that I was missing, if they'd even notice. They don't care. You have people that care about you. I don't." She stopped, and looked away. "You don't know how lucky you are. I mean really lucky."

"I care about you, Blake. I'd know if you left, or if you ran away."

She wiped away the tears that had started to fall. "You're the only one."

He took hold of her hand. "I'm sorry. I shouldn't have said that shit to you."

"It's fine." She tried to pull her hand away, but he was determined to hold onto her. "This is silly."

"Let me hold your hand. I've been in a horrible prison cell, babe. I could have gotten raped. I'm a pretty boy."

"Please, this is West County. If anything you shared a cell with a drunk. Sean and his crew were sent to the hospital. You knocked them up pretty bad."

"Good. They had what was coming to them."

"I'm not going to deny that." She'd never known so much embarrassment. The things they had said had completely fucking sucked.

"You met my dad?"

"Yeah, he wanted to get everything into perspective first before he got involved. He asked for my perspective on what happened. I told him. I'd already given a statement." She shrugged. "I'm pleased nothing bad is going to happen."

"My dad knows how to win."

"Renee was nervous about him coming to get you. She asked if he could send one of his partners or something. You really don't like your dad?"

"It's complicated."

"Is this over Shauna again?"

He sighed. "I'll tell you about her soon, just not right now."

"Your knuckles look a mess because of your fight."

"They washed away the dried blood at the station. It's not bad. I didn't complain about them. The last thing I wanted was some cop touching me." There were specks of blood when they had reopened with dried blood over his knuckles.

He glanced down at the dried blood, and sighed. "I'll treat them properly when I get home." Logan pulled up outside her home. The doors were all dark, and she saw her dad's car was out of the driveway.

"They must have gone out. Would you like to come in, and I'll treat your cuts?" she asked.

"Sure."

"Are you just looking for a reason to put off going to see your dad?"

"Maybe. I've never been inside your house."

"Come on then, I'll show you how small my place is." She climbed out the car, and made her way toward her home. Logan stood right behind her.

"Where would your parents have gone?"

"Date night, maybe? I don't know. I don't get why they stay together, but they do. Parents are really strange." She opened the door, flicking on the light. "That's them when they were happy." She nodded toward a wedding photo. There was a single picture of her as a baby beside them.

"They look happy."

"Yes. They had a future together. Since you've come into my life I've not paid much attention to them." She nodded toward each room. "Sitting room, dining room, study, and kitchen. This is our home. Upstairs there's my room, my parents' room, and a bathroom. The first aid kit is up there. Are you comfortable me treating you upstairs or would you prefer down here?" she asked.

"Why wouldn't I be comfortable?" he asked. "You intend to take advantage of an injured soul?"

She chuckled. "Your injuries are all your own fault. Follow me."

Taking him upstairs, she opened the bathroom door, and became aware of how small the room was. Dropping the toilet seat down, she told him to take a seat.

Removing her jacket, she threw it in the laundry basket, and grabbed the medical kit.

"Are you allergic to anything?" she asked.

"I don't know, Doc."

"You can pretend to be all macho you want." She opened up the first aid kit and took out some sterile wipes. "I really wish you hadn't done anything to them."

"They were talking shit about you. I wasn't going to stand by and let that happen."

"Your parents talk about you going back to Vegas. What happens then?"

"What did they say while I was inside?" he asked.

"Renee was scared. She said that it was like being back in Vegas. You're going to have to talk to her. She doesn't think you're adapting to small town life."

"Did you tell her what those assholes were saying?"

"Yeah. She seemed to calm down then. You weren't just fighting for the sake of it."

"I never fight just to fight."

"Really? You've told me yourself that you enjoy it. You even used to go looking for it."

"Not anymore."

She dabbed at his open wounds on his knuckles. "You don't miss it?"

"No. I happen to like spending time with a friend. I know, crazy right? I enjoy hanging out, studying, watching movies, goofing off."

"Life is not going to always be about that. We're both going to have to make changes soon," she said.

"Why?"

"We're graduating, and even if we want things to stay the same, that's not always going to happen. What will you do with the rest of your life, Logan? You're not the kind of guy to live off your father's guilt. I see how much you hate it even now."

"Maybe I'll become a cook."

"I can see that," she said, smiling. "If you follow Renee you'll be one hell of a cook. However, there is a problem with your future plan."

"What is it?"

"I've never seen you cook. Can you even cook?" She tried to hold in her giggle as he frowned.

"No."

"You're going to have to start practicing."

"Can you cook?" he asked.

"You know I can. I help Renee cook when you're doing your sweaty workout, and leaving me feeling like a whale."

"You're not a whale."

He released a hiss as she pressed one of the wipes against his knuckles.

"It's fine. I can cook. You really need to start thinking of your future."

"I don't want a future without you."

"You could go to college."

"So could you."

"Your parents could help fund you. Look around you, Logan, I can't go." She tore open another wipe after tossing the dirty one into the trash. "I accepted my life. Please, don't lose the chance of a lifetime."

He reached out, capturing a lock of her hair. She continued to work on his hands, used to him touching her. Logan rather liked details. The nights she stayed over at the Black household, he would get her to sit between his legs as he combed her hair. It wasn't so strange, she didn't think. Just another element of who Logan was.

"Were you scared?" he asked.

"With you fighting?" He nodded. "At first I was. Five guys to one, those are not good odds. Then I realized you could be in danger because, you know, you were kicking their asses."

"They started it."

"You finished it."

He winked at her. "Got it."

"Are you going to go through life constantly starting and ending fights?"

"If that's what I have to do."

She finished cleaning up his cuts and stepped back. He got to his feet, capturing her hips. She stared up at him, seeing the intense look on his face. "What?" she asked.

"No one will ever say shit like that to you again," he said.

"Logan, it's not your job to make people treat me right," she said.

"I know. I just enjoy it."

She pressed a hand to his chest. "What am I going to do with you?"

He leaned down, and pressed the lightest kiss to her lips. "Keep me."

****

Logan stared up at his home. His father's car already in the driveway, and the house aglow, letting him know there was no way he was going to get away with this shit. He'd left Blake's house, not wanting to. She was alone in that place. Her parents still hadn't called even after all this time. He didn't like it.

Cutting off the ignition, he made his way inside.

He didn't hear shouting so that was a bonus. Going toward the kitchen, he leaned against the doorframe, seeing his mom and dad talking.

"Did Blake make it back okay?" Renee asked.

"Of course. I took her home. Her parents weren't there."

"It is true what you say about them? They really don't care?"

"She was outside a police station, and not once did they text or call her. When I got home, there weren't even there," Logan said, taking a seat. Seconds later his mom passed him over a hot chocolate.

"What are you talking about?" his father asked.

"Blake. The girl you saw today. Family is awful to her."

"Has social services gotten involved?" John asked.

"Why? They don't mistreat her."

"Neglect is a form of mistreating her."

"She doesn't have any bruises, and she's not malnourished. All social services would do is cause some problems."

"If she's being neglected they'd take her in," John said.

"Put her in a home that's thousands of miles away. No thanks. She's eighteen in March. For the last eighteen years she has coped, and now she has me," Logan said.

"She believes herself to be ugly," Renee said.

"Mom?"

"What? If we can help—"

"Do you really think a home would be good for her? Unless you're willing to take her in. She spends most of her time here anyway, and no one actually cares," Logan said. "May as well leave it like it is."

"I can help," John said.

"No! You only help when you want to. I don't need your help, and neither does Blake."

"Logan," Renee said. "Your father and I have been talking, and we—"

"I'm not going back with him."

"You put three boys in the hospital."

"Not in a coma."

"You have two choices, Logan," his father said, speaking over all of them. "Either you come to Vegas with me, or I move here."

"John?" Renee said.

"He's our boy, and I can do my work from here. It's a nice home."

"You're divorced."

"Your mother and I can live through our differences."

Logan shook his head. "One fight. They were talking shit about Blake, Mom."

"I know. You've got to go back to school with these people, Logan. I'm only doing what is best for you."

"You think living with *him* is what is best for me? Are you out of your fucking mind?"

"Language!" Renee said.

"No, this is horseshit. I'm not putting up with this crap."

Still holding his mother's keys, he rushed out of the house. The last person he needed to see right now was his father. Climbing back into his mother's car, he headed toward Blake's house. He didn't keep an eye on the speed limit or care where the road took him. His only focus was on the girl who helped to calm him.

When he got to her place, he saw that her parents were back home. Instead of knocking on the door, he moved around the side of her house, climbing up the gazebo at the side of her house. Her bedroom window was partially open, and he slid it open.

"Blake, it's me," he said, finding her standing there with a baseball bat in hand. It was a good job he let her know it was him otherwise she'd have taken his head off.

"What the hell are you doing? I could have hurt you," she said, putting the bat beside the wall.

"I know. I just." He rubbed at his eyes. "I need to see you."

"Okay, fine."

He saw she'd changed into a pair of pajama shorts and a tank top. Her nightclothes.

"Here, let me take your jacket," she said, placing it against her chair. "Mom and Dad are back, so you have to be a little quiet."

"Did they say anything?" he asked.

She frowned. "They seemed a little different. Mom was a little freaked out. Said they went looking for me over town when they got a call from the neighbor to say I'd arrived home. She even came to see me, telling me next time I was to call her. It was weird." Blake sat down on the edge of her bed. "What happened?"

"Dad happened."

"He wants you to go back with him."

"I either go with him, or he comes here." He started to pace, and her bedroom was so small that it didn't take him long to grow bored. Taking the seat beside her on the bed, he stared at her. "I don't want him here."

"Going back to Vegas, that's going to your old life, right?"

"Yes."

"Maybe it's for the best. You had friends there."

"None of them are like you, and I didn't have friends, not really."

She pushed some hair out of her face, and he saw how beautiful she was, even wearing the glasses that hid her brown eyes from him at times. He'd convinced her to try contacts, which she wore now more than ever.

"You're confusing me, Logan. What do you want?"

"I want to stay with you."

"I'm not going anywhere. If you want to stay with me then your father is going to have to live here."

"You ever thought about running away?"

Blake tilted her head, staring at him. "Running away?"

"You know, packing your bags, and leaving."

"Yeah, all the time. It would be so much easier to just leave. You're thinking of running away?"

"Why not? We only need each other."

"Logan, be serious."

"I am being serious." The more he thought about it, the easier he truly believed life would be.

Blake paused. "Neither of us have any money. I have four months' worth of savings, that's not a lot."

"I have money. My parents set it up when I was born. I've got plenty for the two of us."

She stared at him. "What will we do?"

"Go, find a place to live our lives away from all of this."

"What if we do something wrong? I'm not eighteen yet, and you are."

"I'll say I kidnapped you."

"Logan, this is serious. You really want to do this?"

"Why not? It's just you and me, and us. What more could there be?"

Her gaze stayed on him. "I've never pushed about Shauna. You're asking me to run away with you. That's serious. Who was Shauna? Why are you willing to run away rather than speak with your dad?"

Logan stared at her. "Shauna was my best friend. From the time we were kids to when she died."

"You blame your father for her death."

"I asked him repeatedly to do something about the bullies. They had gone from calling her names, to hurting her. We didn't always have the same classes, so there was only so much I could do." The memory of finding her in the field outside his school would stay with him forever. "I lied."

"What?"

"I was into sports at my old school. I was like Sean, apart from the fact I had Shauna as my best friend. During practice, I stayed extra to do laps, to make sure I could do the drills. The guys that bullied her, dragged her to the fields and raped her."

"Oh my God."

"I asked my father to stop it. To get them to learn a lesson. He could do it, but he was too busy fucking girls younger than my mother to help me. She was in hospital for a month, and I knew she was different. The first night she got home, she slit her wrists in the tub. She left me a letter telling me that she loved me, and she hoped that I'd one day find a friend good enough."

Tears spilled down Blake's cheeks.

"I blame my father because he should have listened to me. He didn't. Shauna got hurt, and she killed herself, and I don't blame her. I blame him."

Chapter Seven

Blake packed as much of her stuff as she could in her bag, leaving her school books on the bed. Logan had left an hour ago, and they were leaving as soon as he came to pick her up. She would run with him, even though she was terrified. There was nothing for her here.

"You can do this."

She licked her parched lips, and stuffed her bag full of clothes. Next stop would be the kitchen. Glancing across at the clock, she saw it was six-thirty. Her parents were usually gone by now.

Her cell phone beeped.

Logan: **on way.**

Blake: **I'm ready.**

Leaving her bedroom, she made her way downstairs, toward the kitchen, and froze. Her mother and father were sitting at the table. Both of them were wearing robes, and they each had a smile on their face. Why weren't they at work?

"Blake, sweetie, come in. I'm making breakfast."

"What are you doing home?" she asked. This had to be the first time that both of her parents were home when she was up for school. Placing her bag beside the door, she entered the kitchen, and took a seat in the only chair left. This was the space where she ate all of her dinners.

"I know I'm usually gone, but things are going to change around here. I'm taking different hours at work, and so is your father."

He turned toward her with a smile. "Morning, Blakey."

She could only stare. "What?"

"We, erm, we had an intervention of sorts, and we know how awful we've treated you."

"An intervention?"

"Yes. We want to change what we've done, and we want to make a fresh start," her mother said. "We've been trying to show you we've changed for a few months now."

"I've done nothing but push you away, and the truth is, we shouldn't have done."

This was just too much.

"So an intervention, and you want to be better parents? Just like that?" Blake asked. She was on the verge of running away with the only person who cared about her, and now her parents wanted to throw out that little nugget of information that they wanted to care.

"It wasn't always like this. There were times we were happy—"

"Bullshit."

"It's true," Mitchell said.

"I don't believe it. I don't remember it."

"Just because you don't remember it, doesn't mean it didn't happen," he said.

"We are sorry…"

Blake didn't look at them or even hear them. On the one hand, this was everything she wanted, but now, she didn't want it. Logan was coming to get her. He would be there within minutes, and she wanted to be with him. They were friends, and they relied on each other. In the recess of her mind, she *did* have a few good memories. Her mother telling her the other month about the whole pancakes had made her remember. She just refused to believe it.

"For seventeen years I've had to live with what an ugly disappointment I've been," she said, lifting her head. "I'm not the beloved son you wanted, or the beautiful girl you wanted. I'm ugly."

"Blake," her mother said.

"No, I don't want to hear it. *Now* you want to be my parents. You're not good parents. You'll never be good parents. I don't want to hear this."

"Blake, we're sorry," her father said.

She climbed off her chair. "I'm sorry, too." Lifting her bag onto her shoulder, she made her way toward the front door, then paused, heading back. "You know a few months ago a friend of mine, the only friend I actually have, asked me what I wanted more than anything in the world. Out of everything, all I wanted was for my parents to say they loved me. What kind of parents let their children believe they are ugly and unlovable?"

Blake didn't give them a chance to respond. She left the room, and her home, not looking back. Logan was already parked outside, and she rushed toward him. Opening the door, she climbed inside, throwing her bag into the backseat. "Let's go. I want to get out of here."

"What's wrong?"

"I just want to leave right now. Not to look back."

"Is everything okay?"

"It will be if you keep on driving."

She strapped herself in, and took several deep calming breaths. Counting to ten over and over inside her head, she finally found herself calming down. "Did your parents stop you?"

"No. I climbed into my window, grabbed my stuff, and climbed out. You?"

"My parents wanted to have a chat. They had an intervention of sorts, where they wanted to be better parents, loving."

"Isn't that what you wanted?"

"It was—I just, I need to get away. Life hasn't exactly been fun for either of us, has it?" she said.

"No." He grabbed her hand, locking their fingers

together. "We're in this together."

"Yes."

"You do know we may not get far," he said.

"I don't know. We're on the verge of leaving town. I'd say we were doing well." She took a deep breath. Yes, she was scared to be running, but right now, running seemed to be her only option.

"We need to get a head start. There's some snacks in the back, and I stopped off at a drive through on the way over to you. We've got some breakfast burritos if you want to grab one."

She leaned into the back, grabbing two snacks, and opening one to hand over. "Here you go."

Logan took it, taking a large bite.

They ate their food in silence, and Blake stared out of her window. With each passing minute, she started to calm down. Neither of them was stupid, and yet they were doing an entirely stupid thing.

"What are we going to do about an apartment?" she said. "I don't want to stay in hotels, and I also don't want to be living on the streets. We didn't think this through."

"When we get to the city, I'm going to make a large cash withdrawal. We'll have enough for rent and food. When we're ready to move on, I'll do the same."

"Can't your parents freeze your accounts?" she asked.

"Not really. Besides, we can work day to day. I'm eighteen. They can't touch me, and I was graduating this year anyway." He squeezed her hand. "We can do this."

"I believe you, I do."

"I know about all the crap from runaway kids. We can make this work. I'm sure not all kids end up on the street. Besides, we're pretty much adults anyway."

Blake nodded.

This is the craziest thing I've ever done.
"We'll have to start in a hotel though."
"I've got some cash on me."
"I'll have some cash. What I'm thinking is we keep on riding until we're far enough away from West County. We don't cross any borders that require identification, and we stay in a hotel, a cheap one. We find what we're looking for, and then we get an apartment."
"You have it all figured out?"
"Not really, but I have a plan. We can do this."
She was just a small town girl, and she didn't have a clue what she was doing. Resting her head on her hand, she stared outside, wondering what her parents were thinking. It felt good to finally tell them off, even though she shouldn't have to do any such thing.
"Thank you for coming with me," he said.
"It's what friends are for."
Their hands were locked together. They were bound together now. There was no turning back, at least to her there wasn't. This was their future together, regardless of what happened next.

****

John Black: **Where are you, son? School phoned, you didn't go.**
Renee Black: **Logan, please, tell me where you are?**
John Black: **Your mother is really worried now, and I don't like to see her this way. This is unfair, get your ass home.**
Renee Black: **You ran, didn't you?**
Logan glanced through several of the text messages that had come through in the last ten hours. It was late at night, and they were sharing one bed in a room. It had been the cheapest option. They were

intending to save a lot of money to get through the next couple of weeks, and months.

Blake came out of the bathroom. Her hair was wet, which she dried with a towel. She wore a long nightshirt and shorts.

"You called them?"

"No. I'm just reading what they had to say."

"Begging for you to come back?" she asked, sitting on the bed.

"Yep. I don't think they realize we've gone yet. Apart from Mom, she suspects. Check your phone."

She grabbed her cell from the table, handing it to him. He read them out.

Izzy: **u weren't in skool. Y?**

Mom: **I'm really sorry about what happened. Your father and I want to talk.**

Dad: **We're really sorry, honey. Please.**

"Is that it?" she asked.

"There's a couple more. Want me to read them out?"

"No."

"Izzy wanted to know what happened with Sean. He's bitching, apparently."

"It's always about the gossip with her," Blake said.

"You still okay?" he asked.

He watched as she grabbed a hairbrush and started to run it through her long hair.

"Yeah, I'm fine. Not got much reason not to be."

Logan watched her brush her hair, and reached out, taking the brush. "Let me."

"You have a thing for brushing hair."

"I know what I'm doing, and you're attacking yours."

She blew a raspberry. "Tell me about Shauna.

What was she like?"

"She was a really sweet person. The kind that would never do harm to anyone else."

"Were you together?"

"Together?"

"Boyfriend, girlfriend, that kind of thing."

"No. We were just friends." He ran his fingers through her hair. It was wet now, and soon it would be dry, silky. "We were close."

"Would she have run away with you?"

"No. Shauna wouldn't have taken that risk."

"I guess I'm not as good a friend as Shauna."

"You don't need to compare. You're both different."

"Why did you say we were alike?" she asked, glancing back.

"You both wanted to see the good in each other. The world around you is ugly, and you had grown to accept that your parents were who they were. Shauna's parents were always pushing her to be something else. They never listened to what she wanted to be, or do. It was always about what they wanted. Your parents are different, but you both struggled with it."

"I don't think it's up to us to make people love us."

Logan sighed. "You think you're ugly, that people don't like you because of it. The truth is, the world is ugly around you, and you're the bright spark that shines for those who are willing to see. You're not ugly, Blake. You're beautiful."

She didn't say anything for the longest time, and he finished brushing her hair.

"I think you're the nicest person I've ever met," she said.

He leaned forward, kissing her cheek. "I'll take a

shower."

Logan left the room, entering the tiny bathroom, which only had a shower. Removing his clothes, he climbed in the stall, and turned the shower on. The icy water hit his skin in a blast, making him hiss.

"Are you okay?" she asked.

"Yeah, I'm fine." He needed the cold water to clear his head. It wasn't every day that you ran away from home, and took your best friend with you. Not only was Blake his best friend, but he had feelings for her. She was his world, and right now, he wanted to give her a life that was by far better than anything she left behind.

Standing under the water, he grabbed the soap, and started to clear his head. He knew what he was doing, and he'd do whatever was necessary to make sure they were both able to deal with the next few weeks.

After his shower, he wrapped a towel around his waist, and entered the bedroom. He found Blake sat on the bed, flicking through the channels on the small television.

"Hey," she said.

"Hey." He sat down on the edge of the bed, watching the latest news about what was going on in the world.

She changed the channel. There was chaos going on in Europe, and he didn't want to watch either.

His cell phone started to ring, and Blake passed it to him. He saw his father was calling, and he wasn't interested in listening to another lecture.

Turning off his cell phone, he threw it onto the bed.

He grabbed a pair of boxer briefs out of his bag, and slid them up his body.

"Nice ass," she said.

He laughed, turning around to find her blushing.

"I could say the same to you."

She rolled her eyes. "Whatever." He sat beside her on the bed, taking the remote that she offered. "I can't find anything to watch. I don't know. I'm kind of nervous. What happens next?"

"Tomorrow we leave, and head in whatever direction we chose. Providing we don't have to pass through security, we'll be okay."

"Have you run away before?" she asked.

"No. This is my first time. You?"

"No. I've thought about it. I wondered what it would be like to be away from West County, out on my own." She leaned back against the wall. "I guess we'll both find out. It's kind of scary though. Both of us out in the world, neither of us knowing what to expect."

Logan lay down on his side, resting his head in his hand. "We can do this together."

"You're so calm, how do you get to be so calm?"

"Years of fighting, or practice. In the ring you don't have time to panic. You only have time to prepare."

"Are we prepared?"

"We're as prepared as we'll ever be."

****

"He's run away, I'm telling you, he has," Renee said, pacing up and down the long hallway. "I called the school. Neither Logan nor Blake made it there. He's gone, and he's taken her with him."

John stared at his ex-wife, once again feeling a lot of regret. "He's an intelligent boy."

"He's our son, John. He's not some statistic, or some damn boy. Our son." She pressed a finger to her chest, the passion inside her, as well as the fear clear to see. "I should never have called you."

"Who would get him out of trouble?" John asked.

"You're not the only lawyer available. He doesn't

want anything to do with you. He blames you, and I should have listened."

"Renee, you did what you thought was right. I will always come."

She shook her head. "You'll always come? That's your problem. You think with your dick, and not your damn head."

He had no argument. The mistakes he'd made were many. He had screwed over his family in pursuit of young women, promotion, and hadn't considered the damage it had done to his family.

"Is Blake answering her phone?"

"No. I'm going to have to go to her parents, and find out if they have heard from her."

"I'm coming with you."

"Don't you have to run back to Vegas? What about the flavor of the month?" Renee asked.

There was a time when utter contempt came at him. Now when she spoke, it was just a simple question. He had broken her heart more times than he could count. Over the past eighteen years he had promised to be faithful, and had broken his vow.

She had threatened divorce, and he'd laughed about it. Six months ago, he finally got the papers through his office, Renee declaring infidelity.

Even though he was screwing anyone he wanted, when he had discovered she was falling for another guy, he'd lost it.

Renee had told him clearly. She was willing to let his affairs slide, and remain with him, providing she could find love elsewhere. She no longer loved him, and wanted to find someone to share her time with. Like an asshole, he wanted Renee all for himself.

"I'm not going back to Vegas," he said.

"No?"

"No. I want to find my son with you."

"Fine, let's go."

He took the passenger seat as Renee climbed into her car. "Do you like the house?" he asked.

"Yes. Logan liked it as well."

"Good, I'm glad."

"What is going on, John?" She pulled out of the driveway and headed toward town.

"Nothing. I want to start over."

"No offense, but our son is out in the world on his own, and my focus is him right now."

"Logan knows what he's doing."

"Yeah, well running away is not showing what he's doing. Not only that, he's taken a minor with him. Blake is seventeen."

John cursed. That wasn't good.

"She went willingly with him."

"I don't want anything to happen to Logan. Yes, he has his own money, and he's eighteen, but he has yet to graduate. This is, it's a nightmare."

She parked out front of a small house. Two cars were in the driveway, and the lights were all on.

"This is Blake's house?"

"Yes."

"I made a mistake with Shauna," he said.

"What?"

"Logan blames me for her death, I know he does."

"Shauna is not your fault. Was there anything you could have done? Really done?" Renee asked.

"I don't know. Yes, no, maybe. There are days I can't help but wonder if her death is on my hands. Logan told me, and I just kept telling him to go to school officials. I called her parents, and they weren't concerned. I went over the reports of her death, and I remember Logan pleading with me to take the time to handle it. I never did. School bullies were not the only problem. I regret not doing more, and I regret everything that has happened to us."

"John, what happened to Shauna wasn't your fault. You can blame yourself if you really want to, but it's not right. With regards to us, this is not the time or the place for this conversation. Come on, let's go."

****

Three days later, Blake watched as Logan typed into the computer. They wanted to know what was going on in West County. Neither of them had answered their cell phones even though they had been ringing often. In the end they had to turn them off, and they only turned them on in the morning.

"Is there anything?" she said.

"I'm just looking right now."

He typed fast, and she watched as the screen loaded the town paper. Their faces were on it.

"Holy crap," she said.

"Fuck," Logan said. She quickly grabbed a chair and sat next to him. "It was revealed late Wednesday night that two students from County High have run away. Logan Black and Blake Carson, both residents of the small town, have not been seen or heard from since Tuesday. John Black, a lawyer from Vegas is pleading for his son's return. Blake's parents, Linda and Mitchell Carson, are also pleading for their daughter's safe return."

Logan took over. "No one knows the reason for the teenagers to leave without a note. It has been confirmed however that Tuesday evening, Logan got into a fight with fellow peers over Blake, subsequently leading to his arrest, and three boys in the hospital. Nothing is known other than the two are close friends, and their families are pleading for their safe return."

Blake pushed some hair off her face.

"If he can, Dad will put our faces on the news."

"Do we need to drive further away?" she asked. They had settled in a small bedroom, and paid one month's rent. She was looking for a job as a waitress, while Logan was taking on odd jobs. It was harder for her to get work because of her age.

"We've already paid one month's rent. I don't want to waste money," he said.

"What if they find us?"

"We've not done anything wrong. No one is out looking for us." He did another quick search, and typed their names into the search engine.

Several of their images came up.

"Logan, this isn't good."

"It's not bad. Every parent puts out a desperate plea for their kids." He took hold of her hand, and she looked into his blue eyes. "Do you want to head back?"

"Part of me does. I don't know."

"If you want to go back, we can go back. I'd never stop you."

She smiled. "You didn't kidnap me, Logan. I knew what I was doing." Staring at the screen she felt sad. "It's just strange for me."

"Your parents being part of the plea?"

"Yeah, and they're with your parents. It's just messed up." She shook her head. "No, I want for us both to keep on going. I've got nothing to hide, and neither have you. We've got a plan, right?"

"We have."

Locking their fingers together like they had done many times together, they were as one, and they'd get through this.

SAM CRESCENT

Chapter Eight

For the next three months, they did exactly as Logan said. They worked in jobs that didn't require too much notice. Sometimes he took nightclub jobs, while Blake did waitressing or some postal work for companies. Whenever the lease on their apartment ran out, Logan went to the bank, withdrew money, and they moved onto the next city or town. Christmas came and went. Logan made sure they both had an awesome Christmas. They exchanged a couple of gifts and covered the small apartment in trashy decorations so it looked all festive. They even cooked Christmas dinner with a faulty oven, and a stove that liked to only get warm.

All in all, it was shitty, but they had a lot of fun doing it. The apartments they lived in were mostly one bedroom, so they shared. To the outside world, they were a couple just trying to make it in the world. Neither of them had tried to take it that next step even though Logan wanted to. He was starting to wonder what Blake felt for him. She never showed anything other than friendship for him, and he was more like the girlfriend she never had. He combed her hair, and even painted her nails, with nail polish he'd gotten for her Christmas present.

Every Saturday without fail, whether it was morning or night, they went to the library to check for updates from their old town.

As the weeks had worn on, so had the updates about the missing teenagers from West County.

In the latest newspaper that they pulled up, Logan saw only a snippet. "Blake Carson and Logan Black are still missing. Parents refuse to stop looking, and will not rest until both are safely home."

"I guess we're officially old news now."

"Yep."

He turned off the internet, and they both left the library, linking arms.

"How are you feeling? It has been three months. Spring is almost here, and it's nearly your birthday."

"I expected it to be a little harder. You know how you hear all that craziness about kids running away." She shrugged.

"We're not exactly kids though really. A lot of eighteen year olds run away and don't look back. They want to move on, have a big life in the city."

Blake linked her arm through his as they made their way out of the library and into the busy city street. It was still freezing cold, and Logan held her closer as they made their way across the street.

"It's your birthday next month."

"I know." She turned to smile at him. "I'm legally allowed to be with you then. I have to say that you surprised me."

"Why?"

"I figured you'd find some way to start fighting again. You told me how it was in your life, and you loved it. I figured without that deal with your mom, it would be something you'd go back to."

"It's not something I'm interested in. I know you'd be worried about me at night, and that was the last thing I wanted you to do." He squeezed her hand tightly. "Let's head home."

"Oh, wait, I just need to grab something."

She released his hand, and headed toward the shop just across the road. It was where everything fell to shit. Logan smiled as she rushed across the road, and that smile slipped as he saw the car. He even saw the person within the vehicle wasn't looking up. The speed was too fast.

"Blake, move!"

He started to rush toward her, but it was too late.

Her ear piercing scream would stay with him forever. Rushing across the road, he moved toward her, and pulled out his cell phone.

Blake was panting, and holding her stomach. Cuts marred her flesh, and she looked at him with fear in her eyes. "You've got to call them," she said.

"I know."

She would need to go to the hospital where they would ask her name, and her details.

He put the call through to the ambulance and knelt beside her, locking their fingers together like they had done so many times before. Tears filled his eyes, but he forced them down. She didn't need him to cry right now.

"It hurts."

"I know. Fuck, I know."

She closed her eyes, and he called her name. "You can't go to sleep, not right now."

"Shit, I'm so sorry," the guy said, coming toward them.

"Stay back," Logan said. If the guy came close to him right now, he'd fucking kill him.

"Call them," she said. "Call your father first. We don't want any trouble."

"Stop worrying about what is going to happen."

She held onto his hand, and her breathing was becoming erratic. Opening his phone, he tapped on his Dad's number, and placed it to his ear.

"Logan! Renee, it's Logan."

"I'm here," he said, surprised by how fast his father answered.

"Where the fuck are you? This was so crazy. You know you can get arrested for kidnapping if Blake—"

"There has been an accident, Dad. Blake's hurt.

The ambulance is on its way, but it's bad."

"Logan, you're in serious fucking trouble."

"I'll call you when I know what hospital we're going to be at."

The ambulance arrived, and he smiled down at Blake, who was trying not to whimper. She was so damn strong, and he was so proud of her.

"I'm not going to tell them anything. We both did this." She was the minor. He wasn't.

"I know."

She held onto his hand a little tighter.

"I'm going to be with you every step of the way," he said.

"Love you, Logan," she said.

His heart started to pound, and he nodded. "I love you, too, babe."

Leaning forward he kissed her head, wishing he'd not let her cross the road or pull away.

The ambulance arrived, and there was no time for promises or wishes. He had to wait for her parents to get here.

****

Logan sat in the emergency room for several hours. He'd already called ahead to his father, and knew they would be arriving soon. Rubbing at his eyes, he watched as the nurses went about their job. Patients went when they were called to be seen. Logan was told the doctor wouldn't talk to him as he wasn't a family member.

Her family had been alerted, and now he had to wait.

He only hoped his father could help, and smooth over whatever damage had been caused. Law was not his strong point, and he didn't know if he'd get blamed, or if it would be considered kidnapping. They'd run away together.

When his mother and father entered the hospital followed by Blake's parents, he got to his feet. Linda and Mitchell Carson went straight to the reception desk, to ask about their daughter.

"I don't know if she's okay," Logan said.

"We spoke to her parents. They're … not happy."

"I don't give a shit if they're happy or not."

"Enough, Logan," Renee said. "You ran away."

"Blake came with me, okay? Those so-called parents didn't give a shit about her, so they have no right to judge me. I love her."

"Nothing happened, did it, son?" he asked.

Logan shook his head. "Nothing has happened."

"She's seventeen."

"God, Dad, you want me to spell it out! I've not fucked her."

"Logan!"

"Listen here, boy, I get that you're angry with me. You shouldn't have brought that girl into this."

"I love that girl."

"Just like you loved Shauna."

He slammed his fist against his father's face.

"Logan!"

Ignoring his mother, he glared at his father. "Don't you dare speak her name. You have no right. You're a pig, John Black. A pig in a rich man's clothes. You're not my father."

John lifted his head and wiped his cheek, which had already started to bloom with a bruise.

"You're angry at me."

"I despise you."

"This is not getting us anywhere," Renee said.

"Nothing you say is going to make this go away," Logan said. "I'm not coming back home."

"You think Blake's going to go with you? She's underage. A minor. You're lucky her parents aren't prosecuting you with kidnapping."

"They have no right to her. They have been awful to her," Logan said.

"I'm sorry about Shauna."

"What?"

"I'm sorry about her. If you need to blame me, then blame me, but it doesn't matter. Her death was not my fault."

Logan shook his head. "I don't need to hear this." He knew it was the truth. His father couldn't have done anything, but to Logan, there had to have been something. He'd told him constantly what was going on.

"Logan, I made every single mistake in the book. I lost you, I lost your mother, and I lost both of your love and respect. With Shauna, I couldn't do anything."

Glaring at his dad, Logan couldn't take it, so he stormed out of the hospital. There was nowhere for him to go. No place he wanted to be other than with Blake. She was inside the hospital, and he didn't know if she was okay.

"I love you, son. Shauna's death is not your fault either."

"Shut up! I know it's not my fault."

"Do you believe that? Or do you believe that if you hadn't been training she would still be alive?"

"She would be!"

"Shauna had a history, Logan. She had a history of depression."

"She was my best friend. I knew her."

"You didn't know everything about her. I spoke to her parents. Shauna tried to commit suicide multiple times even before the bullying. Every time she was away, she was in a clinic."

He shook his head. "No."

"Yes."

"I said fucking no."

He remembered how pale she always looked, how sad. Logan had asked, and she always said that she felt tired.

Collapsing onto the sidewalk, he drew his knees up and hugged them close to his chest.

"Blake's not Shauna," Logan said.

"I know. You'd have never dreamed of running away with Shauna." His father sat down beside him, and placed his hand across his shoulders. "We all have one life, Logan. One life to shine through or to fuck it up. The power, the money, it all went to my fucking head. With you and your mother gone, I've had a lot of time to reflect about the things in my life, and I fucked up. I fucked up with you, with your mother, with everything."

"We were making it work," Logan said. "Me and Blake. We were having fun."

"You've both got presents back home. Blake's folks had to be woken up. Before you ran away, they were trying, Logan. They had a long history of problems, miscarriages, misdiagnosis from doctors that could have caught it. Their treatment of her, they have admitted to me what they did, how they've been over the years. I warned them that if Blake spoke out, she could end up in foster care. I will do everything I can for that girl. Tell me what you want me to do."

"I can't let that happen, Dad, I love her. Foster care would kill her."

"I know, son. I know."

Logan wiped his eyes. "Crap, we're going to have to go back to school, aren't we?"

"I've got a tutor in place. You and Blake can learn together back at our place. You'll get caught up, go through your exams, and still graduate, if you're both willing."

"You haven't brought up college."

"I'm not going to push my luck."

Logan chuckled. He couldn't believe it. With everything going on around him, he actually found the energy and feeling to laugh.

****

"Where's Logan?" Blake asked.

She sat up in the hospital bed. The biggest damage was a broken leg, a concussion, and impact bruising across her abdomen. Her parents had been in her room for the past hour begging for her forgiveness, and it made her really uncomfortable to be around them. She didn't know if she liked this changed persona from either of them. They were different from the quiet, distant parents she'd come to know.

"He's outside," Linda said. "He's with his father."

"I wanted to go with him."

"Blake."

"You think you can come in here and tell me how sorry you both are. Make up stories from our past? I have lived with my friends believing I was unwanted, and no matter what you say, that is how you've treated me. For years I was the unwanted daughter, the ugly girl, the disappointment. I could come and go as I pleased because neither of you cared enough to even check on me."

"We're so sorry."

"You think seeing the error of your ways in therapy is going to make me feel better. It's not. I want to see Logan."

"It's up to us if you see Logan."

"One month is all you've got. I can be in foster care for a single month, and I will put myself there on neglect if you don't get Logan. He has a right to see me."

Her parents looked at each other, clearly hoping they could argue.

Blake was done being passive. Three months she'd been with Logan without her parents, and she saw the truth. The world they had created for her in County High had been ugly. *She* wasn't ugly at all. The world around her was ugly, and their views had been so strong that she started to believe them.

She wasn't ugly, or useless, or a waste of space. Her value was her own. She was the person in charge of her own life. It only mattered what she thought about herself.

"I want Logan."

After several seconds' hesitation, her mother left to go and get him.

"I tried to be the son you wanted. I even read books on car mechanics, and football. I wanted to be everything you've ever wanted."

"Blake?"

"You want me to forgive and forget. I can't do that. I'm not that kind of person, and I don't want to forget the last eighteen years. You can't change it."

Her father nodded. "It's the biggest mistake I made. I only hope in time you will come to believe it wasn't always like that."

"Having me?"

"What?"

"Was having me your biggest mistake?" She watched as he recoiled.

"No."

"Making you think that I didn't want you," he said.

Blake took a deep breath. "I wouldn't have come home. There was nothing for me to come home to."

"I hope in time I can change your mind. I love

you, Blake. You're my only daughter, my only child."

The door to her room opened, and she saw him.

"Logan."

He rushed toward her, wrapping his arms around her. "Is everything okay? No one told me anything." He cupped her face, staring into her eyes.

She smiled. "I'm fine. I'm hurt, but I'm a warrior."

Logan sat on the bed, and she heard her parents leave, giving them some privacy.

"I've been talking with my dad, and he believes that we can work together, and still be able to graduate."

She nodded. "What do you think? Stay and work, graduate, and then what?"

"Do you want to go to college?"

She scrunched up her nose. "I can't. I can't afford it. I think after our little traveling, I rather liked traveling. Would you like to go traveling with me?"

"I'd love it." He stroked her cheek. "I meant what I said."

"Which was?" She bit her lip, knowing what she wanted him to say.

"I love you, Blake Carson. I never thought I'd find someone like you."

She smiled, turning her head to kiss his hand. "I love you, too."

Chapter Nine

Blake and Logan became the talk of the town once again. Once the doctors were happy with her and her recovery she went with her parents back home. The only reason she didn't put up a fuss was the fact Logan was going with her. He was following close behind with his own parents, and it helped to calm her nerves.

She was on crutches, and she made her way back up to her old room, which was the same. Nothing had changed, only her parents, who were more determined now than ever to actually make life good. Izzy came by to see her. Blake made sure she was aware that their friendship hadn't been a true one, not really. She hadn't seen or heard from Sean and his group.

Logan had.

His father wanted him to apologize, but Logan refused. He wasn't sorry for hurting them, and instead wanted them to come to her with an apology. She didn't want one.

The high school was happy for them to catch up on the work they missed, and providing their assignments were completed within the month, they were able to take their exams.

Blake went every single day to Logan's house, sitting with him to study, and together they worked on their assignments. Neither of them spoke of their declaration of love either.

Logan was on a strict house rules, and he was also grounded. He wasn't allowed to take her home, and his father hadn't moved back to Vegas either.

They were not left alone. When the tutor left, his mother sat in the room, making sure neither of them had time to talk or to plan.

"Are you happy to be back?" he asked, one Friday

afternoon.

She glanced toward his mother who was reading a book. Blake wasn't fooled. Renee was listening.

"I guess."

"How have your parents been?"

"They're okay. I mean, they're trying, which is weird in itself. I never thought I'd have to cope with them trying to be my friend. How are things going with your dad?"

"We're getting along. I don't think I should ask for much all things considered."

"He does care, and he loves you."

"Just hard."

"You've got to give your father time," Renee said.

"Are you two getting back together?" Logan asked.

"No. We're not. Too much history between us. Now study. We all want you to graduate, and not be kept behind for another year." Renee tapped the table.

For the first time since they had been back, Renee left them alone to get drinks.

"The way they're acting they think we're going to run," Blake said.

"I would, with you."

She smiled.

Logan reached across the table, taking hold of her hand. "My feelings for you haven't changed."

"Mine haven't either." She squeezed his hand back. "I never thought this craziness would ever happen to us."

"It did. I don't regret it."

"Me neither."

"Shauna died in April, two years ago."

"Oh."

"She's buried in a cemetery in Vegas. I was

wondering if you'd like to come out with me."

"I'd love to."

"You'll be eighteen. I figured we could fly out, and you know, come back."

She chuckled. "Your dad may come with us. We're rebels and all."

"Not so much."

"I was thinking, for my eighteenth birthday I want to get a tattoo."

"You do?" he asked.

"Will you come with me?"

"Sure."

Blake didn't know what the future held with Logan. "Did you love Shauna? Like, be in love with her."

"No. I loved her like a friend. She was more of a sister. A sister who had a few secrets of her own. Are you thinking that I love you the same way that I loved her?"

"I don't know what to think."

"I love you differently. You're more than just a friend to me."

They had shared beds, and Blake had tried not to think too much about it. They were friends, neither of them showing that they wanted to change their relationship until the moment of the accident.

Renee came back and pointed at their work. "Come on, I expect you both to graduate this year."

There was no more time for talking. Blake finished her work, handing the assignment in to Renee, who would hold it for the tutor. At the end of the day, his father came to take her back toward her home.

Most of the time they didn't talk. Blake didn't know what to say to John, and she imagined he was the same with her.

"You've been good for Logan."

She glanced toward him, shocked that he spoke

first. "Okay."

"I don't know how to talk to you, but then I never knew how to talk to Logan. He's a force to be reckoned with. I made a mistake doubting him."

"Why are you telling me all this?"

"You've become a big part of his life. I never thought he'd run away, but he did. I appreciate you going with him."

She frowned. "I thought you were mad because we went away."

"I was mad. Of course I was mad."

"Oh, okay. I'm confused."

"Logan, he's always been a fighter. He's gotten himself into a lot of trouble with that temper of his. If you hadn't gone with him, he'd have gone to fighting, only he'd have gone for the dirty fighting. The stuff that's illegal, and I'd have ended up having to identify him in a body bag."

"You hurt him a lot because you ignored him. I understand why he's upset."

"We're working on a relationship. Your parents, they told me what happened, and I warned them that when I found you, if you wanted to split from them, I'd make it happen."

"You did?"

"Even though I was scared out of my fucking mind that something bad was going to happen, I knew if you were there with him, he'd do whatever needed to be done to protect you."

"You have that much faith in your son."

"And in you. He loves you. Logan, he's not a guy to do stuff by halves. Once he gets started, he gives all of himself."

She had already grasped that.

He pulled up outside of her parents' place, and

helped her with the crutches that had become a huge part of her life. Her leg was on the mend, and she hoped to be off the crutches and be walking without a problem.

Blake thanked him for the help, and for the ride.

Once back inside her home, she was met with the smell of chicken and garlic. Linda and Mitchell were at the table. "Hey," she said, entering the dining room.

"John let us know that you were on your way home."

So far her parents hadn't fallen back into their negligent tendencies. She eased down into her chair, which was between her mother and father. Placing the crutches on the floor, she stared at her plate.

"How was studying today?" Mitchell asked.

"Good. I completed another assignment. Renee is going to give it to the tutor."

"Do you think you'll be ready for your exams?"

"I think so."

"What are your plans for after graduation?" Linda asked.

"I want to go traveling. Being with Logan, and the three months we were away, I had a lot of fun. I'd like to see the world."

"What about work?"

"I can get odd jobs on the road. I'll figure it out as we go along."

"That's your plan?" Linda asked.

"It's not much of one, but I can do it." She finally looked up to see the concern in both of their faces. "What?" she asked.

"We've been talking, and we have been saving for your college education. You can rush in your application."

She watched as her mother left the room and came back with a pile of magazines, booklets, and stuff.

"You told me I couldn't go to college," she said.

"We've been saving for it."

Blake stared at the pile of information, and she shook her head. "I came to you when I was sixteen, when college was first mentioned. You told me not to bother. I don't get it. Why now? Why were you so damn mean to me?"

She slammed her hand down on the desk, needing answers. These people were supposed to have loved her without conditions, and right now, she wasn't feeling the love.

"Tell her, Linda. She has a right to know the truth."

"What truth?"

"After you were born, I got pregnant again. Everything was going great, and, we were all happy. I had a fall, and I lost the baby."

"A son?"

"Another baby girl."

"I wanted a son," Mitchell said. "I'm not going to lie. I wanted a son."

"And with the fall, there were complications, and I lost a baby. It wasn't the first baby I lost. For several years after you were born, I had several miscarriages, and after some time the doctor told me any chance of another baby was no longer available to me. Your father and I, we went through grief."

"Instead of consoling each other, we just went about life, pretending we were both okay."

"And now?"

"We're dealing with our own problems. We love you very much," Linda said. She stopped, and took a breath. "We were so cruel to you. Our upset ended up costing us so much. Neither of us wanted to admit our feelings, and we ended up burying them deep." Linda dropped her head in her hands and started to sob.

"I can't believe what happened. I just, it has been so horrible. We've been awful parents, and we can't take that back."

Blake sat at the table as both of her parents started to cry. Her own tears welled up, and started to pour down her cheeks.

"I'm not hungry."

She left the table, grabbing her crutches, and making her way upstairs. Blake had to get away from the drama.

Going to her cell phone, she dialed Logan's number. "Life is going crazy right now. I wonder if I'm going to wake up."

****

"Tell me about it. I don't know if I've entered another universe. My parents are getting along," Logan said, leaning back on his bed. He stared up at the ceiling, listening as Blake told him everything that had happened with her parents. He understood her nerves, and why she was a little freaked out by everything.

"They want me to consider a college application."

"What do you want to do?"

"Travel. I want to travel with you."

"I want to see you without a chaperone. What time do your parents go to bed?"

"Around eleven, why?"

"I'm going to be there straight after. I need to see you."

He got to his feet and made his way toward the window. Logan knew he'd be able to get down, and get to Blake's without using a car.

"Okay. I better go. Dad wants to talk."

He closed his cell phone, and made his way back downstairs. His stomach was protesting, and he needed food. His mother was making spaghetti and meatballs, his father's favorite. Logan didn't know what to make of his parents' sudden understanding of one another.

"I like Blake," John said.

For the next hour, he listened as his parents talked about what was going on in their lives, and he watched them both, frowning. "Are you two together?"

"No," Renee said.

"Yes." His father spoke at the same time, and Logan just stared at them.

Renee blushed. "We're not together. We're working stuff out, and we're both glad that you're back, and you're not going to disappear again."

"I wasn't being rebellious," Logan said.

"Have you apologized to those boys?" John asked.

"No, and I told you, I'm not going to. I'm not the one in the wrong. He is, and all of them were."

His father stared at him.

"He has a point," Renee said. "Blake's a lovely girl, and she shouldn't have that kind of crap thrown at her."

"Thank you," Logan said, smirking at his father. "I'll apologize to people who deserve it. Not scumbags, and Sean and his crew were scumbags."

"So, college," John said, swiftly moving onto another topic.

"I'm going traveling with Blake. It's what we both want to do."

John rubbed at his eyes. "You're just going to be difficult, aren't you?"

"Yep." He took a seat at the kitchen counter and waited for food. Renee served him up a large pile of spaghetti, topping it off with sauce and meatballs.

"So good," he said, breaking a meatball and

stuffing it in his mouth.

"Traveling isn't the key to everything."

"Neither is college. People can still make a decent living without a college education. There is a path for me."

"Logan," Renee said.

"Do you want me to be miserable? Is that why you're forcing college at me? I don't want to go. There's nothing I want to study. I wouldn't even be graduating if it was up to me."

John sighed.

"Look, I know you don't agree with what I want, but this is my life, and I want to live it my way."

"You're being unreasonable," John said.

"You broke my mom's heart. You're both divorced. Life doesn't always go how we want it, and the two of you have shown that to me, time and time again. I even walked in on you screwing one of your secretaries, who I might add, fucked me as well. Please, don't give me a lecture on what is good for me. Personally, the two of you, it's not going to work." Logan lifted his plate in his hands and headed toward the door. "I'm going to eat this in my room."

****

Renee scooped up a meatball and popped it into her mouth. She wasn't stupid when it came to John. In the early years of their marriage, she'd been naive, innocent, and easy to manipulate. That girl left the building a long time ago.

She was stronger, more in control than ever before. John, he was different, but that didn't mean she was ready to take him back.

"Are you going to say anything?"

"Nope. What do you want me to say?"

"Our son has some bad manners."

"So does his father." She looked up at the only man she had ever been in love with. There was a time her life had been perfect, beautiful, and it had soon turned ugly. "Why try to force a path that our son clearly doesn't want to take?"

"I know what is better for him."

"This coming from a man who bought me this house in an attempt to stop the divorce."

"Renee, I made a lot of mistakes, and I'm trying to rectify those problems."

She shrugged. "Sometimes you can't force something, John. I know what you're trying to do."

"Tell me what to do. I'll do whatever you need me to do."

"This isn't about me forcing you, John."

"I still love you, Renee."

"You'll always have a place in my heart. It's not the same. It'll never be the same. You can't undo everything."

He hung his head.

"We can start over, friends who have a son together. That's all I can promise." She squeezed his shoulder. "I have to say, screwing the secretary who also did our son is gross."

"You were always a free thinker, more open to change."

Renee smiled. "That's because I'm the cool mom."

"What are we going to do about him?"

"Accept his decision. Logan's a good boy. He'll make whatever choice that is best for him."

"College is best for him."

"No, college is best for you."

John sighed.

"Have a little faith in him. You should just be

happy he's talking to you. When we first moved here, your face was planted on a dart board, and he got really good at it as well." She lifted her glass of wine, taking a sip. Renee knew her son, and she knew that whatever Logan decided, she'd handle it.

****

Blake's window was open, and he climbed through it, trying not to make too much noise. She was balanced on the crutches, staring at him, and then glancing at the door.

"They've just gone to bed," she said, whispering.

"Okay."

He moved up toward her and couldn't resist. Wrapping his arms around her, he pulled her close, and finally kissed her how he'd been wanting to kiss her for months. Gripping her ass with one hand, the other he sank into her hair, and pulled her close. They both moaned, and she wrapped one arm around his neck.

Licking her lips, he waited for her to open. Plunging inside, he tasted her for the first time.

Seconds passed, maybe even minutes, and he pulled away, keeping his hands on her hips. His lips tingled from the touch.

"Wow," she said, licking them.

Seeing her tongue peek out, he wanted another taste, but held himself back.

"Does that answer your question?" he said.

"I don't know. Kiss me and we'll find out."

He dropped another kiss to her lips, messing up her hair as he did. This time, they were both panting as they broke apart.

"I just needed to see you." Logan saw standing was making her a little uncomfortable, so he eased her to the bed, taking the crutch from her. She lay down with her back against the pillows.

Climbing onto her head, he placed his hand on her hips, gripping her flesh.

"They want me to go to college," Logan said.

"You've got to do what is right for you."

"After graduation, I want us both to go. To head out on the open road even if we don't know where it takes us."

"I've already put in my passport application. My parents agreed to let me get one. We can do this. It should be here soon."

"You're coming with me," he said.

"I thought you were coming with me." She raised a brow, smirking. "Or we can both agree that we're coming together."

"Coming together, I like that."

"You've turned it to sex."

"I do like sex."

Blake looked away, her cheeks red.

"I've not been with anyone in a long time, since before I met you."

"Really?"

"I'm not a cheater, Blake. I've seen what cheating can do to a relationship, and that's not me. I'll be here, beside you, every step of the way."

She licked her lips. "Do you have a plan for what happens next?"

"No."

"Me neither."

"I know only one thing—I want to be with you."

"You're a charmer, Logan Black. You've done so much for me that I don't know how I'll ever repay you."

"What have I done?" he asked, frowning.

"You made me see my own value. Without you, I don't think I'd be sitting here now considering this kind of future. I always believed I was a disappointment. My parents, they didn't want me, and to have that kind of value, your parents need to want you. You've made me realize that I only need myself to believe that."

He kissed her head. "From the moment I saw you at the cafeteria, the way you behaved, I wanted to change your thoughts about yourself. You drove me insane, believing you didn't have a right to be Izzy's friend, that others should treat you that way. They were the ones in the wrong."

He gripped her hand, locking their fingers together.

"This is how we're going to be from now on, forever."

They squeezed their hands, knowing without a doubt they were together, and nothing could tear them apart.

Chapter Ten

Blake's eighteenth birthday came and went. Her parents wanted to throw her a birthday party, and she refused. The last thing she wanted in her life was a bunch of people who'd treated her with indifference to be there to party with her. Instead, Logan was invited to her home, and they had dinner with their parents, all at her house. Her parents weren't comfortable with the wealth of Logan's parents.

She wasn't entirely comfortable with their wealth either, but she lived with it. Logan was more than a dollar figure to her. On the day itself, Logan took her to get a tattoo. It was a dolphin at the base of her back. Logan teased her about it, but she didn't care.

Their relationship also became known around West County as well. To celebrate her cast coming off, and being free of the crutches, Logan took her out to eat. Sean and his gang were there, including Izzy.

She gave Izzy a wave, and didn't acknowledge anyone else at their table. There was no point trying to make friends seeing as neither of them was sticking around. In the queue waiting to be served, Logan grabbed her, slamming his lips down on hers, and claiming ownership over her. She was sure of it.

When he lifted up, he'd smiled. "Just letting them know who you belong to, and who I belong to."

It had been the single most thrilling moment of her life, and one she hoped would be on glorious repeat.

Standing beside him now, Blake wanted to make him happy. She held his hand, offering him as much comfort as she could. They had flown out to Vegas so that he could visit Shauna's grave.

"Are you okay?" she asked.

"A loving daughter, and best friend," he read.

"It's just, no matter how many times I come here, it gets harder."

"Is that why you decided to come to West County?"

"No, it's not." He took a deep breath. "Everything is so fucking messed up."

She watched as he pulled away a few of the weeds that had grown in the time he'd been away. The grave was clearly better tended than the others. It had clearly been months since the other graves were tended to.

Logan stepped forward, and she wrapped her arms around herself, to ward off the chill. The grave was filled with loneliness, and Blake couldn't help but wonder what it would be like to have no one tend to your grave.

"Are you okay?" she asked.

"Yeah, I'm fine. I wished I could have been there, you know. None of this would have happened."

"You can't blame yourself."

"Yeah, I know."

"The only people to blame are those boys that hurt her."

He let out another breath. "You're right. Hey, Shauna, it's Logan. I'm here. It has been a few months since I've been here, longer maybe. I'm here with my girl, Blake. I met her at the new school I told you I was going to."

Blake stayed silent, listening to him.

"You always told me that I'd find someone who wouldn't try to change me, who would accept me for me. You were right as always, and if you were here, I'd have to pay you a hundred bucks straight." He turned back to look at her. "I told her I'd never find love. She bet me a hundred bucks I did."

"Was there a time limit?" Blake asked.

"No. No time limit. Shauna always said there was

no time limit on love. Isn't that right?"

No one answered.

Blake didn't know what to say, and stayed silent. This was his time, his moment. "I'm going to forgive him, Shauna. I know you wouldn't want me to stay mad at him. You were always pragmatic, saying where the blame lay with people. I just wish you could be here, but I get it. I know why you did what you did."

Another length of silence, Blake tucked some hair behind her ear, waiting.

"I'm going away for a while. Blake and I, we've got some plans. I'll be back to see you soon." Logan kissed his fingers and pressed them against the gravestone. "See you soon, Shauna."

He stood up, taking her hand.

"I'm ready to go."

"You sure? I don't mind waiting."

"It's fine."

"You loved her a lot."

"I did."

Logan's parents had brought them both to their old penthouse suite, and that was where they were staying. Blake's parents hadn't wanted her to go, but they accepted it, knowing she was going to be there with John and Renee.

She'd never been to Vegas before, and it was so chaotic and busy. It was a complete lifetime away from West County.

They made their way back to the penthouse, only to find that it was empty. Renee had left a note saying she was running some errands, and would be back soon.

"Dad is trying to seduce her."

"Oh, okay." She didn't know why he had to tell her that. His father was strange at times, nice though. "Are you ready for them to get back together?"

"No. I'm not ready for them to make that leap again. Mom, she spent so many nights crying. It took me a long time to figure out what was wrong with her."

"You didn't know why?"

"Nope. I was too busy dealing with my own life to care."

Logan put the kettle on to boil, and she took a seat at the counter, watching him. He wore a tight shirt. April was choosing to be difficult as it didn't know whether to be warm, cold, or hot.

"Do you care now?" she asked.

"Of course I care. That's never going to stop."

"I'm not trying to argue, I just want to be sure I understand."

He moved away from the kettle and cupped her face, tilting her head back. She loved it when he touched her, and now she found herself looking forward to his touches. His lips smashed against hers, and she gripped his arms, not wanting him to stop, or to let go.

"God, I love you," he said.

She loved him as well, and his kisses were only driving her crazy. Blake had expected for him to start initiating sex, but so far, their kisses were the only thing that was happening. All of her life, she hadn't really cared for intimacy, sex, or any of that. Even when Izzy lost her virginity and told her all about it, Blake had not been interested. Sex had always been there but not present for her. Now, maybe it was the fact Logan was hers, or that she was old enough to care. Whatever had happened, that change had occurred, and now it was driving her crazy. Once again, he stepped away, and finished making them coffee.

"Thank you for coming with me."

"Don't mention it."

I'm going insane because I want sex, but that's

okay.

From nerd to nympho within a matter of months.

Running fingers through her hair, she smiled at Logan, and took a sip of the steaming hot liquid. "Do you feel better now?" she asked.

"Yeah, I do."

"Good."

She blew across the surface of the cup, and took a sip.

Sex can wait.
It's not important.

****

Logan lay in bed, staring up at the ceiling. This was his old room, in his old home, and he felt oddly detached. The West County home was more garish and ghastly, but that was more of a home than this one. Memories in this one were filled with arguments, and bitter fallings out.

His parents seemed to be trying to change that now though. Logan had yet to hear one cross word, or one falling out. So far, nothing.

When his door opened, he went onto his elbows and saw Blake entering.

"Is everything okay?" he asked.

She stopped, pausing at his door. "I want to ask you something, and it's going to sound stupid, and silly, and crazy."

He stared at her. "What is it?"

Blake closed the door and padded toward the bed. She didn't sit down, and he noticed her hands were scrunched up into tight fists.

Reaching out, he went to take her hand, and she pulled away, stopping him. "No, I need to say this, and if you touch me, I'll back out for it being stupid."

The shorts she wore stopped at mid-thigh, and the

vest displayed the curves that had been driving him crazy for months. Logan had wanted her for a long time, but her age, and their friendship had kept him at arms' length. He'd not wanted to pressure her, and instead of just getting a quick fuck, he'd shown her the respect he'd never shown another girl or woman.

Sitting up, he turned the lamp on, to which she turned it off.

"What is it? You've actually got me tense here." He turned the light on, and she switched it off once again. Giving up, he held his hands away from it. "I want to look at you, and you want darkness. Fine." He wanted to see her. Darkness was not something he wanted in the way with her. Logan loved looking at her, and he loved staring into her brown eyes. They showed him so much love and passion to a woman that had almost seemed dead not so long ago.

"Do you find me attractive?"

Logan stared up at her. "That's the question?"

"We've been dating officially for a few months now, and I can only come to one conclusion, that you don't find me attractive."

"How?"

What the fuck was happening?

"You only kiss me. You don't try for more, and you've not tried to sleep with me. Then I think to the fact we were sharing a bed for three months, and it was just us, so I mustn't be all that appealing."

This was just attack after attack, and he wasn't happy.

"Wait! You don't think I want you?"

"You're not even trying to sleep with me. I bet if I was Izzy you wouldn't have a problem—"

He cut her off by getting out of bed, and shoving his boxer briefs down to the floor. "This is exactly how I feel about you." Grabbing her hand, he wrapped it around his hardening length. "I am attracted to you. It's so bad it fucking hurts, that is how much I want you, and how desperate I am for you."

"Oh," she said.

Her hand stayed still on his cock. "I want you, Blake. I kept my hands to myself because you were a fucking minor, and I didn't want to risk losing you."

"How?"

"Statutory rape. I was older. I don't know if charges would have stuck or whatnot, but I didn't want to risk it. I kept my hands to myself even though every single night you fell asleep in my arms, and all I wanted to do was claim you. To me, you've belonged to me from that moment in the cafeteria where you stared at me, and I saw all of that fucking pain building inside you. You've been mine since then, and this is not going away."

"Why haven't you? I'm old enough now."

Logan cursed. "If I got you into bed immediately on your birthday, I didn't want you thinking that it was all I wanted. It's not. I want you, Blake. I don't want just sex. Sure, it's fun, and I love it, but with you, it is always going to mean more to me, and be more."

He saw the tears shining in her eyes.

"I didn't think you wanted me."

Cupping her cheeks, he tilted her head back. Her hand was still wrapped around his dick, and it was getting harder for him to think. All of his blood pumping in that one region of his body demanded more attention than ever before.

"I want you. I want you so much that it is scary as fuck."

She licked her lips, and he groaned. His cock jumped as the action made him think of her tongue on other parts of his body. "I thought you didn't want me."

Closing his eyes, he rested his head against hers. "I'm trying to be the gentleman, the guy you deserve."

"Logan, can I admit something to you?" she said.

"Yes."

"I'm a virgin."

"I know."

"I don't want to be a virgin anymore."

He pulled back to stare into her eyes. "Blake?"

"Listen to me. All of my life I've thought I was this ugly, horrible person, and I've told you this before. I never thought I'd be with someone, not in the way I feel about you. I want to be with you, and I want you to be my first." She pressed her lips against his, her tongue licking over his.

Pre-cum spilled out of the tip of his cock, and she rubbed it into his shaft.

"I want to move on from that. Put the past behind me."

"Fuck!" He cupped her hips at the same time he took possession of her mouth. He was so fucking horny right now. It had been too long since he'd been inside a woman. From the moment he met Blake, he'd known she was going to be special to him, and he didn't want that to end. No other girl or woman had ever appealed to him, and would never.

She talked to him in ways that didn't need words, and he wanted her in his life. Because of her, the fire raging inside him changed, and turned into passion not anger.

The change was something he wanted.

There was no need for any more anger, just calm.

"Please, I want you, Logan."

It took a lot of guts for Blake to admit that, and he couldn't just turn away from her, or cut her off. She was the love of his life. Even at eighteen he knew it. There were people, fifty plus years of marriage, and they knew at a young age they would be together forever. With Blake, he knew.

Pushing his fingers beneath her shirt, he lifted it above her head, and tossed it aside. She released his dick, and he captured her hands long enough to stop her reaching for him.

"It has been a long time for me, so I need to do this at my pace, baby."

"Okay. I don't know what I'm doing."

"Let me guide you."

"Is this another Vegas thing?"

"I'm so grateful I took the time to learn from the women here." He reached around, gripping her ass, and pulling her against him. Her naked tits pressed against his chest, and he closed his eyes simply enjoying how close they both were. Running his fingers down her back, he teased the waistband of her shorts, and started to push them down. He stepped away long enough to sink down to the floor, pressing a kiss on her stomach.

"Step out of them."

She lifted one leg, then the other.

Sliding his fingers up her legs, he held her hips, and turned her so that she had her back to the bed.

"Sit down, and spread your legs for me."

"I can see why you're so good at this."

He chuckled. "You've not seen anything yet."

"I don't know if I want to open them."

Logan kissed her knee, then her thigh. "Believe me when I say, you want to open them."

"I do?"

"Hell yeah, baby, you do."

She took a deep breath, and slowly, achingly slowly opened her thighs. Logan didn't look away from her. He made sure his gaze was focused entirely on her, watching her. She licked her lips, and his cock pulsed with fresh arousal.

"Lie back."

"You're giving a lot of orders here."

"Trust me?"

"Always." She eased back, and he looked at her pussy, seeing the glistening evidence of her cream. Opening her lips, he spread her wide, recalling several lessons he'd been willing to take.

"When you find a woman you love, you're going to have to be willing to lick her, treasure her. Don't go down on her as if she's some kind of snack. Enjoy it. You want your dick sucked, be the gentleman that makes her want to suck it."

Not the most poetic teachings, but for him it did the trick.

Leaning forward, he swiped his tongue across her clit, and she gasped, tensing in his hands. He smiled, and did it again, waiting for her to get accustomed to the feel of him touching her, tasting her. Logan teased her clit, sliding his tongue against her, feeling as she grew even wetter.

His cock was desperate for her mouth, but he had time for that later. Now, he was only interested in pleasing her.

Chapter Eleven

Logan's tongue made her tense, and a little nervous. Blake found the sensation out of this world, and yet also kind of scary. He was licking her pussy, and even as she thought it, it turned her on even more. She loved the feel of his tongue, and the way he touched her heightened her need. Never had she known such arousal before. It was almost too much to bear.

Her tits felt full and heavy, and her nipples were rock hard. His hands moved from between her legs, to holding her hips, and down. His tongue flicked rapidly against her clit, and as her orgasm started to build, he'd slow it down, making her wait.

She'd never known such pleasure, and such frustration.

Fisting the silk sheets beneath her, she bit her lip, trying to make sense of everything, only to come shattering on his mouth as he sucked her clit hard.

The orgasm took her completely by surprise, and she jerked up in the bed at the peak of her arousal, screaming out his name.

Logan pressed a kiss between her thighs and eased back. She sat up, and stared at him.

"You okay, baby?"

"I think so."

"You can breathe."

"I'm not sure that I can right now. I'm sort of out of it." She was breathing deeply, her chest rising and falling.

Logan glanced down her body. "I want you, Blake. If you want this to end now, say so."

"I don't want it to end."

"You want me inside you?"

"Yes."

"No turning back."

"I'm not going to turn back."

He got to his feet, bending down to press his lips against hers. She moaned, touching his cheek as she kissed him back. The taste of her wasn't offensive. Logan teased his tongue across her lips, and he opened up. He plunged inside, making her moan.

Logan urged her back toward the center of his large bed.

She watched as he took out a condom, tore into the foil packet, and slid it over his impressive length.

"I want us to be safe. I'm not ready for kids. Are you?"

"Kids are the last thing on my mind right now." No, sex, Logan—that was all on her mind. "I've never done this before."

"I know, baby."

She didn't know why she kept telling him, only that it was extremely important for him to know that she was a virgin. She'd told him several times, and she didn't want him to forget.

He moved between her thighs. "Do you trust me?"

"Yes."

"Then keep your eyes on me."

That was easy for her to do. Staring into his blue eyes, she lay back between the pillows. The tip of his cock pressed against her entrance, and she tensed up.

Everything is going to be okay.

One of his hands moved to beside her head, and the other slowly pushed his cock inside her.

In one smooth thrust, Logan claimed her virginity for his own. She cried out, gripping the sheets beneath her.

"You can hold onto me, baby. Hold onto me, let

me feel everything."

She held onto his arms as he filled her completely.

"I'm there now. You're mine, and nothing is ever going to take you away from me."

"I belong to you?"

"Always. You'll always be mine." He took possession of her lips, and she moaned, opening up to his kiss.

Logan waited until she could wait no longer, and started to thrust up against him, demanding more of his cock.

At first, he took his time, making love to her, drawing out each climax from her body. She ran her fingers down his back, and he kissed her throughout. Blake learned his body, remembering every muscle, every move, every kiss. She wanted to stay in this moment for the rest of her life, and never let go.

"I love you," he said.

There were no words for how she was feeling.

"I'm not going to last."

She wasn't ready or near a second orgasm, but Blake was held captive by his orgasm. He thrust inside her, and his cock tensed up, pulsing, and filling the condom with his cum.

"I'm so sorry," he said, staying still within her.

"Why?"

"I wanted us to come together."

"We've got a lifetime to do that. I don't want to waste a single moment of our time together by rushing."

He kissed her deeply.

Pulling out of her, Blake couldn't hide her wince. Logan left, getting rid of the condom and throwing it away in the trash. He came back, easing into the bed beside her, locking their fingers together.

"Should I go back to my own room?" she asked.

"Not a chance. The only place you sleep now is here with me."

Blake smiled. "I like that."

"I didn't hurt you, did I?" he asked.

"No. It was perfect." There was a little pain but not enough to concern him with. Logan kissed her neck, and his arms wrapped around her. "I wish we could stay in this moment forever," she said, after a length of silence had passed.

"We will."

"How?"

"We're still together. You don't want to sleep naked every single day, and not do anything. That's not what you want to keep, is it?"

"No."

"We'll have each other, and these moments will be part of us for the rest of our lives. I don't see why they have to change. They don't define us. They're just part of us. I'll always be with you. I'll always want you."

"How do you know to say the right thing?" she asked.

"Easy, I was a fast learner, and I grew up fast." He dropped a kiss to her lips.

"Do you miss playing ball?"

"No. It was something I did that my dad liked."

"It helped you to build that anger up toward him. How do you feel now? About your father? He is trying."

Logan rested his chin on her shoulder. "There's not a lot I can say. He'll always be my dad. Just like your parents will always be yours."

"I'm forgiving them. It has taken a lot, and it has been scary as hell at times." She loved the scent of Logan surrounding her. Blake had had a long time to think about her parents, and the trauma they had both dealt with. Neither of her parents had been cruel, not intentionally, and now they were trying. Blake didn't want to cut them out of her life, not if she didn't have to. "I'm pleased I came here."

"Why?"

"Besides the fact I just had sex?"

"Totally rocked your world, didn't it?"

"Yep. I've been able to do a lot of thinking about the future. My feelings with my parents, and even though it's hard, I know in their own way, they do mean well."

"It's time to put the past behind us, and embrace the present and future?"

"Exactly. We're together, and I can't blame my parents for everything. I now have you." She pulled his hand in front of her lips, and pressed a kiss to his wrist. "I guess something good did come out of it."

Logan leaned forward, claiming her lips. "How would you like to attempt doggy style?"

Blake giggled. "I hope this isn't going to gross me out."

"No, it should have you howling my name."

She burst out laughing as Logan pulled her to her knees. The laughter stopped, turning to moans of pleasure. He then showed her how very good doggy style could be.

****

Three months later

"Smile for the camera, babe," Logan said.

They had graduated high school, packed their bags, taken their passports, and were currently enjoying the sunny beaches of Spain. Blake wore a bathing suit, and covered her legs in a long sarong skirt. She had a large hat, and was laughing at him.

"Will you stop?"

"Not in this life. I want something to show our kids when we're too old, and look out of place."

Holding up the camera, he took shot after shot even as she came up to him. Pulling her into his arms, he held the camera up, screaming for a selfie. They were both laughing, which had become the story of their life.

Their families didn't want them to leave, preferring for them to consider college instead. Logan was glad he hadn't gone down the college route. Spending time with Blake, exploring the world, filled him with passion and inspired him. They worked as they went, having saved a lump sum to start so that they could have the proper experience. Of course, his father sent him money if they did need it, which they rarely did.

Collapsing to the ground, Logan held her tightly.

"Do you want to go back to the hotel room?" she asked.

"Are you telling me that you can't wait until night?"

She giggled, leaning down to kiss him. "I would, if my boyfriend hadn't told me it was just as good in the day as it was at night."

"Damn him. He's giving away all the juicy details." Gripping the back of her head, he pulled her down for a kiss. "Race you."

They both ran up to the hotel where they were staying. The moment the door was closed, he pressed her up against him. His cock already rock hard, and desperate to be inside her.

Blake smiled at him, that seductive little temptress smile, and then she sank down to the floor, pulling his pants along with her. His cock sprang free, and her lips covered the tip.

"Oh fuck."

That night three months ago had awoken the need inside her, and now there was no way of turning it off. Sinking his fingers into her hair, he closed his eyes, enjoying her lips on his cock.

She bobbed her head, filling her mouth, taking him deep. The past three months they hadn't been able to keep their hands off each other, and that was the case now. He wanted her more than ever, each day only increasing his need for her.

Logan pumped his cock into her mouth, knowing he couldn't hold the words back anymore.

"Marry me," he said.

Blake paused, and released his cock. "What?"

"I know in the eyes of the world, we're just kids. But I know what I want."

"Marriage?"

"Yes. Take a chance with me. Let's make our lives beautiful, together."

For the longest time she didn't say anything, simply staring up at him. Then finally, he saw her smile, the one that had bewitched him in the beginning, and heard her answer.

"Yes."

Epilogue

After traveling for many years, Logan and Blake Black finally went back home, settling down in West County. They were married in Vegas two months after his proposal, their parents being the only ones present. Once they were married, off they went to enjoy the rest of their lives again.

Over the years they kept in touch, and Blake built a relationship with her parents that had been missing for most of their lives. Logan did the same, building one with his father.

Logan's parents finally got remarried, but it took John Black five years to convince Renee that he'd changed.

They were all back in West County. Logan had taken over ownership of the local gym, and Blake had taken up online college courses. She worked at the bakery, training, and helped Renee in any way she could with her cook book. They built a life together, that wasn't based on financial success but their relationship. Neither of them wanted city jobs. They wanted to commit to each other, without the pressures around them.

After eight years of marriage, they had their first child, a girl, whom they called Shauna.

After Blake gave birth late one Sunday evening, Logan sat beside her, watching as she nursed their first girl.

"Thank you," Blake said.

"What for, babe?"

"For showing me that the world is beautiful, and that I'm beautiful. Thank you."

Logan leaned forward with tears in his eyes, kissing her head. "I never did that, Blake. That was all on you."

"Do you want another one?" she asked.

Even though she'd been screaming in pain, Blake had pulled through, and they proceeded to have another five children. By the time they were forty, Logan knew there wouldn't be any more kids. He wanted to spend the rest of his life, devoted to Blake, and he did.

Their love didn't start with beauty, but in the horrid lies that had been spoken to make both of them to believe the ugly in the world. After fighting their demons, they found the magic, and the will and freedom to love one another.

They were the only couple of County High to remain together, in happiness.

The End

www.samcrescent.wordpress.com

SAM CRESCENT

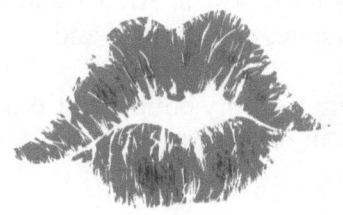

EVERNIGHT PUBLISHING ®

www.evernightpublishing.com